CW00351733

Such Morning Songs

SUCH MORNING SONGS

Desley Moore

The Book Guild Ltd.
Sussex, England

The Book Guild Ltd.
25 High Street,
Lewes, Sussex.

First published 1992
Reprinted 1993
© Desley Moore 1992
Set in Baskerville
Typesetting by APS,
Salisbury, Wiltshire.
Printed in Great Britain by
Antony Rowe Ltd.,
Chippenham, Wiltshire.

A catalogue record for this book is
available from the British Library

ISBN 0 86332 808 3

For my friend Betty
Who shared all my 'Morning Songs'

And nothing I cared, at my sky blue trades, that time allows
In all his tuneful turning so few and such morning songs
Before the children green and golden follow him out of grace.

Dylan Thomas, Fern Hill.

CONTENTS

ACKNOWLEDGEMENT

The author would like to thank David Higham Associates Limited and Dent publishers for granting permission to use the extract from 'Fern Hill' in *The Poems* by Dylan Thomas, which is quoted at the beginning of this book and includes the title phrase *Such Morning Songs*.

PART

1

1

Psalms and Herrings

The early morning sun was sending fingers of light round the edges of the bottle-green blind. Davy stirred and muttered then came awake with a sense of urgency. He raised himself up on a skinny elbow and peered over the top of the humped form of his brother Llew, whose bed he shared. Screwing up his eyes, he made out the time on the old metal alarm clock on the dressing table. Half past five. He slumped back down again and made a half-hearted grab at the blankets as Llew stirred, coughed and pulled the bedclothes over his shoulder.

Davy lay on his back and stared at the cracks in the ceiling. This morning he saw no horses head or stunted trees in the cracks as he usually did. His high, pale forehead was creased and the damp, dark curls clung to it stickily. The words of the Twenty-Third Psalm chased each other round in his head like rats in a trap and his lips moved in an anxious whisper.

'The Lord is my Shepherd I shall not want, He maketh me to lie down in green pastures, He feedeth my soul, He – He – oh, Duw!'

His big dark eyes searched the cracks in the ceiling desperately but the horse's head and the stunted tree told him nothing. He pulled his nightshirt more closely round his thin ten-year-old frame and climbed carefully over the inert body on the outside of the wide old brass bed. His toes curled on the cold linoleum as he padded over to the window and sticking his head under the blind, looked out on to the May morning.

The first rays of the sun were striking diamonds on the small window panes of the cobbler's shop opposite. As Davy watched, old Matt Owen, the cobbler, opened his door and came out on to the pavement to survey the morning, dragging

11

his club foot on the cobbles and raising his big square face to the sun, which glinted on his steel spectacles. He smoothed down his leather apron, looked up and down the road and hobbled back to his doorway. There he paused and turning, coughed and directed a large globule of spit across the pavement to land accurately in the gutter. Davy was lost in admiration. As he watched Matt go in and close the door, he wondered if he could spit from the window into the gutter on his own side of the road. He pushed the sash window up cautiously and leaning out, gathered all the moisture together in his mouth and spat forcibly. His effort fell short of his target and landed on the shawled head of a late-hurrying millworker as she clattered by. She looked up sharply and Davy quickly withdrew his head, giving it a sharp bang on the window frame. His squeak of anguish woke twenty-year-old Llew.

'What the devil! Why you up so early, our Davy?'

Davy rubbed his head and sniffed miserably.

'It's the old scripture exam today. Can't remember the Twenty-Third Psalm and the old Bishop is sure to ask for that and Mr Hall says the Bishop is a good man and just, but he has a terrible wrath! Oh, Duw, I keep getting stuck with that old Psalm, Llew.'

'Well, get on downstairs and learn it,' grunted Llew, turning over and drawing the blankets over his head.

Davy drew on his heavy serge trousers and tucked a striped flannel shirt into them, then drew up the braces. He sat on the bed heavily to pull on the thick grey socks, bringing a muffled exclamation from Llew. Picking up his boots by the laces he trailed, hiccupping, across the landing and descended the steep, narrow staircase. He paused to gaze at the illuminated certificates framed on the stair wall, all testifying to the religious knowledge of his brother and two sisters, who had obviously had no difficulty with the Twenty-Third Psalm or any other questions the old Bishop might ask. He sniffed dejectedly again and shuffled on down the stairs, doubting that he would ever see a certificate testifying to the attainment of religious knowledge by David Rees hanging beside the copperplate names of Llewelyn Rees, Ellen Rees and Megan Rees.

A fire already burned cheerfully in the big black range in the front kitchen and a large white enamel bowl of dough for the day's bread stood on the fender, with a clean white cloth covering it. Mama came bustling out of the back kitchen, her thick, black wool skirt swinging round her ankles.

Susan Rees was a tall, spare woman with narrow shoulders which seemed to be permanently braced to take her through the difficulties of her daily life and the effort to maintain her own strict standards of cleanliness and pride which she imposed on her family. Wages were low in the little mill and market town of Newtown in Mid Wales in the year 1896, and it took all the ingenuity of Mama's careful housekeeping to stretch the wages brought in by Dada, Llew, Ellen and Meg to keep up the 'respectability' of the Rees family, which she guarded with stubborn pride. She was regarded with grudging admiration by her neighbours, but without the affection they felt for her husband, the little stocky Welsh-speaking man from Llanllugan, a small, remote hamlet in the hills.

Will had courted Susan with a cheerful persistence when she was working as a maidservant at Gregynog Hall, unable to explain to himself his attraction to the reserved young girl, tall, slim and straight backed, with a determined, almost severe mouth, slightly long, straight nose, thick dark curly hair struggling to escape from the confining nest of hairpins, and speaking the cold English tongue. But the softness of her large dark eyes betrayed an inner vulnerability and provided the encouragement which carried him through to the desired end. When, on a soft September evening as they stood at the gate of the meadow below the Hall, Susan on the inside of the gate and Will leaning anxiously against the gatepost on the outside, he tried once again stumblingly in the strange tongue which made him feel uncomfortable, he felt he had not understood when she gazed directly into his beseeching blue eyes and said, steadily,

'Yes, Will Rees, I will have you.'

His joy during the ensuing months before the marriage was tinged with incredulity and not a little apprehension, since this girl was so different from the farm girls and servants in the district with whom he had tumbled in the hay-lofts and cheekily seduced behind kitchen doors. She allowed no liberties during his courtship and arrived at the altar cool, quiet and a virgin. When finally Will took her with a mixture of awe and ardour on the marriage bed, she responded with a generosity and warmth which filled him with joy and love and a feeling of having attained the unattainable, a conviction which secretly stayed with him throughout the rest of their life together.

When they eventually rode into Newtown in a pony and trap from Ty Coch, Will's home, and perched atop a few sticks of furniture donated by the Evans' of the Walkmill, Manafon, Susan's family, it was to a three-bedroomed house which went with Will's new job as coachman-gardener to the Rector of Newtown, the Reverend Gwilym Pryce. No 46 Pool Road bordered the Rectory Field and stood with its two bow windows and brass-knockered door, sturdily welcoming them in.

Will swallowed his Welsh non-conformist scruples and not only carved himself a niche in the Rectory household but accompanied his wife to church on Sundays and lustily sang the hymns in his own version of the English tongue and sat serene and uncomprehending through sermons couched in terms which the limited English he was picking up in his daily life could not stretch to. Will was adaptable and he adapted.

Now Mama gave Davy a push in the direction of the back kitchen.

'Go you now and wash, good boy. Dada will be home at seven and you must fetch the pickled herrings.'

A tin bowl of cold water stood in the earthenware sink and Davy splashed his face and smoothed a wet hand over his rough curls. Oh, Duw, it was Friday of course and he would have to fetch Dada's herrings from Betsi Hughes' before he had his breakfast. Dada went out at six every morning to feed the horses and back for breakfast at seven. On Fridays he always had two pickled herrings for breakfast, hot from Betsi Hughes' shop round the corner. The rest of the family dipped their bread in the hot spicy 'gravy' at Friday's breakfast as a supplement to the usual porridge.

Davy towelled his face pink on the stiff linen roller towel hanging on the back of the door and shuffled through into the kitchen in his stockinged feet. While he dragged on his boots,

Mama reached down from the mantelpiece the blue tin with the pink dog-roses painted on it and took out two pennies. She fetched in a white enamel dish from the back kitchen and gave it to Davy. He pocketed the two pennies and made his way to the door.

'It's the old scripture test today, Mama,' he complained, pausing with his hand on the knob. 'That old Twenty-Third Psalm it is that I can't remember. Got to learn it before I go to school.'

Mama was hooking the big black kettle on to the chain above the fire.

'Well, go you quickly then, boy, and I will hear you say it when you come back. Goodness, you have heard it often enough in Church. You will be all right. Go on, boy, hurry!'

Davy clattered down the front steps in his boots, studded to last, and jogged along the pavement, waving the enamel dish and catching it against the Rectory wall to send white chips of enamel flying. He paused at the Rectory gate and gazed up the drive. No sign yet of Geraint, the Rector's son, his own age and his best friend. Geraint would know that old Psalm, with his father the Rector and all. He would get his certificate all right. Davy sighed heavily, then ran on until he came to the tiny corner shop. Up three steps then and push the door open, setting the bell jangling loudly. And oh! the smell of hot spicy herrings, cooking in the oven of the old black range in the room behind the shop. Betsi came waddling through the doorway into the shop, face flushed from the heat of the range, reaching out a red, chapped hand for the dish.

'Two as usual is it, Davy?' she panted, her little black eyes twinkling at him like two shiny currants in Mama's lardy cake, thought Davy.

'Yes, please, Betsi.' He stood on tiptoe and leaned against the counter for a better sniff of the herrings when she opened the oven door to fork two fat herrings out of the big baking tin, then to spoon the vinegary gravy generously over them, with little bits of peppercorns and cloves floating on the top. Davy's mouth watered hungrily as she snatched up a piece of newspaper and carefully covered the dish. He put his two pennies on the counter and carrying the dish cautiously made his way more slowly down the steps and back along the road that skirted the Rectory wall. He paused again at the gate which

15

shut off the drive to the big white Rectory. Geraint would be having his breakfast now, perhaps even bacon. Davy's stomach grumbled at the thought and, yielding to temptation, he lifted the newspaper from one corner of the dish and broke off a hot morsel of herring. He stood for a moment, chewing slowly and blissfully to make it last, under the arching branches of the old chestnut trees which lined up inside the Rectory wall, carrying on this sweet May morning, their pale new leaves and tall, fragrant, pink candles of blossom. Davy tucked the newspaper carefully over the corner of the dish again and hurried the remaining few yards home to porridge and a dip in the gravy.

His brother and two sisters were already seated at the scrubbed deal table in the kitchen eating steaming platefuls of thick porridge. Davy handed over his dish of herrings to Mama and took his seat on the wooden bench on one side of the table next to sister Ellen, known as Nell. Nell spooned a large dollop of the thick porridge into his bowl and he reached for the big white enamel jug that held the milk. It wobbled in his hands, bringing a sharp look from Nell. He put his other hand to it to steady it and poured carefully, his tongue protruding in concentration, afraid to spill any drops, which might bring a sharp pinch from Nell's bony fingers. He replaced the jug carefully and attacked the porridge in hungry mouthfuls.

Breakfast was always eaten accompanied by the heady alcoholic smell of rising dough and usually Llew holding forth on some topic. This morning their talk was of the new laundry chimney which was now completed atop the laundry building which had, to Mama's disgust, been sited right opposite, beside the little cobbler's shop. She had complained bitterly as to what the world was coming to when people would send their washing to an old laundry.

'And what is going to happen to those poor souls who take in washing to make a living for themselves and their families? And then there's Mary-Ann the Mangle, and her with four young ones and no man. Not but what,' she added darkly, 'a fair bit of what she earns by that mangle finds its way into the till of the Cross Guns of a Saturday night. But that's as may be. I don't fancy a big smoky old chimney opposite my house.'

'Progress, Mama,' Llew pushed his bowl away and swallowed a mouthful of hot, strong tea. 'There will be jobs for people in this laundry and maybe better money than they can make taking in washing at home.'

'Tush!' Mama refilled the big kettle over the glowing fire. 'They are better at home with their children around them. What will the children do if their Mamas work at the laundry? You see what happens to some of the little ones, poor souls, playing in the gutters while their mothers go to work in the mills, and their Dadas are in the pubs, like as not, spending what the poor women earn.'

'Well,' said Llew, 'whilst there's not much work for the men round here, it's better that than go on the Parish. Fat lot they get from that and they usually end up in the workhouse. Anyway,' he went on, briskly, wiping his mouth and getting up from the table, 'I know a chap that's been working on the chimney and he's taking me up the scaffolding on Monday to see the view from the top.'

Davy's eyes widened and with a spoonful of porridge arrested between bowl and mouth, he burst out, 'Can I come too, our Llew? Aw, c'mon, can I?'

'No damn fear,' grunted Llew. 'And have you break your fool neck indeed.'

'Go where?' asked Mama, bustling in with a big mug for Dada's tea.

'Up the laundry chimney!' cried Davy, splashing his porridge in his excitement and getting a sharp jab from Nell for his pains.

Mama turned a flushed and horrified face to Davy.

'Lord above, what are you talking about, boy! You stay down on this ground, you hear? Anyway, you come in the back kitchen while I cut Dada's bread and I will hear you say that Psalm for the test. Let's have no more talk about climbing chimneys.'

'Scripture test today, is it, our Davy?' Meggie smiled sympathetically as Davy climbed off the bench and reluctantly followed Mama into the back kitchen, a thick piece of bread soaked in pickled herring gravy clutched in his hand. He nodded miserably and disappeared through the doorway.

'He'll be all right.' Meg reached for a slice of bread. 'He's a good scholar.'

'Much good that'll do him round here,' Nell said, sourly.

'Oh I don't know.' Meg's voice came indistinctly through a mouthful of bread. 'I reckon our Davy could get on if he had a chance. You were a scholar, too, Nell,' she went on, generously, for sixteen-year-old Meg had a sweet nature, cheerful, warm and sympathetic.

Nell sniffed and closed her eyes for a moment, squeezing the bridge of her thin nose with long, slender needle-pitted fingers. She worked in old Madame Beynon's millinery shop and her eyes were strained from long hours bent over the fine sewing on net and chiffon, pushing needles through stiff, white buckram shapes and running tiny stitches through coverings and trimmings, ruching and tucking, under the eagle eye of Madame, whose high class establishment served the gentry and tradesmen's wives and all who could afford to pay for her confections. Often the girls in the workshop stayed on late into the night to complete a special order for the next morning and as Nell, at nineteen, was Madame's best and most meticulous worker, it was she, more often than not, who thought up the designs for these 'specials' and stayed on to see them finished, putting the finishing touches to a beautiful creation under the inadequate light from one hissing gas lamp in the workshop. Consequently she suffered blinding headaches which made her screw up her fine dark eyes and were the reason for the shortness of her temper and the sharp, bitter tongue which was the scourge of her family and the girls she worked with.

Seeing that Nell was in no mood for conversation, Meggie rose and began to clear the table, carrying the dishes through to the back kitchen where Davy was sitting on a low, three-legged stool, rocking back and forth precariously and reciting the Twenty Third Psalm, prompted now and again by Mama, who was hacking thick slices from a large loaf of yesterday's baking. Then heavy boots sounded on the cobbled yard outside and the door opened, letting in the morning sunshine and Dada.

Will Rees was a short, stocky man with broad shoulders stretching the rusty black jacket he wore over a collarless striped flannel shirt, and with short thick legs, encased in black trousers and leather leggings round his calves. His complexion was fresh, with round pink cheeks and his bright blue eyes were sharp and twinkling under a thick thatch of prematurely white hair which this morning stood up, crisp and wiry like a halo. Mama frowned and wrinkled her nose at the stable smell which surrounded her husband. Half a head taller than him, she glanced down involuntarily at his boots as they scraped on the scrubbed slate flags of the kitchen floor, but after all these years Will knew better than to commit the cardinal sin of carrying stable muck into the house on his boots and they had been washed with a yard broom under the pump in the stable yard. Likewise he had learned to scrub his hands and face under the same pump before returning home and the mingled smell of carbolic soap, leather and horses seemed part and parcel of Dada to Davy and the nicest and most comfortable smell in the world.

'There is a beautiful morning,' said Dada, cheerfully, with a Welsh lilt to his voice. 'Leave the door open to let it come in to the house.' He propped the door open with a heavy stone kept for the purpose and stood for a moment in the doorway, looking out on to the sunlit cobbles of the yard and the stone steps that led up to a path through a small cluster of twisted elder trees which bordered that side of the Rectory field. The retaining wall on each side of the steps, and the little lean-to W.C. with the green door, were whitewashed and reflected the morning sun. Davy caught a whiff of the tangy perfume from the big bush of 'old man' which stood beside the back door. Dada turned, rubbing his hands briskly.

'We will go to Manafon on Sunday,' he announced. 'The fine weather will hold now for a bit. Blod will enjoy the outing, too.'

Blod was the same pony they had brought with them from Ty Coch and although old and greying the little mare was still brisk and able to pull the trap.

Meg gave a squeal of delight and Davy jumped off his stool in excitement, sending it flying to the floor. Mama tut-tutted, but there was a pleased expression on her face as she carried the plate of bread through into the front kitchen, with Dada stomping energetically after her and Davy at his heels. With a leap and a whoop, Davy snatched down his cap from behind the door and burst forth into the sunny May morning, all thoughts of the Scripture Test pushed aside by the delight of the forthcoming Sunday outing.

It was too early for school, so he decided to pay a visit to the bakehouse. He turned off into narrow Stone Street and ran on until he came to Angel Court, clattering up the dark, covered passageway, he emerged into the cobbled court, with two small cottages on either side, a stand pipe for water in the middle and facing him was the bakehouse. He pushed open the heavy wooden door and entered the hot interior, filled with the rich aroma of newly-baked bread. Oven-Bottom Billy, the baker, turned a flushed and glistening face from where he had been closing the big oven door on a fresh batch and seeing Davy, he grinned and lifted a huge, floury hand.

'Morning, young Davy,' his voice was a chesty wheeze. 'You'm out early.'

Dai the Bread, Billy's pasty-faced, unhealthy-looking assistant, looked up fleetingly and then went on with the kneading and shaping of loaves on the big wooden table. Dai was a morose and silent middle-aged bachelor who lived with his mother, now little more than a toothless bundle of clothes, barely able to hobble around. They occupied one of the cottages in the court, a one-up one-down dwelling. The old woman, known locally as Lizzie Cuckoo, slept on a narrow iron bedstead, under an assortment of old clothes, in a corner of the kitchen, whilst Dai occupied the tiny bedroom upstairs. Dai's father, the original 'Dai the Bread', had died of the 'galloping consumption' and young Dai, who had been helping his father, went to work for Oven-Bottom Billy, who had taken over the bakehouse when Dai found there was no money to pay for the next load of flour or even a sack of coal for the ovens.

Oven-Bottom Billy was a big, florid man who worked hard from four in the morning until one o'clock when, his deliveries completed in a ramshackle covered cart, drawn by a dyspeptic-looking nag, he closed down the bakehouse and went home to his plump, good-natured, if slovenly wife and six offspring like steps of stairs. There, after a meal, he dozed in a chair by the fire, after which he spent his evenings reading Shakespeare, for Billy was a scholar and being well-versed in the Bard of Avon's plays, greeted Davy this morning, as always.

'What's new on the Rialto?'

Davy took 'the Rialto' to be Oven-Bottom Billy's name for the Brickfield, that part of Newtown which comprised Stone Street and Kerry Road and their connecting Cross Street, the site of the brickfield, long since built over, which gave the area its name.

'Nothing much new, Billy.' Davy watched Billy slide hot steaming, golden loaves onto the long trestle at the side of the

20

bakehouse which already held rows of oven-bottoms, cobs and cottages, giving off a mouth-watering heady smell. 'Our Llew's goin' up the laundry chimney on Monday and we're going to Manafon to Grannie's on Sunday.' He scratched around in his mind for any other news but could only come up with, 'It's nice out and I've got a scripture test today,' the last as a sober afterthought.

'Ah,' said Billy, returning the tray to the table for Dai to fill with more loaves for the oven. 'Scripture, is it? A lot of good reading in the bible, there is. Not enough folks reads the bible for pleasure. Very beautiful some of it is. Lot of good sense in it, too. I don't know as I holds with the Adam and Eve bit, mind. Dunna add up, somehow. But there, tek no notice of me, it is still good to read for the stories. Joseph and them no-good brothers of his, and all them plagues of Egypt. And Esther, now there's a lovely bit. Ah! All good reading.'

Davy listened respectfully, thinking again that Oven-Bottom Billy was a very clever man. He knew that every Sunday morning Billy opened up the bakehouse and that a lot of men crowded in, sitting on up-turned bins or on sacking on the floor where, in the retained heat of Saturday's baking, Billy sat on a rickety chair and read to them from the *News of the World*. Whether this was the result of a thirst of knowledge or of a thirst for the ale in the flagon which Billy generously provided, is open to speculation, but it was a popular Sunday morning rendezvous for those with no commitment to religion to take them off to chapel or church and it beat stopping at home with a nagging wife and snivelling kids.

Oven-Bottom Billy broke the round brown top off a hot, crusty cottage and handed it to Davy. He took it gratefully, the smell of fresh-baked bread making him feel hungry again.

'Ta, Billy,' he said, chewing a crusty bite. 'Well, I'll have to go now.' He still lingered in the warm, scented bakehouse, eyeing the crisp loaves which would go to the small shops to be bought by the mill-hands and others who had no time to bake their own as Mama did.

'Well, ta-ta Billy, ta-ta Dai.'

Billy raised a hand in salute and Dai grunted without looking up. Clutching the warm crust, Davy let himself out into the morning once more and ran on down to the bottom of Stone Street and across Pool Road to the Bridge Wall on the other side. This was a retaining wall that ran along that part of Pool Road which bordered the River Severn. Davy heaved himself on to the broad parapet and swung his legs round until they dangled over the fifteen-foot drop down to the river which ran, sparkling in the morning sun, over its bed of rocks and weeds below. He sat chewing on the warm bread and watching the black-headed gulls gliding and swooping over the water. At certain times of the year the gulls came down from the Pontdolgoch lakes and mewed and wheeled, following the river. Davy broke a very small piece from his crust and tossed it out above the water. Three or four gulls swooped after the morsel, shrieking excitedly, but the swiftest caught it in one smooth movement. Davy contemplated sacrificing another piece of warm crust, but decided against it and instead crammed the remaining crisp and yeasty bread into his mouth and with cheek distended, chewed contentedly, swinging his legs and feeling the increasing warmth of the sun on his back. The town clock struck eight and Davy counted the chimes. Another hour until Miss Morris would come out into the school playground and ring the bell for morning school.

The little town was waking up. Blinds were being raised in the shops along Bridge Street; Sam Morgan, the Haberdasher, Owen Owen's the Ironmongers, Liverpool House, Millinery and closer to hand, in a little square set back from Pool Road, Mrs Evans, Toffee Basket, opened the door of her tiny sweet shop and poked her head out like a small bird, looking for someone to gossip with. Her nearest neighbour, Annie-Bertha Lloyd, as if at a sign, came out tying her sack apron round her ample waist and folding her brawny arms across her bosom and the two women soon had their heads together, sometimes nodding them, sometimes shaking them, absorbed in early-morning news-gathering.

Davy half turned on his perch to wave to Jack Richards the Milk, clopping by in his small milk float, drawn by his brown pony, Nip, the two big brass milk-churns gleaming in the morning sun. The women began to come out of the cottages as he sang out 'Milko!' in a high nasal voice and jugs were handed up to be filled with a generous white flow. Pennies rattled into the pocket of his brown apron and cheery greetings and banter were exchanged with the aproned and shawled housewives gathered on the pavement.

Davy climbed down from the Bridge Wall and dusted the behind of his trousers with his hand. He began to make his way towards the Church School, visible behind its high wall at the bottom of Kerry Road, the huge old oak tree, source of acorn battles in the autumn, rising up in the middle of the school yard. His lips moved as he shuffled along, but this time he got through the whole of the Twenty Third Psalm without mishap and much cheered he broke into a run and entered through the open gates into the playground.

There under the spreading branches of the oak tree a group of boys and girls of all ages stood in a circle, jostling each other for a better view of the activity in the centre. From the ooh's and ah's and shouts of encouragement Davy gathered it was a fight and running across the dusty playground he pushed his way through the press of bodies and elbowed himself towards the centre. Two boys were flailing punches at each other wildly but they were unevenly matched, one a big, handsome boy of Davy's own age, the other small, thin and pale and at least two years younger. A small girl at Davy's side was hopping up and down, large blue eyes snapping with excitement and a ribbon bow as blue as her eyes slipping from her long glossy dark curls. Small fists beat the breast of her starched white pinafore as she screamed encouragement at the bigger boy.

'C'mon Geraint! C'mon! Thump him, Geraint, knock him down!'

Many of the onlookers were shouting encouragement at the underdog, which made Geraint's sister, Elinor, scream more shrilly, her pretty little face distorted with fury. Then the two milling figures fell to the ground, rolling over and panting, locked together in a dusty heap. Finally a vicious punch to the small boy's chest finished the fight for he clutched his thin ribs with his arms, sobbing and gasping for air and finally rolled over on to his side, dirty knees drawn up and a thin trickle of blood coming from his mouth. Geraint rose to his feet, his lips twisted in a triumphant grin and drawing his foot back, planted a kick in the small of his victim's back. As the boy jerked and screamed, Davy rushed forward and caught Geraint's arm, dragging him back from the pitiful, moaning figure on the ground. Geraint turned, jerking his arm away furiously.

'Leave him, Geraint,' Davy panted, urgently. 'Leave him be. You've hurt him bad!'

23

Geraint's face darkened sullenly and he turned away, pushing his way through the circle of onlookers. Elinor squeezed her way after him, tossing her curls defiantly at the group, which had suddenly gone uncomfortably quiet.

Davy, a sick feeling in his stomach, gazed miserably after his friend, and then as another moan escaped the small, curled-up figure on the ground, he knelt in the dust beside him and peered anxiously into the small, grubby face, grey under the dust, eyes squeezed shut and pale lashes wet with tears. A thin line of blood continued to ooze from beneath the clenched teeth and trickle through the grime onto the dusty surface of the yard.

Suddenly a furious push sent him flying onto his back, his head banging on the hard earth.

'What you done to our Alfie, Davy Rees?' a voice yelled at him and as he raised himself on his elbow, shaking his head to clear the ringing in his skull, he saw Nan Mostyn kneel to gather the limp form of her small brother against her thin frame and rock him, crooning comfortingly, pressed to her grubby pinafore.

Alfie opened his eyes and the tears welled weakly out of them as he looked up at his sister's face.

'Our Nan,' he whispered, his breath coming painfully up from his small chest, which he still clutched between skinny arms. 'I'm hurting, our Nan.'

His breath caught in a small sob and Nan wiped the blood from his mouth tenderly with the corner of her pinafore. A bell jangled suddenly in the background and reluctantly the small crowd dragged themselves off towards the sound. Davy struggled to his feet and Nan looked up at him over her brother's head, clear grey eyes blazing in her pale face, straight fair hair falling like a curtain on each side.

'I'll get you for this, Davy Rees, you'll see,' she spat at him and Davy stood, speechless, shaking his head in silent denial.

Alfie struggled in her arms.

'No, Nan. 'Twasn't Davy Rees. 'Twas Geraint Pryce.' He paused for a moment, struggling for breath. ' 'Twas that old Geraint. He said it was a goal but I saved it, I did. He didn't get a goal. He started to fight me when I said it wasn't no goal. But I did fight back, our Nan.' A flicker of satisfaction crossed his pale, pinched features and he struggled from Nan's encircling arms and got painfully to his feet. Nan rose and with her arm about Alfie's thin shoulders, turned and led him in the direction of the still clamouring bell.

Davy stood looking after them for a moment, an uncomfortable feeling still stirring in his stomach. There were times when Geraint made him feel like this, moments when his cheerful, boisterous and satisfying friend showed a side that bewildered Davy. Then he shrugged and, dusting his grubby knees with his cap, he ran across to take his place in the line which was forming under the eagle eye of Miss Morris.

All this was forgotten by the time the bell for the end of school went and Davy and the rest of the Church School scholars pushed and jostled their way out into the sunshine at four o'clock. He felt that the old scripture test hadn't been too bad and in fact he had been quite fascinated by the Bishop. Although dressed in black suit and gaiters, his Lordship's flowing white hair and snowy whiskers corresponded somewhat to Davy's idea of what God looked like and when the piercing dark eyes under white bushy brows had moved on from Davy to his next victim, Davy mentally dressed the Bishop in his mother's long white nightgown and found the resemblance quite startling. No wonder he was a Bishop. And if he got in a temper, well, according to Mama's constant reminders, God could get in a temper with you too if you didn't come up to scratch.

But now he tugged his cap onto his tousled hair and blinked in the sunshine, looking around for Geraint. The nasty feeling in his stomach came flooding back as he saw Geraint leaning against the school wall, a dark scowl on his face as Nan Mostyn squared up to him, spitting fury and shaking a fist in his face. Davy ran across the playground towards them and as he saw Geraint's scowl deepen and his mouth twist savagely, he grasped his friend's arm.

'Aw, c'mon Geraint! Let's go. There's time for a game of football down Pilot's Fields before tea. I've got a pig's bladder from the slaughterhouse to blow up. Come on!'

Geraint had taken a menacing step forward but as Nan stood her ground, pale and determined, Davy tugged again at his arm and suddenly his brow cleared and, grinning and pummelling Davy on the shoulder, he ran for the gate, Davy close on his heels.

Nan stood looking after them for a moment, her thin shoulders heaving with spent fury. Then she shrugged and brushing the hanging locks of hair back from her face, started off in search of Alfie.

2

Cakes and Corpse Candles

Sunday morning lived up to expectations, crisp and sunny, and excitement bubbled up in Davy when he descended the stairs in his best suit. There was a bustle of activity as Nell set the table for breakfast while Mama fried thick slices of home-cured bacon, sent down from Ty Coch by Dada's brother, who now farmed there since Dada's father had died some years ago. Meg cut thick slices of bread to be dipped in the fat from the bacon. Dada and Llew were already seated at the table, Llew dressed in his Sunday suit but Dada in shirt sleeves for he would be dressing after breakfast in the full regalia which he wore to drive the Rector and his children to Church.

The Rector's wife, a delicate lady, had died when Elinor was born and the Rector, a gentle unworldly man, abandoned the bringing up of his children to Mrs Buxton, his housekeeper, who spoiled her 'poor little motherless mites' and totally failed to impose any discipline on the two self-willed children.

This morning Dada was in good spirits, his fluff of white hair on end and his blue eyes twinkling. He was humming 'Jesu, Lover of my Soul', with many pom-pom-poms thrown in, clearing his throat from time to time and beating out the rhythm on the table with his fork. Davy slid into his seat on the bench and Nell, spotting him from the back-kitchen doorway, hastened to fetch a clean tea-towel which she tied roughly round his neck, with a large knot at the back, to protect the best suit from gravy droppings.

'In good voice this morning, Dada,' grinned Llew as Dada burst forth into a full-voiced snatch of the hymn.

Dada paused as Mama came in with a plate of bread and his breakfast of hot, sweet-smelling bacon, the fat cooked until transparent and the lean streaks pink and succulent. He tipped his plate to one side so that the gravy from the bacon formed a small pool, and dipped a thick hunk of bread in it.

'So you will not be coming to Manafon, is it, Llew?' His voice was muffled as he relished a mouthful of bread and bacon.

'No, Dada. I am going out with the cycling club today. We have a thirty-mile ride in front of us. Anyway, one less for old Blod to pull. She's getting too old for these trips now; fall down in the shafts she will, one of these days.'

'Tut-tut, boy. Rubbish you are talking,' grunted Dada. 'Sound as a bell is Blod. Good for a few years yet, indeed. She does still like a trip out and will pull us all like a bird today, you will see. Sit in comfort we will, while you pedal that old machine of yours up and down the hills, boy.'

'I would like a bicycle and join the cycling club,' observed Davy.

'Ay, dare say,' said Llew, tucking a handkerchief into his collar and spreading it across his waistcoat before attacking the breakfast which Nell laid in front of him. 'You will have to earn your living first and save up for it, like I had to.'

Davy sighed. That would be a long way off. But a plateful of bacon set in front of him soon put bicycles out of his head and he was chewing happily when Mama and the girls sat down to their breakfast and Mama poured hot strong tea from a big brown teapot.

'I can't come to Manafon, Dada,' complained Meg, sadly. 'Mrs Purvis is having a tea party and I must go in to help, she says. I am tired of old Mrs Purvis and her tea parties and her dinner parties and all her old parties. It is enough to work from seven in the morning till six at night every day, Saturdays and all, without doing extra for her and her parties.' Meg pouted as she pushed a piece of bacon around her plate, her usually bright face clouded. She was in service on a daily basis at the house of Mrs Purvis, wife of the owner of one of the woollen mills in the town. She was paid five shillings a week, and Mrs Purvis extracted her pound of flesh.

'Aw, Meggie!' cried Davy. 'You're not coming? It's hard luck. Tell old Mrs Purvis to go to –'

'Now, now!' interrupted Mama, sharply. 'That's enough, Davy. It is a pity indeed that Meg can't come but she must do her work. Five shillings a week and her dinner and tea is not to be sneezed at and there's not many jobs about. We will maybe go to see Granny again before the summer is gone, Meg, and you will surely be able to come then. But if Mrs Purvis wants you today, that is that and no more to be said.'

Meg's face grew pink. 'I could get a job at the mills,' she said, sullenly, 'then I would get more than I get at Mrs Purvis' and I wouldn't have to go to work on a Sunday for some old tea party, either.'

Mama's mouth tightened and she jabbed at a piece of bacon with unnecessary force.

'We will have no old talk about the mills.' Her voice was final.

'I don't see why not?' Meg turned a defiant face to Mama. 'Tidy people work there and I'd get more money to bring home. I could learn to be a weaver and there's more again to be had for that.'

'Now, Now, ferch i,' Dada looked uncomfortable. 'You heard what your Mama said, isn't it?' He got up and pushed his chair back. 'Now then, it is time we were moving. Do you want me to be late at the Rectory?'

Mama rose, darting a sharp glance at Meg, who hung her head, close to tears. She couldn't bear upsetting people but she hated the hard and overbearing Mrs Purvis, who put on the mild-natured girl. But she got up obediently and began to clear the table. Nell went off to prepare the vegetables for dinner and put the meat in the oven so that dinner would be well on the way when they returned from church. Mama disappeared up the stairs on Dada's heels, as she was needed to help him into his Sunday finery.

Davy gulped down the last of his tea and carried his mug out to the back kitchen.

'You are still coming with us, aren't you, Nell?' He raised an innocent face to Nell's. She scraped irritably at a large carrot and cut out a blemish.

'Yes, I am, our Davy. And I will see you behave yourself, too, mark you, boy. You will sit by me in the trap and behave like a little gentleman.'

'Yes, Nell,' said Davy, meekly and wandered out to the W.C. 'That old Nell!' he complained bitterly to a sparrow which was pecking the breakfast crumbs thrown out on to the cobbles. He went into the tŷ bach, as Dada called it, and slammed the door shut.

When Dada had finally been seen off, dressed in a biscuit-coloured long jacket, well-pressed black trousers, a blue cravat with white spots on and carrying a pair of yellow suede gloves, his black boots shining and his white hair tucked under a black cap, there was a rush and bustle of Mama and the girls getting ready for Church, a quick inspection of Davy and then they gathered behind Mama in the tiny parlour overlooking the road, clutching their prayer books, while Mama peeped discreetly from behind the lace curtains. As soon as the Rectory trap was spotted emerging from the Rectory gates it was judged time to set off.

'There they go!' hissed Mama and Davy caught a glimpse of Dada sitting at the front of the carriage, whip in hand and head high, and Mr Gwilym Pryce with Geraint and Elinor in their best clothes sitting upright and stiffly behind him. The Rees family issued forth and walked in dignified procession, Mama and Llew leading, followed by Nell and Meg, with Davy bringing up the rear.

Mama nodded gravely to neighbours and friends they passed along the road, the bells were pealing, the sun shining and Davy gave a little skip at the thought of the trip after dinner.

'Walk tidy, our Davy,' Nell admonished over her shoulder and he fell to concentrating on keeping in step with the girls in front. Pity Meggie wasn't coming instead of Nell, he thought. He would be black and blue with pinches from Nell's fingers before the day was through. But nothing could daunt his spirits on that lovely May morning and as they turned into the Church gate he executed another caper and ducked away from Nell's vengeful hands.

Dinner was over, Llew and Meg departed and Mama, Nell and Davy waited in the parlour for Dada to bring the pony and trap round. Davy sat upright on the hard horse-hair seated chair, so well-polished by Mama that whenever he wriggled he was in danger of slipping off. Nell's sharp and critical glances could not dampen his excitement and he let out an excited yelp when the sound of Blod's hooves echoed in the quiet Sunday afternoon. Soon Dada poked a cheery face round the door.

'Ready then, is it? Blod is in good form, straining at the bit. Let us go then.'

They climbed up into the trap, Mama and Dada on one side and Nell and Davy on the other. With a 'Gid-up, Blod' from Dada they were off down the Pool Road at a fine lick, Blod's high stepping style belying her age, her brown coat shining and her old eyes bright.

They were soon out of the town and bowling along in the warm sunshine. Dada's chin was high and a self-satisfied smile creased his fresh face. Hatless, his white hair floated up in the soft breeze. Mama clutched a large black handbag on her lap with one gloved hand and held on to the side of the trap with the other. Her face was serene and she smiled across at Davy, his dark curls blown across his forehead, sitting beside Nell, whose face was relaxed, her eyes softened and dreamy. She patted the thick dark hair which showed beneath her wide hat and Davy, looking up into her face, thought that Nell looked real pretty today and was surprised.

The May hedgerows were fresh and green and the hawthorn trees showered lacy white blossoms across the fields. On the wooded hill slopes wild cherries flowered among the new green of ash, oak and beech and along the sides of the road ladies' lace, red campions, foxgloves and vetch made a colourful border, interspersed with the bright blue eyes of the tiny speedwell. Davy sighed with happiness as the trap rolled along the dusty road and the sun was warm on his back.

It was half past three when they first sighted Manafon, the small village sleeping in the Sunday calm. The village street was empty except for two men talking by a cottage gate, with an old Welsh sheep-dog stretched out asleep in the sun by their feet. The men nodded gravely and touched their caps as Blod clopped by, drawing the Rees family. Dada raised his hand and grinned back at them and Mama inclined her head, holding on to her hat for the road was rutted and the trap bumped over loose stones and rough patches. Soon they were opposite the little church with its lych gate and dark cedars on each side and on their left the Beehive Inn, whitewashed wall gleaming in the sun. Blod stopped suddenly outside the pub. Dada raised his eyebrows and flapped the reins.

31

'Hup, Blod, hup girl. What is with this old pony? Hup now! She will not move.'

Mama sniffed and clutched her handbag more tightly and the frown reappeared on Nell's face, but neither spoke.

Dada looked round, a picture of innocence.

'Likely she has a thirst,' he said, pursing his mouth. 'I will see for a bucket of water from the landlord. Sit you here, I will be but a minute.'

'Is it only the pony has a thirst?' Mama snorted and tossed her head in exasperation. Dada climbed down from the trap, winking at Davy as he passed him.

'Can I come, Dada?' Davy cried and began to climb down.

'Aye, boy, come you,' said Dada, extending a helping hand and they disappeared through the low doorway of the porch into the dim interior of the pub. Dada banged on the counter and waited. Chairs sat neatly around polished oak tables and the floor was scattered with clean sawdust. More sawdust filled the spittoons which were dotted about at strategic points, and the mingled smell of beer and beeswax polish tickled Davy's nostrils pleasantly. He looked round with interest. Sporting prints hung on the wall and close to the bar what appeared to be a poem on a smoke-yellowed piece of card. Davy moved closer and read:

> Within this Hive, we're all alive,
> Good liquor makes us funny,
> If you are dry, come in and try
> The flavour of our Honey.

Davy puzzled for a moment and then his brow cleared. Of course this was the Beehive. He was intrigued.

The bar was empty, but there was a murmur of voices from the back room. Suddenly the smallest and roundest woman that Davy had ever seen appeared behind the bar as if by magic. Only her head and shoulders were visible, but these were sufficient to fascinate him. Broad, fat-padded shoulders appeared to support a round, ball-like head without any neck. On top of this a round, coal-black bun of hair was skewered, making her look, Davy thought, like one of Oven-Bottom Billy's cottage loaves. Her nose was also round and bright pink in colour and her plump cheeks were like two rosy apples. She appeared to have no eyebrows, but her eyes, though small, were bright, dark and shrewd. A large brown mole decorated her chin and sprouted a few wiry black hairs which quivered as she spoke.

'What is it you want? We are not open on a Sunday.'

As if at a signal, the voices behind the door to the back room died out into silence. Dada cocked a knowing eye at the door.

'Aye, well, a bucket of water for my old pony I am asking. We have come a long way and it is warm indeed. Thirsty she is and so am I, come to that.' He looked at the woman slyly and pulling out a large red and white spotted handkerchief mopped his brow with a flourish and leaned more heavily on the bar.

The woman reached under the bar and brought out a cloth with which she proceeded to mop the already spotless counter, so that Dada had to remove his hands quickly.

'There is a pump out in the backyard and you will find a bucket there. A mug is by the pump. You are welcome to water.' She tucked the cloth away again.

Dada turned to Davy. 'Go you, good boy, and fill the bucket and take it to Blod. I will rest here a minute. Water does chill my insides,' he explained to the woman, 'especially when I am sweating.' He looked round appreciatively. 'It is a good while since I was in here last. Very nice it is and there was always a drop of good ale on tap, indeed some of the best I have tasted.'

'Well,' said the woman, slowly, 'I will see.' She picked up a large jug and disappeared behind the counter. Davy heard the creek of a trap-door being lifted and banged backwards heavily. Dada grinned and winked in his direction.

'Take the water to Blod, boy, and come back after. I will not be long.'

Davy found his way round the back of the pub to an old pump standing in the corner of a small grassed area, hedged in with elders and hazel trees. A large bucket stood under the pump and he began to pump clear, sparkling spring water in to it. It was cool under the trees and when he had half-filled the bucket he pumped water into an enormous enamel mug which stood on a flat stone nearby and drank deeply of the cold fresh contents. Then he dried his hands on the seat of his trousers and, picking up the bucket, staggered round the side of the pub and out onto the sunlit cobbles where he set it in front of Blod who bent her old head and drank gratefully. Mama and Nell were still sitting stiffly upright in the trap, gazing straight ahead of them.

'I will fetch Dada now,' he called to Mama. 'He is just talking.'

'Oh, yes?' sniffed Mama. 'And what else? If he is just talking he can come now, tell him. How long are we to sit here in this sun?'

When Davy returned, blinking, into the dimness of the bar the woman was chuckling at something Dada had leaned across the bar to whisper to her, the hairs on her black mole quivering with merriment. A half-empty pint pot was in Dada's one hand and with the other he mopped his moustache with his red handkerchief. He saw Davy and beckoned him over.

'Here, boy, you can have a mouthful.' He held out the pint pot and Davy accepted it with both hands, his heart swelling with pride. He gulped at the cold, bitter, amber-coloured drink then, choking and spluttering, his face scarlet, handed it back to Dada, who threw his head back and laughed loudly.

'Not as well practised as his Dada,' chuckled the landlady, as Dada passed the handkerchief to Davy to mop his chin and wipe the drops from his Sunday jacket.

As soon as Davy got his breath back he thanked Dada and returned the red spotted handkerchief.

'Mama is waiting,' he said, apologetically. 'I think soon she will be in a temper.' He too was in a hurry to get on to the Walkmill, to see Granny and Auntie Martha and Luke and Ifan.

'Aye, aye,' Dada threw back his head and finished the rest of his ale in one swallow. 'We will go now boy. *Diolch yn fawr iawn*, woman dear, thank you indeed.' He set his pot down on the bar and reached over to pat her pudgy hand. Her fat shoulders heaved in a chuckle again.

'Good day to you. Don't forget to put back that bucket, boy.'

Davy dashed outside and collected the now empty bucket. He ran with it clanking at his side round the side of the pub and set it down near the pump. When he returned Dada was already seated in the trap, reins in his hands.

'Well,' snapped Mama. 'Now that you and Blod are both watered, can we get on? It will be time to go home before we

34

get there. Hurry up, Davy.'

Davy climbed in and took his seat next to Nell as Dada flapped the reins and Blod started off again at a trot, refreshed after her drink. They passed through the village and turned off up the small winding lane that led to the Walkmill and soon they were pulling up outside the low green fence which fronted a small garden, bright with polyanthus and daisies, blue Canterbury bells, love-in-a mist and gilly flowers, with small beds of mint and parsley, thyme and sage, under the front windows of the black and white, half-timbered house. The bedroom windows were open to the afternoon sun and lace curtains fluttered in the soft breeze. A thin plume of smoke rose from the chimney and an old grey sheepdog rushed, barking, round the side of the house. As they all climbed down from the trap the door opened and Auntie Martha stood framed in the doorway.

She was Mama's older sister, also tall but more heavily built, with strong, muscular arms and a deep bosom. Her piled-up dark hair was greying and her face, squarer than her sister's, was weather-beaten, with strong features. Two deep lines from nose to chin enclosed a generous mouth and these were intensified now as she smiled a welcome, the fine dark eyes, so like Mama's, shining with pleasure.

'Well, well!' she cried, delighted, 'Here is a surprise. The fine weather has brought you out, then?' She advanced down the cobbled path to meet them. 'Susan, you are looking well, indeed. And Nell, very smart you are today. Will, it is good to see you. Undo that old pony and let her loose in the field. Davy, my boy, you have grown! Soon you will catch up with your Dada.'

Davy was caught up in the strong arms, his face pressed against the enveloping bosom, nose flattened against a sweet-smelling white apron.

'Come in, come in,' Martha swept them in front of her up the path. 'This will be like a tonic for Mam. We were talking about you only yesterday. Mam said you would surely come now the weather is picking up.'

They were shepherded down a steep step into a narrow, stone-floored passage which led into the kitchen. Davy loved the kitchen at the Walkmill. It was a long room with a low ceiling, crossed by dark oak beams, and a window at each end.

35

The deep recess of the windows showed the thickness of the old stone walls. Between the beams the ceiling was yellowed with smoke, but the floor of stone slabs was scrubbed and spotless and the fire burning in the big old range was reflected in the polished horse brasses hanging on each side of the deep fireplace. A long table stood in the middle of the room, its top scrubbed to whiteness and on the big Welsh dresser opposite the door, china gleamed and the brass handles on the drawers reflected the light from the window. On the windowsills stood twin blue earthenware jugs filled with gilly-flowers, their scent heavy in the warm air of the kitchen.

'Here is a nice surprise for you, Mam,' Auntie Martha called out loudly and Davy was propelled with a firm hand in the small of his back towards the wooden armchair on the right of the fire. There sat Granny Evans, a tiny figure in a voluminous black dress buttoned up to her jutting, sharp chin. A dark red crocheted shawl was drawn close round her shoulders, despite the warmth of the room and she wore a ruched white cap on top of her sparse, silvery hair. Bright, bird-like eyes peered up at Davy and a bony, blue-veined hand reached out from the shawl questingly.

'Here's Susan and Will come to see us,' Auntie Martha raised her voice close to the old woman's ear. 'And here's Davy and Nell.'

A thin, reed-like quavering voice issued from the sunken lips.

'Davy, is it?' The old hand touched Davy's sleeve shakily. 'So you have come to see Granny Evans? Good boy, good boy.' She sank back in the chair again as Mama advanced to kiss her wrinkled old cheek and Nell followed suit. Dada came in just then and went over and patted the shawl.

'How are you then, Mam Evans?' he bellowed cheerfully in her ear.

Her thin frame quivered at the noise and the beady eyes blinked, startled. Then as her glance ranged over the visitors she nodded, her head wobbling a little, and grinned toothlessly.

'It is nice to see you all. I am right tidy, indeed. Right tidy. Sit you down. Martha, wet the tea now. They can do with a cup.'

Her chin sank back on her chest but she continued to watch the movements around her from under her half-sunken eyelids.

As the others seated themselves Davy followed Auntie Martha out to the scullery, where she ladled water from a large, clean enamel bucket into the kettle.

'Where is Ifan, Auntie Martha?' he asked as she straightened and hung the jug on a nail above the bucket.

'Well, he is out at the back somewhere, Davy. Go you and find him. Here, let me open the door for you.'

She lifted the latch and let Davy out into the yard at the back of the house. There Auntie Martha's big brown hens poked and foraged in the dusty earth and scattered, clucking and fussing as Davy ran between them towards the wicket gate in the hedge which led down to the stream. He guessed he would find Ifan there. As he passed the door of the stable he heard the sound of a man's whistle and the rustling of hooves among the hay. That would be Luke with his Welsh cob, Gypsy. But it was not Luke he wanted to see, dark, handsome Luke with his black curling hair, strong white teeth and knowing black eyes that matched the uncomfortable teasing with which he would greet Davy. He would find Ifan, with the big head and the fair hair that stuck out in wisps. His blue eyes were gentle and child-like, always seeming, Davy thought, to gaze at something no-one else could see. Although he didn't talk very much and his speech was slow and halting, Ifan was wonderful in Davy's eyes for he knew about things which were fascinating. He knew where the old otter's run was, under the overhanging bank of the stream and once Davy had stood breathless, Ifan's warning hand on his shoulder, as she slipped smoothly through the reeds, three small ones following, through the gleaming circles of water at her wake. That had been on a hot day last summer and later Ifan had led him up on to the top meadow where they had picked cowslips for Auntie Martha to make wine and then lay on the grass on their stomachs, smelling the sweetness of the earth through the green shoots. Davy remembered that there had been a minute rustling sound near his left ear and Ifan had extended his large hand palm up among the grass and a most wonderful thing had happened. A tiny grasshopper had hopped onto the motionless hand and quivered for a moment on microscopic legs before hopping high onto a blade of grass. A slow happy smile had spread across Ifan's funny face. On their way back with their basket of cowslips Ifan had motioned Davy over to

37

the hedge and silently handing Davy the basket, he had parted the leaves and shewn him a perfect nest, in which sat a small brown bird. Davy held his breath and saw three pairs of tiny sharp eyes peeping out from under her wings. Ifan gently drew the leaves together again and smiled and nodded his big shaggy head up and down, pleased with the delight in Davy's face. Ifan knew so many things that Davy couldn't understand why everyone said that Ifan was 'Simple'.

Davy knew that Ifan and Luke were Auntie Martha's sons, but had always been puzzled as to why they had no Dada. When he had asked Mama about this he had been sternly shushed, but he had overheard at some time that she had been 'taken advantage of.' It meant nothing to Davy nor did it occur to him to question why she had been 'taken advantage of' twice. He thought she was lucky to get two sons, since there was no man to run the farm after Grandad Evans had died and Uncle Billy and Uncle Tom gone away. This Luke did well, sharing the heavy work with Auntie Martha. Ifan was referred to as 'her cross', which seemed to Davy to indicate a burden, although he couldn't understand why Ifan could be considered a burden to anyone.

Martha had gone into service when she was sixteen, a handsome, full-breasted girl with strong arms and a capacity for hard work. She lived in at Penybryn, the big farm over the hill, where she worked from dawn to dusk, coping with the household chores and the dairy work, milking the cows, churning the butter and turning her hand to the field work when necessary. Sara Jerman, the farmer's wife was a thin sharp-featured woman, rigidly puritanical, with cold, watchful grey eyes and thin, bloodless lips. She constantly reproved Martha for singing at her work and for tucking her skirts up in the fields as she raked in the hay or bent to plant potatoes in the furrows left by Morris Jerman's plough. However, her disapproval was not shared by Morris Jerman, whose hot, lustful eyes followed the girl's every movement.

Then came the night when Martha woke to see, silhouetted against the moonlit window the broad-shouldered figure in a nightshirt, which advanced on her relentlessly, and a silent and desperate but useless struggle saw the end of her virginity. All she could remember afterwards was the strong rough hands which tore at her nightdress, the suffocating weight and loud uneven breathing and the searing pain and the taste of blood from her bruised lips behind a hard hand which cut off the cries of pain and terror.

After that Martha no longer sang at her work and was sufficiently quiet and withdrawn to satisfy the farmer's wife. The man she avoided wherever possible until the day she was packed off home with her few belongings and a swollen belly, accompanied in the back of the cart by a heifer calf, as compensation to her family. She stayed at home after that helping on the farm, since her two brothers, Billy and Tom, had left for the mines in South Wales and Susan had gone into service at the Hall. She reared her gentle retarded son with loving care and never looked at a man again until the summer the gypsies came to park their caravans on the long meadow behind the inn.

She never knew his name, only that he was there, bending over the river, his hands seeking out the trout among the stones on the cool summer evening, with dusky shadows under the overhanging elders and willows. After the hot day in the fields she had come to look for watercress that grew close to the bank under the bridge. He rose to his feet when he saw her, dark eyes watchful in his handsome young brown-skinned face, black curls clustered over his forehead and round his ears, where golden earrings glinted, and a bright red kerchief knotted round his tanned, muscular neck. When, hours later, she crept back up the fields in the soft summer night, her body warm and fulfilled, her hands were empty of watercress but her eyes were filled with a dream of gentle hands, young searching lips, the sweet smell of the soft earth under her head and whispered words which meant nothing and everything and blended with the murmur of the stream over its cool bed and the evening call of the birds in the trees which cast a leafy roof against the milky evening sky. The night was like a healing draught which had washed away the horror and revulsion left by that former contact and her body felt cleansed and liberated.

She felt no bitterness when, next morning, leaving her chores in the middle, she ran down to the stream and walked along the bank to the meadow, now empty of caravans. There, knotted to a low-hanging branch of the tree under which they had lain the previous night, was the red kerchief and threaded on to one corner a single gold earring. She untied the kerchief and laid it against her face for a moment and closed her eyes, conscious again of the clean young smell of his skin like the sweet smell of the earth itself. With a long, shuddering sigh she thrust the kerchief and the earring into the pocket of her apron and climbed back up the hill, her heart full of a sadness which was still sweet and there was no resentment even when she knew, some time later, that she bore in her belly the fruit of that sweet, dreamlike night. She bore the brunt of her parents' wrath stoically, for there was no instinctive sympathy this time as there had been before. The years passed afterwards in hard work and rearing her two sons and the only sorrow in her heart came from the irony of the contrast between the sweet, gentle nature of Ifan, born out of violation, and the darker, bitter nature of Luke, born of the dreamlike beauty of the summer night by the stream.

As she grew older Martha learned from her mother all the mysteries of birth and death and became the midwife to the village and the one they came for in the night to lay out their dead. The village and the surrounding countryside forgot, or accepted, Martha's 'lapses' and as she never again cast her eyes at any man, she became well respected and valued by all around.

Davy found Ifan in his favourite place by the stream, sitting on the exposed root of an oak tree, hugging his knees and watching silently over the gleaming water which ran over mossy stones and among reeds and willow herb which grew beside the banks. As Davy approached he looked up and a slow smile spread across his wide face.

'Hullo, Ifan.' Davy lowered himself to the grass beside the quiet fellow, with the body of a thirty-five year old man and the gentle, innocent eyes of a child. Ifan nodded his shaggy head happily then with a finger to his mouth pointed up the stream to where the long hanging bows of a willow dropped to touch the surface of the water. Davy's eyes followed the direction of the pointing finger and saw the sudden dart of a bright blue kingfisher as it swooped from the willow branch down to the surface of the stream, skimming the gleaming water with its long beak and swiftly rising again to lose itself among the leaves. Davy held his breath and then Ifan turned to him again.

'Bird,' he said in his guttural voice. 'Blue bird. Fishing. Pretty!'

Davy nodded delightedly and settled in happy silence beside Ifan, content to share the sights and sounds of the summer afternoon with the big gentle man. There was no need of talk with Ifan. Davy didn't know why but it felt good just to sit beside him and if this was because Ifan was simple, then Davy felt it was a pity more people weren't as simple as Ifan.

Thus they sat for a long while, the man's big and heavy head propped by the chin on his knees, Davy leaning contentedly against the bony shoulder in its rough flannel shirt. Bees hummed above the sweet smelling willow herb and dragonflies skimmed the surface of the water, their wings brilliantly coloured and shining in the sun. From time to time an uneven and formless tune issued from Ifan's throat and Davy listened with a sympathetic smile to the strange 'song' which seemed to be part of the gentle summer sounds which were all about them.

At length the peace was shattered by a shout from the top of the steep slope behind them. Luke was standing with legs apart and hands on his hips, his eyes narrowed and his full lips drawn down in a sneer.

'God, boy, if you sit there much longer you'll end up as daft as he is. Our Mam says to come for your tea.' He turned on his heel and strode away, his shoulders hunched scornfully.

Davy felt a little shudder pass through Ifan's body and the pale eyes blinked rapidly, but he heaved himself to his feet like an obedient child and with a sad little smile he took the boy's hand and silently drew him up the steep bank and on to the meadow. In companionable silence and hand in hand they followed Luke's striding figure in the direction of the house.

The rest of the family were already seated round the big table when they got back, which had been spread with a snowy white damask cloth. As he took his seat beside Ifan, Davy's mouth watered at the sight of the plate of hot Welsh cakes, rich with currants and topped with yellow butter, melting over the sides.

'Bread and butter first, boy,' said Auntie Martha, presiding over a big blue enamel teapot, and Davy reached obediently

41

for a long slice of scone bread, thick with yellow farm butter, and Nell pushed a pot of gooseberry jam towards him. He scooped a spoonful of the thick, tangy preserve on to his plate and spread it over his bread. He and Ifan gave themselves up to the joy of Auntie Martha's baking while the conversation of the others buzzed above their heads.

After three pieces of bread and jam, two Welsh cakes and a huge piece of rhubarb pie covered in creamy 'top of the milk' Davy felt full and content to lean back in his chair and listen to the conversation. He was immediately aware and intrigued by what Auntie Martha was telling Mama, while Dada sat grinning, a large piece of yellow cheese waving about on the end of his knife.

Auntie Martha leaned her elbows on the table, both hands wrapped round her cup, her eyes gazing solemnly across its rim.

'I knew on Tuesday night, you see, that there was going to be a laying out last week. I'd seen the corpse candles on the marsh and it's a sure sign. And it was old Jones, Cae Glas.'

Dada snorted laughter through his nose.

'Corpse candles, indeed! Marsh gas, Martha, my girl. Only Marsh gas. That's what them little lights are, so they do tell.'

'Be that as it may, Will Rees, but corpse candles they have always been called round here and sure sign of a death. I should know.'

'*Diawl*!' said Dada, blue eyes wide. 'Women's notions!'

Suddenly a thin reedy voice startled them all, and made the hairs stand up on Davy's neck.

'Corpse candles,' Granny Evans quavered, 'I have seed the corpse candles. Death!' The thin voice dropped sepulchrally. 'Aye, death. Always.'

Her head sank down again, her eyes closed and a gentle snore bubbled through the sunken lips.

Auntie Martha set her cup down with a rattle in the saucer and broke the silence that followed.

'Aye,' she said firmly, 'the corpse candles are always for a death and sure enough they came down from Cae Glas to fetch me on Wednesday night. Old Jones had gone. And indeed he was a fine old man. Made a beautiful corpse, he did. Then the old woman, old fool, had to go and spoil him for me.' Her face tightened and she shook her head regretfully.

'How was that, then?' Mama voiced the question in Davy's mind, as they all sat gazing spellbound at Auntie Martha, all except Ifan, who was smiling and nodding his big head at his own thoughts as his pale blue eyes stared out of the window.

'Well, when I was done with him, and indeed he did look a fine corpse, I fetched the old lady to see him. Well, she is pretty shaky, you know, near ninety I shouldn't wonder, older than him a fair bit I believe. She took the candle over to have a closer look but she went too close, and set fire to the wadding. Scorched his beard, she did, and set fire to his head bandage. Old fool, I had a job to do him tidy again after. I do like a nice tidy corpse,' she added, smugly.

As if on cue, the reedy voice issued forth again from the old woman by the fire, although her eyes remain closed.

'Corpse candles,' she muttered, 'I've seed 'em. Death!'

'Aye well,' said Auntie Martha, briskly, 'More tea, anybody? Will, let me top you up. Now, Nell, you are not eating much. Let me give you some more pie. Pass your plate up.'

Nell shook her head.

'No, thank you, Auntie Martha. I am full now.'

'*Twt*, you have not eaten enough for a sparrow. What is with you, girl? Not in love, is it?'

Nell's face flushed to a bright scarlet and Mama, suddenly alert, looked across at her searchingly.

Luke, who sat next to Nell, peered round into her face, eyes narrowed and grinning maliciously.

'Ho, ho!' he teased. 'So who's the fellow, eh? Come on, tell us, Nell!'

'Aye,' smiled Auntie Martha. 'Looks like I hit the nail on the head! Courting is it, then, Nell?'

Nell shook her head and stammered a denial, her burning face lowered towards the fingers twisting together on her lap.

Mama's eyebrows shot up and Dada gave an embarrassed cough and reached out to spear another piece of cheese. Luke nudged Nell slyly.

'You've gone all red, girl. No need to be shy. When will be the wedding then? We must all come into town for that. Looks like we've got a sly one here, Auntie Susan. You never knew our Nell was courting then?'

Before Mama could answer Luke's persistent voice, Nell had pushed back her chair and hurried from the room, head bent to hide a sudden rush of angry tears.

'Now see what you've done, boy,' scolded Auntie Martha, frowning at Luke who grinned back at her, elbow resting on the back of his chair.

'Well, well,' he said softly, his dark eyes glinting round the table. 'Looks like we've uncovered a secret, eh?'

'Come on, Martha,' said Mama, crossly, rising to her feet and gathering up the plates, 'I will help you wash up and then we must go, indeed.'

Davy leaned his elbows on the table and gazed unseeingly in front of him. He felt a rising excitement. If Nell had a fellow she could be expected to get married and leave home. Life would be easier without the long thin fingers pinching him for every small misdemeanour and Nell's sharp voice scolding him, which made life uncomfortable. He hoped Meg would never get married. He'd like Meg to stay at home for ever. But Nell –
.

'Corpse candles. Death!' The quavering old voice interrupted his reverie and with a backward glance at the motionless figure in the chair by the fire, he ran out into the late afternoon sun, Ifan lumbering after him, smiling happily and nodding his big head.

The sun was settling down in an orange glow behind the hills as they journeyed home, Blod slower now and not so highstepping. Nell was silent, her face averted against the questionmark in Mama's eyes, and when Davy's head dropped sleepily against her shoulder she made no effort to remove it. Davy dozed through the bumping rhythm of the wheels. Once he muttered 'Corpse candles!' and Dada laughed loudly.

'Corpse candles, indeed! *Twt*! Women's notions.' He cracked the reins against Blod's swaying haunches. 'Gid up, old girl. Step out or we won't get home till midnight. Then the corpse candles will get you, Blod. Ho, ho!'

Davy shivered and crept closer to Nell as the evening air grew chilly and the sun finally disappeared behind the hills.

3

Tall Chimneys and Judas Iscariot

The fine spell held and the sun was shining at four o'clock on Monday when Davy and Geraint emerged from the school door and strolled together across the playground.

'Come up to our place till tea,' urged Geraint. 'I've got a pigeon in the loft. Swopped it with Tetta Evans for a dove.'

'But those are your Dada's doves! He sets store by 'em. Won't he make a row?'

Geraint grunted. 'No. He'll never notice one gone, he's got a heck of a lot. And it's a corker of a pigeon. Come on, I'll show it to you.'

Davy shook his head reluctantly.

'Maybe I'll see it tomorrow. Got something I want to do before tea. Something important. Secret.'

Geraint stopped by the school gates.

'Aw, c'mon, Davy. It's a real beauty of a pigeon, I tell you. Bet you haven't got anything real important to do. An' if it's secret you can tell me, anyway.'

Davy was saved from further argument by a tinny rumble of wheels from further up Kerry Road. They stepped out onto the pavement and saw Dico Lewis astride his tandem, a piece of board between two sets of pram wheels. Legs stuck out on either side he guided it, as it hurtled down the steep pavement, by means of a length of string attached by both ends to the swivelling axle of the front wheels. The two boys watched his progress with interest and then in the space of seconds disaster struck. Two chatting women emerged from Bob Williams' baker's shop half-way down the slope, so engrossed in their gossip that Dico's chariot had caught up with them before they could scramble out of the way. The tandem shot between the

45

legs of the one short fat woman and she sat down suddenly on Dico's knees. The tandem careered on its way, the woman's helpless screams and Dico's anguished shouts attracting the amazed attention of the inhabitants of Kerry Road, out chatting and enjoying the afternoon sun. Davy and Geraint managed to jump back out of the way as Dico and his yelling passenger careered past, before Dico, his vision obscured, gave a spasmodic pull on the string and the tandem fetched up in the gutter, spilling out its load. The fat woman heaved herself to her feet, eyes wild and hat askew, and picking up the long loaf which she had waved above her head during the rushing descent, proceeded to belabour the hapless Dico over the head with it. Her companion still stood, rooted to the spot, mouth hanging open, outside the shop. All this was too much for the two boys, who fell back into the dust of the playground and rolled about in a paroxysm of mirth.

Eventually Davy picked himself up and rescuing his cap from the dust, knuckled the tears of laughter from his eyes.

'See you tomorrow,' he spluttered out as Geraint still lay, laughing hysterically and banging his fists helplessly on the ground.

As Davy made his way home he passed Dico sitting on the edge of the pavement, nursing his bullet head and gazing with disgust at his shattered tandem. Davy choked on a laugh again, then took to his heels as Dico balled his fists and shouted a furious epithet in his direction.

He slowed down to a thoughtful walk as he neared his home on Pool Road, then stopped at the Stone Street corner and leaning against the wall gazed calculatingly up at the laundry chimney which soared towards the blue sky, ringed by its framework of scaffolding. No good to try and climb that scaffolding now. If Mama happened to look out of the front windows she could see him, and anyway he might not be able to get up to the top and down again before Llew got there with his builder friend, when his work finished at five o'clock. He bit his lip and scowled across at the chimney. He was determined to reach the top of it, but although he had tackled Llew again on the subject in bed that morning the answer had once again been a vehement 'No!'

Suddenly he heaved himself away from the wall and dodging across the road, slipped through the gates into the laundry yard. Keeping under cover of the wall he made his way at a crouch towards the engine room at the foot of the chimney. The door to the still-unused buildings was ajar and he slid into the dim light of the interior. Feeling his way cautiously past machinery which stood in massive hulks in the dusty twilight of the big room, he made his way over to a large shaft and crawling through, found himself at the base of the chimney. He peered up, fascinated at its awe-inspiring height. The blue sky was a round disc at the top and Davy stood for a while looking up at his objective. He then walked round the base of the chimney and his face lit up with a delighted grin as he came upon a ladder-like formation of wide staples which had been built into the inside wall of the chimney for eventual cleaning purposes. He stuffed his cap in his pocket, spat on his hands purposefully and began to climb the staples. He was stretched to his limit, as these had been placed to suit the length of a man. Soon his arms and the backs of his legs began to ache with the stretching. He paused for a while, afraid to look down, his eyes fixed on the ever-growing circle of light at the top. After a while in which his stretched muscles protested, he climbed doggedly on, stretching up for each rung, a slowly rising tide of fear beginning to edge his consciousness as the pain in his thin arms sharpened and his grasping fingers began to feel numb. Some twelve feet from the top he was forced to stop again. He tried to ease the weight of his body on his feet to relieve the strain on his arms, but since he only had a toe-hold on each staple he was unable to slacken his over-extended arms. A wave of nausea passed through his quivering frame and beads of cold sweat broke out on his high forehead.

For a moment he contemplated going back down and inadvertently glanced over his shoulder down into the cavernous depths of the chimney. His head spun dizzily and panic brought bile up into his throat. He couldn't go back. He remained plastered to the wall of the chimney, every nerve in his thin body screaming out in pain and terror. A whimper escaped him but he forced his aching muscles to take another step up and reached up for another rung. Once again he leaned his body against the wall, salt tears of fear and pain trickling down his cheeks and into his open mouth. Numbly he reached up again, another slow and painful haul to the next rung. He was only some four feet from the top but his strength was spent.

Quivering and sweating he hung there, while his heart pounded sickeningly against his ribs. Weak sobs broke from him and he raised a despairing, grubby face to the blue sky which mocked him only feet away. Suddenly the full realization of the fact that in minutes his numb grasp must fail and his wracked body refuse another effort, brought a last remnant of a scream from his dry throat, which echoed down the hollow shaft beneath him. The sky and the wall swam together into a grey mist, when suddenly his coat collar and one of his arms were grasped in a hard grip and miraculously all the weight was lifted from his feet and he felt himself being hauled up the remaining few feet of wall, unaware of his knees scraping the rough brick and the side of his face grazing the parapet as he was dragged over the top. Merciful darkness descended, blotting out the agony and terror.

When he came to he was lying on the rough plank of the scaffolding with the white face of his brother Llew hovering over him.

'Oh, Jesus! Oh God! Our Davy!' Llew's voice cracked wildly. 'What the hell – ? You stupid little bugger! What you think you doing? You nearly killed yourself. You daft sod!'

Davy grinned weakly up from his prone position, tears of relief trickling down his dusty face.

'Thanks, Llew,' he whispered, then with an effort, his voice croaking, 'Thanks for pulling me out.' His head sank sideways and his gaze took in another pair of legs by his side.

'You were damn lucky we were here, boyo,' said a rough but sympathetic voice. Llew's builder friend, Davy thought. He tried to sit up but the pain in his thin arms sent him flopping back on to the board. Muttering and cursing, Llew lifted him in arms which trembled with shock and fright.

'Here, lift him onto my back, Llew. Can you hang on round my neck, boyo?'

Davy nodded and he was lifted onto the broad back of Llew's friend. His arms still ached, but he clung thankfully to the thick powerful neck and clutched the man's waist with his trembling knees. The man manoeuvred himself onto the ladder and when they reached the bottom Davy was set down on wobbly legs. Llew thanked his friend for his help and grasping Davy's arm none too gently, led him across the road and up the steps of home.

An hour later Davy emerged again. He stood at the bottom of the steps and looked across at the chimney. The marks of Dada's belt still smarted on his behind, his joints ached, the side of his face and his knees felt raw from the iodine which Mama had used, over-generously, he felt, to doctor his scrapes, and his belly rumbled hungrily, for he had been refused tea as part of his punishment. As he looked up at the length of the chimney to its top, outlined against the sky, blue and summery, a painful grin split his face. Well, he'd done it, hadn't he? He'd climbed it. He hadn't noticed the view from the top mind, but what was an old view compared with telling them all in school that he'd climbed it? A sigh of satisfaction expanded his chest and he began to make his way stiffly and painfully towards Pilot's Fields.

The two fields, in which the young of the neighbourhood spent most of their time were reached by way of the Shitten Alley, a narrow pathway between the houses of Sheaf Street and the high corrugated-iron fence which bordered the Rectory Field on the side furthest away from the Rees's home. This narrow alley came out on to The Steps, a sturdy, wide wooden stairway, leading up onto Kerry Road. A path on the left ran past the Horse Repository and opened on to Pilot's Fields. The pathway was narrow and overgrown with nettles and lady's lace. The large black Nissen style buildings on the right were used for the horse sale once a month, where the horses which had travelled from outlying districts were housed overnight ready for next day, when they would be paraded around the large open space in front.

As Davy made his way along the path he could see some of the horses being led in ready for the Tuesday market and the monthly sale next day. Mostly cart and plough horses, they had been groomed until their coats shone and tails and manes were plaited with brightly coloured ribbons. Brasses shone on the harnesses and the leather had been polished until it gave back a reflection. He sat for a while on the stile which led into Pilot's Fields and watched the dignified progress of the horses, led by men sweating in heavy suits, gaiters shining clean and caps ticet-slick on the sides of their heads. The clopping of the great hooves, the neighing of the horses and shouts of the men held his interest for some time and then he slipped stiffly from the stile and made his way through the long grass of the first of the fields, getting pollen from the buttercups across the toecaps of his boots. He paused for a while on the plank bridge which crossed a small stream dissecting the two fields and watched the sticklebacks and tadpoles darting over the stones. Afterwards he descended from the little bridge onto the dried mud at the side of the stream and lowering himself slowly onto his haunches, reached through the rushes which grew on the bank and dabbled his sore hands in the cool water. He stayed like that for some time, enjoying the relief from the burning in his palms. He held his hands still and let the tiny fish tickle his fingers and his wrists and the sun warmed his small stiff body. After a timeless interval of contentment he rose and made his way across the now-dried marshy patch which bordered the stream, rich with the milky-mauve flowers of the 'milkmaid' and the big shining golden cups of the marsh marigolds. Flapping drops of water from his hands he emerged through a gap in the hedge into the second Pilot's field, where the grass was long and lush and starred with buttercups and daisies and red clover. Overhead a couple of pee-wits swooped and cried querulously and bees hummed sleepily in the late afternoon sun. His mind was emptied of everything but the sights and sounds of the meadow and the warm scented air which anaesthetized his aching body.

Halfway across the field he was startled by a voice calling his name.

'Davy! Davy Rees! Coo-ee!'

He looked all around him and then a shrill whistle turned him in the right direction as a small fair head reared up from the long grass on his right. He made his way across to where Nan Mostyn sat crosslegged among the buttercups and daisies, a crown of daisies on her head and a daisy chain hung round her neck. She picked and searched among the grass with thin fingers.

' 'Lo Nan,' said Davy, standing over her. 'What you looking for?'

'Four leaf clover to bring me luck.' She peered up at him through a curtain of fair hair. 'Well, it's for our Alfie, really. He needs a bit of luck.'

Davy lowered himself cautiously onto the grass beside her.

'What's up with Alfie, then?'

'Oh, he's bad again.' She sighed heavily and resumed her

50

search among the clover leaves.

'What's the matter with him?' Davy grunted as he shifted his sore behind to a less painful position.

'Con-sum-shun. That's what the doctor says.'

'Heck!' Davy's eyes widened. 'That's bad, isen it?'

'Yeh,' said Nan, wearily, 'It's bad all right. Got an awful cough he has. Cough, cough all night long. An sweating. Something awful. An' he fetches blood up too, sometimes.'

'Can't the doctor do nothing for him?' Davy felt sad for poor thin little Alfie.

Nan shook her head. 'Seems not. That's what our Dad died of. In the family, I s'pose. Don't seem fair, though, our Alfie getting it. He's only little.'

She bent her head so that the long strands of hair hid her face, but not before Davy saw a tear trickle down her cheek.

'I'll help you look for a four leaf clover,' he said gruffly and began to search among the clover leaves at his side. They sat in companionable and busy silence for a while, Nan sniffing from time to time. At length she sat up and looked at Davy.

'What you done to your face, Davy? Fell over?'

'No. Scraped it climbing the laundry chimney.' His voice was casual.

'You never! All the way up to the top? How d'you do it? Up the scaffold?'

'No, climbed it from the inside. It was flippin' hard too. Climbed some big rungs inside. Nearly fell a couple of times too. But I got to the top.' He gave a cocky grin. 'Feel a bit stiff now, mind. It was bloomin' hard work. Bet I'm the only one that's done it, though.' He could no longer keep the pride out of his voice.

'Coo! I wouldn't try it. Wonder you diden kill yourself. Why did you want to do it?'

'Oh, I dunno,' he said, airily. 'See if I could do it, I s'pose. And to see the view from the top.'

Well, I s'pose you could see miles and miles from up there couldn't you?'

'Yeh, miles and miles.' He blushed guiltily and searched the grass again. 'Hey, I b'lieve I got one.' He held up a clover leaf on a long stalk. 'Four leaves there, isen there?'

Nan took it and examined it. Her face lit up.

'Oo, yes! That's four leaves for sure. Oo, thanks, Davy! I'll take it for our Alfie. P'raps it'll bring him luck.'

'Where's Alfie now?' Davy asked as they rose to their feet, Nan carrying the four-leaved clover carefully between finger and thumb. She straightened her daisy crown and began to walk back along the field, dragging her feet through the long grass. Davy fell in beside her.

'He's at home in bed.' She quickened her steps. 'I'd best be getting back to him. Our Mam will be back from the mill by now, but she goes out most nights. Our Alfie doesn't like to be by himself at nights. 'Specially when our Mam comes home under the weather.'

'Under the weather?' echoed Davy, mystified. 'Is she bad as well then?'

Nan shook her head.

'Oh, she's all right. Has a drop too much sometimes, though. Gets that ole rot-gut from the Eagles. It's cheap but it makes her bad. It frightens our Alfie when she's like that.' Her head dropped lower over her four leaf clover and she quickened her pace yet again. Davy turned a horrified face to her.

'But doesn't she care about you and Alfie?'

'Oh, yes. But she's had it hard since our Dad died. You don't get enough to live on off the Parish. Anyway,' she added, loyally, 'She's done her best for us. Wouldn't let them take us to the Workhouse. She went to work at the mill. She needs a drop of something to cheer her up, I s'pose.' She squared her thin shoulders and pushed the strands of hair from her face. 'I'll run on now, Davy. Got to get back to our Alfie. Thank's for finding the clover. If it brings him luck I'll – well, I might give you a kiss!'

With a laugh and a wave of the hand she ran swiftly through the grass and disappeared through the gap in the hedge.

'Huh! You'll have to catch me first!' muttered Davy, darkly, as he followed after, slowly and stiffly.

He took the way home down Kerry Road, alongside the fence which bordered the back of the Rectory. The evening was cooling a little and the tall trees which bordered the back drive were casting long shadows across Kerry Road. He felt tired now and very hungry and fell to wondering whether he could soften Mama's heart enough to beg some bread and jam to take to bed. His head was drooping and his steps slowing as he came abreast of the Rectory gate.

A sound made him look up, to see Elinor swinging on the gate, dried tear tracks streaking her rounded cheeks and a downward turn to her pretty little mouth. She kicked at the gravel petulantly and clanged the gate open and shut. She stopped her swinging as Davy approached and climbing to a higher bar, hung over the top of the gate, tangled dark curls swinging from their blue ribbon.

'I hate Geraint!' she announced, as Davy stopped beside the gate.

He looked up at the stormy blue eyes and the small, rosy mouth and something strange happened to his heart.

'What you been crying for, then?' he asked hoarsely. 'Geraint done something to you, has he?'

'He broke my doll!' Her voice wavered and fresh angry tears welled up into her eyes. 'He's a devil, a devil, a devil! And I hate him. I'll kill him, I will!'

Davy dropped his eyes from the swimming blue ones above him and shuffled his feet uncomfortably.

'Mebbe he couldn't help it?' He felt he must make an effort to excuse his friend but he knew only too well Geraint's merciless teasing of his sister and the tantrums this brought on even though this had no effect on Elinor's adoration of her brother and her intense loyalty to him.

'Oh, yes, he could help it,' Elinor cried. 'He did it on purpose, he did. All because I pulled his hair when he wouldn't let me up the stable loft to see his old pigeon. He snatched my doll and threw it down off the ladder. And now she's broken and nobody can mend her.' The tears brimmed over again and, snuffling, she drew the back of her hand across her small nose.

'Aw, heck,' Davy regarded her miserably. 'Don't cry any more, is it? Tell you what, I'll get you another doll.' He had a sudden inspiration. 'I'll get you a doll that won't break. How's that?'

Elinor sniffed and knuckled her eyes.

'Where would you get a doll from?' she asked, contemptuously.

'Got one at home,' said Davy eagerly. 'I'll get you that. 'Tisn't mine of course,' he explained hurriedly. 'Used to belong to our Meggie but she's grown up now.'

The blue eyes, now dry and direct, gazed down into his

uncompromisingly.

'All right, go and get it then,' she commanded. 'Get it now.'

'All right, I will,' Davy nodded, 'stay here then 'till I get back. Shan't be long.'

'Hurry up, then.' She watched him as he turned and ran off down the road and then commenced her swinging on the gate again.

Davy ran as quickly as his stiff legs would allow down Kerry Road, along Pool Road and up the steps of the house. Once in the girls' bedroom he searched feverishly through the old chest of drawers, paying scant heed to the newly ironed petticoats and vests and passing quickly over linen bloomers and bust bodices and other mysterious articles of underwear. At length he found what he was searching for and drew it out from its hiding place at the bottom of the lowest drawer. He carried it over to the window and looked at it doubtfully.

It was the only thing approaching a doll which the girls had possessed, apart from wooden dolly pegs which they dressed in scraps of material and inked in faces on the round knobs at the top. This was a foot high wooden statue of Judas Iscariot, now dressed incongruously in a green taffeta dress with a bit of faded lace around the bottom and a striped flannel cape and bonnet made from the tail of one of Dada's old shirts. The bearded face with the hooked nose looked out sadly between the edge of the bonnet and the faded bow of ribbon which held the cape around his shoulders.

The Reverend Gwilym Pryce had discovered the statue at the back of an old cupboard at the Rectory, and feeling a strong distaste for the traitorous presence in his house and a feeling that there was something decidedly Popish about statues, anyway, had thrown it out onto the garden rubbish heap for burning. Dada had discovered it there and thinking that Mama had been able to disguise it and make a doll for the girls, he carried it home. Mama, stifling her first feeling of revulsion, got out her basket of scrap materials and soon gave Judas Iscariot a new image. However, she failed to deceive Nell, who rejected the bearded dolly with horror and it was Meggie who took it to her bosom and cradled the unyielding figure with unquestioning love. Soon the paint was worn off the sad, hook-nosed face by the kisses of Meggie and the occasional tears wept over the poor dolly which was scorned or laughed at by the rest of the family. Even Mama was unable to hide the feeling of unease at the sight of Judas Iscariot in her small daughter's arms, but the rejection only increased the protective love in Meggie's gentle heart and 'Judy' was her constant companion and bedfellow, although Mama had forbidden her to appear in public with the doll.

Davy gazed at Judy now with mixed feelings. Well, it was doll, wasn't it? And it wouldn't break, would it, no matter how much it was thrown about? 'Twasn't pretty, of course, not like Elinor's blue-eyed, pink-cheeked, china-faced doll with the golden curls. But the dress was pretty, he thought, and it had got a bit of lace stuff on it as well. Heck, it must be all right, 'cos Meggie had loved it, he defended it stoutly to himself, so Elinor was sure to love it too. He cheered up and, tucking it up under his jersey, he clutched the resulting lump on his stomach carefully and stole back down the stairs, letting himself out of the front door with his free hand. Forgetting his aching joints he ran back up Kerry Road to where Elinor was impatiently swinging backwards and forwards on the Rectory gate. She spied him coming and jumped down. She stood watching him suspiciously as he approached and, seeing no evidence in sight of the promised doll, frowned and stamped her small foot.

'Where is it then?' she demanded imperiously. 'Where's the doll? You didn't get it, did you?'

'Yes I did, then!' Davy fetched up panting in front of her. 'Here it is!'

He drew Judas Iscariot from under his jersey and held it out to her, searching her face eagerly for the desired response.

As she took the doll from him Elinor's eyes widened and her fine dark brows flew up like wings. She stared down at it speechlessly for a long moment, while Davy waited, a pleased smile spreading over his bruised face at what he took to be stunned gratification. At length Elinor looked up. A flush of fury and disappointment crept up her rounded cheeks and her blue eyes blazed at him.

'That's not a doll!' Her voice was shrill with temper. 'That's a nasty, horrible – thing! You promised me a dolly, you bad, wicked boy. You promised! Not this – this – !' Words failed her in her fury and she hurled the unfortunate Judas at Davy's feet.

'Liar! Liar! Liar!' she screamed at him, her small face distorted. 'I hate you, Davy Rees!' Turning on her heel she ran back down the drive, sobbing with frustration.

Davy gazed after her, his heart swelling with pained bewilderment. Then he stooped, slowly and stiffly, and picked up the rejected wooden figure. For a moment he cradled it in his arms and looked down at the sad, carved face. He gulped once and blinked rapidly, then, stuffing Judas Iscariot back up his jumper, he turned and made his way home. The ache in his limbs unnoticed as the ache in his breast overwhelmed him.

That night in bed, with Judas Iscariot restored carefully and secretly to his resting place in the girls' bottom drawer, Davy lay gazing at the cracks in the ceiling once more. He reviewed the events of the day. The memory of Elinor's furious rejection of his gift caused a stinging in his eyes and he turned and buried his face in the pillow, ashamed of the lump lodged in his throat. Then the picture of Dico came into his mind, with the fat woman on his lap, careering madly down Kerry Road. A strangled gasp of hysteria was muffled by the pillow. Finally, as he turned onto his back again, his aching muscles reminded him of his climb up the chimney, and anticipating the admiration of his friends in school the next morning when he told them of his exploit, he smiled and fell asleep, the pillow cool against his sore face and his hands resting on the patchwork quilt, burning palms up, as if in a gesture of supplication.

4

Rabbits and Pageboys

Davy's eyes flew open and he jerked awake as a heavy hand shook his shoulder. Dada was leaning across Llew.

'Rise up, boy. It is four o'clock. Come you, now.'

As Dada disappeared silently, Davy yawned then scrambled carefully over Llew and, dragging his clothes on, picked up his boots and hurried downstairs. The fire was lit and the kettle was beginning to sing as it hung from its chain above the cheerful glow. Dada was lowering two eggs into the kettle with the aid of a large spoon and he grinned cheerfully over his shoulder as Davy appeared in the doorway.

'Good boy. We will have breakfast in us in two ticks and you can come and help me at the stables before we go. Get the things on the table now and I will cut a bit of bread for us.'

Davy opened the cupboard of the dresser and took out two egg-cups, two plates and two mugs. He set these on the table then took teaspoons from the drawer and two knives, which he set in place.

It was the first Saturday of the summer holidays and last evening Dada had brought Fan, his ferret, down from her cub at the stables and to Davy's delight announced that they would go off after rabbits for the pot early the next morning, as soon as Dada had fed and tended the horses.

Davy looked forward eagerly to these early morning outings with Dada. He loved the feel of the quiet, silent world of the fields and woods at the early hour, broken only by the birds' morning songs and the rustle of creatures in the undergrowth. Dada would point out the species of birds, naming them in Welsh to Davy and would expound on the lore of nature as their boots picked up the morning dew from the grass and the world stirred sleepily to begin another day.

Now they sat eating their boiled eggs, with thick chunks of bread and mouthfuls of hot strong tea. Dada had cut extra bread and made doorstep sandwiches with thick chunks of red cheese, which he tied into two paper packets to be put in their pockets. While they ate their breakfast he stood the big enamel teapot containing the rest of the tea in the stone sink to cool, in order to fill a big bottle with the spare tea, to provide their refreshment.

Breakfast eaten, Davy carried the dishes to the sink and filled up the big kettle again to be ready for Mama when she got up and Dada descended the cellar, returning with Fan wriggling in a small sack over his shoulder. Shrugging into his jacket and stuffing his packet of sandwiches into his pocket, Davy followed silently out of the back door and they made their way up the steps and through the little grove of elders, emerging into the Rectory field as the morning sun broke through and sparkled on the dew, turning the drops into diamonds as they hung on long rye grass and sparkled on spiders' webs spun like fine filigree between the stronger green stems.

As Dada unlatched the stable door the horses stirred and shuffled their hooves in the straw and whinnied in welcome. The warm animal smell mingled with straw and manure tickled Davy's nostrils pleasantly as he followed Dada from stall to stall, filling water buckets from the pump outside and setting them down among the fresh straw which Dada forked into the stalls. He threw down hay from the loft above for Dada to fill the mangers and worked with a spare brush on the warm, gleaming flanks of the four horses, two for the carriage, one small Welsh cob for Geraint and Elinor to ride, and Blod. Gentle brown eyes followed them at their tasks and the creatures blew steamy breath through their noses contentedly.

Their work completed, they let themselves out of the warm stable into the crisp morning air. Dada made the stable door secure and with his squirming sack over his shoulder, led the way down the back drive onto Kerry Road. They turned up left between the tall, imposing building of Pryce Jones' Royal Welsh Warehouse and its twin factory, equally imposing, where the goods were made which were sold in the warehouse, the two blocks connected by a tunnel-like bridge which spanned the road to the railway station. Branching off to the left from the Station Road was Brimmon Lane which led to Great Brimmon, the large farm which also gave its name to the fields and woods which climbed the slope of the Crow's Lump, part of the Kerry Hill range which dominated the southern side of the town. On the northern side was the Bryn Bank, part of a complementing range of hills with steep fields, named for the Bryn Farm, a sixteenth century black and white house visible on the summit.

As they climbed Brimmon Fields, Davy looked back from time to time at the town, nestling in its long narrow valley, the river Severn meandering through and splitting the little town into two parishes. Houses and mills lay huddled together along the banks of the river and up the steep slopes of the valley on either side. By now thin spirals of feathery smoke began to rise from the chimneys and mingle with the misty miasma which rose from the river and which medical opinion blamed partly for the high incidence of tuberculosis in the town, whilst acknowledging the main cause to be the poverty and poor working conditions in the mills.

As they continued to climb through the bracken, grazing sheep raised their heads and watched them incuriously and the morning sun grew warmer on their shoulders. They climbed a gate into the field which lay below the wood and Dada mopped his brow with his big red handkerchief and, pausing on the other side of the gate, took his coat off and hung it on the gatepost. He then trudged on up the field and Davy, following, glanced back at the abandoned coat hanging there.

'Dada, somebody might take your coat before we get back.'

Dada stopped and looked back.

'*Duw*, boy,' he smiled and shook his head. 'If there is a man needs that old coat more than me, then he is welcome to it.'

Puffing up the hill behind Dada's stocky figure, Davy thought of the Reverend Gwilym Pryce reading the lessons last Sunday, and how Jesus had said, 'If a man steals your coat, give him your cloak also.' He supposed Dada was thinking of that, but he hadn't got a cloak to give away. Mebbe he'd have to give his livery jacket. *Duw*, it would be a bit thick, a man pinches your coat and you have to give him something else on top of it. Some of these old rules in the bible were harder on the good folks than the bad ones.

They reached the foot of the wood where the rabbit holes

were hidden among the bracken and brambles. They sat for a while on a fallen tree to get their breath back, then Dada opened the sack and took Fan out by the scruff of the neck, her bright eyes shining like bootbuttons in the sun and her sleek cream-coloured body wriggling and warm to the touch.

At the end of an hour she was back again in the sack and three large rabbits lay with glazed eyes and broken necks on the sun-warmed grass. Dada took a length of twine from his trouser pocket and tied six back legs together. Something tightened in Davy's stomach as he watched but he pushed it aside and set a grin of satisfaction on his face to match Dada's.

'There is a good roast for tomorrow, boy,' grunted Dada, straightening up, 'and one over for the stew-pot on Monday, eh! Now then, we will have our bit of bait.'

They sat down again on the fallen tree and munched contentedly on their cheese sandwiches, with gulps of cold tea from the bottle to wash it down.

A sleepy warmth was growing in the air and time stood still, with nothing but a faint stir in the undergrowth and the occasional flap of wings in the treetops of the wood behind them. Davy saw the bright eyes of a rabbit peering out from one of the holes in the bank and quickly disappearing at the sight of human forms on the log. A lark rose suddenly from the bracken a few yards from where they sat and they watched it as it hung suspended in the clear air above their heads and heard its sweet morning song.

Davy looked down at the huddled forms of the rabbits lying near Dada's boots and felt a sadness stir in him.

'Pity about the rabbits, too, Dada,' he ventured, wistfully.

Dada stirred the furry bundle with the toe of his boot thoughtfully.

'Aye, Davy, my boy. 'Tis a pity. But there we are, man has got to eat and the good Lord has put the beasts of the field and the birds of the air for man to take. Think on now, boy, some day we will be down in the earth and feeding some creature, isn't it? Up now and let's be getting back then,' he added briskly, and he rose from the log and with Fan slung over his shoulder in the sack and the rabbits hanging from his other hand, began to make his way down the fields back towards the town. Davy rose and hurried after him and they jogged quickly downhill, pausing at the gate to pick up Dada's coat which still hung there, warmed by the sun.

As they made their way through the field below the farmhouse, a shout made them stop and look back. There at the top of the field, brandishing a thick stick, stood Morgan of Brimmon, stocky legs apart and a flush of anger on his face.

'Rees! You have been at it again! If I catch up with you I will cleave you to the ground, Rees!'

Dada turned an innocent face in the direction of the irate farmer.

'Morning, Mr Morgan. Grand morning, indeed. Something the matter, then?'

'The matter!' the spluttering voice called down the field. 'I'll give you "something the matter" indeed! You varmint, stealing rabbits is the matter!'

Dada frowned down at the rabbits suspended from his grasp and then back up at Morgan.

'Stealing is it, now?' he called up. 'Not stealing, Mr Morgan. If I had took one of them sheep, then there's your stealing, for them sheep has been bred by you. But the rabbits now. No, indeed. But I thank you for them, isn't it, Mr Morgan. Good they will be in our pot to feed us. *Diolch yn fawr 'n wir.* Good morning to you Mr Morgan,' and he turned on his heel and proceeded unhurriedly down the remaining slope towards the stile onto the lane. Davy followed, glancing warily back at the figure dancing with impotent rage at the top of the field.

'I will tell Mr Gwilym Pryce on you,' shouted the farmer. 'We will see what he thinks of a thief for his gardener!'

Dada clicked his tongue as he climbed the stile and while he waited for Davy to clamber over, raised the fistful of rabbits in salute and bowed his white head in Morgan's direction. A yell of rage was his answer as they made their way down the lane in the direction of home.

'Will he tell Mr Gwilym Pryce, then, Dada?' asked Davy anxiously.

Dada's eyebrows shot up.

'*Duw*, boy, there's *twp* you are. Not at all. Morgan is a friend of mine,' and he led the way home between the lush flower-patterned hedgerows, head erect and blue eyes innocent and cloudless, a cheerful whistle emanating from pursed lips.

It was half past ten when they arrived back at the house, to find Mama taking hot bread out of the oven, her face flushed and an air of excitement about her. She poured boiling water into the waiting teapot and after pouring out three mugs sat opposite them at the kitchen table and folded her arms on its newly-scrubbed top. She pushed back a wisp of straying hair and launched into her news and the reason for her excitement.

'Mr Hall has been here,' she addressed Dada, but with a sidelong flick of her eyes at Davy. 'And he wants our Davy to try for the scholarship to the County School next year!'

Davy's heart gave a lurch and he leaned forward, his eyes moving from Mama's face, flushed with pride, to Dada's, which was buried in the big white mug. There was a moment's silence as Davy and Mama waited for Dada's reaction.

Dada lowered his mug to the table and frowned down at it as though the mug itself had been the bearer of this disturbing news. Davy waited, holding his breath and Mama gazed at her husband, clasping and unclasping her hands on the table top. Pushing back his chair, Dada rose and clomped over to the window, where he stood in silence with his back to them, staring out at the patches of sunlight on the cobbled back yard. After a while he broke the silence.

'This is a lot of old nonsense, my girl, and you know it. How will we afford for the boy to go to the County School if he passes? There will be tidy clothes and old books to buy. Mind, I have nothing against the learning, but it is a struggle enough for you now. No, the boy can go out to earn in another year and bring a bit more money into the house for you.'

Davy's heart sank in his breast. The scholarship classes started next term and he knew Geraint was going to join them. For some months he had secretly nurtured a longing to try for a scholarship and go with Geraint to the County School and now that the question was out in the open and the possibility actually being aired, the unspoken desire became a painful lump in his throat. He gazed in silence at the heightened colour in Mama's face, his heart in his eyes.

Mama, reading his face, tightened her lips, squared her shoulders and clasped her hands more tightly together.

'Now, Will Rees, you know I would manage without what bit our Davy would bring in. I have kept this house and all in it tidy and respectable all these years and I can go on doing it, the Lord willing and me spared.' She addressed her husband's unyielding back. 'As for tidy clothes, haven't our Davy always been turned out tidy then? As for the old books you talk about, well we would manage them. Daresay our Llew and the girls would give me an extra shilling now and again to help out. I say he should go, Will, and Mr Hall says so too. He says our Davy is good at his lessons, one of his best scholars. The boy should have a chance anyway, I say.'

She got up and gathered up the mugs, carrying them into the back kitchen, her head high and defiant.

Davy gazed miserably at his father's back. Dada turned and came to sit down at the table opposite him. Davy lowered his eyes and said nothing. Dada cleared his throat and drummed his fingers on the table top.

'Look, boy,' he said, his voice gruff. 'I know you are a good scholar and I am glad for it. But times is hard and your Mama has had struggle for years. I thought for you to earn in another year and make things to be a bit easier for her. You know young Tom Martin who is the Buttons at the Rectory? Well, next year he will be fourteen and will be too big for his livery, so he will come to me as under-gardener. I have already had word with Mr Gwilym Pryce and you are to take Tom's place as Buttons when you finish school next summer.' Dada cocked an apprehensive ear in the direction of the back kitchen, where the clatter of utensils was unnecessarily loud. He smoothed his white fluff of hair down and as Davy remained silent, with bowed head, he went on more firmly.

'It is a good opening, boy. Mr Gwilym Pryce is a kind man and Mrs Buxton keeps a good table. You will have plenty of tidy food and your livery will be free so it will save on the clothes. There will be two shillings a week for your Mama and only a field away from home. Remember, if you was to go to this old County School it will be four years anyway before you will bring money into the house instead of taking it out. What do you say, boy?' as a muffled sound escaped Davy's hunched form.

Davy shook his head speechlessly, unable to look up at Dada.

'Dammit all!' shouted Dada, incensed at the clatter in the back kitchen and the obdurate silence at the table. 'Dam' that old fool Hall with his notions. No more of it now, the both of you! Am I master in my own house or not? Susan!' he bellowed, getting up and reaching for his cap from the peg

63

behind the door. 'I am going up to the Rectory. See you have all come to your senses now, by the time I get back. And you, boy,' turning with his hand on the doorknob, 'you shall come up to the Rectory with me after dinner and Tom Martin shall tell you what he does do all day and you will see it is a tidy little job with good prospects to step in to. Why, you will mebbe take my place some day when I am past it. There now!' and he went out, banging the door behind him.

Davy got up and wandered into the back kitchen. He leaned against the door jamb and stared out into the yard. Mama clattered about crossly, getting the vegetables ready for dinner.

'Whisht, boy,' she said after a while. 'Do not think too hardly of your Dada. He is only for the best as he sees it and is thinking of me too. Never fret, you shall try that old scholarship next year, anyway. If you don't get through it, no harm done and tidy work waiting for you at the Rectory. If you do pass it, well, there. We will see, we will see. The Lord is good and the Devil is not so bad.' She smiled as Davy turned round, hope and doubt struggling across his face.

'But Dada – ?'

'Oh *twt*, boy. Get along with you, now, from under my feet. There's more ways of killing a cat than choking it with cream, and you must leave this with me. I promise nothing but that you shall try. Leave it go at that now, isn't it. Off you go and mind yourself.'

Davy clattered out through the door and up the steps and passing through the elders he threw himself face down among the long grass of the Rectory field, giving himself up to confused dreams, veering from hope to doubt until, hope uppermost, he closed his eyes and dozed in the warm sunshine, tired after the early morning start.

Dinner at one o'clock in the Rees household saw everyone round the board except for Meggie. Neither Dada nor Mama brought up the subject of the scholarship and talk was general, mainly between Dada and Llew, with Nell more silent and withdrawn than usual. Davy was careful not to make any wrong moves, as the long thin fingers seemed to be hovering, ready to pinch. Mama's eyes rested on the pale face of her eldest daughter from time to time, taking in the bluish smudges under the fine dark eyes and the downward droop of Nell's mouth. The girl picked at her food and finally, with a small sigh, pushed her plate away and sat gazing out of the kitchen window. During a pause in the conversation, Llew looked across at Nell, and with a teasing grin on his face, waved his fork in her direction.

'Lovesick, is it then, Nell? What's this I hear about you courting? And a bobby, too, isn't it? Young Elwyn Jones, I'm told. That right?'

A sudden silence descended on the dinner table, as knives and forks were suspended in mid-air and everyone's eyes turned to Nell's face, suffused with an angry flush. She rose from her chair and faced Llew, hands resting on the table top.

'You hush up, Llew Rees,' she hissed, her eyes glittering dangerously. 'Like an old woman with your gossip, aren't you? Tittle-tattle tale-telling. I just wish people would mind their own business and leave me to mind mine!'

Before anyone could recover from the outburst she had pushed back her chair, snatched her jacket from behind the door and rushed out, banging the door behind her viciously.

'Well, I never!' said Llew, eyes wide and eyebrows to his hairline. 'What's with her? It's common talk in the town that she's going with him. What's up with her, anyway? He is a tidy lad, indeed. Nothing to be ashamed of. Fit enough match for Miss High-and-Mighty, surely?'

Dada cleared his throat and drummed on the table with his finger tips.

'I have been told nothing of this.' He turned bewildered blue eyes on Mama. 'Did you know Nell was courting, girl?'

Mama had been gazing speculatively at the closed door.

'Nobody would bring old gossip to me,' she retorted, rising and gathering up the plates. 'It is a nice thing when you have to hear from others what is going on with your own daughter.'

Llew ran his fingers through his thick, dark hair, making it stand on end.

'Why in hell is our Nell being so close about it? That's what I can't fathom. Good God, he is a tidy boy, I say, and a bobby is a tidy job. What's she keeping it secret for? Beats me.' He shrugged and got up from the table. 'She's a funny one, that Nell, as awkward as they come. You never know when you are doing right with her.' He reached for his cap and went out, muttering to himself.

Mama clattered crockery, lips tight and eyebrows drawn

65

into a frown.

'Mark my words,' she waved a bunch of knives and forks at Dada who drew back apprehensively. 'There is something funny behind this. The girl is nineteen, going on twenty now. Time for courting. If he is a tidy lad like our Llew says, what is all the closeness about? Why doesn't she bring him home here? Are we not good enough for him? Is that it? Well, I will have words with that girl before I am much older,' she added, darkly and bustled off into the back kitchen.

Dada looked at Davy.

'We will get out of here, boy,' he grinned. 'Your Mama is fit to be tied now. Something is going on she isn't told about. This is no place to be. Come you, we will go up to the Rectory. Whilst I tackle them damty old weeds round my cabbages you can have talk with young Tom Martin. Up with you, boy, let us go.'

The fine weather was holding and the sun beat down on the cobbles as Dada and Davy entered the square courtyard at the Rectory. The buildings enclosed the large cobbled courtyard on three sides, whilst the fourth side was walled, with a wide double door let into it and a smaller door through which they had just passed. The house itself faced them, with its heavy oak door and brass bell-pull let into the doorpost. Tall, Georgian style windows overlooked the courtyard and a white climbing rose, which grew to the right of the door and almost reached the upstairs windows gave off a sweet perfume as the sun beat on the walls. Forming the right side of the square were the stables where the horses could be heard moving around, and on the roof some of the Rector's white doves perched, cooing sleepily above diamond-shaped apertures in the white-washed walls, through which they could fly in and out of the loft above the stables. Among them strutted Geraint's pigeon, plump and softly grey, with blue-green iridescent collar and breast. Davy wondered whether Geraint's father had yet noticed the alien among his doves. He thought it quite likely that he hadn't, for that gentle man was notoriously vague and absent-minded, beside being short-sighted. Through the open doors of the coachhouse Davy could see the Rectory trap with a few brown hens sheltering in the shade beneath it.

On the left, completing the square, were the kitchens and servants' quarters, ending in an eight foot stone wall with a green painted door which led into the kitchen garden.

The kitchen door stood open, as did all the windows, to let in what little air there was from the sun-drenched courtyard. As Dada led the way in, Mrs Buxton raised a flushed and perspiring face from her pastry making, her plump arms floury to the elbows and her white cap askew on top of her greying hair. At the sink the figure of the thin young housemaid, Emmie, drooped over the washing up, hands crimson to the wrists as she sloshed a dishmop dispiritedly over plates in the hot, steaming water. A fire burned relentlessly in the enormous and shining black range, with its polished brass taps and knobs, contributing to the steamy heat of the big stone-floored kitchen.

'*Duw*!' said Dada, mopping his brow. 'It is hot with you Mrs Buxton. That old fire doesn't help.'

Mrs Buxton drew the back of her hand across her damp forehead, leaving a floury trail.

'Well, I must have a hot oven for my pastry,' she answered with a resigned sigh. 'Hello, Davy. Geraint and Elinor are down in the field with the pony.'

'Ay, well, afterwards,' said Dada. 'Let us find Tom first for you to have talk with him, boy.'

'Tom is it you are wanting?' Mrs Buxton waved a floury hand in the direction of the door at the far end. 'Tom is in the scullery cleaning out some steins for me to make nettle beer in. Those two children are forever with a thirst this weather and they have nearly finished that last lot I made. Go you through to him. That lazy young hound will welcome a chance to stop work. I have to be at his heels all day long or he would be skulking off somewhere to hide from work.' She waved a truculent rolling pin in the direction of the scullery door. 'The Rector should have left him in that home in London, if you ask me.' She banged crossly on the expanse of pastry on the table with her rolling pin and Emmie jumped and wielded her dish mop with a little more vigour.

Dada and Davy went through into the scullery. As they opened the door Tom Martin, who had been leaning over an earthenware stein full of suds which was standing in a deep sink, idly paddling his hands in the soapy water and gazing dreamily out of the window, gave a guilty start and began to sluice the water round in the stein busily. When he turned his head as they came through the door he relaxed and gave them a cheeky grin.

' 'Ullo, Rees. Wotcher, Davy. It ain't arf 'ot, ain't it?' His broad cockney accent sometimes made it difficult for Dada to understand him. 'Too bleedin' 'ot to be stuck in this place, anyroads.'

He was a thin, wiry lad coming up to fourteen. His fair hair stood up in wiry tufts on his head above a narrow, sharp-featured face with small, pale eyes which darted shrewdly here and there, weighing up the world around him and how best it could be manoeuvred to suit Tom Martin. Orphaned in babyhood in the back streets of London's East End, he had been brought up in a Church of England children's home, where charity did not extend to affection and food was short, so that Tom had acquired at an early age an instinct for survival and a cunning to match. Ultimately geared to such survival in the predatory world of London streets, he was more than a match for his present existence, under the unworldly protection of the 'Old 'un', as he cheekily called his benefactor, the Rector, and Mrs Buxton was too distracted with the day to day running of her household and the mothering of two unruly children to be an enemy worthy of his mettle. At the moment he had a wily appreciation of his well-fed and comparatively easy existence but with the inherent instinct of the predator he knew there were richer pickings to be had by such as he in the world outside and had no intention of remaining longer than necessary in this quiet and unstimulating rural backwater.

Dada greeted him now and drew Davy forward. Davy returned Tom's grin, but he had never felt comfortable with the older boy, even though he knew that Geraint had a strong admiration for the cockney lad and relied on Tom's foxy cunning for help in many of his more rebellious escapades.

'Now then, Tom, my boy. Next year you will be coming to help me in the stables and the garden, isn't it, and we are thinking our Davy will maybe be taking your place here in the house. I will leave the boy here with you for a bit and you can tell him about the job, now, and the sort of things he will have to do. No need to stop your work,' he added with a twinkle, 'or I will be in bad books with Mrs Buxton, indeed.'

Dada went out whistling cheerfully leaving Davy to hover round the sink, eyeing Tom uncertainly.

'Well, young Davy, wot abaht it then, eh?' Tom ceased operations and dried his hands on his coarse, sacking apron. Leaning negligently against the sink he gave Davy a mocking grin. 'Want to come and work 'ere do you, lad? Or Dada wants you to, is it, and you have to do what you're told, eh?'

Davy shrugged and looked around the scullery with its two deep sinks, its white-washed walls and stone floor, at the big mangle and the dolly-tub in the corner and the many shelves holding a variety of big crocks and utensils. Despite the heat outside and the steamy water in the sink it was cool in here and would certainly be very cold in the winter.

'Do you have to work in here much?' he asked Tom, eyeing the dim corners and the high, discoloured ceiling.

'Aow, yes,' answered Tom, with a little secret smile curving the corners of his wide mouth. 'In 'ere a lot of the time, I am. Cor, it's 'orrible in the winter, too. Freeze yer monkeys it would. Had chilblains on me fingers and me 'eels all last winter, I did.'

'What do you do, then?' asked Davy. 'I mean all day, like. Is it very hard work?'

'Aow, yes, terrible 'ard.' Tom shook his head solemnly. 'Terrible 'ard it is. On all day, not a bit o' rest. It's "Tom fetch this, Tom do that" from ole Buxy from morn 'til night, 'til you're dropping o' weariness. Then a cuff on the ear for naht, likely, an' you doin' yer best when yer near droppin'. Aow yes, it's 'ard orlright, young Davy. Got to be tough you 'ave, my lad. More kicks than 'a'pence, as they says.' His small eyes regarded Davy's concerned face with malicious interest.

'But the Rector's kind, isn't he?' Davy asked, anxiously, a sinking feeling in his stomach.

'The Old 'un? He's orlright, I s'pose. But you don't see much of 'im. Jus' old Buxy chivvying you arahnd orl day. Wears you aht it do. But I 'spect you'll be orlright, young Davy. Won't bully you too much when yer Dad's arahnd, I s'pose. But o' course he ain't arahnd orl the time, is he?' Tom inspected his nails intently, the secret little smile hovering round his mouth again.

'Don't even know yet if I'm coming here,' said Davy stoutly. 'Might try the scholarship and go to the County School like Geraint, yet.'

Tom's eyebrows came together in a scowl.

'Scholarship, is it,' he sneered. 'Trying to ape yer betters, are you, young Davy. Huh! The gardener's son going to the Cahnty School! That's a larf, that is. Wotcher goin' to be after, eh? Prime minister or somefink? Aow, cut orf, will yer. I got me work to do. Not goin't to get a clip on the ear from Buxy over the likes of you. Cahnty School! Well, we'll see, won't we. We'll just 'ave to wait an' see.'

He turned his back on Davy and resumed his task but as Davy moved towards the door, thankful for the end of the interview, Tom turned and waved a soapy finger in his direction.

'They needn't fink I'm staying 'ere much longer, anyway,' he sneered. 'Aow, naow, not me. I've got other fish to fry, I 'ave. Just watch me!'

Davy made his way back through the kitchen, ducking his head at Mrs Buxton as he passed, and hurried out into the sunshine. He took a deep breath of warm air and let it out in the significant whistle. Whew, that Tom! He didn't much fancy working with him. Come to that he didn't much fancy working there at all. He didn't think Mrs Buxton was as bad as Tom made out, but all the same! Oh well, he shrugged, hitched up his trousers and trotted out through the gate and down to the field where Geraint and Elinor were taking it in turns to ride their pony. They hailed him and he ran down the field towards them, his brow clear and his future career consigned to the fates.

5

Buttons and Tramps

Davy emerged from the door over which was carved in stone 'County School for Boys'. Clutched in his hand was a ruler, a pencil and a pen. He was jostled by a rush of a score or so other boys of his own age, and from the twin door on the opposite side of the building with its complementary carving 'County School for Girls' issued forth a similar stream of girls. A fresh breeze sent clouds scudding across an unsettled sky, heralding rain. He waited on the gravel path for Geraint to join him and looked around with interest. The red brick, two storeyed building sat squarely facing the railway station, a playing field for girls on the left and one for boys visible through shrubs of laurel at the back of the school. The gravel paths which ran on either side of the building met in front where two wide steps led up to double wrought iron gates.

He had sat with others of his age group from schools throughout the county for two hours that morning doing arithmetic and for a further two hours in the afternoon trying the English examination, for the scholarship to the County School. Mama's promise of a year ago had been fulfilled and she had persuaded Dada that there was no harm in the boy trying for the scholarship at least, seeing that he was staying for another year in the Church School anyway. This was as far as Dada would go and in fact when school broke up for the summer holidays in a week's time, Davy was to begin work at the Rectory as a pageboy, in place of Tom Martin who would then join Dada in the stables and gardens.

He had enjoyed sitting at the individual desks, with their lids ink-stained and carved with the initials of previous occupants, in the lofty-ceilinged boys' hall. Heads around him were bent

71

over examination papers, lifted only to gaze for inspiration out of the long windows. The silence had been unbroken except for the rustle of papers, the scratching of pens and the occasional cough, sniff or sigh of frustration. Davy had found the questions well within his grasp and had let himself go in the 'composition' test in the afternoon, scratching away for an hour on the subject of 'A Day in the Country', chosen from a list of possible titles which included 'My Home', 'People of Foreign Lands', 'A Day in the Life of a Penny' and 'The Summer Holidays'. He had written of a visit to Manafon and described life at the Walkmill and had become so absorbed that he came to with a start when the thin grey-haired man with the spectacles sitting at a big desk at the front signalled that only another five minutes remained. He had hastily written his 'conclusion' and gathered up his papers, handing them up to the grey-haired man, who dismissed him with a curt nod. It was with a feeling of anti-climax that he walked past empty classrooms and through the cloakroom to the door.

It would be grand, he thought, as he stood waiting now, the small crowd of prospective scholarship boys melting away around him, real grand to be coming here every day with Geraint, a satchel of books over his shoulder, as he had seen the County School élite carrying. But, and he gave a deep sigh, what about Dada? By the time the results came out Davy would be firmly established in his pageboy role at the Rectory. He was cogitating morosely on the subject when Geraint came flying out of the door.

'How d'you do, then?' asked his friend, breathlessly. 'Wasn't bad, was it? Did you get through all the questions? What'd you do for the composition? I wrote about the penny, did a heck of a long thing. Think it was all right too.'

'No, 'twasn't bad at all,' Davy brightened. 'Thought I might do the one about the penny but I did the one about a day in the country. Wrote a lot about that as well.'

'Bet we'll both pass,' said Geraint, airily.

'H'm,' sighed Davy. 'A lot of good it'll do me. Dada'll never let me come here, I'll bet.'

'Well, I think that's flippin' rotten,' said his friend, indignantly. 'Fancy wastin' your time up at our place. Flippin' pageboy, cleaning boots and carrying coal and the like. Anyway,' he dismissed Davy's problem with a wave of his hand, 'Let's go home for our tea then we can go up Brimmon Wood. I want some right kind of sticks to make bow and arrows with.'

'Right,' Davy cheered up and they clattered up the steps on to the Station Road, the pressing problem of hunger and the search for bows and arrows blotting out the uncertainty of the future.

However, the future for Davy crystalized a week later when he made his way beside Dada on a cool, cloudy Monday morning at half-past seven, through the Rectory door. Mrs Buxton was waiting for them in the kitchen.

'Morning, Will. Morning Davy, my boy. Tom here is ready for you Will. I'll show you first where you will sleep, Davy and then you can start on your work.'

Davy was to sleep in along with Tom as his services might be needed in the evenings and early mornings.

Mrs Buxton led the way up the back stairs and along a passage to a low door at the end which she opened, ushering Davy inside. He looked around at his future living quarters and took in a low beamed ceiling, walls papered in a pattern of fading stripes interspersed with unlikely looking yellow flowers. Two single black-painted iron bedsteads stood side by side, covered with clean white sheets, red wool blankets and white honeycomb counterpanes. A large old chest of drawers completed the furnishing, since the room was small. One or two rag rugs on the bare boards of the floor and a framed text which proclaimed that 'God is love' intertwined with sprays of faded forget-me-nots, were the only concession to decoration.

Mrs Buxton pointed to a pair of long black trousers laid out on the bed with a small coil of string on top of them.

'Them's your livery trousers,' she said briskly, and pointing to the back of the door, 'and that's your coat. Now get into them and come straight down to me in the kitchen. There's the boots to be cleaned first and the copper to be filled for my Monday wash. If them trousers is too long, hitch 'em up with that piece of string.' She ran her eyes over Davy. 'You're a fair bit smaller than that Tom. Daresay them things'll be a bit big. But you'll grow into them and meantime you must do the best you can with them.' She bustled out, shutting the door after her, leaving Davy looking dispiritedly round him.

He found an empty drawer in the chest of drawers and laid

the contents of the small parcel, an extra pair of socks, change of underwear and a clean shirt, at the bottom of it. Then he pulled off his boots, jacket and trousers and struggled into the livery trousers. They were indeed too long and he hitched them up with a grunt until they cut into his crotch, then tied the piece of string round his waist. He then took down the livery coat, shrugged it on and proceeded to do up the long row of small brass buttons with clumsy fingers. The coat reached almost to his knees and the sleeves to his fingertips. He sighed deeply and folded back the sleeves into a long cuff. He looked down at himself for a moment and shrugged then sat down on the edge of the iron bedstead and pulled his boots back on. After smoothing down his hair with his hands he made his way back down the stairs to the kitchen.

Mrs Buxton looked up from where she was sorting laundry at the big table with the help of Emmie, who drooped over the pile of soiled clothes, her pale face expressionless.

'Hm,' Mrs Buxton looked him over doubtfully. 'Oh, well, I suppose you'll do. Bit small you are. Still. Now get on into the scullery like a good boy and make a start on them boots. The blacking and the brushes is in the drawer at the bottom of the press. When you've finished them you can take them upstairs to the front bedrooms and put them outside the door. You'll know which is which, and don't linger over it. I want my copper filled soon. You'll be starting at six from now on. You can take your coat off for now anyway and hang it up. There's an apron behind the scullery door. Put that on. But if the Master sends for you, then you put the coat on. Now look lively and get on with things. I hopes as you're going to be more willing than that there Tom. Eh, but he had me hespered to death with his dodges. You just settle down and do as you're told and we shall do very nicely young Davy.' She looked him over again and sighed. 'Pity you're so small, too. Well, what can't be cured must be endured. Get on with you now. Polish them boots and do 'em proper mind.'

And so Davy's first day in service began. He carried water, cleaned boots, fetched coal, chopped wood and was at Mrs Buxton's beck and call, with a pause for meals, which were good, until nine o'clock in the evening when she signalled that Emmie, Davy and Tom could draw up their chairs and sit beside the fire with her.

74

The three young people sat in silence, while Mrs Buxton revised the past day and outlined the tasks for tomorrow. Emmie's head nodded forward sleepily for a while and her adenoidal breath rasped in and out of her pinched little nose. Tom bit his nails and stared into the fire, his eyes hooded secretively. Davy's body ached with weariness and his eyelids drooped from time to time as Mrs Buxton's voice droned. He started guiltily as the voice sharpened.

'Drat the wench!' She shook Emmie's skinny arm. 'You'd better get to your bed, my girl, if you're going to fall asleep. Go on, off with you. It's the same every night. Not a sound from you but a snore. Fine company you are!'

Emmie looked round dazed and pale then rose and stumbled to the door. With a sleepy mumble she disappeared. Mrs Buxton looked across at Davy.

'I think you'd better get off, too, Davy,' she said, not unkindly. 'It's bin a long day for you I s'pose and you not used to it. Up the wooden hill with you now. I'll call you at six and look alive then, remember. Good night.'

'Good night, Mrs Buxton, Tom,' answered Davy, smothering a yawn and making for the door.

Tom smiled slyly after him.

'See you later, Davy boy. And don't keep me awake crying for yer muvver, either.'

As he climbed the back stairs Davy heard Mrs Buxton say, 'Hush you, you cheeky young rip. Leave the lad be now, and no bullying mind, or you'll have me to reckon with.' And Tom replied with a harsh chuckle, 'What'll you do, Buxy, tell old Will on me?'

As he wearily dragged off his clothes and drew his nightshirt over his head Davy thought longingly of his own bed at home and the warmth of Llew's presence which seemed so comforting in retrospect. He climbed into the narrow bed, then realized he had forgotten to say his prayers. Mama wouldn't like that. At the thought of Mama a lump came into his throat and he climbed numbly out of bed again and sank to his knees with his hands clasped on the white counterpane. He began the Lord's prayer, but his mind wandered across the Rectory field to home and Mama. A wave of misery engulfed him as he thought of the days and months and years ahead, carrying coal, chopping wood, filling coppers and cleaning boots, while

Geraint – well, Geraint would be at the County School, carving G.P. on the lid of his very own desk, playing football in the playing fields and learning Algebra and Latin, Geography and History. He'd have no time for Davy, the boot boy, then. There'd be no going up Pilot's Fields with a pig's bladder for a football, wandering through Brimmon Wood or gathering conkers in the Shitten Alley where they fell from the Rectory conker trees.

He stayed on his knees, his head buried in his arms and tears welled up and spilled onto the sleeve of his nightshirt. What did it matter if he passed the old scholarship? Dada had put his foot down and he wouldn't change his mind. And they couldn't afford for him to go anyway. There was no hope at all. A muffled sob escaped him.

So absorbed was he in his own misery that he failed to hear the door open. Suddenly his thick dark curls were grasped and his head was jerked backwards roughly.

'Ho, ho, ho! So it's crying for its muvver, is it. Aow, the poor little babby. An' he looks so nice in 'is little nightshirt, sayin' 'is nice little prayers. No muvver to tuck you up, then?'

Davy twisted round, fury and shame flooding his face.

'Leave me alone,' he shouted, his voice cracking and in his turn he reached up to grasp the tow-coloured tufts on the mocking head which bent over him. Frustration and misery boiled up into a hatred which lent strength to his tired arms and for the next ten minutes the two of them rolled on the floor spitting fury like wild cats. But the weariness resulting from the hard day's work conquered both of them in the end and they rolled apart, gasping and spent, and lay for some minutes, chests heaving, getting their breath back.

Then Davy dragged himself painfully to his feet and stumbled over to his bed. He threw himself down, drew the covers up to his chin and closed his eyes. He kept them closed while Tom got up from the floor, undressed and climbed into the other bed. As the silence lengthened and Tom's breathing slowed and took on the rhythm of sleep, Davy opened his eyes and stared across at the window, where the square of light was fading into dusk. There was a strange emptiness in his mind as he lay unmoving and unblinking for a long while. Later darkness fell and a single star was visible through the window but the emptiness in his mind persisted and hardened and he still had not moved when hours later his eyes slowly closed and shut out the stars.

The days passed and took on their own rhythm. Davy carried out his tasks to the best of his ability and managed to avoid incurring Mrs Buxton's wrath. He saw little of Tom during the day and at night they maintained an uneasy truce, Davy refusing to be drawn by Tom's teasing and maintaining a stony silence, so that in the end Tom gave up and they ignored each other wherever possible. Davy was allowed home on Sunday afternoons but was quiet and withdrawn and spent most of the time lying on his stomach reading on the old bed he had shared with Llew. Mr Gwilym Pryce, feeling a little sorry for the boy in a detached and absent-minded way, had asked him one day if he liked reading and when Davy replied that he did, had lent him a copy of Charles Dickens' *Great Expectations* which quickly absorbed Davy and which he kept under his pillow to read at night until the light faded. Mama became a little anxious at the change in him but after confiding her worries to Dada and receiving the reply that the boy was all right and doing well at his work, she stifled down her anxiety to a small niggle, which stayed with her.

Davy's misery had been aggravated by Elinor's behaviour. With an airy farewell, Geraint had left a week after Davy started work, to spend the holidays with an uncle in North Wales, leaving Elinor to her own devices and her own company.

She very soon got bored without her beloved Geraint and wore out the doting Mrs Buxton with her mischief, tantrums and complaints. She then turned her attention to Davy and took a malicious delight in teasing and humiliating him. She was forever ordering him to fetch and carry for her, reversing her orders to him from time to time and in the resultant confusion stamped her foot and called him a stupid and silly boot boy. If he rebelled she complained tearfully to 'Buxy' and Davy came in for a tongue-lashing and was told to 'mend his manners and remember his place'. He nursed his hurt pride and his unhappiness increased as the weeks went by and the summer was lost in endless drudgery, until a numb acceptance of his fate began to set in.

When he had been at the Rectory some four weeks, he went to bed early as usual on a Thursday night. After undressing and saying his prayers, now rather perfunctory, he climbed into bed and reached under his pillow for *Great Expectations*. He had barely opened the book when Tom came into the room, much earlier than usual. Davy looked up in surprise, then with a nod, returned to his reading.

'Wotcher, Davy,' Tom's voice was unusually friendly. 'Readin', eh?'

Davy looked up warily and nodded again.

'Never got the hang of it much, meself,' Tom proceeded to undress. 'But I s'pose it's orlright for them as likes it. Bit of a scholar you is though, ain't you young 'un? Must be a bit orful like for a scholar to be doin' a lowly job like this.' He climbed into bed and Davy frowned, refusing to be drawn.

'Ow long you goin' to stick it, then?' Tom settled down, leaning on one elbow and regarding Davy from beneath hooded eyelids.

'Not got much choice, have I?' Davy responded irritably.

'Aow, I don't knaow,' Tom's secretive little smile played about his lips. 'Don't like it, though, do yer? An' that makes two of us. I been thinkin'.' He eyed Davy speculatively. 'Neither of us likes it 'ere. Then what are we stayin' for? That's what I asks meself. What are we doin' 'ere? It's a free country, ain't it? Even if you passes that there scholarship, yer old man won't let yer go to the Cahnty School, will 'e? So yer gotter spend the rest of yer natural 'ere, while yer friend, young Geraint, as is priverlidged so to speak, will be goin' off to that Cahnty School. 'E won't be no friend of yourn then, will 'e, young Davy? 'An I've seen 'ow young Elinor treats yer. Like a bit o' dirt. An' you worshippin' the grahnd she walks on. I sees that too.' He grinned slyly at Davy, who coloured to the roots of his hair.

Before he could articulate his fury, Tom raised a silencing hand.

'Orlright, orlright. Keep yer 'air on. Just sayin', I am. Yer can't deny it, I've watched yer. An' I've thought to meself, poor young shaver. An 'ell of a life 'e's goin' ter 'ave rahnd 'ere. Oh yers, I keeps me eyes open, I does.'

'It's none of your business,' replied Davy, bitterly.

78

'Ah, well, naow. That's as may be. Mebbe I can make it my business. Wotcher say if we runs away to London, the two of us? I ain't stayin' 'ere for the rest of me natural, either. I'm orf to seek me fortune, I am. Aow, I knows me way abaht, never fear! I'm orf an' right soon, too. I was just finking as 'ow yer might like to come wiv me. Seein' as 'ow yer ain't got much ter look forward to 'ere!' Tom lay back on the pillow, his hands behind his head, and stared up at the ceiling through narrowed eyes. 'Fink abaht it, young 'un. Just fink abaht it quiet-like for a bit. But don't take too long abaht it 'cos I'll be orf in a day or two an' yer won't get a charnce like this again. Yer couldn't go on yer own. Like a new-born babby, yer'd be. But I knows me way arahnd, I does. Yer'd be orlright with me. But,' he added darkly, casting a threatening look over at Davy, 'don't yer whisper a word of this to a mortal soul, hear? Or on me muvver's grave I'll get yer for it. Aow yes, you tell and I'll get yer if it's the last fing I do.' He drew his finger across his throat dramatically and leered across at Davy's pale face.

Run away! He'd never thought of running away. His fevered brain pictured it, the long tramp to London and then – what? He supposed Tom knew what they would do then. Seek their fortunes! His imagination leapt ahead. When he'd made his fortune he could come back home. He saw himself in a carriage and pair bowling into Newtown, his fortune in a box on top, Mama smiling and welcoming him, Dada and Llew shaking hands admiringly, Nell and Meggie exclaiming in delight at the presents he would bring them. And Geraint and Elinor. Well! He'd be upsides with them, then, wouldn't he? As for Elinor, there'd be admiration in those big blue eyes all right, and she'd toss her dark curls and smile at him and he'd bring her the best present of the lot. Maybe a diamond ring. He caught his breath. Yes! a diamond ring and he'd put it on her finger and he'd asked her to marry him and, well, she'd say yes straight away. She'd be flippin' glad to and him with a fortune.

He lay for a long time clutching the coverlet spasmodically, giving rein to his imagination as the light dimmed outside the window. Tom slept, his small secret smile on his face and eventually Davy slept too and in his dreams he ran his fingers through sovereigns and jewels in a fine strong box, while Elinor and Geraint and Mama and Dada and all of them peered over his shoulders and exclaimed in admiration and gratitude.

It was noon on the following Sunday and the misty early morning drizzle had given way to a watery sun which was strengthening as it shone overhead. Tom and Davy sat under a hedge on the far side of Welshpool, their damp hair and shoulders beginning to dry a little as they chewed on two hunks of slightly stale bread, extracted from two bags of miscellaneous scraps of food carefully saved and secreted over the last three days. They had silently let themselves out of the servants' quarters of the Rectory at dawn, before Mrs Buxton had stirred and had hastened to put some miles between them and the town before slowing to a stoical trudge. The fifteen miles they had covered had been uneventful, for little was abroad on the quiet Sunday morning and their passing had been remarked only by a few ruminative cows who stopped their chewing to look over the hedge speculatively, and a sleepy farm youth, calling on his own charges for milking time and was too morning-eyed to spare them any curiosity. The town of Welshpool had been in a drowsy mid-Sunday-morning state when they had passed through less than an hour ago, the last trickle of worshippers hovering round St Mary's as they made their way up the Church Bank. They were now seated close to a fork in the road where a signpost indicated that Oswestry lay straight on and Shrewsbury down the right fork.

'Which way now?' asked Davy through a mouthful of bread which, though uninviting, was going some way to allaying the pangs of hunger with which he had been attacked for the past two hours.

Tom pointed in the direction of Shrewsbury.

'That must be the way. I fink so, anyways. Shrewsbury's in England, ain't it? I dunno abaht Os-Os – whatever it is. Yers, that's the way, I reckon. We orter get to Shrewsbury tonight, I should fink.'

Davy looked up at the signpost dubiously.

'We aren't halfway there, 'cording to that,' he pointed out.

'Aow, we'll rest a bit naow and then take it steady, like,' Tom said airily, poking about in his bag of scraps for a more tempting item and coming up with a small and greasy piece of black pudding which he popped into his wide mouth and chewed appreciatively.

Davy selected a cold potato with some remnants of gravy adhering to it and crammed it wholesale into his mouth. They both had a bottle of water in their pockets and they washed their meal down with this.

'May as well rest awhile an' get a bit of kip,' yawned Tom, and screwing the top of his paper bag over the remainder of his food, he proceeded to make a pillow of his jacket and stretching out luxuriously on the grass verge, was soon asleep. Davy's eyelids were prickling and so, rolling up his jacket and following Tom's example, he dozed off, the sun now warm on his face and the dampness of his clothing less uncomfortable as it dried and warmed in the sun.

Davy awoke with a start and looked round him with a dazed air. He found himself lying in the middle of two prone figures. He rubbed his eyes, shook his head and looked again. On his left Tom still slept, the inevitable small smile lifting the corners of his wide mouth, pale lashes lying undisturbed on his thin cheeks. Davy stared then at the figure on his right and wrinkled his nose at the musty smell which the warm sun was drawing from the scarecrow-like clothes of the interloper. His bemused eyes took in the details of the recumbent body by his side. A battered and greasy hat, under which lay long strands of greying, sandy hair, was tipped over the eyes, hiding them so that Davy could not tell whether they were open or closed, but the steady if wheezy breath which issued through a small gap in the straggling whiskers of the same colour suggested sleep. A pair of overlarge trousers were held round the waist with a twist of baling twine while similar twine held the bottoms of the trousers in a thick frill round each skinny and grimy bare ankle, which was visible between the bottom of the trousers and the top of each boot, gape-soled and laced with muddy string. The fellow's hands were joined peacefully across a hollow stomach and the upper part of the body was clothed in what appeared to have once been a woman's shirt-blouse in a violent shade of puce, its former glory now besmirched with droppings of assorted meals. A large overcoat of a nondescript and rusty colour lay beside the sleeping figure, together with an enamel can with a battered lid and a smoke-stained bottom. A bundle tied with a large green-spotted handkerchief which was surprisingly clean in comparison with the rest of the creature's possessions, lay beside a three-foot long thick stick, with a bulbous knob at the top. Davy sat up cautiously and leaned over to peer closer at their unexpected companion. He jumped back quickly as the figure stirred and grunted, and the disturbance of the strange clothes sent out an increase of the pungent smell.

'Whew!' Davy breathed out through his mouth and held his nose. 'What a stink!'

He reached over and shook Tom, who started up frowning but warily awake in the instant. With a cautionary finger to his lips Davy pointed to the motionless figure at his side and raised his eyes questioningly at Tom, who now sat upright and stared across him at the scarecrow figure. Then he grinned and shrugged.

'Jus' a tramp,' he whispered in Davy's ear. 'C'mon. Time we was shiftin' anyways. Dunno 'ow long we've slept but we better get orf if we's to get to Shrewsbury 'fore dark.'

They had begun to gather up their possessions silently when a grating voice startled them and made them freeze.

'Shrewsbury, is it, young shavers? Have a job gettin' there afore dark, boyos!'

The boys looked round at the stretched-out figure to find that the battered hat had been tipped back and a pair of shrewd grey eyes were regarding them benignly from under wrinkled, lizard-like lids. The gap in the whiskers had split wider into a grin, revealing an assortment of broken and discoloured teeth and a moist tongue which flicked in and out of the gap in the whiskers increasing the lizard-like image. The pale, fleshy nose was pitted with tiny black spots.

Davy swallowed nervously and glanced back at Tom who rose to his feet and moved over to stare down at the tramp, a cheeky grin on his face.

'Yer got sharp ears, old'un. Wotser time, anyway? Got any notion?'

The tramp sat up and squinted at the sun then stared around him at the shadows cast by the hedges and the trees.

' 'Arf past three. Four o'clock,' he conjectured, shrugging. 'You've slep' the afternoon away, lads. I bin 'ere a fair time an' you was sleepin' like a couple o' babbies when I come.'

'Aow, cripes,' Tom's face fell. 'We was 'opin' to get somewhere near Shrewsbury 'fore dark. Thought there'd be more shelter there to kip down for the night.'

The tramp shook his head and pulled the brim of his battered hat further over his eyes to shade them from the sun.

'Towns isn't the best places to kip, always, old sons. Depends on what the rozzers is like there. Some'll wink an' leave you lie, but others is nasty-like and'll make short work o' shiftin' you on. Where you makin' for anyways?'

The two looked at each other warily and didn't answer. The tramp chuckled.

'S'orl right with me, boyos. Dunt want to know yer business. Runnin' away, is it?' He held up a staying hand as the two boys stiffened defensively. 'Orlright, orlright! Told you, it's nuthin' to me. Jes thought I could give you a few tips, that's all. You don't have to tell me nuthin'. But there's things as it's best to know if you're on the road, things as makes it easier.' He broke off a long juicy blade of grass and poked it into the gap in his whiskers. His jaws moved as he chewed and the boys, hypnotized, lowered themselves to the ground, one on each side of him.

'Y'see lads,' began the tramp. 'The road's no place for ammerchewers, as you might say. Bein' on the road is like a perfession. There's tricks to every trade, as they say an' trampin's no different. It's a trade. A perfession,' he reiterated, selecting another blade of grass. 'You got to know the rules an' abide by 'em. Yer gotter remember you're not the only one on the road. Us tramps is a brotherhood, in a manner of speaking. We 'elps each other an' 'as our own ways o' goin' about things.'

'Got to know the dodges, eh, old 'un,' queried Tom grinning slyly and tapping the side of his nose.

'Well, as to that,' replied the tramp, 'Haven' I said, there's tricks in every trade and dodges in every perfession. Tramps is no different.'

Davy gazed at the incongruous figure with interest.

'How did you get into tramping, then?' he asked. 'Sort of born to it, were you, or did you sort of go into it gradual like?'

The tramp gave a wheezy chuckle.

'Don't know as you could be born into it, boyo. Tramps is loners, you see. Don't often take their wives along o' them. Mind, I 'as known of couples on the road, but they'm more rare an' mos'ly old uns. No, I s'pose you drifts into it mainly. Things 'appen an' it seems the best way out. Take me, f'instance. Born in the South Wales valleys, I was, an' intended for the colliery like me father an' gran'father before me. Me Dada was killed in the pit an' left me Mam with five kids. Me two bigger brothers went down when they was younger'n you and when me turn came I went down too. Nigh on twenty years I was down the pit and hated every day of it.' He gazed reflectively out at the peaceful, sunny countryside around him and sighed.

'I married when I was twenty-three,' he went on after a while. 'She was a good 'ooman, was Mari. Strong in the Chapel and very strict in 'er ways. Everybody said she was a good wife and so she was, no doubt. But what with spending me days down in the darkness an' cold, most times up to me waist in muck an' water, and then not much light or warmth when I got home at night, well, I s'pose you could say it jus' got on top o' me. We never 'ad no kids, y'see. Seems even that were out of 'er nature, so to speak. Cold, she were. Cold an' black chapel as well.' He sighed again, then rubbing his nose on the sleeve of the puce blouse, 'Well, come the day when I set off for me shift at four in the morning an' found meself walkin' past the colliery gates an' headin' for the mountain road. One or two of me mates were surprised like an' shouted after me, "Where you goin', boyo?" But I never answered, 'cos I didn't know meself. Jes kep' goin' out into the air and the sun. An I bin goin' ever since, like.'

Davy was silent, contemplating the story thoughtfully.

'What about your wife,' he asked after a while. 'Must have wondered where you'd gone to. Disappearing like that all of a sudden.'

The tramp cocked an eyebrow and gave a wry look in Davy's direction.

'That's a fair question, I s'pose, boyo. But let me ask you one then. Got a Mama and Dada, 'ave you?' He went on as Davy nodded silently. 'What they goin' to think of you disappearing all of a sudden, like, eh? Thought about that? My wife would've bin all right, I promise you. Didn't need me, see? An' as I say, there was no kids or I don't suppose I'd 'ave gone. But what about your Mama and Dada? What was it, was they bad to you, like? Leathered you, or something?'

Davy shook his head.

'No!' he said, indignation in his voice. 'Mama and Dada are good. 'Twasn't them that made me run away. 'Twas something else.' His voice trailed off and he plucked at the blades of grass at his side, his face lowered.

The tramp's gaze turned on Tom calculatingly, sizing him up. Tom grew restive under the stare and suddenly leapt to his feet.

'Aow, c'mon, Davy,' he cried impatiently. 'We gotter get on. Can't sit here talking all day. We'll never get nowhere. C'mon, C'mon.'

Davy rose to his feet reluctantly. His boot had rubbed a blister on the back of his heel and thoughts of Mama and Dada had lowered his spirits somewhat. London seemed a long way off and the future clouded, but then he thought of the alternative. Back to the humiliation at the Rectory and a hiding for running away into the bargain. He shrugged into his jacket and gathered up his packet of food and his now empty bottle. The tramp, who had been watching his face, also got up from the grass verge. He picked up his belongings, threw his coat over his shoulder and hitched up his over-large trousers.

'If you young gennelmen don't mind, I'll join up with you for a bit. I'm doin' the Shrewsbury road meself and I'd be right glad of your company. Might put you in the way of a place to kip tonight too. That's if you don't mind?' he added with a mock bow.

'Suit yerself,' grunted Tom, indifferently, but Davy for some reason felt his heart lightening a little as he fell in beside the scarecrow figure and the ill-assorted trio set off down the Shrewsbury road as the shadows lengthened a little and a small cool evening breeze began to stir the tree tops.

6

Haystacks and Homecomings

Davy sat cross-legged on a hard straw palette, naked except for a rough grey blanket wrapped around his shivering frame. He snuffled miserably and clutching the blanket round his shoulders with his left hand, reached down with his right to scratch his behind where something was biting him. Heavy rain beat incessantly against a row of tall narrow windows facing him and intensified the gloom of dusk in the long bare room. It became increasingly difficult to pick out the details of his surroundings but as he looked round uneasily he made out bare walls and a row of similar palettes down both sides, on which humped and inert forms lay. A variety of sounds emanated from the occupants of the palettes, snores, uneasy mutterings, coughs and wheezes and from somewhere in the shadows at the far end a continuous drunken monologue, interspersed with crazy high-pitched cackles which sent further shivers up Davy's spine.

On his right the tramp slept, curled up with the blankets pulled over his head, while on the other side he could just make out the form of Tom lying on his back, arms behind his head and a soft snore indicating that he, too, slept. Davy's shivering intensified until his teeth chattered and he knew that he had never been so lonely and so miserable in his life. He was in a workhouse, some twenty-odd miles the other side of Shrewsbury and his sodden clothes hung among a row of strangely assorted garments on a piece of rope strung across the far end of the room.

His confused mind cast back over the events of the past two days and he clenched his teeth together in an effort to stop their loud chattering. His nose had become accustomed to the

86

heavy, fetid smell of unwashed bodies and the wet and malodorous clothing which hung in the darkening room, but the strange sounds made him nervous and he drew the blanket up over his ears in an attempt to shut them out.

It was the second night of their journey, the first having been spent among the sweet-smelling hay in a dutch barn half-way between Welshpool and Shrewsbury. The tramp had led them unerringly to their night's shelter, where they had taken turns to sip from a scalding can of tea obtained by the tramp from a house down the road, obviously known to him as a 'touch'. He had also obtained from the same source three thick hunks of home-baked bread and a generous lump of cheese which they shared hungrily, eked out with the rest of the scraps from the boys' bags, which Davy pressed on the tramp despite a warning frown from Tom. Their supper demolished, they made themselves comfortable among the hay and Davy had found solace in the soft night sounds which made him think of Dada and in watching the clouds scud across the night sky. A fresh breeze had blown up and the tramp had said that he smelt rain coming. With his boots removed to ease his blistered heel, he lay back luxuriously in the hay, enjoying its sweet earthy smell. Before he fell asleep his last thoughts were of the tramp. Davy liked him and was conscious of a feeling of contentment in his company and he wished that the tramp would stay with them all the way to London. However, it was clear that Tom did not share his feelings and in fact had declared his intention of 'ditching' the tramp during the time that he had left them to fetch the tea and bread and cheese from the house.

The next morning they had awakened early to louring skies and a cool wind. The tramp urged them on to the road to get as far as they could, he explained, before the rain came. They had reached Shrewsbury by mid-morning, where the tramp had cadged fresh tea for them and also a bag of stale buns from the back door of a bakery. They breakfasted on these under a hedge on the far side of the town and the tramp took a grubby piece of rag from his pocket and packed it round Davy's sore heel which eased the rubbing somewhat. They had put some ten miles or so between them and Shrewsbury when the rain started, a few spots at first and then it began to fall steadily. However, it was warm rain at first and they kept going well into the afternoon, when the tramp obtained another can of hot tea for them, together with two large cold potatoes and the carcase of a chicken which came from a big house and still had satisfying pickings on it, and half a rather stale brown loaf, which they broke into three pieces. They sheltered under an old oak tree to partake of this meal. It had grown much cooler as the afternoon wore on and Davy's clothes clung to him, chilling his body. His boots were wet and had developed a hole in both soles which caused him to squelch as he walked. He felt the tramp's lizard-like eyes resting on him from time to time but their expression was inscrutable and the meal was eaten in silence. Tom seemed to have withdrawn into himself since morning and spoke little throughout their passage through the dripping countryside, his small eyes hooded and his wide mouth drawn down at the corners. He appeared to regard the tramp with suspicion, which made Davy uncomfortable. He had grown fond of their strange travelling companion and grateful for the hot tea and food which the tramp provided for them.

After the meal the tramp wiped his mouth with the back of his hand, belched loudly and began to gather up his possessions.

'Better get on a bit further, lads,' he urged. 'This ole rain's goin' to get worse instead of better and we'll need some cover for tonight. We'd best make for the work'ouse. They'll give us a kip there.'

'Workhouse!' Davy was horrified. 'But won't they keep us there?'

'Bless you, no!' The tramp chuckled. 'O' course not. Keep us? What would they want to keep us for? Got enough on their 'ands without 'anging on to us, lad. But we'll get a bed of sorts and a sleep in the dry. C'mon, look slippy. It's about five mile further on. We goin' to get mighty wet but we'll be wetter still if we don't get under shelter tonight.'

Davy looked at Tom dubiously but the boy looked sullen and only shrugged, so they set off again, the rain driving in their faces and running down the backs of their necks. When they finally reached the gaunt and forbidding building which housed the workhouse nearly two hours later, they were three miserable and sodden figures and while the tramp went off to see the Master of the workhouse, Davy and Tom stood

88

dripping in the stone porch. They were silent and shivering and too exhausted to care where they were. The tramp came back with the Master, a grey-looking man with thinning hair and a drooping moustache and the tramp moved over to Davy and put his hand on his shoulder. The Master nodded expressionlessly and Tom's eyes were suddenly alert and suspicious. Davy, however, was too wretched to notice his surroundings and when the Master turned on his heel and disappeared down a passageway, the tramp beckoned both boys forward and they followed him along another passage and down a short flight of steps to the room which they now occupied in company with some seven or eight other travellers driven in by the weather.

Suddenly Davy was overcome by his own misery and exhaustion and he eased himself down on his straw bed and wrapped his blanket more closely around him. Gradually his shivering eased and he fell into an uneasy sleep, dimly conscious of the itchings on his body which he was too weary to scratch and finding some comfort in the folds of his musty-smelling blanket.

He must have slept for some hours for when he woke with a start it was to find a grey dawn filtering through the panes of the long windows. He sat up and looked around him in some confusion aware of a heavy and aching head and a rasping pain in his chest. He discovered that the palettes on either side of him were empty. Clutching his blanket round his naked frame he swung his legs onto the floor and stood up unsteadily. Some of the forms on the other mattresses were beginning to stir, with mutterings, coughing and scratching. Davy stood swaying by the side of his bed, panic mounting in him when found no sign of Tom or the tramp, only the two blankets lying crumpled on their palettes. He was staring round wildly, cheeks flushed and hair on end, when the door at the end of the room opened and the master of the workhouse entered. He was followed by a large, red-cheeked and cheerful-looking policeman. Davy's eyes widened and he froze. The two men came over to him.

'This is him,' said the Master coolly. 'This is the lad. Other 'un's scarpered by the looks of it. But this is the one old Billy the Miner wanted took back. T'other 'un'd make out, he reckoned.'

The policeman looked down at Davy with a twinkle in his

eye.

'Well, young feller-me-lad. Wotcher been up to, eh? Running away, is it? And where was you bound for, may I ask?'

At that moment Davy felt past caring what happened to him. His head throbbed, his eyes were heavy and his whole body felt hot and uncomfortable. Besides, the policeman looked kind and jolly and, well, if they stuck him in prison it couldn't be any worse than this place.

'We were going to London,' he mumbled. 'Going to seek our fortunes. But it came to rain.'

The policeman threw his head back and laughed richly.

'Oh dear, oh dear,' he spluttered. 'Seekin your fortunes, was you? An it come to rain. Oh dear me. Hard luck, young shaver. But you'd have had to be a sharp 'un to find your fortune in London I doubt. You'd 'ave to be a lot cleverer than you've turned out to be.'

'Tom was clever, anyway,' muttered Davy. 'He knew his way about.'

'Ah, well, maybe your fine feathered friend does. He's buzzed off, anyway. I think you may be well rid of that young villain. Now then, young feller, you get your clothes on and come along o' me.'

The Master had left the room and the policeman took hold of Davy's arm under the blanket and led him across to where the assorted clothing hung in a depressed line on the rope.

'Still a bit wet, I'm afraid,' said the policeman, as Davy reached for his own garments and shakily began to dress himself. 'Oh well, there's nothing else for it. Get them on and let's get out of here.' He looked around frowning and wrinkled his nose distastefully. 'Cor, what a stink! Hurry up, young 'un, me stomach's turnin' over.'

When Davy had drawn the last of the cold damp clothes on to his shivering body he followed the policeman from the room and out into the morning. The rain had stopped and the air smelt clean and fresh and both Davy and the policeman took deep breaths.

'Are you taking me to gaol?' asked Davy in a small voice and the big man laughed again.

No, boy, you don't go to gaol for running away. What's your name now? Davy, is it? Well, Davy, you're goin' back home and no more of your tricks or mebbe it will be gaol next time.

90

Come on, there's a trap on the road and I'm goin' to drive you back into Wales where you come from. Now, be a good lad and tell me where you live and we'll have you home safe and sound in a few hours.'

Davy thought as hard as his aching head would allow. He didn't fancy the thought of arriving home with a policeman. There'd be Dada's strap at the other end. Then back to the Rectory and it would be worse than before. He'd never face Elinor and Geraint, and Mrs Buxton would be sure to take it out of him. Misery washed over him and he sat down on the workhouse steps with his face in his hands.

' 'Ere, 'ere, young shaver,' said the policeman kindly, leaning over him and trying to lift his head. 'Wot's up, don't you want to go back to your Ma and Dad? 'Ere, you 'ave got a Ma an' Dad, haven't you?'

Davy nodded, miserably, and the policeman went on. 'Well then, that's the place for you. Come on now, let's get off. It's a fair way and I want to get back here this afternoon, so let's make a start.'

Davy rose to his feet and followed the policeman down the drive. Alongside the gate a horse was hitched with a large old trap harnessed to it. The policeman grasped Davy under the armpits and swung him in and soon they were bowling off down the road at a fair speed. The rhythmic clopping of the horse's hooves and the swaying of the trap had a hypnotic effect on Davy and he curled up in the back of the trap, and fell into a fevered sleep.

Some hours later they reached the outskirts of Welshpool and the policeman pulled to the side of the road and reined in the horse. He leaned over the sleeping boy and looked into his flushed face. Davy's forehead was beaded with sweat and the dark curls clung to it. The policemen felt one burning cheek with the back of his hand and gave a grunt of concern. He shook Davy's shoulder and the dark eyes opened slowly. He looked up into the kindly face above with a dazed expression.

'We'd better get you home quick, me lad, before you gets the newmony,' the man said, gruffly. 'Now then, tell me where I'm to take you. I only know your old friend picked you up by Welshpool. Where you from? Let's have it.'

Davy had a sudden vision of the Walkmill and Auntie Martha's tall and comforting figure at the door. He thought of

Ifan with his wide smile and his faraway gaze which asked no questions and Granny Evans nodding and dozing in her own little world by the fire.

His voice was cracked and hoarse as he whispered, 'The Walkmill, Manafon,' and then drifted off again into a fevered doze.

The policeman grunted and turned back to flap the reins. The horse started into a trot again and they were on their way through Welshpool and out onto the road where the policeman kept on the alert for a signpost or a passer-by to tell him the way to Manafon.

☆   ☆   ☆

When Davy opened his eyes again he was lying on a fat feather bed between sweetly scented sheets, which were cool to his aching body. He squinted through a shaft of sunlight and made out a small clean room with rose patterned wallpaper and spotless lace curtains stirring in the breeze from the open casement window. He blinked rapidly and gazed through the window at a blue sky with puffy white clouds like cotton wool drifting across above the top of a leafy sycamore tree. His head still throbbed and his chest felt sore and tight but with lifted spirits he realized he was at the Walkmill. He stretched his hot limbs luxuriously in the enveloping bed and sighed with relief. He turned his head on the big fat pillow and looked around him. Everything was neat and clean, the mahogany dressing table and chest of drawers polished to give off a rosy glow and the brown lino on the floor shone between the scattered rag rugs of bright mixed colours. On the wall opposite the bed hung a picture of a buxom lady with long golden hair clinging to a ladder propped against an apple tree and reaching up for a very rosy apple, while a young man stood below steadying the ladder and gazing up at the buxom lady with a besotted expression on his rosy-cheeked face. Davy was regarding this picture with drowsy interest when a step sounded on the stairs and the door opened to let in Auntie Martha.

'Oh! So you're awake at last, you young scamp!'

Davy nodded and watched her warily as she crossed to the bed. She put a cool hand to his forehead. Hesitatingly he put his own hand up and touched hers as it lay there. She gave a wry smile.

'Well, what have you got to say for yourself, then, Davy Rees? The very idea! Running away like that. What are your Mama and Dada going to be thinking? Worried sick they will be. Didn't you think about that? Well now,' she plumped down on the side of the bed and regarded him steadily. 'What was it all about, Davy? You'd better tell me.'

Davy plucked at the sheet and dropped his eyes.

'Well, I had to go to work at the Rectory. Dada said. And I started when school broke up. It was awful. Dada let me try the scholarship for the County School, but it's no good. Even if I pass there's no money for me to go, see. Dada said I must work to earn for Mama and, well, I wanted to go to the County School but if I can't I don't mind to work, but I don't want to work at the Rectory.'

'I see,' Auntie Martha narrowed her eyes and looked out of the window. 'Well, I suppose it has been a bit of a struggle for your Mama and your Dada is only thinking of what's best for her. But why don't you like the Rectory? Your Dada works there and he seems content enough. He tells me that Mr Gwilym Pryce is a good kind man. I can't think he would be hard on you?'

' 'Tisn' that,' Davy shook his head. 'It's – well, it's a lot of things. An' I did want to go to the County School with Geraint, and I think I did well in the scholarship test. But it was Tom, and Elinor, and – oh, well, everything, somehow. Can't I stay here with you, Auntie Martha? I can help round the farm an' I'd work hard, honest, an' if you paid me two shillings I could send it to Mama every week. I wouldn't mind working for you, Auntie Martha,' he added, eagerly.

Auntie Martha smiled and pressed his hand.

'Look, Davy. You could stay here and welcome, but what good? There's only work enough on this little place for Luke and me and Ifan helps with some things, he's very good with the animals. Understands them, like. There is no real job here. Anyway,' she rose briskly, 'it's not for me to say. I must get word to your Mama and Dada that you are safe here. Look how they will be worrying!'

Davy sighed and nodded his head.

'I suppose so,' he agreed, heavily. 'But there will be Dada's strap at the end of this, and worst of all, back to the Rectory for me.'

'There, there,' Auntie Martha straightened the bedspread. 'Now don't go and upset yourself. You have been real poorly. You're not that well yet, either. Now get a bit more sleep and then you shall have some nice broth for your tea. We'll soon have you right again, boy.'

She left the room and Davy snuggled down in the big bed. He gazed sadly through the window. Well, there would be no fortune and no presents, just a good hiding and back to the Rectory. But the bed was comfortable and his eyes were heavy and he decided to worry about that tomorrow. He fell asleep and dreamed that he was standing on a ladder and reaching an apple down from a tree in the Rectory garden, but it was Dada that stood at the foot of the ladder with his strap in his hand and there was no escape.

It was the following Sunday when Dada arrived to fetch Davy. Auntie Martha let him in and he came stomping into the kitchen where Davy sat by the fire opposite Granny Evans who was dozing with her chin on her chest and the usual little bubbling snores making her sunken lips quiver. She woke with a start as Dada bellowed,

'Well, what's this, what's this! Mam Evans, you are harbouring a young viper in your bosom!'

Granny Evans' old eyes looked bewildered.

'Bosom!' she croaked. 'What is with you, Will Rees! What talk is this in a respectable house. Bosom, indeed!' She looked down shakily to where her shawl was pinned across her hollow old chest. 'Bosom, is it?' she muttered darkly. 'What about my bosom? Cheeky young rip. Coming here talking about bosoms. The idea!' She promptly fell asleep again and Dada turned to Davy.

'Well now, boy!' He frowned fiercely. 'What's all this! Frightened your poor Mama half to death, you young villain. We have scoured the hills for you, my lad. What's the meaning of it? Come on! I want an answer!'

Her eyes on Davy's face, Auntie Martha hurried forward with a chair for Dada.

'There, Will. Sit you down. I will make a cup of tea for you to have in your hand.'

'Hm,' grunted Dada, sitting down and sticking his head out belligerently at Davy. 'I will have words with this young scoundrel first, Martha, my girl.'

'Yes, well, let us talk it over quiet-like,' ventured Auntie Martha. 'The boy is not well, see. Caught a terrible chill, he did, getting wet through. Awful shape there was on him when the policeman brought him here. Feverish he was and no wonder for his clothes were sticking damp to him and flea bites on him! *Ach y fi!*' Auntie Martha shuddered and went over to sit at the table.

'Policeman, did you say?' roared Dada. 'Policeman! *Diawl!* What wickedness was you up to boy, that there was policeman with you?'

'Nothing, Dada,' whispered Davy, hastily. 'Honest, Dada. No wickedness. He came and fetched me from the workhouse, is all. I think the tramp did it.'

Dada's eyebrows flew up to his hair.

'Workhouse! Tramp!' He threw his hands up, his mouth working and his eyes looking round wildly at Auntie Martha.

'Now, Will! Keep calm! You will have a stroke!' Auntie Martha looked alarmed.

'Calm, is it?' cried Dada, his voice cracking. 'Policemen and workhouses and tramps! Good God, woman! His Mama will have a fit!' He ran his fingers through his white hair until it stood on end then took a deep breath.

'You had better tell all, boy.' His voice had become ominously quiet. Davy cleared his throat nervously and glanced at Auntie Martha. She nodded encouragingly so he embarked on his story in a low monotone, avoiding Dada's eyes and fixing his gaze instead on Granny Evans, who slept through it all completely oblivious.

When he came to the end Davy glanced warily at Dada from under his eyelashes. Dada's rosy face was set and he frowned into the fire without speaking for a while.

'I will take that cup of tea now, Martha,' he grunted at last, and Auntie Martha, with a wink at Davy, bustled off into the scullery to fill the kettle. Dada thumped his fists on his knees and glowered at Davy.

'Never a thought, I suppose, to how this would worry your Mama, eh? You are *twp*, boy. She has been out of her wits. It is a dam' good hiding you are asking for, to bring us worry like this. I have a good mind – ,' he fumbled with his belt and Davy, watching, sucked in his breath and stiffened. However,

Auntie Martha came in again to put the kettle over the fire and the teapot to warm on the hob. Granny Evans stirred and raised her head. Her eyes opened and rested on Dada.

'Bosom, indeed!' she quavered, indignantly. 'You watch your tongue, Will Rees.'

Dada looked wildly at the ceiling and clutched his head.

'*Diawl!*' he cried.

Auntie Martha clicked her tongue soothingly as she set out the cups and saucers on the table.

'We will all be better for a cup of tea now,' she said, and Davy blew out the breath he had held since Dada had gone for his belt.

While they drank their tea Auntie Martha steered the conversation round to enquiries about the rest of the family and the atmosphere had eased somewhat when Ifan came lumbering in, nodding and smiling at Dada. Auntie Martha poured another cup of tea and handed it to Ifan who smiled into it happily. Davy felt better with Ifan there. His gentleness seemed to fill the room and make everything better.

At length, when Dada had drained his third cup of tea, he handed the cup and saucer to Auntie Martha and turned to Davy.

'Well, boy, I have brought news for you but indeed you do not deserve to hear it. Still,' he shook his head. 'It pleases your Mama and is all decided now, seemingly. Between her and that old Hall. Not much say did I have,' he grunted with mock severity. 'They have put their heads together and decided all. No longer am I master in my own house,' he complained to Auntie Martha, who smiled and said, 'Tut, tut, Will.'

Davy's heart beat faster and he waited in a fever of impatience for Dada to proceed.

'No, indeed,' went on Dada, looking solemn. 'I do have no say in what is going on any longer. Heads are together and tongues clacking. And I am just to say "Yes, Mama" and "Indeed, Mr Hall". Old Hall's knees have been under my table more often than mine this past week.' He peeped slyly at Davy's agonized countenance out of the side of his eyes and relented. 'Well, boy. Seems like you passed that old scholarship. Third from top in the whole county!' He coughed in an effort to keep the pride out of his voice.

Davy's world hung suspended for a moment as Auntie

Martha cried 'Well done, our Davy!' and came over and kissed him on the forehead. Ifan clapped his big hands and grinned, comprehending only that something good was happening to Davy, and Granny Evans woke again at the noise.

'Are you turning that bad-tongued man out of my house, then?' she asked, with satisfaction. 'That's right. Stand no nonsense. Turn him out. Bosoms indeed!'

Davy's eyes were fixed on Dada.

'Aye, well. As I say it is all decided. You are to go to the County School after all. Llew, Nell and Meggie are to give another two shillings each to your Mama every week to make up for your earnings and to keep you. There now! And you don't deserve it, boy,' but his blue eyes twinkled at Davy and he leaned over and patted his shoulder. 'Well, now, we had better be on our way home. Your Mama will be hopping about waiting for you, though the good Lord alone knows why, you young villain. But remember, boy. Frighten your Mama again like that and I will have the hide off your back in no time!'

Davy's face was split in a triumphant grin as he bounded from the chair.

'Thanks, Dada. I promise I won't worry Mama again, honest. And Dada. I am sorry I ran away from the Rectory.'

'Aye, well,' said Dada, rising. 'Dare say that young limb Tom was most to blame for that. Come on, boy. Thank your Auntie Martha for having you, now. Good she has been. Better than you deserve.'

With congratulations and goodbyes ringing in his ears, Davy sat up in the trap beside Dada. The sun shone, Dada's white hair floated in the breeze, Blod raised her hooves high in a buoyant trot and Davy's heart sang in his breast as he turned to wave to Auntie Martha standing at the gate, with Ifan grinning happily over her shoulder.

7

Sideshows and Exits

It was the last Tuesday in October and the biggest fair of the year in the little market town. The day was grey and cold and a blustering wind blew down from the hills and sent the heaps of fallen leaves swirling through the streets. As Davy and Geraint sauntered home from school at four o'clock the town was thronged with country folk, standing in groups talking, often in the soft Welsh tongue, or pushing their way through the crowds on the pavements to get a peep into the shops which were doing a great trade on the busiest day of the year. The horse sales and the sheep and cattle auctions were over and the farmers and their wives were crowding into the shops before they set off back to the quiet of the hill farms and villages.

The pubs had been full all day and talk, laughter and bursts of song eddied forth from their doors. On the Gravel, a wide piece of river bank behind the gasworks, the pleasure fair was in full swing, hobby horses ablaze with lights in the gloomy afternoon and sideshows playing to an enthralled crowd. Davy and Geraint hoisted themselves up on to the Bridge Wall, where they had a view of the fair, and watched fascinated, the heady music of the hobby horses and the calls of the various sideshows ringing excitingly in their ears.

'You comin' down after tea?' asked Geraint, eagerly.

Davy nodded. ' 'Course! I got sixpence to spend. Saved it up. You got anything?'

'Oh, I'll get something off the old man,' replied Geraint. 'But I'll have to sneak off without Elinor seeing me or she'll want to come with us. See you 'bout six then, is it?'

Davy agreed and they climbed down from the wall reluctantly and made their way home for tea.

Dark had fallen by the time the two pushed their way through the crowds on to the Gravel. The fun was fast and furious and the lights and the noise set their pulses racing. The ground was muddy from the previous day's rain and churned up by the milling feet which swarmed over it. The stalls were lit by naphtha flares which hissed above coconut shies and shooting galleries and stalls where fat, sweating ladies drew out fresh hot toffee into long twists and curls or rattled brandy balls and aniseed drops into paper pokes. The flares and the lights from the hobby horses were reflected in the swirling, muddy waters of the river and on the Rackfield across on the other bank, the trees swayed in the wind and seemed to dance to the gay grinding music.

The boys each parted with a halfpenny to a large black-haired woman who handed them both a twist of sticky toffee with a massive paw. Chewing contentedly they pushed their way through a crowd which stood catcalling in front of a sideshow. The ribald remarks were directed at a thin, apologetic-looking man who was inviting them in to see the 'fattest woman in the world'. Yellowing photographs were pinned to the canvas of the square shelter, showing a massive woman with about six chins, whose white flesh overflowed the wooden armchair into which she was squeezed and whose tiny black eyes were lost in the dough-like folds of her cheeks. The boys shivered in gruesome delight and moved on to the next spectacle. This was a large black man dressed as a witch doctor, who stamped around on a wooden platform, shaking his feathered headdress at the crowd and waving an awesome-looking spear which made the gathering press backward with a gasp each time he lunged at them. The next delight was a boxing booth where a crowd of country boys were egging on one of their friends to 'have a go'. The young man, high coloured face sheepish and nervous, took off his coat and handed it to the nearest fellow then stepped into the ring, a stocky figure in moleskin trousers and a flannel shirt. His protagonist, who waited for him with a grin of fiendish anticipation, was a barrel-chested man of about forty, black hair greased down and luxuriant moustaches above a very red-lipped mouth, parted to show gleaming white teeth. Davy and Geraint watched as the two men circled each other and sparred with their bare fists but as the fight progressed it was obvious that the young country lad, game as he was, was no match for the experience of the older man, who played with him for a while and then began to land telling blows which rocked the lad on his feet. The fight ended with a sweeping uppercut to the jaw which sent the country boy reeling backwards with arms flailing, to land among his yelling mates. They set him on his feet where he stood shaking his head dizzily and responding with a slow grin to the catcalls of the crowd. The older man stooped down from the ring and shook the lad's hand good-humouredly and the group of country boys moved off laughing towards the hobby horses. Davy and Geraint followed them and watched them clamber aboard and mount the wooden horses. The music started up and around they flew, clinging on to the gilded poles, the horses soaring up and down in a gallop, the lads clutching their caps in the wind and calling encouragement to each other.

'How much is it to go on?' Geraint was reaching into his pocket and counting his coppers.

'Penny a ride, I think,' answered Davy, eyes shining.

'Let's go on next time and stay on for two rides'

'Right!'

Davy got two pennies out and as soon as the hobby horses stopped they climbed up the steep steps and chose their highly-coloured mounts. Again the music started up and away they went, faces flushed and jackets flying. A cloth-capped man came to take their pennies, moving with practised ease among the galloping horses and Davy's breath came faster as they gathered momentum and circled round with increasing speed, the upturned faces of the watching crowd fading into a blur and the naphtha flares and gaily coloured sideshows melting into a dazzling kaleidoscope against the darkness of the sky and the gleam of the river.

They had two turns and finally and reluctantly climbed down on legs made wobbly by the effort of clinging by their knees to the wooden sides of the horses. Breathlessly they pushed their way through a group of coyly giggling girls, who were twisting and turning with occasional squeals of mock terror as they weaved away from marauding bands of cheekily laughing youths. They fetched up in front of the coconut shy and decided to expend another halfpenny each on three balls which they hurled with more enthusiasm than accuracy at the hairy coconuts atop their perches. By a fluke Geraint toppled an enormous coconut and promptly engaged in a heated exchange with the stall holder who reluctantly handed him a very small coconut as his trophy. The man grew surly as Geraint furiously demanded the large coconut he had dislodged and ended up by chasing them away with a vicious looking stick. Choking with laughter they dodged through the crowd and ran towards a group of caravans close to the river. Geraint drew forth his cherished penknife and with the instrument which is generally taken to be for getting stones out of horses' hooves, bored a hole in the end of the coconut and they took turns to drink the sweet-tasting 'milk'. Then they banged the coconut against the wheel of a caravan to break it, bringing a large woman to the door, black hair hanging over her shoulders and a bare-bottomed baby on one arm. She cursed them roundly and fiercely and stopping only to gather up the pieces of shattered coconut they fled back into the crowd, where they milled around chewing coconut and spitting out bits of shell at oblivious passers by.

Drunk with the lights and music and the shouts and laughter of the crowd they finally found themselves by the swing-boats. Another penny each was handed over to a bored-looking young man with a cap pushed onto the back of his thick curls. With an expressionless face he steadied one of the boats and they climbed aboard, seating themselves at either end and clutching the long ropes with the furry ends like the bell-rope in church, Davy thought. They pulled with all their might in turn and were soon flying up into the night and descending with stomach turning speed. Davy was feeling decidedly queasy by the time the bored young man stopped the ride and they climbed down to the muddy ground. As they moved away from the swing-boats a sudden surge of the crowd separated them. Davy pushed his way through the press of bodies, searching for Geraint. Suddenly, a drunken man, singing hoarsely and smelling like a brewery, staggered against him and sent him flying to land up against the side of a toffee stall, where he crumpled to the ground. He sat in the mud dazed for a moment. Then two small hands shook his shoulders and the white face of Nan Mostyn hovered above, mouthing wildly in the clamour.

As he pulled himself upright against the wooden post of the

stall, Nan grabbed his arm and shook it, nearly toppling him over again.

'Geroff!' he shouted, hoarsely and tried to pull his arm away.

Her eyes were pools of terror in a chalky face, made more ghastly by the light of the naphtha flare above the stall.

'Have you seen our Mam?' she gasped. 'Have you seen her? I can't find her anywhere. Oh God, our Alfie's awful bad. And I can't find our Mam.'

She began to sob wildly, her thin body shaking. She had no coat on and her teeth chattered with cold and fright. Davy pictured the thin draggle-tailed figure of Mrs Mostyn and wondered how he could be expected to have seen her in all that crowd. He shook his head, frowning.

'No. I haven't seen her. She wouldn't be here at the fair, would she?' He couldn't picture his own mother among this sort of crowd.

'Oh, I don't know!' cried Nan. 'She weren't in the Eagles. I got to find her. It's our Alfie. He's that bad tonight.'

Davy looked round. There was no sign of Geraint and not much chance of finding him now.

'I'll come and help you to look,' he said and, grabbing her arm, began to push her in front of him through the crowd. When they emerged out on to Bridge Street and there was a chance to speak Nan turned to Davy.

'I'll have to run back to our house first. I've left Alfie by himself. Come with us, Davy,' she pleaded.

'All right, come on then.'

They set off at a run along Bridge Street and turned off left into Ladywell Street. This was a long narrow street with a variety of small cottages and larger houses. A number of passages led off into courts. It was the old historical centre of the town which had grown up around 'Our Lady's Well' and with two or three small corner shops, a bakehouse and a communal pump it was a close community. The gaunt back of the Victoria Hall, one of Newtown's two entertainment centres, was flanked by rows of small cottages and Nan led the way up a narrow alleyway between these called Picton's Row, at the top of which was the Picton Arms pub. Sounds of revelry could be heard coming from the pub as they let themselves in through the door of one of the tiny cottages in the dark, cobbled alley.

Davy, following on Nan's heels, found himself in a small, low-ceilinged kitchen. A wooden table under the window held a candle and it was by the flickering light of this that Davy took in his surroundings. Apart from the table, a wooden armchair, two wooden kitchen chairs and an old sideboard made up the furnishings, and there was a small iron cot bed against the wall near the fireplace. There was little warmth in the room. A few damp pieces of wood smouldered in the grate, giving off a musty, acrid smoke. Nan went quickly over to the small bed, avoiding a large chamber pot which stood beside it and which held, to Davy's horror, what appeared to him to be a large quantity of blood.

Nan put a finger to her lips as Davy approached the bed.

'I think he's sleeping,' she whispered. 'See, he coughed up all that blood. Oh, he was terrible bad. I wish I could find our Mam. I'm frightened. He looks bad, don't he?'

Davy stared down at the still figure of Alfie which hardly made a mound under the blanket which covered him. Thin, stick-like arms rested on top of the blanket. The small face on the grubby, blood-stained pillow was hollow-cheeked and deathly pale, with blue shadows under his eyes and round the mouth which was caked with dried blood. His small nose was pinched looking and the nostrils flared as breath fluttered in and out. Two bright pink spots of colour on the boy's cheek-bones burned below where the pale lashes lay over his closed eyes and served to accentuate the pallor of his skin.

Davy caught his breath. 'He looks awful!' he whispered, hoarsely. 'Can't you get the doctor to him?'

Nan shook her head. 'Can't afford it,' she whispered back. 'Owe him too much money as it is. Last time he came he told our Mam to give Alfie plenty of milk and eggs and fish and all them sort of things. As if we got the money to buy all that!' she added with bitterness.

Davy looked round.

' 'Tisn't very warm in here. I'll try and poke the fire up a bit. That wood looks wet, though.'

'Yes, it was. Found it down by the river. Can't find much dry wood about with all the rain we've had lately.'

Davy poked at the soggy wood which smouldered sullenly and simply gave off a further puff of thick grey smoke. Nan scraped some candle-grease out of the tin candlestick and dropped it among the wood. She threw a match in after it but, apart from a brief yellow flare, all that it did was add another evil-smelling ingredient to the smoke.

A sudden weak cough brought him back to the bed. Alfie's eyes were open and his pale forehead glistened with sweat in the flickering candlelight. His lips moved and Nan bent over him to try to catch his words. Another wracking cough shook his weak frame and a trickle of fresh blood showed at the side of his mouth. He lay for a moment, his breath fluttering his thin chest, his eyes fixed on Nan's face. Then his lips moved again and Nan and Davy leaned nearer.

'Lift me up, our Nan,' he whispered and Nan sat on the bed and gathered him up in trembling arms. He rested against her shoulder and gave a little smile.

'You bin to the fair, our Nan?' the words came weakly.

Nan looked up at Davy.

'Yes, Alfie, I found Davy there.'

Alfie struggled for breath and a further trickle of blood ran from the corner of his mouth and mingled with Nan's tears which dripped on to his face.

'Tell me,' he whispered at length. 'Tell me 'bout it.'

Nan shook her head, unable to speak. Davy lowered himself on to the bed beside them.

'Well, there was a lot of lights and music,' he began in a low, shaky voice, 'and hobby horses and the fattest lady in the world. An' there was stalls with toffee and coconuts and Geraint won a coconut and we drank the milk out of it and ate the coconut. An' then there was a black man all dressed up, with a big long spear, an' there was boxing an' crowds an' crowds of people. An' we had a go on the swing-boats. They go awful high. An' music was playing an' women pullin' toffee out in long strips.'

Alfie's eyes shone in the flickering candlelight which threw grotesque shadows on the wall.

'Nice,' he whispered. 'Take me our Nan?'

Nan nodded and hugged him closer, her eyes dark wet pools above his tow head.

'I'll take you, Alfie,' she whispered, as the tears slid down her cheeks. 'An' you shall ride on the hobby horses an' in the swing-boats. An' I'll buy you the longest stick of toffee there is

104

an' we'll go to see the fat lady and the black man an' I'll win you a coconut. There!'

Alfie smiled and gave a tiny sigh of happiness.

'Nice,' he whispered, and then, his eyes darkening, 'Our Nan – !' he cried as another cough shook his body and the blood gushed from his mouth, carrying his weary little life with it.

Nan cried out in terror and peered into his face.

'Alfie! Alfie! Oh, no! Oh, our Alfie! Don't go! Oh, God, please, please!'

Davy stood up, shaking uncontrollably and watched as Nan laid Alfie back on the pillow, her body racked with sobs.

'He's gone,' she said dully, after a long silence. 'An' our Mam wasn't here.'

'What shall we do?' whispered Davy, shaken by his first encounter with death and staring in numb horror at the still small figure on the bed.

The candle flickered as it burned low in the candlestick and suddenly a tiny flame fluttered in the grate and then disappeared again. The room was very silent, the corners in shadow. A clock ticked on the mantelpiece and far off a burst of laughter came from the Picton Arms. Nan sat motionless on the side of the bed, holding one of Alfie's thin hands and stroking it mechanically. Davy shivered.

'What shall we do?' he asked again after a while. 'D'you want me to go an' look for your Mam?'

Nan shrugged. 'If you want,' she answered, tonelessly. 'But it's too late now, isn't it. Too late. He's gone an' she weren't even here.'

Davy swallowed painfully and put his hand on her shoulder.

'Will you be all right by yourself if I go and find her?'

She nodded woodenly and continued to stroke the small cold hand.

As Davy let himself out of the door he looked back. The candle was guttering low in the candlestick and Nan's shadow blotted the wall behind the bed. There was an unnerving stillness about her as she sat with her hair hanging over the dead child like a curtain, the only movement the continuous stroking of his limp hand. He closed the door silently after him and leaned for a moment against the doorpost, his body shaking and his legs weak. He took a deep breath of the cold night air and looked up and down the alley, trying to decide which way to go. Suddenly the door of the pub at the top flew open and yellow light spilled out on to the cobbles of the alley. Davy watched as two forms emerged and struggled briefly in the pool of light, then the smaller one broke away and came running and stumbling down the alley towards him. The man weaved after the woman, arm outstretched, shouting and laughing drunkenly. As the woman neared Davy a light appeared in the bedroom window of the next door cottage and by it Davy recognized the woman as Mrs Mostyn. She stopped, swaying, a silly smile still on her face as Davy stepped in her path.

'Mrs Mostyn!' he said urgently. 'Please, Mrs Mostyn! It's your Alfie. He's dead!'

He was instantly shocked by the baldness of his own words. The woman stood staring at him stupidly for a moment and then reached out and took him by the shoulders. She shook him backwards and forwards, raving at him, the fumes of drink on her breath fanning his face. Suddenly he wrenched himself from her grasp, pent up emotion spilling from him.

'Alfie's dead! Alfie's dead!' he screamed at her. 'He's in there and Nan looked for you and you weren't there! Alfie's dead, I tell you, Alfie's dead!'

Mrs Mostyn staggered back, her arms thrown up and let out a wild keening yell. The man, who had halted his drunken run to watch them stupidly, turned and lumbered back up the alley. Suddenly doors were opening and feet running. Mrs Mostyn went on screaming and tearing at her hair and at length her neighbours closed in on her and led her into her own house, from where there emerged one long drawn out wail of desolation and then silence, except for the low murmur of voices.

Davy had shrunk back in the shadows of the opposite wall after his outburst, shaking from head to foot, hot tears welling up and spilling down his cheeks. He remained there for some time until his tears dried and the horror in him dulled to a weary numbness. He brushed his cheeks with his sleeve and then, shoving his hands deep in his pockets, made his way slowly down the alley and along Ladywell Street, kicking through the dead leaves that blew along the street and eddied round the lamp posts in the pools of yellow gaslight.

He wandered along Bridge Street, the wind cold on his face. The sky had cleared and a few stars twinkled overhead. A watery moon showed above the trees on the Rackfield and the outline of the laundry chimney was thrown in relief by the flaring lights of the fair. The music ground on but it seemed far away and he stopped to lean against a lamp post opposite the entrance to the Gravel, watching the people milling in and out of the fairground. He thought about Alfie and for some reason a picture of the three rabbits lying at Dada's feet up Brimmon wood came unbidden into his mind. He struggled for some time with his thoughts, formless feelings of sadness and injustice causing him to shake his head from time to time. A group of girls hurried past giggling and crossed the road to push their way into the fairground and for a brief moment he wondered what time it was, but he continued to lean, dark curls blowing back from his pale forehead, shoulders slumped and hands thrust deep in his pockets.

Suddenly he was startled by a hand gripping his shoulder and looked up to find Nell's face above his own and the broad-shouldered figure of a young man looming up behind her.

'Whatever are you doing here, our Davy? D'you know what time it is? You should be home in bed by now, boy!'

Davy stammered some reply and pulled himself up from the lamp post.

'What's the matter with you, then? Here, you look as though you'd seen a ghost. Are you on your own? I thought you went out with Geraint?'

'Lost him,' Davy mumbled. 'What time is it?'

'Gone nine and time you were home. Mama will be out of her wits. Here, our Davy,' she went on, peering into his face which looked ghastly in the yellow light of the street lamp. 'Not sick are you? You look awful.'

'I'm a'right,' muttered Davy, but she continued to stare anxiously into his face. Then she turned to the young man who had been standing by in silence.

'Look, I'd better get our Davy home. He doesn't look well. I'll see you some time tomorrow, Elwyn. All right?'

'Don't know whether I'm on duty or not tomorrow night. But I'll leave word at the shop.' The young man nodded and bade them good night and Davy watched him walk away then turned to Nell.

107

'That your fellow, Nell?' he asked, with a stirring of interest. 'You going to marry him?'

'Mind your business!' Nell's words were sharp but her voice sounded different to Davy and she was looking after the young man and her eyes were soft and shining in the gaslight.

'Seems a nice chap, Nell,' ventured Davy. 'Don't you want to marry him? You ought to hang on to him. A policeman an' all. Has he asked you yet?'

'You nosey young rip!' Nell turned to face him, half laughing. 'I've a good mind – !'

Davy hastily moved back a step out of the way of the sharp fingers.

'Only asking, Nell.' He looked at her solemnly. 'He's nice looking all right. You could do worse.'

Nell laughed softly and began to smooth her gloves over her long slim fingers. She was silent for a moment and Davy looked up into her lowered face, curious at this new, softer Nell. Then he heard her sigh and she bit her lower lip, her eyes troubled.

'What's up, Nell?' he asked softly and stepping closer touched her on the sleeve.

She shook her head and turned away, sighing again. They stood in silence for a long moment, Davy's interest quickened as he waited. At length she looked at him speculatively.

'Oh, our Davy! I just got to tell somebody. I don't know what to do at all. I'll tell you but you've got to swear you won't tell anybody, not yet, not till I'm ready. Do you swear on your honour not to tell anybody? Not Mama or Dada or anybody? Swear then!'

Her long fingers closed round his arm like pincers and dug into him. He winced and tried to pull his arm away.

'Ow! I swear, Nell, I swear! Honest I won't tell. God's honour. Not Mama nor Dada nor nobody. Ow!'

'All right then,' Nell released his arm and he rubbed it indignantly. He hoped the revelation was going to be worth it. 'Just you remember.' Nell shook her head warningly at him under the yellow glow of the street light. 'You just tell a soul and I'll – well, you'll be sorry, that's all, I warn you, you'll be sorry!'

'A'right, a'right.' Davy replied fervently. 'I can keep a secret as well as anybody, our Nell!'

Nell fell silent for a moment, her eyes dark pools under the shadow of her wide-brimmed hat with the ostrich feather circling round the crown. Her gloved hands were clasped in front of her and she stared unseeingly above Davy's head. The noise from the fair washed around them as they stood isolated in the pool of yellow lamp light. Davy looked up into her face curiously until at length her gaze dropped to his.

'It's like this, you see. Elwyn wants to marry me all right and I want to marry him.'

'Ah!' interrupted Davy, sagely, 'you're gone on each other. Well that's all right then, isn't it?'

Nell flushed. 'Its not that easy, boy. Will you listen? Elwyn wants to emigrate to Canada and he wants me to marry him and go with him.'

'Canada!' Davy's eyes grew round. '*Duw*! What's he want to go to Canada for?'

'Oh, I don't know.' Nell's gloved fingers plucked at each other. 'He's been on about it for over a year now. Seems he's got an uncle in the police out there that keeps on at him to go out. Prospects are good out there, he says. Elwyn's made up his mind to go, nothing will change him. But he wants me to go with him. I've put him off and put him off but he wants an answer now. Oh, our Davy, I don't know what to do. He's given me 'till Christmas to make up my mind but he's going after that, whatever.'

She bit her lower lip and kicked at the swirling leaves at the foot of the lamp post with the toe of her dainty buttoned boot.

Davy was silent, contemplating the implications of her story. If Nell went to Canada, chances were they'd never see her again or at least not for years and years. People just didn't come back and forth from Canada. He looked thoughtfully at his sister's brooding face and frowned. Nell made life a bit uncomfortable for him, no denying, and he'd often wished she'd get married and get a place of her own. But Canada! It wasn't as though he'd never want to see her again. No, not that. He realized he didn't like that idea at all. She wasn't that bad. It was one thing, Nell in a house of her own in Newtown, but Canada! Never see her again!

After a while he asked softly, 'You don't want to go to Canada, do you, our Nell?'

She shook her head, her eyes bleak.

'No, Davy, I don't want to go really. But, well, I want to

marry Elwyn. I don't know what I'd do if he went without me, I don't really. I never thought when I started to go with him. There was no talk of Canada at first. But, now, well it's too late, see. I think the world of him now and I can't bear to lose him.' Her voice caught in her throat and she drew a small handkerchief out of her pocket and blew her nose with fierce concentration.

'Whatever would Mama and Dada say?' asked Davy in awe. 'They won't like you going to Canada. Mama would be out of her wits.'

Nell gave her nose a last wipe and sniffed hard.

'That's just it. How do I tell them? It would vex them terrible. I don't know what Mama would say, I really don't. But I've not got long to make up my mind now. Oh, our Davy, I don't know what to do. It's been on my mind now for ages. If I want Elwyn I'll have to go and that's that. You see, he says if I think that much of him I should be ready to go out there with him. And I suppose I should, really. But it's so far away, and maybe it's for ever. He's saved up enough for us both to go, he's a steady boy, see. But would we ever come back?'

Her words seemed to carry on the wind that swept round them and Davy shivered feeling suddenly cold and miserable. The shock of Alfie's death, which had passed to the back of his mind with Nell's news, suddenly flooded back and he went on shivering, his face pinched and his eyes blurred with sudden tears.

'Here!' said Nell, suddenly, peering down at him. 'You're cold, our Davy. What am I thinking about, keeping you standing here listening to my troubles. You looked awful when I came, now I've made you worse. What's wrong, boy?' she asked, concerned.

He poured out the story of Alfie and Nan and Mrs Mostyn, while Nell listened, horrified.

'Heavens alive!' she whispered. 'Oh, that's awful. Poor little Alfie. And poor Nan, too. And Mrs Mostyn, out drinking! Whatever are people coming to? The woman wants a stick to her back. Never mind, our Davy. Come you home now. I'll tell Mama you've been with me if she makes a row. Come on, now. Let's get you home to the warm.'

She put one arm round his shoulders and led him along the street and held on to her hat with her free hand as the October wind buffeted them and the first drops of rain stung their faces. Dark clouds hid the moon now and the lights of the fair were behind them. As they made their way along Pool Road the noises from the fairground grew fainter and were replaced by the rushing noise of the swollen river as it swirled along its stony bed in the darkness. As they reached the steps of No 46 the wind and rain were stirring the branches of the trees in the Rectory field and whipping the last leaves off into the night. The mournful hoot of an owl sent them tumbling thankfully in through the door to warmth and the anxious greeting of Mama.

8

Logic and Judgements

By the following Saturday the weather had cleared again and after a night's sharp frost which brought down the last remnants of yellow and bronze autumn leaves from the Rectory trees the morning was crisply cold and sunny. Davy had shivered over his morning wash in the basin in the back kitchen sink and moved gratefully into the front kitchen to warm his hands at the bright fire, stretching across the big bowl of rising dough which he sniffed appreciatively. Nell came in with a saucepan of steaming porridge and spooned large dollops into the waiting bowls. Davy took his place on the bench and poured sweet milk over his portion then tucked in with gusto, the hot oatmeal bringing warmth to his body. Mama poured out mugs of hot strong tea and he added milk and three generous spoonfuls of sugar. This might normally have brought a sharp reprimand from Nell, but since their talk under the lamplight on October Fair night relations between Nell and Davy had taken on a new dimension. No longer did the thin fingers hover menacingly at meal times and although Nell was quiet and withdrawn there was a calmer air about her movements as though a decision had been reached and the consequences faced. Davy for his part was almost solicitous towards her, bringing calculating glances from Mama, who missed nothing of atmosphere where her family were concerned. Repeated confrontations with Nell over the past year in the form of inquisitions had elicited nothing but a plea of headaches and protestations against the nosiness of the family and with these lack of answers Mama had to be content, although too shrewd to be satisfied.

The talk over the porridge this morning was of the tragic

112

events of October Fair night. The scandal of the death of Alfie Mostyn while his mother was gallivanting round the pubs was complicated when the town awoke next morning to the news that Mrs Mostyn was missing. The nearest neighbours had remained in the cottage that night, awaiting the coming of Mrs Ellis the Box. Ellis the Box was the local undertaker and while his wife laid out the departed, Ned Ellis made the coffin and buried the remains with lugubrious efficiency. An ominous calm had settled over Mrs Mostyn who sat withdrawn in a dark corner of the room totally oblivious to the whispered talk and offers of tea and comfort. Her fixed and stony gaze never left the iron bedstead where the small motionless figure was now decently covered, face and all, by the blanket. Nan crouched on her haunches in a corner on the other side of the room. She had spoken no word to her mother and her eyes were cold and fathomless in the flickering light of a new candle which a neighbour had fetched in. Sometime about one o'clock Mrs Mostyn had risen slowly and moved wraith-like through the solemn whispering of the women and had gone out the back way, closing the door behind her. One of the women had half risen to follow her but had been bidden to sit down again as her neighbour whispered, 'Only gone out the back to the closet, she has. Leave her be.'

Mrs Ellis the Box had arrived five minutes later and in the hushed activity that followed, the fetching of hot water from next door and the search for a clean nightshirt which proved fruitless, Mrs Mostyn's continued absence was hardly noticed and if it was it was thought better that she should not witness these last rites. Nan remained crouched in her corner ignoring the soft words of comfort sometimes thrown to her by a bustling neighbour and she appeared unmoved as Alfie was washed and laid out in a clean white linen nightdress belonging to a tidy little woman from next door but one, his little wasted body lost in the voluminous folds of his stiffly starched shroud with broderie anglaise frills at neck and wrist. Her task completed, Mrs Ellis the Box sighed with mournful satisfaction and solemnly accepted a cup of strong tea. The women gathered round the small corpse, its white face peaceful above the stiffly frilled collar like a sleeping choir boy, and sniffed and dabbed their eyes and nodded their sorrowful congratulations. 'He looks lovely,' they murmured. 'Like a little angel, poor little dab.'

'Better fetch his Mam now,' said one woman, as she fitted a new candle on to the hot guttering wax in the candlestick and moved the flickering light over to the mantelpiece above the deathbed so that the small body could be viewed in its last pathetic dignity. But Mrs Mostyn was not to be found and despite an all night search by neighbours and eventually the local constabulary, it was not until the following afternoon that a group of small boys, perched along the Bridge Wall to watch the fair being dismantled, had spotted what they took to be a bundle of old clothes caught firmly in the tangle of branches of a tree overhanging the river, now above the waterline since the river level had dropped overnight. A thin white hand protruded and moved with the water as it eddied round the base of the tree and when this became apparent the boys gave frightened yelps and slithered down from the wall, crying out to draw the attention of curious passers-by to this phenomenon.

The capricious river had not borne Mrs Mostyn far from where she had flung herself in. When the news was broken to Nan it came as a relief to concerned neighbours that her stony silence at last broke down and the floodgates of her double grief opened and Nan finally wept for her vanished family.

Now Mama was shaking her head as she laid Dada's place against his arrival for breakfast.

'Poor little girl. What would have become of her but for Mr Gwilym Pryce I do not know. She could not have stayed in that old house of sorrow on her own. But as she is to take Emmie's place at the Rectory, now that Emmie is going to the mill, she will have a tidy place with a roof over her head and good food in her. Mrs Buxton will be right good to her, I don't doubt. She would have had to get out of that cottage anyway. Mrs Mostyn owed a lot of rent, poor woman, and Mr Evan Francis, her landlord, says he would have turned them out weeks ago if it hadn't been for poor little Alfie.'

'H'm,' snorted Llew. 'It's a wonder for that old skinflint. All those little houses he owns down Ladywell. Nothing but hovels, some of them. And people struggling to keep them clean and tidy and he's too mean to do any repairs.'

'I expect his wife spoke up for the Mostyns,' said Mama. 'She is a right nice woman and big church. Not like him at all.'

Llew grunted. 'There is too many like him round here. Especially some of the mill-owners. They own the workers body and soul. Rent them the little one-up-one-down cottages under the weaving rooms, do no repairs, pay them wages that wouldn't keep a cat alive then sit on the local board and carry on about the disgusting way the poor live. *Ach y fi!* They make me sick.' He took a deep draught of tea and set the cup down into the saucer with a vicious clatter.

Mama frowned and clicked her tongue at him.

'Mind with my cups, will you, boy. And that is enough with that old talk. If there were no mill-owners there would be no mills and no jobs for the people. Then you would have even more to bang my cups about for.'

'Good God!' shouted Llew, angrily. 'What is with the people around here? Bowing and scraping and touching their caps to these old fat-bellied buzzards. Yes sir, no sir. If the workers would stick together and demand a better deal they would get somewhere. It's not long since babbies were working in the mills, aye, and dying or maimed for life and all for sixpence a week, which like as not was spent in the pubs by their gutless fathers and mothers. Yes, they try and drown their sorrows in cheap rot-gut instead of standing on their own feet and demanding their rights. They make me bloody sick, they do.'

'Llew!' rapped out Mama, scandalized. 'You will mind your language in this house, boy. Wait till your Dada comes in. He will raise the dust from your britches, big and all as you are.'

'Argh! He is as bad as the rest, touching his cap for ha'pennies to the Reverend!' Llew was carried away on the tide of his own disgust.

However, this was too much for Mama who raised the tea towel she was carrying and lashed him across the head with it. Davy ducked out of the way as Llew tipped his chair back and rushed out of the house, banging the door behind him. There was a shocked silence around the table as Mama stood clutching the tea towel, eyes blazing and bosom heaving under the bib of her white starched pinafore. Davy kept his head lowered and spooned his porridge up with earnest concentration and Meggie stared round-eyed at Mama, her sweet face flushed. Nell reached for the teapot and quietly poured herself another cup of tea.

Dada, stomping in cheerily through the back door, stopped

in the kitchen doorway at the sight of the tableau.

'What is with you lot?' he cried looking from one face to another. 'You look like a lot of old hens with the gapes.' He stared at Mama's face and frowned. 'Have you lot been vexing your Mama, is it? I will have my strap to you if you have.'

'Llew did and you're too late. He's gone,' said Nell, coolly, sipping her tea.

'Llew?' bellowed Dada. 'What has that young rip been doing now, then? Getting too big for his boots, the young whippet!'

Mama turned on her heel and tight-lipped went off to make a fresh pot of tea, while Dada sank down on to his chair and looked round at them, blue eyes questioning.

Nell shrugged. 'You know Llew. He was on his hobby-horse again, that's all. You know how he goes on about the mill-workers and so on. Thinks they should get together and demand their rights, instead of drowning their sorrows in drink. Full of these ideas, our Llew. Nobody takes any notice.' She finished her tea calmly and wiped her mouth with a dainty handkerchief.

'Well! I will take notice of the young rip!' growled Dada. 'What sort of ideas are those in a tidy Christian house?'

'An' he said you were – ' blurted out Davy and stopped with a yelp as Nell pinched his arm viciously.

'*Diawl*!' said Dada, bristling. 'Go on? What did he say about me then? He is not too big for me to tan his hide.'

'Nothing,' said Mama, bustling in with the teapot, calm restored. 'The boy has nothing but old wind in him. Talks a lot of old rubbish, he does. He will grow out of it.'

'Yes, if he lives long enough,' said Dada, darkly, but he attacked his bowl of porridge with gusto and drew hot tea noisily through his whiskers afterwards, making the fastidious Nell frown.

Breakfast finished, Mama gathered up the dishes and de-parted to wash up and prepare the risen dough for the oven. Eventually Dada, Meg and Nell set off for their work and Davy wandered up the back steps into the Rectory fields in search of Geraint.

The dewy grass clung to the toes of his boots as he made his way across the field towards the big white house. The October sun shone on the last blood-red leaves clinging to the vine of the

Virginia Creeper which covered the front of the Rectory. The berries had all been picked from the little grove of elders for Mama to make elderberry syrup which was good for coughs and now the branches looked bare and twisted, sad in the fall of the year. Smoke rose straight up from the Rectory chimneys in the still air and Davy shivered as the early winter chill crept into his bones. He let himself into the courtyard through the door in the wall and closing it softly behind him stood still for a moment looking around him. Doves cooed softly from the roof of the stables and the last few leaves from the climbing rose lay still on the cobbles. He cupped his hands together and blew into them carefully, making a soft owl hoot. A few brown hens foraging round the stable door looked up indignantly and as he repeated his owl call a voice came from inside the coach house.

'Here!' called Geraint.

As Davy entered, Geraint's head popped up from the trap which stood there resting on its shafts. Davy drew nearer and saw that Geraint was sitting in the tilted trap, a box on his knees, examining its contents.

'Chemistry things,' he nodded to Davy. 'You know those experiments we did in chemistry last week? Well, I've got most of the things to do them, I think.' He pawed over some tubes and a bunsen burner and a number of phials of chemicals which lay in the box.

'Didn't know you had them!' Davy exclaimed with interest. 'Where'd you get them?'

'Oh, that old uncle I stayed with last summer. They were at the back of a cupboard. Must have belonged to my cousins sometime, I s'pose. Asked if I could have 'em and he said yes. Don't think he even knew what was in it!' Geraint chuckled. 'Bit daft like that he is. Like my old man. Brothers, see.'

'What you goin' to do with 'em, then,' asked Davy, picking up the phials gingerly one by one and peering at the contents.

'Well, I thought it'd be a bit of fun to try those experiments that we did last week in school.'

Davy looked at him doubtfully.

'Haven't got no gas for the burners,' he pointed out. 'How we goin' to heat them?'

'Oh, well,' Geraint brushed the objection aside impatiently. 'We'll manage. I pinched a big box of matches from Buxy's cupboard after breakfast. Now, where can we do it?' he looked round thoughtfully.

'What about our cellar?' offered Davy, eagerly. 'We can go down there and nobody'll bother us. If we sneak down through the door in the yard nobody'll see us. There's only Mama at home and she's always busy.'

'Good,' said Geraint briskly and gathered up his box to climb down from the trap. They let themselves out of the courtyard and set off across the field towards Davy's house. Davy suddenly thought of something and chuckled.

'Hey, d'you know what logic is?' he asked Geraint, clapping him on the shoulder.

Geraint frowned. 'I dunno. Something ole Potts the maths teacher talks about. Don't understand what he's on about, though.'

'Well,' said Davy. 'He told us something yesterday that shows what logic is. Us going down our cellar made me think of it. Goes like this. Our cellar is better than nowhere. Nowhere is better than heaven. Therefore our cellar is better than heaven. Get it?' He grinned at Geraint's puzzled face. After a great deal of muttering to himself light dawned on Geraint's face and he gave a delighted whoop.

'Hey! that's good, that is. I s'pose you could jus' as well say. Our stable's better than nowhere. Nowhere's better than heaven. Therefore our stable's better than heaven. Ha! I'll tell that to the old man. See what he makes of that!'

They crept down the steps and into the yard at the back of Davy's house. Crouching down they made their way beneath the two back windows and came to the low door into the cellar which stood at right angles to the kitchen door. Davy opened it cautiously and they descended the steps, closing the door behind them. There was plenty of light in the cellar from the grating which gave on to the pavement on Pool Road and this showed a large, clean cobbled room with a low whitewashed ceiling from which hung various implements belonging to Dada. There was a wooden table in the corner which held empty jam jars ready for Mama's jam and pickle making and this Davy cleared and dragged across to position beneath the grating.

'Better do it here where we got light.'

Geraint laid his box down on the table and began to prepare the test tubes and glass phials. When he had everything set up

118

to his satisfaction he began to add small quantities of powders and crystals to some liquid in a test tube.

Davy watched him dubiously.

'Are you sure you got that right? I don't remember any of them blue crystals.'

'Well, actually, old Stinks didn't use them,' said Geraint, squinting at the test tube as he raised it to the light. 'I put them in to give it a bit of colour, like. Thought that all them clouds of whirling gas that comes out would look good if they were blue. Stink's were a bit tame, just white.'

'Well,' said Davy, doubtfully. 'I dunno. What are them blue crystals, anyway? Got to be a bit careful you know,' he cautioned.

'I dunno what they are, really,' replied Geraint, fitting the tube into a stand which he had taken from the box. 'Writing was too faded on the tube to read it. Anyway, it's nothing we've had in chemistry so I 'spect it's some sort of colouring. Where's the matches? If you keep on striking them and passing one on to me as the one I've got burns out, we should get enough heat going to do the trick. Hey!' he chuckled. 'Wonder what people'll think when they see clouds of blue smoke coming out of your cellar and smell the stink!'

Davy was convulsed with laughter.

'We'll run for it after we've got it goin' well and take all the stuff with us. They'll never know what the heck it was!'

'Right you are!' grinned Geraint. 'Now, strike a match and pass it on to me and then when you see it nearly burnt down, pass me another quick.'

Davy struck the match and passed it to Geraint who applied it to the base of the tube. It took ten minutes before a thin plume of royal blue gas began to issue from the top of the tube.

'C'mon,' urged Geraint in excitement. 'Keep 'em goin', lad. It's coming, it's coming!'

The smell was atrocious and Davy wrinkled his nose in disgust as five more matches were passed in relays to Geraint. The evil-smelling blue gas began to come out in ever-increasing waves which drifted through the grating and billowed up into the air.

The boys were laughing hysterically and Geraint was calling for more matches when there was a sudden blinding light and an explosion which threw Davy across the cellar. A split second later Geraint landed on top of him and they lay in a stunned heap, faces blackened and minus eyebrows, eyelashes and the front tufts of their hair.

Up on the road was tremendous commotion. At the moment of the explosion a local character known irreverently as Jumping Jesus, was standing on the grating. His blasphemous nickname came from the fact that he was a thin, pious-looking individual who always dressed in a long, black, go-to-chapel overcoat, summer and winter. He walked with a bouncing gait on the tips of his toes and was never seen without a bible which he carried ostentatiously clasped to his breast. He carried his head on one side and his small, sly, lashless eyes were mostly hidden by the wide brim of an ancient black hat. The locals would have been tolerant of these eccentricities since the town was full of characters who were normally regarded with amused affection. But Jumping Jesus had a less attractive pursuit which earned him the dislike of the local people. Summer and winter he roamed the fields and woods, stalking the courting couples as they leaned on the gates or lay in the bracken. After spying on them long enough to satisfy himself, he would jump out on them, brandishing his bible and calling down the wrath of the Almighty on their sinful goings-on. The fact that most nights he was chased back down the lanes to the town by irate and red-faced swains did not discourage him nor did the patent dislike of the townspeople ruffle his funeral feathers or dampen the strange, bouncing gait.

He had come mincing down Pool Road this particular morning and had stopped outside No 46, astonished at the phenomenon of the blue foul-smelling smoke billowing up from the cellar grating.

'Like the pit of the devil!' he muttered to himself, excitedly. 'There is evil going on down there! Evil! Someone is tampering with the devil. There is shame! There is wickedness!'

He stood trembling on the grating in the midst of the blue smoke and tried to peer down. The stink was terrible but he was too excited to pay heed to it. He made out two forms moving ceremonially over an array of sinister-looking equipment. Hysteria flooded through his shaking body.

'Sorcery!' he screamed, jumping up and down on the grating. 'Satan is here in this cellar! This is the pit of hell!'

His voice cracked and his small eyes blazed in his pallid face.

He flung his arms up and turned a contorted face heaven-wards, causing his hat to fall off and roll into the gutter. As the evil-smelling blue smoke enveloped him he cried out.

'Lord, send down thy judgement!'

On that there was a huge bang which lifted him off his feet to land on his back in the middle of Pool Road.

Seconds later Mama came running out of the house and at the same time Matt Owen hobbled painfully across from his cobbler's shop. Between them they raised Jumping Jesus to his feet, while others came rushing up, their astonished stares divided between the last ragged remnants of stinking blue gas issuing forth from the cellar grating and the gibbering and white-faced figure of Jumping Jesus, his wisps of hair floating in the breeze and his eyes popping.

'Dear Lord!' cried Mama, bewildered and shaking but still holding Jumping Jesus upright with the help of Matt, whose glasses were askew and his face pale. 'What happened, then?'

Speechless, Jumping Jesus pointed a trembling finger at the grating and for the first time Mama noticed the blue smoke. Her eyes flew wide and her eyebrows shot up to her hair.

'But this is my cellar!' she cried. 'What – what is going on?'

Jumping Jesus found his voice.

'Hell is in your cellar!' he croaked, as his body jerked spasmodically in their grasp. 'You are cursed, woman! The Lord has sent a thunderbolt to destroy your house of iniquity!'

Everyone's eyes turned to the sturdy facade of No 46.

'Well, He 'anna made a very good job of it!' said a voice from the crowd, unimpressed.

Mama released Jumping Jesus's arm so suddenly that he staggered back against Matt Owen, tramping on the cobbler's club foot. Matt cursed wildly and hopped around on his good foot. Left without support Jumping Jesus's legs buckled under him and he sat down forcibly on the road, knocking the last remaining breath out of his body.

Meanwhile, Mama, a bewildered frown on her face, had run across to the grating and dropping to her knees on the dusty pavement, peered down through the bars. She was confronted by two black and hairless disembodied faces turned up to hers questioningly while the whites of two pairs of eyes shone through the last drifting wisps of blue smoke. Mama's terrified scream rent the air of Pool Road. There was a confused clatter down below and the gruesome faces disappeared.

Who should appear at that moment but Dada, leading Blod who was pulling a cart full of horse manure from the stables which Dada was delivering to one of the allotments. Startled by Mama's piercing scream Blod reared up on her hind legs, almost lifting Dada off his feet and tipping a fair portion of the cart's load on to the road.

'*Diawl!*' gasped Dada, righting himself and struggling to hold Blod. Then his eyes fell on his wife on her knees on the pavement, apron now flung over her head in her terror. His jaw dropped and he stared in amazement.

'*Diawl!*' he cried again. 'Susan! What is with you, girl?' His stunned gaze took in the small crowd which had abandoned Jumping Jesus and was moving curiously towards Mama. Dada loosed Blod and ran forward.

'Get back! Get back!' he shouted, hoarsely, his arms flailing and scattering the bemused onlookers. 'God blast you! Leave her alone! What are you doing to her? Are you all gone mad, is it?'

The crowd fell back, treading on each others toes and cursing and shouting at each other. Blod, spying the lone figure of Jumping Jesus still sitting breathless in the roadway, eyes tight shut, moved over to investigate and lowering her head, blew gently through her nostrils on to his upturned face. This was the last straw for Jumping Jesus. Uttering a hoarse shriek and terror lending strength to his limbs, he leaped up and ran for his life down Pool Road.

Floating back came his anguished cries.

'Lord, save me! The Devil is after me! I felt his hot breath. Save me, save me!'

Her interest aroused, Blod lumbered after him, the cart swaying and splattering the milling group with highly-smelling manure. This served to scatter the crowd, who moved quickly away, muttering and cursing their disgust, leaving a totally bewildered and trembling Dada to raise Mama to her feet and lead her faltering steps indoors.

When at last she could be persuaded to stop rocking back and forth and take the pinafore off her head, he demanded an explanation. He listened round-eyed and at length, gathering that the whole amazing sequence of events had emanated from their cellar, stomped hastily, blue eyes blazing, out to the back door. Flinging it open he was in time to witness two black-faced figures creeping furtively out of his cellar. Reaching out, he grabbed each one by the collar and dragged them, squeaking with fright, into the kitchen where he shoved them up against the wall, Geraint still clutching the chemistry box to his breast.

'Now then – !' roared Dada, legs apart and leaning forward menacingly. 'Now then! Speak, you!'

Explanations were long and confused but retribution came short and sharp. An hour later Davy and Geraint lay on their stomachs in the damp grass of the Rectory field. The chemistry box had been confiscated and conveyed to the Rectory by Dada to be locked up by Mr Gwilym Pryce. Geraint at length broke the thoughtful silence.

'Dunno about your cellar bein' better'n heaven,' he chuckled. 'More like it was worse'n hell this morning!'

They both began to shake with laughter and there they lay until the chilly damp from the grass seeped through to their bodies and fetched them to their feet with a shiver and they wandered off beneath the bare branches of the fallen-leaved trees in search of something to do.

It was six o'clock that evening and the family had finished their tea, with the exception of Meg who had not yet come back from Mrs Purvis's. Nell had gone out and Llew was in the back. Mama cleared the dirty crockery and laid a fresh place for Meg. Davy, having finished cleaning out the cellar as part of his punishment, had cleared a space at the end of the table and was spreading his homework books out. He carried a bottle of ink from the cupboard beside the fireplace and set it in front of him. Then he examined the nib of his pen carefully and found it bent. He pressed it against the edge of the table and it broke.'

'Dammo!' he exclaimed, softly.

Mama's sharp ears pricked.

'What you say, boy?'

'Nothing, Mama.'

He scrabbled round in the bottom of his satchel and found a reasonable nib, which he fitted into the holder. He opened his exercise book and began on an essay which was designed to show how much he knew about the confused relationship between Church and State under the turbulent reign of Henry VIII. He wrote industriously for quarter of an hour before he paused and stared into space. Dada had come in from chopping sticks in the back yard and was sitting in the wooden armchair beside the fire, removing his boots and leggings.

'Dada,' said Davy, frowning thoughtfully, 'we are Welsh, aren't we?'

'Aye, boy,' replied Dada, struggling with a bootlace. 'We are Welsh indeed. And proud you must be of that. It is very bad, I do feel, that you are not taught your own language. The old English is cold and hard to get your tongue round. There is no music in it. But they do be set against *y Cymraeg* in these schools. And I am thinking it better they taught you that than how to blow up your Dada's cellar.'

Davy grinned sheepishly.

'What I am thinking, Dada, is there no Welsh history? We are learning all about the kings of England but there must have been things going on in Wales all the time. Why are we not told about them?'

'Ah well, there boy, you are asking me about things I do not understand.' Dada leaned back in his chair his blue eyes puzzled. 'Seems you are not to know what was going on in your own country. We did have princes in the old days, I am told, Llewelyn and Glyndwr. We did not go in for old kings, seemingly.'

'Hm,' snorted Davy. 'Just as well, I should think. This old Henry was a bad old thing with his six wives.'

'*Diawl!*' said Dada, eyes wide. 'Six wives! One is enough for any man to handle, if you ask me. How would he be allowed to have six, anyway? It is against the law, even for an old king I should think.'

'He didn't have 'em all at once,' explained Davy. 'He had 'em one after another.'

'One after another?' Dada shook his head. 'What he do? Wear 'em out like boots?'

'Well, looks like some he divorced and some he just chopped their heads off.'

'*Diawl!*' cried Dada again, sitting forward horrified. 'Chopped their heads off? They should have locked him up! The man was dangerous!'

'Who is dangerous?' asked Mama coming in from the back

124

kitchen with the big kettle, which she hung over the glowing fire.

'This old king of England, going round marrying women then chopping their heads off,' explained Dada excitedly. 'Some sort of maniac, he is. Six he has got through already!'

'What old nonsense are you talking, man?' said Mama, frowning. 'That is old Henry the Eighth in history. Even I do know that. What was your schooling?'

'I did learn to read and write in my own language, and to add up and so on,' said Dada indignantly. 'What for would I want to learn about some old king running loose with an axe? They should have locked him up after the first time. What were the police doing? Glad I am that I am not a scholar if that is what you do have to learn about.'

'*Twt*, Will,' exclaimed Mama in despair. 'History it is. He was a king, see. They do not lock up kings in England.'

'*Diawl*, glad I am that I live in Wales, then. England do seem to be a dangerous place to live.'

Mama groaned and cast her eyes ceilingwards in exasperation while Davy, spluttering with laughter, returned to his essay.

A few moments later the door opened and Meg entered. She was weeping bitterly and without a word she disappeared up the stairs.

'What in the name of goodness?' said Mama and disappeared after her.

Dada and Davy exchanged glances.

'What is wrong with that girl?' asked Dada, eyes wide.

Davy shrugged and shook his head. They were silent for a while listening to the murmur of voices from above, interspersed with the occasional muffled sob from Meg. Dada was frowning and drumming his fingers on the wooden arm of the chair when at last Mama's voice floated down, sharp and angry.

'Will! Come up here, will you.'

Dada rose and hurried up the stairs in his stockinged feet, leaving Davy to chew the end of his pen and cock his ears, but he could make out nothing but Mama's agitated murmur followed by an angry roar from Dada. After about ten minutes of more rumblings Dada came stumping down the stairs, blue eyes ablaze and an angry flush on his face.

'God damn and blast them!' he cried as he reached for his boots and began to drag them on. 'I will wring their necks! I will have the hide from that young whippet's back!'

He was still muttering dire threats when Mama came down the stairs again, cheeks flushed and eyes troubled.

'Now then, Will, be careful. Do not lay hands on young Purvis. They are high people. They will have you locked up! Perhaps you had better leave it lie?'

'Leave it lie!' exploded Dada, reaching for his coat from the back of the door. 'I will leave young Purvis lie! On his back he will be! Out of my way, woman!' as Mama stood to block his path.

'What's going on?' shouted Llew, coming in from the *ty bach*. 'What's happened now?'

Mama was still barring the front door while Dada danced with rage but afraid to lay hands on her. Llew grabbed Dada's arm.

'Hey! Whey up now, Dada. What's it all about?'

Dada turned on him angrily.

'Leave me be, boy. I will be up to Purvis' and tear that young fellow limb from limb!'

Llew hung on to his arm and turned questioningly to Mama.

'It is Mrs Purvis' son, Ronald,' explained Mama, still pinned to the door, arms wide. 'He have tried to do bad things to our Meg. And Mrs Purvis have blamed our Meg and said she led him on. And she have sacked her and called her dirty names.' Mama's voice broke.

Llew's face went white and his mouth tightened. He said nothing for a moment but stood rigid, his grip tightening on Dada's arm. Then he swung Dada round and back into the chair, almost knocking the breath from his body.

'Stay there!' he ground out through clenched teeth. 'See that he stops there,' he turned and commanded Mama.

Dada was struggling for breath, eyes wild and was heaving himself from his chair when Llew wheeled round and disappeared in the direction of the back door.

'Llew!' cried Mama dropping her arms and running after him. 'Llew, come back. What are you going to do?'

'Sort out Mr Ronald Bloody Purvis!' shouted Llew and the back door slammed violently behind him.

'Stay you there, Will Rees,' she commanded. 'No good for

you both to get into trouble. The Lord alone knows what that boy will do. Mad he is, now.'

Dada was stumping round the kitchen like a caged animal. Davy could see there would be no peace to finish off Henry VIII now, so he closed his books and tucked them away in his satchel along with his pen. The ink he replaced in the cupboard and leaving Dada to his ravings and Mama to rock to and fro in the wooden armchair he mounted the stairs thoughtfully. He paused outside the girls' bedroom then tapped softly on the door. There was no sound from within so hesitantly he lifted the latch and, opening the door a crack, poked his head in.

'Meggie? You all right, Meggie?'

Receiving no reply he pushed the door a little wider and peering round saw Meg sitting on the edge of the bed staring straight in front of her, her arms crossed, hugging her body. Her face was pale and her soft grey eyes looked hurt and lost. Davy advanced a pace towards her.

'Meggie?' he repeated. 'You all right, girl?'

She did not move or speak. Davy moved forward to sit on the edge of the bed beside her. He put his arm round her shoulders and a shudder passed through her body.

'Aw, c'mon, Meggie. All right now, is it?' He squeezed her shoulders and looked into her face pleadingly.

Suddenly the gentle face crumpled and she turned and buried her head on his shoulder. Her body shook with sobs and a rush of tears wet the shoulder of Davy's flannel shirt. He let her cry for a while, patting her shoulder and making soothing noises.

'Oh, our Davy,' she whispered at last, raising her head and drying her eyes with the bottom of her pinafore. She gazed towards the window, eyes puffed and soft mouth trembling.

'I am a good girl,' she whispered, shaking her head. 'I am not a bad girl or a – a, oh, all those old nasty things she called me.' Her voice broke again and the tears ran down her cheeks unheeded.

'Of course you are a good girl,' Davy said, stoutly. 'We all know that. Never mind those old Purvis'. Don't you fret. Llew will see to them. C'mon now, Meggie. Stop crying now, is it? Look I will go and make a cup of tea for you to have in your hand. You will feel better for a cup of tea,' he added, sagely.

127

She nodded, drying her eyes again and Davy descended to the kitchen.

'Mama, I will make Meggie a cup of tea,' he said, reaching for the brown teapot which sat waiting on the table. Mama rose hurriedly.

'Leave me do it, good boy. Poor girl, what am I thinking of. She will be needing a cup of tea. Sit down, Will, out of my way. You are doing no good stamping up and down like this. Sit, you.'

Dada sat down stiffly in the chair Mama had vacated, hands on knees and blue eyes bleak, muttering under his breath from time to time.

Mama had disappeared up the stairs carrying the cup of tea when the back door banged and Llew came through to the front kitchen.

He pulled out a chair and sat at the table, examining a row of skinned knuckles with a grim smile of satisfaction. Dada jumped up and came to stand over him.

'Well, boy?' he queried, whiskers aquiver.

'Well?' Llew looked up with a lopsided grin. 'Aye it is well indeed. That young whipper-snapper will think twice before he will lay his dirty paws on another girl. I have shook him like a rat and then laid him low with a right and a left which have left him missing a couple of teeth and due for a shiner any time now!' He breathed deeply and with satisfaction. 'The old girl did have the hysterics and did threaten me with gaol and all sorts but then his father came to see. And he was right tidy now. Said it served him right and he'd a mind to black his other eye. That set old Mrs Purvis off again but he turned on her pretty sharpish and she went off like an old hen with wet tailfeathers.' Llew fumbled in his pocket and brought out some coins which he laid on the table. 'Mr Purvis did take me in his study and shook hands with me and offered me five pounds. I told him I would take Meg's wages for this week and nowt else and he said he understood and would give her a good character himself if she wanted it.'

'She have got a good character already,' snorted Dada, 'and it was not the Purvis' that give it to her.'

'Aye, aye,' said Llew, rising and blowing on his knuckles. 'But there we are. All is settled now.'

He went towards the back kitchen winking at Davy as he

passed and Davy grinned back admiringly. Llew turned and paused in the doorway.

'God, it felt good when my fist sank into that soft, stuck-up face. He blubbered like a baby when he hit the ground. So much for your gentry!'

With a look of grim triumph on his face he turned and disappeared in the direction of the stone sink to cool his knuckles with a basin of cold water.

9

Handcuffs and Drumsticks

A bitter north-east wind was blowing strongly down Kerry Road when Davy and Geraint made their way home from school for dinner. It was a Tuesday in December, two weeks before Christmas and the sky was grey and leaden.

'Dada says there will be snow,' announced Davy, blowing on blue fingers.

'Hope so!' Geraint's nose was red and his eyes watered in the wind. '*Duw*, it's cold, too. Be good if it snows, though. Tell you what. Let's start making a sledge tonight. There's plenty of pieces of wood at the back of our coachhouse and I can get nails an' so on. It'll be ready then for when the snow comes. And it's sure to come.'

'Aye, sure to.' Davy nodded, eagerly. 'I'll come round after tea tonight, then, and we'll get started.'

A strong gust caught them both in the back and forced them to take two or three running steps down the pavement before they steadied themselves again, laughing. The people who were struggling up the pavement towards them were bent forward, men clutching their caps, coat tails flying and women hanging on to their hats with one hand and their skirts with the other. The millworkers coming home for dinner were better off, with shawls wound tightly round their heads and enveloping their shoulders.

As they neared the bottom of the slope the big burly figure of Constable Dicky Davies rounded the corner with, on his right and handcuffed to his wrist, the small, thin dejected looking figure of Ivvy Whippet, the most persistent poacher in the town. Ivvy had seven children and his only work was to hang around the markets and auctions to pick up pence for odd jobs.

Fair play to Ivvy, he carried his pennies home to his wife conscientiously in the deep pocket of his trailing overcoat, never touching a drop to drink, but they weren't enough to feed his clamouring brood and his despairing and bedraggled wife. The 'Parish' allowed them one and sixpence a week which did little to help and so Ivvy went out poaching to add something to the pot. When he was caught and turned in, as he regularly was, and went for nine days 'down the road', which meant to Shrewsbury gaol, then the Parish increased his wife's allowance to five shillings and thus, without Ivvy to feed, she was marginally better off when he was in gaol.

However, this time, in order to teach him a lesson, the magistrates had sent him down for fourteen days and he would therefore not be out until Christmas Eve and would miss the most lucrative markets of the year and the season when both buyers and sellers were at their most generous. Added to that, he had his eye on a fat old hen for the Christmas dinner, one of seven which scratched around the sheds in Dicky Skinny's allotment up Brimmon Lane, past laying and kept on with a view to putting money in Dicky's pocket at Christmas. Ivvy told himself, without much conviction, that Dicky Skinny wouldn't miss one, the old skinflint, but now their necks would be wrung and they would have been disposed of by the time he got back on Christmas Eve.

With these thoughts in mind he was not going up to catch the Shrewsbury train with P.C. Davies in his usual mood of resignation. He was hunched inside his frayed and trailing overcoat and a dewdrop hung drearily from his nose, pinched and mauve with cold. His short skinny legs moved in a shuffling trot in an effort to keep up with the long plodding strides of the Constable, who leaned stoically into the wind, his large and bovine countenance expressionless.

As the boys drew closer to them a sudden gust lifted Ivvy's cap off his head and sent it sailing over the wall into the Church School yard. He gave an anguished yelp and put up his free hand to hold on to his few grey wisps of hair.

'Me cap!' he squeaked, miserably. 'Me cap's gone. You'll ha' to stop!' as he dragged back on the handcuffs.

Constable Davies stopped and turned to look at him, frowning.

'Come you on. We'll miss the train an' I dunna want thee on

me hands any longer'n I can help.'

'I inna goin' without me cap!' snivelled Ivvy as Davy and Geraint stopped to watch them. 'Thee't ha' to loose me while I go in for me cap. I shunna be a minute, mun,' he pleaded, eyes watering in the wind. 'It's too bloody cowld to go to gaol without me cap. Undo me a minute, oot'ee?'

'Oh ah?' P.C. Davies gave a short laugh. 'Think I'm daft, eh? An' have thee run off? I inna that soft in the 'ead. Thee stay by 'ere and I'll fetch thee cap!' and unlocking the handcuff on his own wrist he lumbered off through the gates into the school yard.

Ivvy stood for a moment, a puzzled frown on his face, blinking down at the handcuffs dangling from his wrist. Davy and Geraint watched, incredulous, grins on their faces.

'Run for it!' urged Geraint, hopping up and down and laughing hysterically. 'Go on, run!'

'Run?' echoed Ivvy, shaking the handcuffs, 'Ow can I? I'm – ' then the truth dawned on him and he looked round, bewildered.

'Well, I'll be damned!' he said, softly, a slow grin spreading over his face. 'I'll be damned! The silly owl 'oolert!' He lifted his wrist with the handcuffs hanging from it and shook his head. 'That daft sod! He inna right in the 'ead. He could'a lost me!'

On that P.C. Davies emerged from the school yard with the cap in his hand.

' 'Ere y'are,' he said, crossly and jammed the cap down over Ivvy's ears. ' 'Owld on to it now an' dunna let it blow off again, you 'ear?'

He clicked the dangling handcuff back on his wrist and bending to the wind they set off again, Ivvy holding his cap on with his free hand. His querulous voice came floating back to them.

'Yo' could'a lost me, y'owl fool!' but P.C. Davies took no notice and just gave the handcuffs an extra jerk causing Ivvy to give a tottering run forwards into the wind in order to keep up.

'Well!' Davy slapped his thigh with glee. 'I'd never have believed it!'

'One was as daft as the other,' chuckled Geraint and they were hustled on down the pavement once more by an impatient gust of wind.

Today was 'Live Market Day' when the Christmas poultry were brought in live. Turkeys, geese, ducks and chickens had been arriving all morning, driven down from the hill farms in carts and traps, heads poking out curiously as they bumped along the roads and down the hills into the streets of Newtown. Those streets in the centre, Market Street, High Street and Broad Street and all round the Market Hall were filled with the sounds of gobbling, quacking and clucking as the long-suffering birds submitted to having their breasts pinched and the tops of their legs squeezed by prospective buyers who then disparaged their qualities and haggled over the price. Buxom country women with cheeks whipped up by the cold to shades which ranged from scarlet to puce, hovered over their wares on sturdily booted feet, dressed in thick woollen skirts which hid good flannel petticoats and woollen drawers, shawls round their shoulders and plain black hats sitting square on their heads and skewered to their bunned hair by hatpins. They bargained with the townspeople obstinately and shrewdly, while their menfolk gossiped in groups or sneaked away to the nearest pub for a hot toddy. The following week would see the killing of the remaining poultry, with farmhouse kitchens under a deluge of flying feathers as the plucking and drawing went ahead furiously in preparation for the 'dead market' the following Tuesday and on the benches of the Market Hall up until Christmas Eve.

A few late straggling traps full of poultry were still bowling down Kerry Road as the boys crossed to the corner to turn home for dinner and they watched these for a while enjoying the comic sight of the long goose necks and smaller duck and chicken heads which protruded through the rope nets which imprisoned them in the trap and gave voice protestingly into the winter wind.

The sky had darkened to a dirty yellowish grey and suddenly Davy put a hand up to his cheek as something feather-soft touched it. He looked up wonderingly and there were the first flakes of snow whirling in the wind and eddying above the ground as though reluctant to settle.

'It's snowing!' shouted Davy and Geraint tore off his cap and flung it in the air, catching it again with gleeful laughter. Whooping excitedly, they ran and capered homewards, impatient for evening to arrive so that they could get to work on their sledge.

'We're in for a heavy fall, mark my words,' warned Dada, as he tucked into a steaming plate of pig's hock broth, thick with lentils. 'When this old wind do drop you will see.'

Mama clicked her tongue in exasperation and went off to look out woollen mufflers and mittens while Davy spooned up his broth with eager anticipation.

Dada was proved right for the wind dropped by evening and the snow thickened, falling steadily and relentlessly as a leaden sky hung low over the valley, and the little town settled, shivering under a thick white mantle which was to last into the New Year and give the traditional white Christmas.

By Christmas Eve the skies had cleared and a hard bitter frost had settled in making the ridges of snow in the streets crisp under foot. Icicles hung from the guttering on the houses and people hurried about their shopping, wrapped to the chins, their breath steaming and their noses red.

Davy had been busy since he got up, chopping wood and carrying coal for Mama to stoke up the fire into a fierce glow to have a hot oven for the mince pies. She was up to her elbows in flour, rolling a large expanse of pastry on a floury kitchen table, two big jars of her home-made mincemeat at hand, thick and sticky with fruit, chopped apples, flakes of suet and redolent with 'a drop o' summat good' so it would keep. Suddenly there was a sound of wheels outside and the muffled stamp of hooves in the snow and after some commotion the door opened and, accompanied by a rush of cold air, in came Auntie Martha, shawled, bonneted and mittened so that only her laughing dark eyes, pink nose and smiling mouth showed. She was carrying a large object wrapped in a snowy white cloth and was followed by an equally thickly wrapped and grinning Ifan with a big square basket over his arm and carrying a small green fir tree, its roots wrapped in a ball of sacking.

Greetings flew and exclamations of welcome, and while Mama hurried to wet the tea in the pot from the already bubbling kettle hanging above the hot fire, Auntie Martha's big white burden was laid on the table and its cloth unwrapped to reveal the biggest goose Davy had ever seen, the ends of its drumsticks upturned and decorated with frills of pink and white tissue paper. On its enormous breast was pinned a flat, cream-coloured breastplate of fat, the edges decorated with

134

similar pink and white frills and its stomach bulged with giblets.

Auntie Martha stood by with a proud smile on her face as Mama, wide-eyed, poked the goose and exclaimed with delight and gratitude. Then Ifan, nodding his big head and still wearing his wide grin, began to unload his basket, laying out the contents on the end of the table furthest from Mama's pastry and next to the goose. There were four big pound pats of fresh butter, wrapped in greaseproof paper, pale cream in colour and oozing salty drops of moisture from their ridged tops. There was a large round yellow cheese in a piece of white muslin, a dozen big brown eggs and a paper bag full of crisp rosy apples from the Walkmill trees. Ifan laid a sweet-smelling bunch of dried sage on top of the pile, to make the stuffing for the goose and finally drew out two bottles of Auntie Martha's cowslip wine from the bottom of the basket.

'Stand these somewhere cool to settle,' suggested Auntie Martha, 'or you will have that old wine shooting up to the ceiling when you open it after all this jiggling about.'

Meanwhile Davy took the Christmas tree out to the back and stood it against the wall of the *ty bach*. He looked at it admiringly before going back in to the warm kitchen. By now the visitors were settled with a cup of tea in their hands and a fresh mince pie each, hot from the first batch out of the oven.

'Well, Davy,' Auntie Martha spoke through a mouthful of mince pie. 'How would you like to take Gypsy up to your Dada at the stables for me? Then he can give her food and drink and a rest and mebbe bring her back down when he comes for his dinner. We must start back shortly after dinner, see,' she told Mama, 'to be back before dark. There is the milking and the hens and beasts to feed before night and Luke will have been tied seeing to Mam.'

'Wrap warm then,' Mama told Davy, 'coming from this heat.' Then beaming round, as Davy tied a muffler round his head to keep his ears warm and set his cap on top, 'I was expecting you, see, so there are two rabbits in that pot stewing with plenty of vegetables and potatoes so there will be plenty for all, to fill you before you go back.' She lifted the lid of the big stewpot standing on the trivet, letting out a belch of savoury steam which brought forth sniffs and murmurs of appreciation.

135

Davy plunged out into the cold air and grabbing the reins of the impatient Gypsy who was stamping her hooves and blowing steamy breaths through her big nostrils, he led her and the trap round the corner and up Kerry Road, the crisp snow crackling beneath wheels and feet. Once at the Rectory he delivered her over to Dada's ministrations, pouring out the news of the visitors and the good things brought with them.

Dinner over, Auntie Martha and a happy, smiling Ifan set off back to Manafon and afterwards the pace of preparation quickened, with Davy being sent hither and thither on errands. Fetch the Christmas pudding, a huge rich-smelling globe with a cloth round it tied on the top in four ears, from the bottom of the wooden chest in Mama's bedroom. Find a bucket to be filled with soil hard to dig on account of the gleaming frost in it and plant the Christmas tree firmly, not to lean. Drag across a cane-seated chair in Mama's bedroom and climb precariously on to it to reach down from the top of the wardrobe the big cardboard box of gaily coloured garlands and Christmas tree baubles with which the girls would decorate the house this evening after work.

In the meantime Mama had stuffed the goose and laid it in a large meat tin, kept from year to year for the purpose. This had to be conveyed round the corner to the bakehouse which Oven-Bottom Billy kept open after the morning's baking. He re-stoked the fires on a Christmas Eve and was on duty until midnight cooking the geese and turkeys for those lucky enough to have birds too big for their own ovens. Each meat tin had to bear its distinctive 'seals', a collection of objects wired to the side handles. The Rees' seals consisted of a small cupboard key, a halfpenny with a hole bored through it, the brass flywheel of a clock and a small, tarnished shoe buckle. Oven-Bottom Billy insisted on these means of identification despite the fact that everyone knew their own tin and their own bird. But it was now a tradition and the seals remained wired to the big meat tins for the duration of their lives for such tins were rarely used between Christmases. Large joints or birds were unknown in everyday living.

At four o'clock Davy made his way round to the bakehouse, staggering under the weight of the goose in its tin, covered by a clean white dish towel. His boots slipped and slithered through the crisp frozen snow and his breath steamed in the cold air.

When he finally struggled into the bakehouse the warmth inside was redolent with a new and rich smell. Cooked birds lay in their tins on the trestle at the side, golden brown and glistening, whilst on the big table rows of tins stood, their contents waiting in dignified ranks to go into the oven.

Davy laid his burden down with relief and turned to greet Oven-Bottom Billy whose flushed and beaming face owed much of its glow to the bottle of whisky which stood at the end of the table.

'Hello, Davy boy,' his greeting was as warm and expansive as ever despite the fact that he had been here in the heat since four o'clock in the morning and would work on until the last bird left, sometimes after midnight. 'Got your seals on, have you?' He fingered them, memorizing them afresh for he knew everyone's seals in the neighbourhood and could pick out a bird unerringly when its owner called to collect it. 'It will go in at five o'clock Davy. Come for it about ha'past eight, is it?'

Davy nodded, moving close to the warm oven. A sudden snore startled him and turned his glance to the corner of the room. Dai the Bread sat on the floor, back against the wall and head lolling to one side. There was a pink flush on his usually pasty face and he breathed heavily through open mouth.

Oven-Bottom Billy winked at Davy.

'Overcome by the 'eat,' he said chuckling. 'This 'eat.' He patted the bottle on the table. 'No 'ead for it 'as Dai. Nemmind I can manage this meself. 'Ere!' he said, picking up a tin mug and splashing whisky into it. 'Tek this across the yard for 'is owl Mam, will you Davy. Poor owl gel. It'll warm 'er up a bit, anyway.'

Davy slid across the packed snow of the yard, holding the mug of whisky carefully to save spilling. He lifted the latch and entered Dai's house, peering into the gloom of the kitchen. Although a fire burned in the grate the room was cold and Davy shivered, causing a few drops of whisky to spill on to the stone-flagged floor. The mound of old clothes on the iron bed in the corner stirred and a tangle of long grey hair emerged with two small black eyes showing through the strands.

'Oo's there?' The high-pitched voice was surprisingly strong and a claw-like old hand pushed aside some of the grey locks to reveal a yellow and wrinkled countenance. 'Oo's there?' Lizzie Cuckoo repeated. 'Watchoo want?'

137

Davy advanced and proffered the mug.

'Drop of whisky off Billy,' he said, and the old claw shot out and grasped the mug eagerly. He watched while she raised herself on a skinny elbow and clutched a safety-pinned shawl round her shoulders more closely with her free hand. She drank deeply, finishing the whisky off with a few swallows, then handed back the mug and burst into a fit of coughing. Davy watched in consternation as her whole body shook under the pile of old coats which covered her. At length the coughing subsided and she wiped her eyes with the corner of the shawl and then blew her nose into it.

'You all right?' asked Davy anxiously.

'Reach me one o' them lozengers, boy,' she gasped, pointing a shaky finger at the wooden chair by the side of the bed and Davy undid a screw of paper and passed her an oblong brown cough lozenge which she popped into her toothless mouth and sucked noisily. Her watering eyes peered blearily up at Davy.

'Oo are you, boy?' she wheezed, wiping a brown dribble from the side of her mouth. 'I'm cowld,' she went on before he could answer. 'Where's that Dai? 'E should be 'ome by now. No good, 'e inna. Like 'is father, no go in 'em. Worsen 'is father. No go at all. I could carve a better man out of a swede!' She chuckled thinly then lay down again and disappeared under her musty covering. Davy crept out thankfully and latching the door behind him returned to the savoury warmth of the bakehouse where he delivered the empty mug to Billy and with a last look around at the glistening golden bodies made his way back home through the gathering dusk of the afternoon.

☆　　☆　　☆

The family were gathered round the festive board and the last mouthfuls of Christmas pudding were being savoured. They were all replete, flushed as much with overeating as with the heat from the enormous fire which burned in the grate. The goose had been cooked to golden brown perfection and accompanied by roast potatoes, sprouts and carrots and a rich gravy which Mama had made with the giblets. Dada sat back in his chair now and patted a loaded stomach.

'*Duw*, Susan, that was the best dinner ever I ate. Good that old goose was. There is nothing like a goose, indeed. An old turkey do have lot of meat on but it is dry old meat, I am thinking. That was a very good bird, fair play.'

'Beautiful pudding too, Mama,' congratulated Llew, blowing his cheeks out. 'Dammo, I am too full to move from the table.'

'You will have room for a glass of ale, though?' queried Dada, rising with some difficulty and stamping off to the pantry to return with a large brown bottle which he had had filled at the Queen's Head the night before.

'Well,' said Mama, cheeks pink and mouth smiling, 'if you men are going to drink that old ale we women will have a glass of Martha's cowslip wine.' Beaming at the girls, who smiled their agreement, she bustled off to fetch her bottle and returned to fill three small wine glasses with the sparkling golden wine.

Davy looked round, eyes wide.

'Where is my drink, then?' he asked indignantly.

All eyes turned on him and Dada thumped the table.

'Bring him an ale glass,' he told Mama, chuckling. 'Today he shall drink with the men.'

Mama looked doubtful.

'Maybe a little taste of this wine?' she ventured.

'*Twt*, girl, he does not want that old woman's coddle,' roared Dada. 'Ale for the boy today, isn't it? It will do him no harm to have a drop.'

Mama said no more but fetched a glass and Dada filled it with ale. Davy braced his shoulders and with eyes shining, drank from his glass with a seasoned air although in truth he found the ale bitter and had to repress a shudder.

They sat round the table contemplating the remains of the goose and the plum pudding, the heat of the kitchen making them drowsy. Mama and the girls sipped daintily at their cowslip wine while Dada and Llew talked over their ale.

Nell peeped under her lashes from time to time at Mama. She had a question to ask and was plucking up her courage to broach it. At length she put down her wine glass on the table and sitting straight, clasped her hands together on her lap.

'Mama, can I bring Elwyn Jones for tea this afternoon?'

The words came out in a rush and Mama looked startled.

'Well, now,' she said, contemplating the last drop of wine in her glass. 'This is the first I have heard of this Elwyn Jones.'

Dada cleared his throat and took another pull of his ale, while all eyes turned to Nell's blushing face. Her chin went up and her dark eyes travelled round the table and then returned to Mama's face.

'Oh, now, Mama,' she said, acidly. 'Do not tell me that the old gossips have not been to you with their tales. I have been courting Elwyn nearly two years now.'

'Old gossips know better than bring their old tales to me,' said Mama, bridling. 'But I am not saying I have not heard. And if he is a tidy boy, as they do tell, why the old hush?'

'No old hush,' said Nell, eyes straight. 'I am asking now, isn't it? Can I bring him to tea?'

'About time,' said Mama, giving Nell look for look.

Breaths were released in a sigh of relief round the table and Dada poured himself another glass of ale.

'Aye, he will be welcome if he is a tidy chap,' he nodded, eyes twinkling, and turned to Mama for confirmation. She inclined her head, a little smile hovering in the corners of her mouth.

'Yes, well, we shall see,' said Nell and her troubled eyes met Davy's. Meggie intercepted the glance and wondered. She sensed something wrong and her gentle eyes clouded. She had been very quiet and a little withdrawn since the episode with Ronald Purvis, but had recently got herself a job at the Gwalia Mill and her confidence was slowly returning.

She looked round the festive board now and her spirits lifted. Her eyes ranged from the highly coloured, blue-eyed countenance of Dada, took in the thin, dark intense face of Llew, the happy, smiling pink-cheeked Davy, the proud firm-chinned Nell, absorbed in her own thoughts and finally rested on Mama, the centre and king-pin of the Rees household. Her heart expanded in her breast and the darkness of the last few weeks fell away, never to return.

After the table was cleared and the washing up done Llew and Nell disappeared and Davy went in search of Geraint. Meg curled up on the old horsehair sofa under the window with a copy of *David Copperfield*, borrowed by Davy from the Rectory library, and Mama and Dada dozed in front of the fire. At half past four Mama and Meg stirred themselves to lay the table for tea. They carried in the Christmas cake, white icing glittering and a sprig of holly for decoration, a dish of

140

mince pies and a platter of slices of cold goose and a pink ham which Mama had boiled the previous night. Bread and butter and a jar of Mama's pickled onions completed the feast and Mama hovered, straightening the already smooth, snowy cloth, touching knives and forks and examining the best tea plates, polishing them to a pristine shine, with a clean tea towel. Davy returned first, leaving snowy boots in the back kitchen and glowing from an hour of sledging with Geraint down the Vastre, where the road ran down steeply from the Kerry Hills into the town. After he had warmed his hands he was ordered by Mama to wash and put something on his feet, which he did, throwing hungry glances over his shoulder at the festive spread on the tea table.

It was almost five o'clock when the front door opened to admit Nell, followed by the tall, broad-shouldered figure of Elwyn Jones, stiffly dressed in best suit with starched white collar and toecaps shining. They came through into the kitchen, Nell's cheeks pink with cold as she drew off her gloves and laying her hand on Elwyn's sleeve, drew him forward.

'Mama, Dada, this is Elwyn Jones,' she said, chin lifted high.

Mama took in the straight grey eyes, crisp brown curls and firm, dependable chin and blew out a soft breath.

'You are welcome, Elwyn Jones.' She inclined her head. 'I was only saying to Nell that it is about time.'

Dada rose from his chair by the fire and advanced to shake hands.

'Aye, indeed, welcome you are boy. This girl of ours has been close about this old courting. I do not see why.' His blue eyes twinkled. 'Come you and sit down, Mama will make tea now.'

'Thank you, Mrs Rees, Mr Rees,' replied Elwyn Jones, nodding gravely around to include Meg and Davy and they all seated themselves while Mama fetched in the teapot and spooned tea into it from the old japanned caddy.

Dada engaged Elwyn in talk about his policeman's job while Nell looked on proudly. They were just seating themselves at the long table when the front door opened once more and Llew entered, ushering in a female, the sight of whom stopped Mama in her tracks in the middle of pouring tea. All eyes turned to the newcomers.

Llew entered the kitchen first, the girl hovering behind him.

'Mama, this is Annie Owen. We are courting. I have brought her to tea.'

He turned and drew the girl forward with a half defiant air. Mama blinked and the teapot jerked in her hand sending a few drops of tea to spoil the white tablecloth. She put the teapot down on the stand carefully and then straightened. There was a silence as she looked the girl over very deliberately.

Annie's eyes looked back at her with a calculating air. They were black and knowing beneath a frizzed bang of coal-black hair on which was perched a bright pink hat with a large turquoise feather. Mama eyed the feather with distrust as though it were alive and about to strike. Her eyes then travelled over the rest of the outfit, a puce topcoat with a lot of braid frogging and reaching to meet grey suede boots of a cheaply smart design. A feather boa decorating the girl's narrow shoulders did nothing to reassure Mama. She nodded briefly and turned to meet Llew's eyes. The glance that passed between them was like the first salvo fired in a war and Llew flushed and his gaze hardened.

'Another who is close about his courting,' said Mama, shortly, and left it to Dada, blue eyes bewildered, to bid the two to sit down at the table. Llew pulled out a chair for Annie, who seated herself with a show of confidence, bright black eyes circling the faces at the table. Llew seated himself beside her defiantly.

'You would like to take that off,' said Mama, eyeing the feather boa. 'It will be getting in your tea.'

Annie's sharp chin went up but she unwound the boa and hung it over the back of her chair. Then she undid the buttons on her coat very deliberately to reveal a bright pink satin blouse which highlighted a sharply uplifted bosom. Mercifully the expression in Mama's eyes was hidden as she stooped to resume pouring the tea. Meggie rose swiftly and fetched in two more cups and saucers, plates, knives, forks and spoons which she set before Llew and Annie with a diffident smile. There was an uncomfortable silence which Dada broke with a clearing of the throat.

'Aye, well, help yourselves now. There is plenty for all. Pass me that meat, Nell, I will make a start. Come you, Elwyn *bach*, try some of Mama's pickles, good they are. Bread and butter, Miss Owen?' He addressed the turquoise feather as though afraid for his gaze to slip lower towards that shining pink bosom.

'Thank you, Mr Rees,' replied the girl, but her gaze was bent calculatingly on Mama's face. However, Mama was attacking a slice of goose as though she were expecting that to sprout a turquoise feather at any moment.

The family bent with relief over the meat and pickles while the clattering of knives and forks seemed to fulfil the need for conversation. Mama at last directed a few polite remarks to Elwyn Jones and it was clear to the family that at least she approved of him. No-one but Davy appeared to notice that Nell's face was clouded and although she glanced proudly at Elwyn from time to time as he expanded under Mama's approval, it was obvious to Davy that she had something on her mind which was spoiling her happiness and he guessed what it was. Nell had reached her decision and was going to break the news to Mama and Dada tonight. Poor old Nell. Davy sighed as he chewed on a piece of pink ham. Mama and Dada were not going to be pleased when Nell told them she was going to Canada. He peeped under his eyes at Annie Owen. *Duw*, Mama wasn't going to be in a very good skin, anyway! Poor old Nell!

Davy propped himself on his elbow and drew the bedclothes over his shoulder. It was bitterly cold in the bedroom but he felt too restless to lie down and cover himself up. Llew had not yet come up to bed and from the rise and fall of voices downstairs the storm over Annie Owen had broken on top of Nell's announcement of her intention to accompany Elwyn Jones to Canada. A shaft of steely blue moonlight fell across the bed as Davy gazed towards the window at the stars which twinkled brightly in the frosty sky.

He thought of Mama's face tonight as Nell had told her in low tones about her future plans. He shifted uncomfortably, allowing an icy finger of cold air to penetrate the bedclothes. He shivered and frowned up at the heedless stars. He had been curled up on the old sofa under the window while the others were seated round the fire, his presence forgotten. He thought he would always remember the stricken look on Mama's face

143

and the way all the breathing in the room seemed to be stilled. Dada's blue eyes had been bent on Mama's face and he had gripped the arms of his wooden chair tightly, chewing on his moustache then allowing his gaze to travel round the other faces in hurt bewilderment. Elwyn Jones had looked uncomfortable but stubborn and Meggie had sat twisting her hands together on her lap and gazing at the fire through gathering tears. Nell sat upright and very still, but her hand trembled on Elwyn's sleeve.

Mama had broken the silence with one word.

'Why?' The question came like a cry of pain on a long, indrawn breath.

Davy had hardly taken in the deep rumbling tones of Elwyn Jones, interspersed with the whispered defence and reassurances of Nell. He had been watching Mama and Dada and seen the realization dawn on them that this was a fight they were going to lose. After half an hour of discussion there had followed an uncomfortable silence. Then Mama rose to her feet and made her way uncertainly to the foot of the stairs and it was the first time that Davy had ever seen her shoulders drooping. Then she straightened them and turned. She looked first at Nell, whose tortured eyes had followed her, then at Elwyn, his honest face sullen and troubled.

'If I had known,' she said, hand on the doorpost and a bitter twist to her mouth, 'if I had known that you wanted to take my girl to some old foreign parts, I would not have welcomed you to my house. But too late it is, I can see.' She turned again and began to slowly mount the stairs. 'Canada, is it? It is an awful long way. An awful long way.'

Now Davy lay back on his pillow and drew the clothes over him with cold fingers. He thought of Llew and Annie Owen. Mama had spoken no more to the girl and soon after tea was cleared she and Llew had left, Annie settling her feather boa on her shoulders with a defiant air and Llew looking sullenly defensive. He wondered if it was serious with Llew and Annie. Mama would have a fit.

He lay reviewing Christmas day with mixed feelings. His feet were cold and his breath vapoured against the icy white linen of the sheets. The room darkened as a cloud obscured the moon and he turned shivering on to his side. He gazed out at the shadows and then his spirits lifted. Tomorrow was Boxing day.

More goose, more plum pudding, more mince pies and more sledging with Geraint. A small smile lifted the corners of his mouth and gradually he stopped shivering and fell asleep.

10

Philosophy and Petticoats

The birds were singing their spring song and the trees burgeon-
ing with delicate green leaves as Davy and Dada sat side by
side in companionable silence. They were seated on a fallen
tree up Brimmon fields on the first Sunday afternoon in May.
Davy was whittling a stick with the penknife which he had had
for his birthday, whistling softly between his front teeth while
Dada hummed contentedly, beating time on his knee and
gazing down with serene blue eyes on the town below, over
which lay a Sabbath calm.

Thin feathers of smoke rose from the houses on each side of
the river and the tall chimneys of the silent mills rose up like
pointing fingers. A fine mist still hung over the river, which
sparkled through it as the sun caught the water. The air was
still a little cool as though hardly recovered from the long
severe winter, but each day the sun got stronger and warmer.
Rooks returned to nest and cawed querulously in the higher
branches and bluebells were getting ready to replace the dying
primroses in the wood. There was a promise of summer not far
off in the wooded hillside at their back and the fields which ran
below them down to the town's edge were at their greenest and
freshest.

A movement in the grass by his feet caught Davy's eye and
he stopped whittling to watch a grass snake, its skin iridescent
in the sun, slide mysteriously along the ground. He watched its
progress with interest as it made its way between bits of bark
from the tree and tiny plants which swayed in its wake. It
disappeared under a spread of large foxglove leaves and a
spider ran startled from its path.

Davy straightened and breathed deeply of the clear air,

scented with woody smells and the sweetness of hawthorn blossom from a nearby tree. He raised his face and closed his eyes against the sun, a pink haze swimming behind his lids. The sun felt warm on the shoulders of his jacket, which was becoming tight on him. He opened his eyes and looked down at his hands curled round the stick and the penknife. They suddenly looked large and awkward and the wrists bony as they protruded too far through outgrown sleeves.

For no reason he gave a sudden chuckle which caught and broke as his voice often did now. Dada turned twinkling eyes on him questioningly. Davy grinned back and flinging the stick through the air, closed the penknife and dropped it into his pocket. He clasped his bony knees and stared down at them.

'I will be glad when I can have the long trousers Mama has promised me. I feel a bit daft in these old short trousers now.'

Dada stared at the offending knees as though it were the first time for him to see them.

'*Duw*, boy, do not be in such a hurry to grow up. Good it is to be young. It is *twp*, when you think about it. The young cannot wait to grow old and the old wish they were young again.'

Davy grinned and shrugged his shoulders in the too tight jacket.

'Do you wish you were a boy again, Dada?' he enquired with interest.

'*Diawl!*' said Dada, 'I do not think so. It was hard then. I remember only work. Up for five for the milking and on all day after. No days off and not much play do I remember.'

'No school then, Dada?'

'*Duw*, no. Not real schooling. I did learn my letters at Sunday School. There was a good minister we had at the Sunday School. We would go to the old chapel on Sunday afternoons and Mr Idris Thomas would teach us to read. The Bible, of course. My sums I did learn from my Mama. At night she showed us how to add up and take away. My Mama was a bit of a scholar. She could read and write. Her father did learn her, him being a lay preacher. My Dada did never learn.' He chuckled. 'But sharp enough he was. You would not do him in the market. It would be a foolish man that would try, mind you!'

Davy was silent, staring out over the valley to the hills on the other side. Dada glanced sideways at the thin sensitive young

147

face and thoughtful dark eyes.

'Still set on the teaching, is it?' he asked.

'Aye, I think so,' said Davy, bending to pluck a piece of grass which he chewed on dreamily. 'If I do all right at the end of next year, anyway. There will not be much money in pupil-teaching at first but its what I want to do. I was talking to Mr Hall last week. He says he will help me when the time comes. Maybe I can get a start in the Church school.'

'Seems a funny thing. You being such a scholar, I mean,' said Dada, pensively. 'But please your Mama it will, mind you. It is good you will still be at home. Your Mama misses Nell, aye and that rip Llew, indeed. She is like an old hen with chicks missing,' he added with a rueful grin.

Davy nodded. It was over a year now since Nell had married and gone with Elwyn to Canada and Mama had only the monthly letters, which came with regularity, to comfort her. She had taken the goodbyes very hard and matters had not been helped when, six months later Llew had quietly married Annie Owen and gone to live in a small cottage in Ladywell Street. Seven months later his son was born, a tiny version of Llew himself, and it was this infant which had conquered Mama's stubborn coldness and forced her to accept Annie into the family. In order, said Dada, that she could get her hands on little Owen. Mama had refused to see Llew or Annie until the day they had arrived on the doorstep, Llew with the tiny bundle in his one arm, and Annie pertly hanging on to the other. She had silently motioned them to sit down and made them a cup of tea in their hands. Then she reached for the bundle and sitting in Dada's old armchair had parted the shawl and gazed at the tiny pink face with the tuft of dark hair, the image of Llew. At last she looked up and nodded and Llew knew that the war was over. For a while it was an uneasy truce but as Annie put herself out to please and curbed the sharp tongue with which she was making Llew so uncomfortable, the atmosphere improved and the three were welcomed at No 46.

Thinking of this Davy suddenly grinned at Dada.

'*Duw*, funny to think I am an uncle, too.'

'Aye, and I am *taid*,' said Dada beaming. 'But they are teaching him to call me Grandad Rees. It is the old English way but there! He looks a right sharp little owl babby and he do please your Mama, whatever.'

148

'And now Nell is to have a baby soon, so she says in that last letter. Do you think we will ever see them again, Dada?'

'*Twt*, boy, of course we shall see them again,' said Dada stoutly, but his blue eyes clouded and he sighed. '*Daro*! but that old Canada is a long way off. For why would that young fellow want to go all that way to be a policeman? He could just as easy be a policeman here in Wales.'

'I dunno,' Davy said, stripping the bark from a twig with his fingers. 'I suppose it is better pay and more prospects out there. There is not much crime about here, after all,' he added, grinning. 'Just Ivvy Whippet and a few other poachers and a bit of pilfering. A few fights, perhaps, and a bit of drunk and incapable.'

Dada snorted through his nose indignantly.

'Poaching, is it? They should not lock a man up for that. The good Lord made all the creatures and they should not belong to just a few old people that own a bit of land. I do not think any worse of a man for a bit of poaching. I have done it myself, indeed,' he chuckled reminiscently. 'I do not remember anything in the Bible about poaching, now. And if a man has a drop to drink and is lying in the gutter, then that is his lookout, mind and only himself harmed. *Twp* it is to drink so much, of course. But then the well-off ones do do that in their own big houses and servants to drag them to their beds and nothing said.'

Davy laughed.

'*Duw*, Dada, you are beginning to sound like Llew now, isn't it?'

'*Diawl*, no!' answered Dada, thumping his knee. 'That boy is full of old nonsense. He do think we should have a rev -rev, dammo what do you call it?'

'A revolution, Dada,' put in Davy grinning. 'Like they had in France. The poor people took over from the rich and chopped their heads off.'

'Ha!' said Dada, eyes wide. 'That is what our Llew wants to do, is it? I am thinking the boy has lost his wits. The day he will start to chop heads off I will deal with him. Where would he get such notions from? We are tidy people and we have been brought up tidy.'

'I do not know that he is wrong altogether,' mused Davy, stripping the last bit of bark from his twig and running his

149

thumb up and down the moist inside of it thoughtfully. 'There is a lot of old injustice around too. You have only to look how the millowners live and compare that with how the workers live. And if the poor folks grumble then they can get out, for there are plenty to take their jobs.'

'Now then,' said Dada sharply. 'Let us have no more of that old talk. One in this family is enough with bad old talk like that. Do not you start it, boy.'

Davy grunted and they were silent for a while. The soft sounds of the May afternoon were all around them. Sheep bleated in the fields and a wood pigeon cooed drowsily from a tall tree in the wood. A soft breeze ruffled Dada's white hair and stirred the dark curls that lay across Davy's forehead. Thoughts of school and the things he was learning drifted through Davy's mind, followed by pictures of himself imparting the same knowledge to other boys through the years. He was moved to wonder what purpose was in it all. He smiled to himself. Here was Dada, who couldn't have told you the dates of the old Kings of England to save himself and would find no use for a bit of Latin in his daily life. And yet he was none the worse for it. But then his thoughts turned to Elinor, as they did so often and he stirred on the log, stretching his limbs, feeling the bitter-sweet sensation stir in his breast. He knew that he loved her. He had for years and felt that he surely always would. He must have prospects if he was to court Elinor. Then his eyes clouded and he sighed deeply. She was a strange girl, was Elinor. There were times when he thought that whatever he did and however he turned out, she would have no use for him. A wild thing, she was, wild and proud. Sweet as butter one minute and the next, claws out to scratch. She was like the wind. You would not know which way she would blow next. Maybe as she grew older she would change and he would have a chance. A picture came into his mind of the dark-fringed violet blue eyes under fine dark brows like wings, small straight nose and soft curving mouth. And yet those eyes could grow dark and stormy if she were thwarted and the soft lips draw back on screams of rage and frustration.

But she was Elinor and with all his boyish ardour he loved her. Geraint knew and alternatively poured scorn on him or teased him cruelly, but he remained impervious to this and to Elinor's own cavalier treatment of him.

150

He examined his knees again. Time he had those long trousers. They looked naked now, somehow. He was nearly sixteen and tall for his age. He would get on to Mama again. Dammo, it would be ages before he was earning and he needed clothes. A new jacket as well and maybe a starched collar like Llew. He rested an elbow on his knee and his chin on his hand and sighed again.

Dada turned and looked at him quizzically.

'What is with you, boy? You are like an old hen with the gapes there. You have the weight of the world on your shoulders now, is it?'

'Just thinking, Dada. All these old clothes are too small for me getting. I wish I could earn money to buy new.'

'Hm,' grunted Dada. 'Never satisfied you young ones. You want to go in for the learning and when everyone is scratting to see you do it, now you are wanting to earn money. Your Mama will do her best no doubt but I will not have you worrying her. Meg does give extra in so that you do not go short. There is a good girl, little Meggie. A good sister indeed.'

'I know, Dada,' said Davy quickly, shame in him now. 'Just saying I am. I will wait while Mama will see her way. But Geraint has been in long trousers a year now and I am taller than him. I do feel a bit of a fool sometimes, that is all.'

'Aye, well, we will see. Your Mama will do her best, you can be sure. She is proud of you boy, remember that. She sets store by the learning. And Meggie thinks of you before she thinks of herself. Be thankful.'

I am Dada, honest. Meggie is good as gold. Glad I am that she is not gone from home. Oh, not because of the money,' he hastened to add. 'No, it is good to have Meggie still with us. She does not seem to go in for the courting, does she?'

Dada smiled and shook his head.

'No. Pretty as a picture is our Meggie, to turn all heads. But she do not bother when the young larrups do make the cows' eyes at her. Oh, she is young yet and a comfort to her Mama. I am hoping she do not take up with some foot-loose one who will want to take her off foreign like our Nell. Why that girl would have to take up with some old wanderer, I do not know. But that one always had her own ideas and her own ways and you would not turn her, whatever.'

'She did not really want to go, you know,' said Davy. 'But

151

Elwyn would not stay and she wanted Elwyn.'

'Aye, aye. Well, that's the way of it. As long as our Meggie does not go far away, that is all. She seems to be contented enough at that old mill, but that is the way with Meggie. A good little girl indeed.'

'Well,' said Davy, straightening his back and digging his hands in his pockets, 'you will have Meggie and me for a long time yet. I will never leave Newtown. I do not ever want to go away. Not like Geraint. He talks of nothing else. He will go in the Army one minute, the Navy the next, or out to Africa to shoot down a few natives or to America to search for gold. Always he is going away.'

'I do not know how Mr Gwilym Pryce got that one, indeed,' grunted Dada, shaking his head. 'There is something in that boy I am afraid for. He do like to hurt,' he added, frowning. 'I have watched him. There is something wrong there.'

Davy shifted uncomfortably and bent to select a piece of grass to chew.

'Geraint is all right,' he muttered defensively. 'He is a good friend.'

'Hm,' grunted Dada. 'We shall see. I do not understand the boy, truth to tell, nor his sister either. There is a right little madam for you now.'

Davy flushed darkly and looked away. Dada peeped at him from the corner of his eyes and blew through his whiskers.

'Some day you will find a tidy girl of your own station,' he said. 'It is not good to set your heart on what you cannot have.'

Davy turned his red face towards him.

'Dada, you are old-fashioned with your talk of stations,' he cried heatedly.

'Old-fashioned, is it?' Dada's blue eyes widened. 'Not old-fashioned at all now. It is just sense. You will see, boy, as you get older.'

Davy shrugged impatiently.

'Why are we talking like this, Dada? I am not sixteen yet!'

Dada grinned and slapped his knee.

'Right you, boy. Long time to go yet before you will be thinking of the girls, isn't it? Though indeed I was a right rip when I was not much older'n you.'

Davy had to laugh.

'A one for the girls, was it, Dada?'

'The old temptation was put in my way a lot, more like,' explained Dada with modesty. 'Wherever I turned there was the girls. I don't know why, but they did seem to have a weakness for me. Try to get away as I would, they was always after me. A very funny thing, that,' he added, eyes innocent.

Davy chuckled and Dada joined in. They were silent again for a while when suddenly the stillness was broken with an explosive giggle from the wood behind. They both turned startled faces in time to see a woman rise from behind a gorse bush and picking up her skirts, rush down the path at their side, high button boots flying and hair tumbling over her shoulders.

'*Diawl!*' said Dada. 'She did rise from that bush like a pheasant before the beaters.' He frowned, puzzled. 'She must have been there a long time too. We have been sat on this log well over an hour, see.'

'Who was she, Dada?' Davy asked curiously.

'Well,' said Dada, tugging his moustache. 'I did not get much of a look at her, she was off like a mare with a burr under her tail. But I think it was Jinny Nannygoat.'

'Jinny Nannygoat! Who is that, then?' Davy stifled a giggle.

'Ah, now,' replied Dada, eyes twinkling. 'Better you did not know, see. No better than she should be is Jinny Nannygoat. *Diawl!*' he said, looking round cautiously. 'Your Mama would have fits if she knew that I would even know her name!'

On that there was another rustle behind the gorse bush and a red-faced, thick-set man rose to his feet and began to pick pine needles and bits of dried leaves from his britches.

Dada's eyebrows flew up but his blue eyes were expressionless.

'Good afternoon to you, Mr Morgan,' he called politely. 'A nice afternoon for a walk in the wood now, isn't it.'

The man looked up, startled, the colour in his face deepening.

'Is that you, Rees?' he said, picking off the last leaf and descending the slope towards them slowly. 'Looking to see for some mushrooms, I was.'

'Indeed?' said Dada, interested. 'Bit early for the old mushrooms, I am thinking, isn't it, Mr Morgan?'

'Aye, well, likely that is why I have not found any.' Morgan coughed and looked at the sky. 'Grand day, indeed, Rees. You

153

been sat here long, then?'

'Oh a fair time now,' Dada said calmly. 'I did not see you go past, Mr Morgan. Indeed we have seen nobody till now, have we, Davy? Except a few minutes ago. A young 'ooman did go past. In a bit of a hurry, it did look like.'

'A young 'ooman!' repeated Morgan, staring at Dada astonished. 'You don't say so? Now what would a young 'ooman be doing up here by herself, I do wonder?'

'Looking for mushrooms?' suggested Dada, innocent as a baby.

Davy took a fit of coughing and Morgan regarded him, frowning.

'That boy of yours do have a nasty cough, Rees,' he muttered. 'Maybe you have sat too long on that damp old tree.'

'Aye, maybe,' agreed Dada, rising. 'But it is a nice spot. Nice and quiet like. And a good view all round, indeed.'

Morgan's countenance darkened and he removed his hat to scratch his head as Davy got up and followed Dada as he began to make his way serenely towards the path.

'Oh, Rees!' called Morgan in a strained voice. 'Wait you a minute.'

Dada turned an innocent face to him.

'Yes, Mr Morgan?'

The farmer cleared his throat loudly and taking out a large white handkerchief, blew his nose like the last trump. He replaced the handkerchief in his pocket and looked at Dada uncertainly.

'Looks as though you have caught cold too,' said Dada, concerned. 'The old grass is still damp. To the hands and knees I mean. Picking mushrooms.'

Morgan made a choking sound and Dada looked alarmed.

'Look here, Rees,' he said, handkerchief out again to mop his brow. 'You and me have had words in the past, I do know. About the rabbits and suchlike,' he explained, eyes on Dada's face.

'Oh, aye, the rabbits.' Dada looked thoughtful. His eyes wandered over the holes in the bank at the foot of the wood and back to Morgan's face.

'Oh, aye, the rabbits. Plenty for all, I would have thought Mr Morgan. But you do not agree?'

154

'Well now, that is what I was about to say,' said the farmer eagerly. 'I have been thinking lately. Plenty of rabbits there are, indeed. All it is, I do not want everybody coming tramping over my fields to get them and doing damage, maybe. But a tidy chap like yourself now, that is a different matter. Do you see now, Rees?'

'Oh indeed, Mr Morgan.' Dada nodded, pleased. 'I do see quite clear what you do mean.'

'Well then,' said Morgan, sweating hard. 'You come when you like, Rees. But keep it to yourself. Not a word to anybody.'

'About the rabbits?' asked Dada, blue eyes wide. 'No indeed, now. Not a word shall pass these lips. I thank you Mr Morgan. Glad of these rabbits will be my wife. And how is your good wife these days?' he asked, very polite.

Morgan frowned furiously up at a pigeon which made guttural noises at him in an accusing manner from a nearby branch.

'She is well,' he growled. 'A good woman is my wife, indeed.'

'Oh, indeed,' agreed Dada, fervently. 'Worth a lot is a good woman.'

He began to descend the path, with Davy at his heels, face red with choked back laughter. They had gone some yards when Dada turned and paused, looking back at the farmer for a moment.

'Good day to you,' he said pleasantly, then added. 'Do you be careful now, Mr Morgan, *bach*. Mushrooms is funny things. They can give you a terrible belly-ache if you do pick the wrong 'uns. Then all hell do be let loose.'

He resumed his way down the path jauntily, whistling a little tune, his blue eyes gazing happily over the valley below. Davy looked back over his shoulder in time to see Morgan throw his hat to the ground and dance on it.

Sunday tea over, Davy strolled out on to Pool Road and heaving himself up on to the parapet of the Bridge Wall, swung his legs round to hang over the long drop down to the river below. He crossed his legs in the too-short trousers and whistled softly to himself. The evening breeze stirred the fresh new green leaves on the trees on the Rackfield and two piebald ponies grazing there stood close together hard against a tree trunk.

People passed on their way to evening chapel, the men stiffly correct in their best dark suits and solemn faces and the women

155

in grey and brown and beige with hats skewered atop strained back hair. All looked purposeful and self-conscious and re-minded Davy of Auntie Martha's big brown hens, filing in dignified line across the yard.

He had turned back to a dreamy watching of the river as it rippled and chattered its way over its rocky bed, when a soft voice behind him brought his head back round.

'Hello, Davy,' said Nan, pausing by the wall.

He smiled and returned her greeting, for he liked Nan.

'How are things going with you?' he asked with lifted brows.

'Oh, not so bad,' she said, leaning her elbows on the broad parapet. 'And you? How's school going?'

'All right, I think,' Davy shrugged. 'Only another year or so now. Shan't be sorry, either. I could do with earning some money.'

'You won't have to go away, will you?' she asked, her grey eyes turned up to him and a soft wisp of fair hair escaping from her ribbon at the back of her neck.

He shook his head.

'Hope not. I don't want to go away. I don't think I would. I would like to get a start at the Church school. I think Mr Hall will speak for me. That is if I get through my exams all right.'

'Oh, you'll be all right,' she said, smiling and drawing her shawl more closely about her rounded shoulders. She was not beautiful but she had filled out since being at the Rectory and her figure was sturdy, broad-hipped and with a sweet round-ness to her bosom which hinted at a ripeness to come. Her face was arresting rather than pretty, with wide, high cheekbones and a pointed chin. Her eyes were her best feature, almond shaped and clear grey with golden lashes strangely tipped with brown. Her brow was high and clear beneath thick, coarse fair hair and her skin was creamy and pale. She wore a narrow black velvet choker around her full throat as was the fashion at the time.

However, Davy took in none of this. To him she was just 'Nan the Rectory'. At this time no other face but Elinor's registered with him as being worthy of attention.

'What are Geraint and Elinor doing?' he asked now, with studied casualness.

'Well, Geraint is out in the field with that old airgun he got for Christmas. I don't know why the Rector got it for him.

156

Except he does not seem to be able to say no to either of them,' she added pensively. 'Geraint is shooting at the poor crows in the Rectory field every evening when he has finished his homework. It is a wonder they will come to nest there at all. But Geraint and Elinor, they both get their own way, don't they?'

Davy shrugged.

'I suppose so. What is Elinor doing?'

'She went to tea with Mrs Purvis. Ronald Purvis is home and his mother invited a few young people to tea. Geraint would not go but Elinor was glad to dress up in her new long dress. White it is, with a blue sash and a big blue ribbon to tie her hair back. She did look beautiful, too,' said Nan, eyes shining.

'Huh!' Davy grunted. 'A bit young to go to tea with Ronald Purvis' crowd, isn't she? Only fourteen! Ronald Purvis is twenty-one.'

'Well, you know how Mrs Purvis likes to keep in with the Rector and be the big church woman. That is why the two from the Rectory were invited.'

'Don't blame Geraint for not going,' said Davy.

'Well, his Dada was cross and wanted him to go to keep an eye on Elinor but he wouldn't. Do you like Geraint?' Nan asked, twisting the fringe of her shawl, eyes lowered.

'Of course!' answered Davy, sharply, 'he's my best friend.'

'But you are not like each other, are you?' Nan said.

'Well, no two people are the same.' Davy shrugged. 'Don't you like Geraint, then? Is it because of what he did to your Alfie?' he asked uncomfortably.

She looked up at him with worried grey eyes.

'I used to hate him. Sometimes I think I still do. And other times, well, I don't know.' Her face flushed and she lowered her eyes again.'

'Here!' said Davy, with a short laugh. 'Not gone on him, are you?'

'Oh, shut up,' she said, crossly. 'He can be a nasty cruel beast, always teasing and – well, I don't know.' She broke off in confusion.

'Oh, well, teasing! That's Geraint. He always teased Elinor to make her mad.' He kicked his heels against the wall.

'Oh, she can fight back!' cried Nan, her eyes sparking. 'Like

157

a wild cat, she is. It's different for her.'

'He means nothing by it,' said Davy, sourly. 'It's just his ways.'

'Well, I don't like his ways.' She tossed her head and straightened. 'Anyway, I must go. I am taking letters to the post for the Rector. I must not miss it.' She drew two envelopes from the pocket in her skirt and stared down at them unseeingly. 'I suppose Geraint will go from home when he leaves school?' Her voice was low.

'Sure to,' answered Davy, airily. 'I can't see him settling to anything here. Wants to travel, he says. Don't know why.' His gaze travelled over the river to the hills beyond. 'I like it here,' he said contentedly. 'I don't want to go away.'

Nan sighed and turned the envelopes over in her hands.

'Oh, well. I'd better go. Ta ta, Davy,' and she turned to make her way down the road to Short Bridge Street.

'Ta ta,' he called out and watched her go, shoulders straight and head back as though the thick knot of hair was too heavy for her head. He gazed after her thoughtfully until she was out of sight. Nan was all right, he thought. But oh! Elinor! The name was like a song to stir his blood and he swung his legs round and jumped down from the wall, suddenly restless. Then he leaned back against it again and stared up at the green hills behind the streets and houses.

And then, for a moment, his heart swelled in his breast. He was Davy Rees, nearly sixteen and all the town and all the hills around were his. He belonged to it all. He grinned and gave a whoop of joy, then, shoving his fists into his pockets he began to saunter jauntily down the road, shoulders back and cap on the back of his head rakishly.

PART

2

11

Rhubarb and Rejection

It was a quarter to five on a Tuesday evening in April, 1909 when Davy mounted the steps of No 46, a small brown case in his left hand holding the books and papers which he needed for the preparation for lessons for the following day. As he pushed open the door with his free hand he thought ruefully that it would probably mean burning the midnight oil to get this done if he went up to the Rectory for the evening as planned. He sighed and went through into the kitchen where Mama had a roaring fire blazing in the hearth despite the soft mildness of the late April day. He dropped his case on to the old horsehair sofa and reached up to hang his jacket behind the door. He loosened his tie against the overpowering heat in the room just as Mama came in from the kitchen with a large enamel jug of water to fill up the already steaming kettle which hung on its chain above the fire.

'Dammo, you have some heat going here, Mama,' he complained.

'To bake a rhubarb pie for your tea, my boy, and there is no need to swear,' she added automatically.

He pulled out a chair from the table as far away from the fire as possible and sat down.

'All right if I drink some of this milk, Mama?' He pointed to the large white jug in the middle of the table.

She took a mug out of the cupboard and passed it over to him.

'As long as you do not take too much, boy. I want to make a bit of custard to go with the pie.'

He poured a mugful of cool milk from the big jug which he lifted easily with no effort of the thin, wiry wrist. A picture came into his mind of the trouble he used to have lifting this big old jug and how, even when he was using two hands to it, it would wobble and threaten to spill its contents, which it sometimes did. And what a pinch that would bring from Nell's long thin, needle-pitted fingers as she frowned down irritably from her seat beside him at the scrubbed table.

Nell had been in Canada nearly eight years now and had two children, Gareth nearly six and Gwennie three. Her letter still arrived regularly every month, often accompanied by photographs of the children at various stages of growth and once a studio portrait taken specially, of her and Elwyn and the two children, from which Nell's eyes stared out as if she would project herself across the sea and back to her home in Wales. She had never spoken of home-sickness but nevertheless Mama had read the emotion into the poignancy of some of her questions and the comparison between Newtown and Banff, where they had settled, mostly to the detriment of Banff. But lately the tone of her letters was more resigned and they were full of the progress of the children and the refurbishing of a small frame house out in the suburbs which Elwyn had bought for her, to get more of a feeling of home, as he put it, than in the centre of the town where they had first lived in an apartment house. Elwyn was doing well, she reported, and when they had all they needed for the house, which they were calling 'Cambria', then they would start saving hard for a visit home. They all knew this would take years, but the promise of it in every letter kept them all going on both sides of the ocean.

There was a clatter of boots rushing in through the back door and a small face peeped inquisitively from the back kitchen doorway.

'Hello, Owen,' said Davy, grinning at the little fellow as he sidled round the doorpost. 'What are you up to then, boy?'

'He is up to no good, as usual, mark my words,' replied Mama sharply, but the eye she bent on the child held a wry affection.

'Come over here then and tell me what you have been doing?' Davy patted the table in front of him and when the boy came across the kitchen he lifted him by his armpits and sat him on the edge of the table, where Owen sat swinging his sturdy boots on the end of slender bare legs, and grinning happily into Davy's face.

162

Owen was seven, but still small for his age. He looked very like his father, Llew, with dark eyes darting restlessly and a pale, pointed face which could break into a smile of great sweetness.

Feeling a surge of affection for the little chap, Davy butted his head into the navy-blue jersey which tightly encased the thin chest, bringing a throaty chuckle from Owen who reached up and grabbed handfuls of the thick, wavy dark hair which tickled his chin.

Undoing the small fingers, Davy asked,

'Does you Mam know you're here?'

The child nodded solemnly then wriggled in an effort to get down. Davy set him on the floor and he ran back out through the back kitchen and could be heard clattering across the cobbles of the back yard. Mama grumbled as she began to lay dishes on the table for tea.

'That Annie does not know where he is half the time. Nor care if you ask me.'

She had never got over her dislike of Llew's wife whose only merit in Mama's eyes was the fact that she had produced Owen.

'Your Dada will be in soon,' she said, setting down a large plate of bread thickly buttered with farm butter, and the old wedge-shaped green cheese dish. Then she took down a teacloth from the string line above the fireplace and opening the oven, lifted out a large enamel dish of rhubarb pie, the crust crisp and golden and sweet pink juice bubbling from the air vents in the crust. She set it down in the middle of the table and Davy's mouth watered hungrily.

'I will just make a bit of custard with that now,' she murmured, eyeing it with satisfaction, and swept off into the back kitchen, a tall, spare-framed woman in her fifties, shoulders still set back purposefully, her piled-up brown hair thick and wavy but well streaked with grey now.

Heavy footsteps sounded on the cobbles of the yard and Dada's voice could be heard raised sharply, scolding Owen. Soon he was addressing Mama in the back kitchen.

'*Diawl*! That boy was piddling on the drain in broad daylight!'

Mama clicked her tongue in outrage.

'Well, I did have him in the *ty bach* in short order. His boots

163

did not touch the ground.' Now he was pouring water into the enamel basin in the old stone sink and scrubbing his hands briskly. After a pause he came stamping through into the kitchen and, greeting Davy with a grin and an 'Aye, aye!', he pulled out his chair and sat down at the head of the table. He bent over and peered at the big pie and his blue eyes gleamed under shaggy white brows.

'Dammo, that do look good enough to eat. I do want my tea sharpish, too. I must go up the wood for pea sticks this evening before it do come dark.'

He rapped a large spoon impatiently on the edge of the table and looked round him, mouth pursed in a reedy whistle behind his white moustache. Dada had changed little that Davy could see. His hair had turned white at an early age so he had always seemed the same to Davy. His blue eyes were as bright and shrewd as ever and if his stocky figure was slightly heavier, the thickening was not of fat.

'I would like to come and help you cut those old sticks, Dada,' said Davy now, 'But I am for the Rectory tonight, as you know.'

'Aye, aye, boy. Geraint did get back this morning about eleven o'clock. Very smart he did look indeed, in his uniform. Fit as a fiddle. He did say to tell you to be up about eight when he will have had his supper. The Rector is in Church tonight with his confirmation class.'

Davy nodded as Mama came in bearing a bowl of thick yellow custard which they proceeded to spoon over huge pieces of pie, swimming in sweet pink juice.

'Do you leave some for our Meg, now,' warned Mama. 'I will put a bit on this plate here for Owen, if he have not run off by now.' She set a smaller piece on a plate for the child and went off to call him. Soon he came clattering in, beaming at the sight of the pie, and wriggling up on to the bench, set to spooning mouthfuls up greedily. Mama looked smugly round and then sat down to pour out the tea.

'I was just saying to Davy,' mumbled Dada, dribbling pink juice and fumbling for his handkerchief to mop his whiskers. 'Geraint is home and do look right smart.'

'Hm,' said Mama, looking down her nose. 'Very important chap now, no doubt. But anybody can go into the old army.'

'Oh, important he is indeed and no doubt. Two of those old

164

doodahs he do have on his shoulders to prove it.' He peeped mischievously at Mama, who bridled.

'Our Davy is a schoolmaster. He do not have to wear old doodahs on his shoulder to be important!'

Davy chuckled and winked at Owen who smiled back through a mouthful of pie.

Mama, jealously eyeing the last piece, whisked it away and popped it back in the oven to keep warm for Meg, who did not finish work at the mill until six.

'And who is the man fighting now, with the doodahs on his shoulders?' asked Mama sweetly, resuming her seat.

Dada drew in his chin and cocked an enquiring eye at his empty plate.

'Well now, damned if I know, come to think of it. Not gone to war, is it? I do think the Rector did say something about keeping them black men in order somewhere.'

Mama snorted. 'Keeping the black men in order, is it? Why do they not leave them poor black men alone, I wonder. They are not bothering us, are they? Minding their own business they are, as far as I can see. I do not mind that the Christian folks here send them a few old clothes for it is not good for people to run around bare naked anywhere. Though I did wonder at that last batch they did send from our Church. I do not see the people in them hot lands wanting them jerseys and shawls and red flannel drawers. Roasted they would be in that hot sun, poor souls. But sending young Welshmen out with doodahs on their shoulders and guns and all to keep them in order! No wonder if them black men would put them in the pot and eat them. No more than they deserve,' she added disgustedly.

Dada's hand went up to his moustache to hide a smile.

'Now, now, Mama,' said Davy, grinning. 'You are for overthrowing the great British Empire with talk like that!'

'Great British Rubbish?' said Mama defiantly. 'What I do want to know, what do we get out of it? Why cannot we leave other people alone?'

'Well now,' replied Davy. 'You don't build an empire by leaving other people alone, you know. As to what we get out of it, well we get the gold and the diamonds and the rubies. And we get tobacco and crops and the black man to dig them and plant them and pick them. Oh yes, we get plenty out of it.'

165

'Oh yes?' said Mama, interested. 'I am getting no diamonds and rubies and such-like out of it. And I do not want their old tobacco, anyway,' with a contemptuous sniff. 'And what do we give the black men in exchange for these old diamonds and rubies and tobaccos and things? They are not giving them out for nothing, I am sure.'

'Ah!' explained Davy. 'They are not giving them to us at all. We are taking them, see.'

'Well!' cried Mama, scandalized. 'No wonder we are having to send the soldiers out there to keep them in order. If the old British Empire was stealing from me like that it would take an army to shut me up, mind you!'

'Oh, dear!' Davy chuckled delightedly. 'Are you sure our Llew has not been putting these ideas into your head, Mama?'

'I do not need our Llew to put ideas into my head,' said Mama, loftily. 'I have my own ideas in my head, thank you very much,' and she rose to clear the dishes from the table.

'Locked up she will be,' observed Dada mildly.

'I never thought I'd see the day,' said Davy, rising and reaching over to rumple Owen's dark hair.

'Women!' snorted Dada. 'They do know nothing. They should stick to rhubarb pie!'

At eight o'clock Davy made his way up the back steps and through the little grove of twisted elders. He strolled across the Rectory field, remembering the many times he had run through this field as a lad to call for Geraint. It had seemed such a great big field then, but now his long legs traversed it in seconds as the soft breeze of the April evening blew the dark waves from his high forehead. The birds in the chestnut trees were giving vent to a full-throated evensong and he had a feeling of pleasurable anticipation at the thought of seeing Geraint again. His friend had been away for a year this time. Dammo, they had had some good times on Geraint's last leave, too, he thought, grinning as he let himself in through the door in the wall and crossed the courtyard to pull the old doorbell. It was Nan who answered the jangling summons, smiling a friendly welcome to Davy, her snowy starched pinafore tied round her trim waist, over a neat navy-blue dress with a prim white collar. Despite the smile and the steady grey eyes there was an air of tenseness about her which Davy did not bother to analyse.

166

She preceded him down the tiled passage and indicated a door on the left.

'Wait in there, Davy, will you? I'll go up and tell Geraint you're here.'

He nodded and she left him, moving down the passage in soft shoes, her crisp pinafore rustling over the brisk motion of her sturdy limbs, just as the warm rays of the setting sun shone through a window at the foot of the stairs, turning her thick cap of shining hair into gold above the heavy bun at the nape of the neck. Davy watched her until she mounted the staircase out of sight, remembering her as a skinny child with lank fair locks and a grubby pinafore. My word, but there was a fair change in Nan, too, he thought appreciatively. He opened the door and stepped inside, closing it softly behind him.

The high-ceilinged room was in twilight, the heavy furniture just shapes in the gloom, and at first Davy did not notice the immobile figure standing at the window with her back to the room. Then she turned and the rays of the setting sun striking the window illuminated her.

'Elinor!' exclaimed Davy, softly, then clearing his throat, 'I thought you were still in London.'

'Davy, is it?' Her voice was cool. 'Yes, I am back. Not for long I hope. I was dragged back.'

The warm glow from outside the window gave her motion-less figure a strange dream-like quality. Her dark hair was dressed in an intricate pompadour and red stones in the dangling earrings which she wore glowed like fire. The smooth curve of her profile was outlined against the gathering dusk and her face rose like some exotic flower above the high-necked frill of a lace blouse. Davy caught his breath. She was lovely and completely grown up.

When at last his voice came it was hoarse.

'Dragged back?'

With an impatient movement of her shoulders she turned back to the window.

'Of course. You don't think I wanted to come back to this dull place!'

'You liked it in London then?' Davy still stood, back to the door.

'Liked it!' Her voice was contemptuous. 'It's the only place to be. There's life and fun there. This place is so boring. There's no life here at all. Anyway, I'm not staying. They'll see. If they think they can keep me here in this backwater, they're mistaken,' she added, her voice rising.

'You were staying with your Auntie, was it?' asked Davy, eyeing the defiant set of her narrow shoulders.

She chuckled maliciously.

'Poor old Auntie Lou. She was like an old hen, trying to keep an eye on me. Much good it did her!'

The sun sank behind the hills and the twilight in the room deepened. Elinor turned abruptly and came towards the door. Davy still stood against it in a dream.

'Can I come past, then?' she snapped and flushing deeply he sprang to one side and opened the door for her.

'Thank you,' she said with a short laugh and whisked out, leaving a faint perfume in her wake.

Davy closed the door again slowly and advancing to a deep armchair beside the empty grate, he sat down heavily. The sudden meeting with the object of all his boyhood worship had disturbed him. His pulse was racing and he breathed quickly. Elinor! A pain expanded in his chest and he stared unseeingly at the window where she had stood.

The door burst open and in came Geraint. He paused for a moment peering through the shadows.

'Davy?'

Davy stirred.'

'Here, Geraint.' It was an effort to make his voice light.

'Good God! Sitting in the dark, eh? Let's have this lamp lit,' and he fumbled in his pocket for matches and lit the big brass lamp which stood on the polished table in the middle of the room. 'Damn the old man, sticking to these blasted lamps,' he said with a wry laugh. 'We're still in the dark ages in more ways than one.'

He threw himself down in the armchair on the other side of the fireplace and pulling out a packet of cigarettes, drew out two and threw one across to Davy.

'Smoke?'

Davy caught it awkwardly and they lit up.

'Well!' Geraint grinned across at Davy and leaned back in his chair. 'You don't change much anyway, Davy boy. How's the schoolmastering?'

Davy puffed on his cigarette and grinned back, relaxing a

little and breathing deeply.

'Not so bad, boy. Keeping the little devils at it, you know. But what about you? You've more to tell than me, I'll warrant.'

Geraint chuckled and slid down further in his chair.

'God, yes. That's the life you know. Out in the colonies. The British are like bloody little gods out there. You can have a whale of a time. The poor fool blacks run on their heads for you. Got to, I suppose. And the dusky maidens!' He gave a self-conscious laugh. 'Ripe for the picking, eh?'

Davy contemplated the glowing end of his cigarette and felt the familiar uncomfortable stirring in his stomach.

'How long you home for now?'

'Twenty-eight days. Then back to Aldershot. Mind, the life's not bad there, either. We have a fair old time in the Mess. Oh, I like the life all right. Couldn't settle down to civvy street now, especially here in Newtown. God! I'd die of boredom.' He stretched his arms up and yawned widely. 'I'd like to see a bit of real action though.'

'I see Elinor's home.' Davy leaned forward to throw his half-smoked cigarette into the grate. 'Didn't know she'd come back.' His voice was deliberately casual as he leaned back in the armchair again.

'Oh Lord, yes.' Geraint laughed, his perfect white teeth gleaming in the lamp light. He sported a blond moustache and his hair shone golden against the brown leather back of the armchair. 'She's been in disgrace, you know. Not that that will worry Elinor,' he chuckled. 'They'll never get her to settle down here now. Poor old Auntie Lou was having fits, I believe. Seems Elinor got in with that Ronald Purvis. He's up in London. Supposed to be handling some business for his father. Seemingly he introduced Elinor into a pretty fast set. Poor Auntie Lou said her behaviour was scandalous. Loose men and women and all-night parties! Oh dear me! Too much for Auntie Lou. She summoned the old man to London to take charge of his straying daughter and bring her back to safety. Which he did, it seems. Dragged her kicking and screaming back to the old homestead!'

He offered Davy another cigarette but Davy shook his head.

'Well, she's a bit young for that sort of thing anyway, isn't she?' It took an effort to control the tremor in his voice.

169

Geraint nodded and drew on his cigarette.

'Lost her head at the first taste of freedom. And that Ronald Purvis, he's a bit of a blighter anyway. At first Auntie Lou thought it was all right, seeing he was from Newtown, like, but when she saw where it was leading Elinor, all hell was let loose. I hear he's back in Newtown. Hope he hasn't followed Elinor. If he hangs round her here he'll have me to reckon with,' he added, glowering and balling his fist.

'He's a lot older than Elinor and a bad lot,' cried Davy, hotly.

Geraint shrugged.

'You know our Elinor. Wild as a park hare and if you tell her not to do something she'll do it all the more. I'll try and keep an eye on her while I'm here, though.' He flicked his cigarette end into the grate. 'Anyway, to hell with Elinor and her tricks. When we going to have a night out together, Davy boy?'

They fell to making plans and the leaden feeling in Davy's chest lightened somewhat. It was near to ten o'clock when Davy finally pulled himself up out of the depths of the armchair and announced his intention of going.

'Still got some work to do,' he explained ruefully. 'Some lessons to prepare for tomorrow. I shall be up 'til the small hours now.'

'Good God!' Geraint's voice was disgusted. 'If that's school-teaching you can have it. Don't know how you stand it. Anyway, don't work too hard, Davy-boy. The little buggers aren't worth it. Come on, I'll see you out.'

He preceded Davy through the door and down the passage. There was an almost arrogant vitality in all the movements of his handsome frame. Where the hall widened at the foot of the stairs, Nan moved away from a small table where she had been lighting a lamp. As she made to walk past them Geraint barred her way teasingly. She stopped and held herself very still and as her eyes were raised to Geraint's Davy was made sharply aware of a strange current which passed between the two. Geraint's look was dominating and mocking but it was the look in Nan's eyes that disturbed Davy most. It was a naked gaze in which submission was mingled with some other, even more uncomfortable emotion.

Geraint's laugh broke the momentary spell.

'Off to bed Nell?' There was a small secret smile in the curve of his lips and a look of meaning in his glance which brought a flush to the girl's face. Davy looked away, embarrassed, and moved past Geraint towards the door. There was a brief scuffle behind him and he heard Geraint give a low laugh. He was letting himself out when his friend caught up with him. Davy hesitated on the doorstep and looked up at Geraint's tall figure outlined against the lamplit doorway. He grinned and winked wickedly at Davy.

'See you Friday, Davy boy,' and the door closed quietly and decisively in Davy's face.

He made his way across the dark courtyard, his emotions disturbed and the old queerness back in his stomach. His feet felt their way automatically over the familiar cobbles. Under the trees the back driveway was dark but it was easier to find his way through this than across the field. As he neared the gate there was a faint yellow glow from a street lamp on Kerry Road. The vague outline of two figures emerging from the shadow of the bushes at the side of the gate showed briefly, then the taller moved swiftly through the half-opened gate and disappeared. Davy hesitated a moment and the second figure retreated back into the shadow of the bushes as his footsteps sounded on the gravel path. He moved on again but, with his hand on the gate, hesitated once more and looked back into the shadows. His eyes, accustomed to the dark now, picked out a faint white outline. The blood mounted to his cheeks as realization came and he stood as though hypnotized, staring at the shadowy form. Suddenly the figure detached itself from the darkness and Elinor faced him, the edges of the street light showing up the downward twist of her lips and the angry light in her eyes.

'Spying, are you, Davy Rees!' Her voice was low and furious. 'Who sent you? Geraint or the old man?'

A surge of emotion shook Davy's body. He took a step forward which brought him so close to her that he was conscious of the perfume which rose from her hair. She stood her ground, breast heaving under the white blouse. On a wild impulse he reached out and gripped her shoulders. His mouth came down hard on hers and for a moment he held her defenceless. Then he felt her lips draw back under his mouth and she struggled like a wild animal in his grip. He released her so quickly that she staggered back a pace, her body shaking

171

with fury. She drew her arm back and he felt a stinging blow across his face.

'Take your dirty hands off me, you lout!' Her voice was a shriek of outrage and for a moment he looked into her face, livid in the faint light of the street lamp, her eyes wild. Then with a sob of fury she turned and ran, stumbling down the dark drive.

Suddenly his legs felt weak and he leaned back against the gatepost, the blood pounding through his body and his breath rasping drily in his throat. He put up a shaking hand and touched the stinging weal across his cheek. He remained leaning against the gatepost until his breathing steadied and a feeling of total desolation flooded through him. He thrust his hands deep in his pockets and shivered in the cool night breeze. Above him clouds drifted and massed in the inky sky, heralding rain, and an owl hooted mournfully in the dark trees along the drive.

Thoughts drifted sombrely through his mind and he saw himself again standing in the same spot, offering Judas Iscariot to a small Elinor. With a harsh laugh he finally pulled himself away from the gatepost and moved heavily through the gate and onto Kerry Road, walking through the pool of yellow lamplight with bent head. The first few drops of rain fell cool against his burning cheek and he lifted up his head to receive them gratefully.

12

Flies and Floods

Davy and Geraint were buffeted by the rain and the wind at their backs and the force pushed them precipitately through the front door of the Buck Inn and into the warm humid atmosphere inside. Davy pushed his wet cap to the back of his head and made his way to the bar to order two pints of ale. He looked around the bar room in the yellow smoky light and wrinkled his nose wryly. There was a heavy smell of wet clothing and the few who were able to get close to the fire were steaming nicely.

It had rained heavily and relentlessly since the first drops which had cooled Davy's face on Tuesday night, coupled with a strong blustering wind which shook windows and drove the rain in sheets across the town. The river was swollen and out above its banks. The Gravel was flooded as were most of the small streets close to the river. The Rackfield was submerged as the turbulent waters took a short cut across the bend opposite the Bridge Wall. Debris rushed along swiftly on the mud-coloured water, with the occasional tree or the swollen body of a dead sheep swirling helplessly past.

'Hell of a night again,' observed Dai Shenko, pulling energetically on the pumps to put a foaming top to the amber flow. ' 'Tinna getting any better, neither.'

He placed the two pints on the bar and mopped up the spillings with a beery-smelling grey rag.

Davy nodded, sorting coins out from his cupped hand. He carried the drinks across to a table near the fire where Geraint had seated himself next to a florid faced individual whose wet coat was smelling rancid in the warm steamy air. Geraint took a deep pull at his pint and leaned back with a sigh of satisfaction, looking round the bar room with its low, smoke-yellowed ceiling and stone-flagged floor. The clients were draped wetly against the bar or seated around the room on padded benches, their garments clinging damply to their hunched bodies.

'Look at 'em,' he murmured in Davy's ear. 'They look as if they've all been washed up from somewhere unmentionable!'

The florid faced man belched loudly and placed a restraining hand on his fat stomach. A small, sallow-faced man with a grey stubble on his chin cocked an eye at him.

'Bloody 'ell, Bill. Inna there enough wind outside without thee bringing it in 'ere?'

The fat man grinned and drank deeply from his pint pot.

' "Let your wind go free where 'ere you be",' he declaimed, wiping his mouth with the back of his hand and belching again.

The sallow man clicked his tongue and shrugged at Davy and Geraint who grinned back at him.

A tall, thin fellow, his too-large cap resting on prominent ears, leaned the torn elbow of a wet tweed coat on the mantelpiece and stared down into the fire morosely.

'No end to it,' he muttered. 'We'll all end up with foot-rot, you'll see.'

'Go on with thee, thee owl Jonah,' replied the fat man, cheerfully. ' 'Tinna so bad as all that. There be more water in this ale than outside, I'll warrant.'

The barman heard the remark and made a threatening fist.

'Watch thyself, Bill Owen, or thee't get thrown out, rain or no rain. Thee't glad enough to drink it, anyways. Drop o' good ale is this.' He looked round challengingly and the banter flew to and fro good-naturedly in the mixed dialect of the little town, compounded of border Welsh with a sprinkling of Yorkshire idiom which had been introduced into the town by the influx of millhands from Yorkshire during the height of the woollen industry.

There was a commotion by the back door which led out to the urinals. Davy and Geraint craned round to have a look. A short man with a long coat and a battered trilby was shuffling in, bent double and making inarticulate and distressed noises.

'What the 'ell?'

'What's the matter with thee, Lloyd?'

'Straighten up, mun, and tell us what's 'appened!'

There was a babble of concerned remarks as everyone turned to eye the doubled-up individual curiously. He staggered back against the doorpost, his face grey with fright and a few beery tears coursed down his stubbly cheeks. One of the men nearest the door got up and went over to him.

'Speak up, Lloyd! What's wrong with thee?'

'I've 'ad a stroke!' cried Lloyd, wildly. 'I canna straighten up!'

'Good God!' said the man, stooping to peer into Lloyd's face. 'Thee dussent say!' He straightened and looked round the bar with a worried frown. 'The poor bugger's 'ad a stroke!'

'A stroke!'

'Never!'

'Canna 'e straighten?'

Another man got up and went over to Lloyd.

'We'd better get 'im over to sit down,' he said, staring anxiously at the jack-knifed figure, but Lloyd waved him away with a distraught moan.

'Dunna touch me! Dunna touch me! Get the doctor, quick!'

Suddenly the first man stooped down and looked more closely at the contorted and shaking figure.

'You silly owl fool!' he shouted hoarsely, straightening up. 'Thee'st fastened thee waistcoat buttons to thee fly!'

While Lloyd fumbled with the offending buttons the room erupted into laughter. After doing up his fly again properly, Lloyd straightened up and looked around him with dazed relief on his pale, sweating face. Then with a sheepish grin he weaved his way to the bar and demanded a pint. Dai looked at him with disgust.

'I should think thee's had enough! Stroke indeed! Go on 'ome to thee missus.'

Lloyd's bleary eyes focused on Dai's face with an effort.

'If thee knew my missus thee wouldn' be so quick to send any poor bugger 'ome to 'er,' he complained bitterly, but he steered a course to the door muttering and hiccupping and letting in a blast of rain-laden air as he opened it. He stood for a moment in the doorway and looked back at them, swaying like a sapling in the wind, his trilby tipped forward over his eyes. He drew himself up.

'To hell with all of you!' he said with solemn dignity and let the door bang violently behind him.

Geraint wiped tears of laughter from his eyes and rose to order a second drink. While he waited for the two pint pots to be refilled the door opened again and Dicky Skinny, a small grocer, was blown in. He fetched up against the counter at a tottering run and held on to it while he got his breath back. His battered bowler hat was jammed down hard over his ears to keep it from blowing away and his small weasly eyes peeped up from under the brim like shiny boot buttons.

'Surry, surry, it's still coming down,' he gasped as he fumbled in his deep pocket for his money.

'Well, thee dussent expect it to go up, dust'ee?' enquired Dai Shenko with raised eyebrows.

Dicky Skinny looked up at him suspiciously and put two coppers down on the bar after first peering carefully at each one.

'I'll have a half,' he announced with a defensive air and looked round at the gathering.

'Dunna thee overdo it now,' cautioned Dai and winked at Geraint as he put his two foaming pints down on the bar.

'These is 'ard times,' muttered Dicky Skinny, his eyes measuring the half-pint glass which was set in front of him.

'Hard for thy customers!' Dai nodded grimly. 'Still keeping thee thumb on the scales, Dicky?'

Dicky Skinny choked on his first swallow.

'I'll have thee up!' he told Dai. 'For slander!'

'Aye, aye,' grinned Dai. 'An' I'll follow thee up the steps with the Weights and Measures man!'

Scowling and sticking his moist bottom lip out, Dicky carried his glass over to the old settle on one side of the fireplace and seated himself next to the only woman in the room. She was a shapeless figure with a shawl round her shoulders, fastened with a large safety pin. A man's tweed cap sat square on her grey hair and pendulous flesh sagged from a whiskery chin. She gazed into a glass of gin with watering eyes and addressed it confidentially whenever she spoke.

'Nemma God!' she murmured into the glass. 'You'm half drownded, Dicky. Turrible night, in't it? Not fit for 'umans.'

Dicky Skinny grunted and sipped his half-pint slowly to make it last.

' 'Ow's yer missus?' she enquired ingratiatingly of the glass of gin. ' 'Er was right bad of the bellyache last week.'

''Er's all right.' Dicky's voice was surly. 'Eats too much, that's 'er trouble.'

A picture of the thin shadowy figure which hovered apologetically about his dimly lit shop brought incredulous thoughts to his listeners' minds.

Sally Sugar sighed into her glass.

'A bit o' summat to eat be awful dear nowadays, right enough,' she sympathized.

'No good thee try to soften Dicky up to buy thee a drink, Sal,' chuckled the fat man at Geraint's side. 'Ever tried getting blood outa a stone?'

Sally regarded her empty glass pessimistically and Dicky ignored the remark and huddled further into his wet black overcoat.

Davy rose to his feet, grinning.

'Give us your glass, Sally,' he invited and she surrendered it willingly. 'What are you drinking?'

'That's right good of you, mister,' she addressed her hand which looked bereft without the glass. 'I do 'ave a drop of gin for me insides. All churned up they be.'

Davy was ordering two pints and a gin for Sally Sugar when the door opened again and a soaked figure struggled in. Rain glistened on his old black sou-wester and dripped on to his shoulders which were inadequately protected by an empty sack draped over them. He drew off his sou'wester and shook a shower of drops from it as he advanced to the bar. Those nearest him ducked out of the way, grumbling.

'Give us a pint, Dai,' his voice was breathless with excitement as he turned to face the gathering. 'Green brook's burst out!' he announced, importantly. 'Ladywell's in a hell of a mess. Three foot o' water an' still comin' up. Hell of a mess, mun,' he repeated as he searched in his trousers' pocket with a wet hand for the coppers, which he slapped down on the counter.

There was an excited babble of voices and a number of people rose and made for the door. Davy cancelled his order and returned to Geraint.

'I'll have to go down and see what shape's on our Llew and Annie and little Owen. They're living down Ladywell now. Annie's having another baby any time.'

'I'll come with you,' Geraint volunteered and they joined those who were pressing towards the door, followed by the agonized stare from Sally Sugar's watering eyes as she raised them from her empty cupped hand to watch her hopes vanishing through the door.

When they reached the top of New Church Street, which bisected Ladywell Street, they could discern a sizable crowd gathered near to where the waters were rushing down Ladywell. The April dusk had deepened into a cloudy darkness and storm lanterns which bobbed about highlighted the steady sheets of rain which were adding to the chaos. Shadowy figures splashed through the flood waters, helping the victims carry their possessions to higher ground and some stalwarts staggered through the water with old people and children on their backs. The shouts and splashings of the rescuers rose from the darkness, coupled with the background comments of the crowd which was being pushed back from the swirling edges of the water by two large and rain-soaked constables, trying to clear a path for the helpers.

Geraint gave an excited laugh at Davy's side.

'I'm going down to see what I can do,' he cried and began shouldering his way to the front of the crowd, with Davy pressing forward in his wake. Once at the water's edge, Geraint plunged into the waist-high swirl and disappeared into the darkness. As Davy was about to follow him a hand grasped his sleeve and he looked down at see Meg's face peering out of a rain-soaked shawl which she held together round her head and shoulders with a wet hand. The yellow light of a nearby constable's hurricane lamp lit up her pale face which gleamed wetly by Davy's shoulder.

'Have you seen anything of our Llew and them?' she gasped, clutching at Davy's arm. 'Annie-Bertha Lloyd told Mama that Annie's pains had started about tea-time. Mama's over there,' she nodded over her shoulder, her teeth chattering with the cold. 'And Dada's gone down into Ladywell to try and see what's happening at our Llew's.'

'Go you back to Mama!' cried Davy. 'I will go down and see what's happening.'

He disengaged his arm and plunged into the dark swirling waters, the cold impact on his legs tearing a gasp from him as he dragged on deeper until the water was up to his waist. He waded through the darkness, his lower half numb, and struggled in the direction of Llew's cottage. He bumped into dim forms as they cursed and struggled through the rising water and finally he fetched up outside where he judged Llew's house to be. There was a faint candlelight in one of the upper windows and two forms swayed in the propped-open doorway of the flooded house. As Davy struggled up to them he could make out Llew in the doorway with Owen in his arms, the boy sobbing with terror. Dada was reaching out for him calling encouragement but the child clung round his father's neck convulsively. Davy reached the doorpost and hung on to it.

'Where's Annie?' he shouted at Llew and as if in answer a sharp scream of agony came from the upper room.

'Oh, dear God!' cried Llew. 'Here, take him, Dada,' and he unwound the child's arms and thrust him at Dada, who grasped him firmly and cradled him against his heaving chest. Llew then turned to Davy with a contorted face.

'For God's sake get me some help for Annie! She's in a bad way. I don't know what to do.'

Another scream came from above and with a choking curse Llew turned back into the house and waded to the stairs.

Dada had disappeared into the darkness with Owen. Clamping his teeth together against the shivering which now shook his body, Davy struggled after him, another shriek pursuing him from the lighted bedroom window. He could no longer feel his limbs and once or twice nearly fell head-first into the flood-waters as his feet slid on rough cobbles. A sudden sharp constriction across his chest crystalized into an agonizing pain and he found difficulty in breathing. A cold sweat mingled with the rain on his face and he was forced to stop in the darkness. With the water creeping up to his armpits he stood leaning slightly forward against the rush of the flood, both hands clasped to his heaving chest. He took a deep painful breath and moved on to where the bobbing lantern lights outlined the edge of the water.

As he struggled out on to the higher ground of New Church Street, Meg's shawled figure detached itself from the onlookers and grasping his arm, she led him, dripping and gasping through the milling crowd to a street lamp, under which Mama stood. Her wet skirts clung to her legs and she comforted a sobbing Owen whom Dada had dumped unceremoniously beside her. As Davy leaned, struggling for breath, against the lamp post, Mama frowned anxiously up at his face, conscious of its sickly pallor and the blue shadows round nose and mouth.

'Dear Lord, boy,' she whispered anxiously, as Meg lifted Owen and made soothing noise. 'What is it? You do look like death!'

Davy took one or two deep breaths and heaved himself upright.

'It's nothing, Mama,' he replied with an impatient shake of his head and in truth the pain in his chest was receding. 'We must get help for Annie. She's in a bad way.' He grasped Mama's arm urgently. 'What can we do?'

Mama looked round wildly.

'Maybe I had better try and get to her.'

'You can't, Mama!' cried Davy. 'It's too deep for you now.'

'Dada has gone to try and find the doctor,' said Meg as she shifted Owen's weight on her other arm. 'But I don't know where he will be. Some of the men have gone to get a couple of boats from Dick the Boats down by the Bridge. Maybe they would take you and Mama in one of them.'

At that moment there was a small cheer from the crowd and a shout of 'Here comes the boats!' as a party of men struggled into New Church Street carrying two small rowing boats. A youth stumbled after them with oars over his shoulder.

Davy pushed his way towards them through the knot of rain-drenched people and grasped the arm of one of the men who were carrying the first boat.

'Look!' he cried urgently. 'My brother's wife is stranded in a house down there. She's in labour and in a bad way. there's only my brother with her and no woman to help. Can you take my mother and me down there?'

The man blinked raindrops off his lashes and nodded.

'Aye, boy. Bring your Mam quick.' His voice was hoarse and he stumbled on with the impetus of the other men.

Davy returned to Mama and urged her down through the crowd to the water's edge. She called back over her shoulder for Meg to take Owen home and get him dried, then pulling her wet shawl closer round her, she allowed herself to be half-pushed, half-lifted into the boat. Davy sat beside her and they were soon moving slowly down the dark street where one or two gas lamps cast a sickly light over the muddy waters which washed the sides of the houses. Here and there candlelight could be seen in upstairs windows, silhouetting heads which craned out anxiously. Soon they reached the flooded door of Llew's house and Davy directed the boatman, who steered his wobbling craft to rest by the doorpost.

Davy peered into the doorway anxiously and shouted for Llew. There was a clattering on the stairs and a splash as Llew descended into the water, wading towards them. He gave a sob of relief as he saw Mama sitting upright in the boat in soaked dignity. Davy hung onto the doorpost and lowered himself out of the boat, which rocked wildly. Mama hung on to the sides in grim silence and between them Davy and Llew lifted her out and carried her to the stairs. Davy shouted his thanks to the boatman who gave an answering yell of encouragement and pushed off into the darkness.

At the top of the stairs Mama drew herself up and took a deep breath. All was quiet now in the bedroom where Annie lay, except for the sound of harsh and laboured breathing. In the small bedroom grate a sickly fire burned and a kettle was wedged precariously into the narrow chimney above it.

'I lit a bit of fire earlier on,' whispered Llew. 'There's a few sticks left in that bucket. All I could get before the water came into the coalhouse. There is a bowl there on the washstand, Mama. I don't know how hot the water is in the kettle. It is not much of a fire.'

Mama nodded.

'Good boy. You have done your best. Now out of the way, both of you.' She stooped to wring the water out of the bottom of her skirt, laid her wet shawl over the bannister post and squaring her narrow shoulders moved purposefully into the bedroom and shut the door.

Llew passed a shaking hand over his face and a shudder passed through him.

'Come on, boy,' muttered Davy, grasping his shoulder. 'Let us go into Owen's room and sit a minute. Annie will be all right now Mama's here, don't you fret.'

Llew shook his head but he followed Davy into the tiny room on the other side of the stairs and they sat down on the narrow iron bedstead in the darkness. Davy could feel Llew shivering convulsively beside him.

'Maybe it won't be long,' he whispered and put a comforting hand on Llew's knee. Llew was silent for a moment then he got up and stumbled towards the window where he leaned on the sill, facing the room. Davy could see the outline of his drooping figure against the faint grey of the window.

'She hasn't been well for a bit now,' he said through chattering teeth. 'Off her food and very low, like. And losing too, all the time. She was grand with Owen, no bother, except for a sharp tongue, which was nothing new.' He gave a short, harsh laugh. 'But this time's different. She's been real bad and gone very weak.'

'Dada's gone to try and find Dr Bellamy,' whispered Davy. 'P'raps they'll be here soon. But she's in good hands now Mama's here,' he added, stoutly.

Llew nodded, but without conviction.

'Aye, but it's awful quiet. She was screaming terrible before and that was bad. Now she's too quiet.' He returned to the bed, feeling his way, and sat down heavily. Then he rose again.

'There's a bit of candle and matches somewhere on the mantelpiece. It'll be better for a bit of light.' He fumbled in the darkness and soon a match flared and half a candle gave light in the small room.

They sat for some time in silence, listening to Mama's footsteps moving across the boards in the next room. Llew clasped and unclasped his hands over shaking knees and they both shivered as their wet clothes chilled their limbs and clung to their legs. Half an hour had passed when the door opened and Mama stood in the half-light. She beckoned to Llew who rose quickly and went over.

'She is pretty bad, boy,' she said in a low voice. 'She does need the doctor. You had better be praying your Dada does find him. I do not think I can bring the baby myself.'

Llew gave a low moan as Mama turned back to the other room and closed the door softly. Davy got up and went to the window, peering out at the swirling water which reflected back the yellow streetlights and the faint candle-lit upper windows. A boat rocked past in the gloom with an old couple in it clinging to the sides and the boatman answering the good-humoured banter from the bedroom windows as the stranded householders settled to wait the going down of the waters. He heard Llew return to the bed and sit down with a groan and the protesting squeak of springs.

A sudden shriek which tailed off weakly sounded through the thin walls and brought Llew to his feet. He stumbled over to the window, cursing wildly.

'Hang on!' cried Davy, suddenly. 'There's another boat coming!'

He leaned out of the small window and as the boat rocked through a pool of gaslight, made out Dada's white head, now hatless and dripping, as he sat up square in the boat, and a thin, drooping figure beside him with a bag clasped between chin and knees. The oarsman pulled with more energy than skill and the boat wobbled slowly into the darkness again.

'It's Dada!' Davy pushed Llew towards the door. 'He's got the doctor. Come on!' and a shout from below brought Mama to the head of the stairs as they clattered down and splashed towards the front door.

Dada had already heaved himself out of the rocking boat but the doctor sat tight, clutching his bag.

'I cannot see to anybody if I am soaked to the skin,' he protested. 'You will have to carry me.'

With a muttered curse Llew waded to the boat and with a heave and a grunt, slung the long thin doctor over his shoulder. The latter kept a stoical silence as his feet trailed in the water and his hat fell off and bobbed round in the wake of the boat. Llew staggered to the stairs and heaved the doctor on to his hands and knees above the water line, leaving him to pull himself upright by the bannisters and stumble upwards to where Mama waited, hands clasped anxiously, in the gloom on the landing. There was a whispered exchange then Mama and the doctor disappeared into Annie's room and closed the door. Llew and Davy returned to Owen's room and sat down once again on the narrow bed in the light of the guttering candle.

They began a wait which seemed to Davy endless. He was conscious of Llew sitting next to him, tense and silent. Neither spoke, and before long the candle spluttered and died, to reveal the first faint light of a grey dawn. Davy rose stiffly and went to the window. Outside the rain had stopped and the flood waters had receded a mere few inches. Down in the street knots of people stood and here and there the stalwart ones were already appearing with buckets and brooms to begin the weary task of clearing out the inches of silt and wet debris from their houses.

183

The candles were out in the upstairs rooms now and children slept after the excitement, while their parents wandered in and out of the doorways assessing the damage and commiserating with each other.

As Davy watched, a tall figure came round the corner pushing a handcart piled high with dry wood. It was Geraint, his face fresh and cheerful, his blond hair blowing in the cool morning breeze. Davy watched the people gather round the handcart and take bundles of the welcome wood to start fires for the drying out process and to make the ritual cup of tea.

'Roll up, roll up!' Geraint called out, a grin on his face. 'Firewood by courtesy of the Rector. Come and get it!'

Amid cries of gratitude and approval the firewood fast disappeared off the cart. Davy tried to call out, but his throat was so dry that he only gave vent to a croak which went unheard and soon Geraint was moving briskly off with an empty cart, his cheery whistle floating back through the grey morning light.

Davy turned as the bedroom door opened and Llew was on his feet. Mama stood there and the first thing Davy was conscious of was the unusual sight of her shoulders, now bowed as though in defeat. She looked across at Llew and tears welled up in her eyes.

'Annie?' cried Llew, wildly. 'Mama! What – ?'

She shook her head and a tear coursed down her face, which was suddenly old and weary.

'It was no good, boy. Dr Bellamy did his best indeed. But it was no good. She didn't seem to have fight in her. She let go.'

'The baby?' Davy whispered. 'That too?'

'The baby is alive,' said Mama, gently. 'A little girl. Lovely she is.'

Llew moved his shoulders in a gesture of rejection and walked across to the window. He stared out and a harsh sob escaped him. Mama left the doorway and returned in a moment or two with a small bundle cradled in her arms. With a sad smile she parted the wrappers and Davy looked on the tiny pink face with its folded-in rosebud mouth and closed eyes. It was so doll-like that for a moment he could not believe in it as a new human life. But then a tiny flower-like hand opened and he stretched out his finger and touched the pink palm. Instinctively the small fingers closed round his firmly and he and Mama exchanged sympathetic smiles. Then Mama carried the baby over to Llew, and laid it in his arms.

Llew cradled the tiny bundle awkwardly and stared down at it with a desperate air.

'What am I to do with her?' His voice was harsh. 'And what about Owen?'

Mama squared her thin shoulders with an effort and took a deep breath.

'You will bring them home, of course, boy. What else would you do, for goodness sake?'

13

Salvation and Nuptials

Summer came early that year, beginning in May with warm days full of blossom and sweet scents. During the long days of June the little town was somnolent under the heat, the hills surrounding it were milky with haze and the river flowed shallow and clear and innocent. As it rippled, sparkling, over the rocks it was hard to believe that it had roared and spilled over, bringing devastation in its wake. The streets which had been flooded in April were now dry and dusty and only in the little houses were there muddy tide-marks on the walls to bear witness to the height of the water.

The workers sweated in the mills during the day and spent their evenings sitting on their doorsteps, gossiping lazily while the children played outside, enjoying the freedom on the excuse that it was too light and too hot to sleep. Dusk came late and sometimes the inhabitants would still be out at midnight on their doorsteps or on chairs carried out into the small cobbled courtyards behind the houses, savouring the cooler air and reluctant to return to the shelter of the small houses which still retained the heat of the day.

Davy found difficulty in interesting his drowsy pupils, enervated by the stuffy classroom and lack of sleep. Sometimes he would bang on the desk with his cane to wake them up or to try to drive some point or other into the drowsy sweat-sticky heads. The children rushed from the classrooms at four o'clock and made thankfully for the fields, richly carpeted with buttercups, daisies and clover, or headed towards the river where, with bare white feet, they paddled and splashed each other with abandon or sat in the shade of the trees and fished with bent pins on the end of string tied to twigs.

It was Saturday morning and Davy gave a sigh of relief when he woke. Llew, who once again shared the big old brass bed, was already up since he worked on Saturday mornings in his job as a shirt cutter at the Pryce Jones factory. Davy stretched luxuriously and savoured the thought of a day free from the frustration of trying to push knowledge into hot, reluctant heads.

Hands behind his head he lay there staring at the same old cracks in the ceiling. Suddenly a rich chuckle escaped him. He was thinking of the events of the previous evening.

Yesterday had been Dada's birthday and at teatime he had invited Llew and Davy to go round to the Queen's Head for a pint to celebrate. Mama, pouring tea, had snorted and banged the teapot back down on the table.

'There must be a lot of birthdays round here if that is the reason for the old drinking.' She tucked in her chin and looked down her nose. 'Every Friday is a birthday, seems like.'

'Now, now, Mama,' admonished Llew, while Dada stared at the ceiling with innocent blue eyes, his lips pursed in a soundless whistle behind his moustache. 'You do not grudge Dada a pint on his birthday, is it?'

Mama sniffed.

'I have forgotten when my birthday is.'

'*Diawl!*' cried Dada, bringing his gaze down to her face. 'That is only woman's ways. You do forget your birthdays purpose, like, so you do not have to admit to your age.' Head on one side he appeared to calculate. 'Let's see. How old is it you are now, girl?' He peeped at her slyly, pulling at his moustache.

Mama tossed her head and rose from her chair.

'Mind your own business,' she snapped as she disappeared through into the back kitchen.

Dada winked at Llew and Davy and reached over to pat young Owen on his dark curls.

'Women!' he said, shaking his head. 'The good Lord did start something when He did take that bit of bone out of Adam to make one. Must have been his funny bone!'

'It was a rib, Dada,' said Davy, grinning.

'Well, whatever.' Dada shrugged. 'He should have been more careful.' He leaned over and regarded Owen seriously. 'Do you watch yourself with these women, boy. Your turn will

187

come.'

Owen nodded back solemnly, his cheek distended by a lump of bread and eyes wide and fastened on Dada's face.

Meg entered with the baby on her arm.

'Here are more of them, boy,' said Dada. 'Well, now. How has this little *ferch'i* been today?'

'She is as good as a little angel,' crooned Meg, her eyes soft. 'Look at her!'

She parted the shawl to reveal a tiny head with soft blonde down on it, two bright blue eyes and a small pink mouth.

'She have got my eyes,' said Dada, boasting.

Llew gazed at the baby's face and smiled with an effort.

'She is not like Annie or me,' he said. 'I don't know who she is like. More like you, I think, Meggie. She could be your baby.'

'I wish she was,' whispered Meg, hugging the little bundle closer.

'You can have her if you like,' offered Owen, generously. 'And I will be your boy as well, Meggie.'

'Right you,' said Meg, briskly. 'Come and get some sticks to go in the oven for morning, then.'

Owen slid off his chair and trotted after her. Llew's glance followed them.

'Meggie is a born mother.' His voice was heavy. 'She should marry and have children of her own. Not be saddled with mine.'

'*Twt, twt*, boy,' said Dada, gruffly, rising and reaching down his cap from behind the door. 'Meggie is all right. She do love these little ones of yours. I must go up to the stables for an hour. I will see you in the Queen's Head at eight, is it?'

Dada was already established in the bar of the Queen's Head when Davy and Llew walked in at eight o'clock. They vied with each other to buy Dada the first birthday pint but he waved a hand expansively.

'Now boys, no need to be arguing. The night is young yet. Plenty of time, plenty of time. There is a pint each for you with the barman.'

They settled down at his side with their pints and listened to the talk and chaff of his cronies. The place filled up as the evening wore on and Dada's eyes grew brighter and his cheeks pinker as the ale flowed steadily. Llew offered him a cigarette which he took and lit cautiously. At the first puff he choked till his eyes watered and he had to be pounded on the back. He cast it into the nearest spittoon scornfully.

'These are silly old things indeed,' he croaked. 'If the good Lord had wanted me to smoke he would have put a chimney out of my head.'

As soon as he had recovered he was persuaded to sing a song. It was a melancholy ditty in Welsh which, he informed the company solemnly, was all about the attempt of a man with a wooden leg to climb a mountain. By the time the barman had called 'Time' at ten o'clock and thrown his bar towel over the pumps, Dada was three sheets to the wind. He rose and with fond goodnights to all around and Davy and Llew grinning on each side of him, he sailed unsteadily out into the night.

When they reached the pavement he stopped and refused to budge. He focused with difficulty first on Llew's face then on Davy's.

'I cannot go home,' he announced mournfully. 'Your Mama will kill me.'

On that there was a sudden clash of cymbals, drums and tambourines so close to his left ear that he leapt into the air and staggered back dazed against the wall of the pub. Voices were raised high in a rousing hymn and a Salvation Army collecting bag was waved under their noses by a pretty fair girl in a bonnet. Dada stared at her speechless for a moment and then a benign expression spread over his face. He fumbled in his pocket with difficulty and brought a copper out which he dropped into the bag with a flourish.

'You are a good girl,' he told the bonneted collector as she thanked him with a sweet smile. He pulled himself from the wall and faced her, swaying slightly.

'Shinging to the Lord, outside thish den of iniquity.' His gaze was owlish and he flung his arms out wide to express the wonder of it, nearly toppling himself. '*Duw*, there ish lovely!'

He joined in a few bars of the hymn, waveringly, and when they finished singing he tacked off in the direction of their little circle, while Llew and Davy looked on hysterically. The circle parted to receive him and he stood in the centre clapping with enthusiasm.

'Mush tell you,' he announced, beaming round. '*Duw*, it ish very good of you. Shinging to the Lord in the midsht of all us shinners!'

Davy and Llew watched a tall man in a peaked uniform cap detach himself from the group and join Dada in the centre. He bent and spoke softly and Dada cocked his head on one side, listening and nodding solemnly. Then the tall man turned to the group.

'We will pray for our poor lost brother,' he announced and they all bent their heads while the man intoned a long and wordy plea for mercy on this straying lamb.

Dada, swaying dangerously, was much moved. He hung his head and a tear trickled down his pink cheek. He stood for so long in contemplative silence that the Army became restive, and with furtive glances began to move away. Dada came to with a jerk and looked round peevishly at the melting audience.

'Aye, aye, you!' he called after the tall man, who halted with a patient smile. 'Ish that it, then? Am I shaved?'

The man nodded warily and hurried off after the rest of the Army.

Dada shook his head in wonder as Llew and Davy led him in the direction of home.

'I'm shaved,' he muttered. 'Shaved at last. Wait till Susan hears.'

Llew and Davy exchanged hilarious glances. But Mama was not at all impressed with the news of his salvation and it was a much chastened lamb which finally mounted the stairs unsteadily while Mama, eyes shooting sparks and chin drawn in, followed after with the candle.

Remembering, Davy chuckled again and once more stretched his length in the bed. He glanced at the old alarm clock. Eight o'clock and it was already hot. He decided ruefully that he had better get up. Mama would not be in a very good skin with them this morning. Dishes were clattering briskly down below and a small cry from the next room indicated that little Esther had wakened for her feed. He heard Meg hurry up the stairs and her soft crooning voice as she tended to the baby's needs. He swung his feet out of the bed and began to dress.

Mama upbraided him roundly for not looking after his Dada better last night and he was glad to escape after breakfast. He had promised Dada to give an hour's help in the Rectory garden to ridge the potatoes. It was going to be hot again so it was best to start early before the worst of the heat. He set off up the back steps and through the grove of elders, the scent of their lacy blossom lying heavy on the warm air. He paused when he got out onto the field and with his hands in his pockets gazed across at the square white house, quiet in the morning sun. There was an air of emptiness to it to his mind, now that Geraint and Elinor were gone away again. Geraint had been posted to a camp in the north and Elinor had defiantly returned to London after only a week at home in April. The Rector, his gentle, unworldly face creased with worry, had finally given up hope of keeping her at home in her reckless mood and she made life unbearable for the household between sulks and flares of temper. If Mrs Buxton suspected that she had gone back with Ronald Purvis she kept her suspicions to herself out of loyalty to the poor motherless lamb.

Thoughts of Elinor were painful to Davy now. She still shone through his longing like an unattainable star. Although he knew his love to be hopeless it persisted and her vivid image blocked out all thoughts of other girls. Memories of the night when he had held her briefly in his arms and kissed her while she struggled like a caged animal still had the power to bring a flush to his cheeks. The scent and feel of her remained with him as clear as the stinging blow from her furious hand. He raised his fingers now and touched his cheek. His eyes were bleak for a moment and then he gave a small bitter laugh at himself. Shrugging his shoulders he strolled across the field to the Rectory.

He let himself through the door in the wall and stepped into the courtyard. Already the sun lay hot on the cobbles and the cooing of the Rectors' doves added to the warm sleepiness which pervaded the air. Davy was making his way across to the green door which led through into the walled vegetable garden when Mrs Buxton emerged from the kitchen, a bowl of scraps in her hand which she threw out for the hens. As they converged on the offering, wings outstretched and clucking excitedly, Davy bade Mrs Buxton a smiling 'Good morning.'

As she raised her face to his he was forcibly struck by her appearance. Her usual rosy face was pale and mottled and her eyes puffy and half-closed as though after prolonged weeping. She nodded briefly to him and hurried back into the kitchen.

Davy hesitated a moment, a frown on his face, and then followed her into the house.

'Mrs Buxton?' His voice was tentative. 'Is there anything wrong?'

With a wild look she suddenly collapsed weeping into the armchair beside the fire, the skirt of her apron lifted against her face. She rocked back and fore, her plump shoulders heaving with sobs. Davy stood by uncomfortably.

'Mrs Buxton?' he said again softly. 'What is it? What's wrong? Can I do anything?'

She shook her head behind the apron and the sobbing changed into a long moan. Davy was looking around him irresolutely when the scullery door opened and Nan came in. Her face was troubled and when she saw Davy she stopped and covered her mouth with her hand. He looked from her to Mrs Buxton, then in two or three strides was across the room. He grasped Nan's arm none too gently and drew her firmly back into the scullery and closed the door.

'What the devil's wrong, Nan?'

She shook her head. Moving over to the sink she leaned on it heavily, her back to Davy.

'Is it Geraint?' he asked, but she moved her head from side to side again.

'The Rector, then?' he persisted, but again the shake of the head.

'Elinor?' His voice cracked a little and this time she nodded faintly.

He took her by the shoulders and turned her to face him.

'What about Elinor?' His gaze was fixed on her face. She lowered her eyes and shook her head again.

'Nan!' he said, his fingers pressing hard into her shoulders. 'What's wrong with Elinor? Tell me! Is she here?'

She twisted out of his grasp and went to lean against the door.

'It's not for me to tell,' she said sullenly. 'Yes, she's here and brought trouble as usual.' Her voice was bitter.

'Where is she?' he asked quietly.

Nan shrugged.

'She went out. Down into the field, I think.'

She moved aside as Davy made for the door. He strode past Mrs Buxton without a glance and she did not look up. Down in

192

the field he could see no sign of Elinor and he wandered round distractedly. Eventually he spied her, sitting with her back to a tree in the far corner of the field. He approached her, his heart beating quickly then halted, standing over her, a flush on his face at a sudden picture in his mind of their last meeting.

She looked up at him and he caught his breath. Her pallor seemed to accentuate the soft child-like curves of her face, but her blue eyes shone as hard as sapphires. She wore a simple frock of sprigged muslin and her hair was no longer piled high in sophisticated fashion but hung in loose dark curls over her shoulders. To Davy she had never looked so lovely and so desirable and for a moment he stood silent, drinking in the sight of her.

Suddenly she gave a hard little laugh.

'Well, Davy Rees, what do you want?'

She raised her eyebrows as he dropped to the ground beside her. He took a deep breath to steady his voice.

'Are you all right, Elinor?'

She frowned and stared at him suspiciously.

'What do you mean, am I all right? What business is it of yours?'

He shrugged.

'None, I suppose. But there's something wrong, isn't there? I thought perhaps I could help.'

She burst into wild laughter, rocking her body from side to side.

'You help!' she gasped. 'You help! You don't know how funny that is!'

She stopped laughing abruptly and fell to plucking at her skirt, a frown on her face.

'Why should you want to help, anyway,' she muttered.

Davy kept his eyes on her lowered face.

'You know why,' he said, steadily.

She looked up at him, her blue eyes mocking.

'Are you trying to tell me you love me?' Her lips twisted in an ironic smile.

Davy nodded gravely.

'You know I do, Elinor. I always have and, God help me, I suppose I always will. All right!' he added as she moved her shoulders restively. 'I know I've no chance. But I do love you and I'd do anything for you.'

Elinor gave a little laugh and relapsed into silence. Now she twisted her dark curl in her fingers and stared in front of her. Davy sat watching her and his throat ached at her loveliness and her remoteness. The midsummer sun rose higher in the sky and its hot rays, shining through the leafy branches dappled the green grass which was starred with daisies. The air was heavy with summer scents and a blackbird trilled overhead, the liquid notes beautiful as they hung on the drowsy air. On the other side of the wall at the bottom of the field the milkman's cart rumbled along Pool Road and he called his wares cheerfully to sweating housewives.

None of this impinged on Davy's consciousness as he sat, plucking at blades of grass and waiting patiently for some response from Elinor. But the silence lengthened and at last he began to feel uncomfortable. He rose to his feet and stood for a moment looking down at her bent head.

'I'd better go,' he said quietly. 'I shouldn't have come here. I just wanted you to know. If I can do anything.'

She squinted up at him through a shaft of sunlight and he was unable to read the expression on her face.

'Oh, you can do something all right.' There was a note of derision in her voice. 'You could marry me.'

He went very still and after watching his face for a moment she laughed.

'What an ardent lover!' she mocked. 'I offer myself in marriage, but do you fling yourself at my feet? You stand there as if you'd been pole-axed!'

He continued to stare at her as though transfixed and as he remained silent she got to her feet and leaned against the tree trunk. She lifted her chin defiantly and her blue eyes met his, straight and hard.

'You may as well know it all, Davy Rees,' she said. 'The whole town will know it soon, anyway. I've come home in disgrace. I'm in trouble, like any servant girl. I'm going to have a baby.'

She gave a harsh laugh and pressed her shoulders against the tree.

Davy's world stood still and all sounds were blotted out. The blood left his face which took on a greyish pallor and his mouth went dry. At length his voice came and it was a harsh whisper.

'Whose?'

She shrugged bitterly.

'Does it matter? He's not going to marry me, anyway.'

'Ronald Purvis?' He got out the name with difficulty.

She nodded and suddenly her eyes were bleak in a defence-less face.

'Yes. Ronald Purvis.' Her face crumpled and she covered it with her hands, her body shaken with wild sobs.

Davy reached out instinctively and touched her arm, but she shrank away from his touch. He balled his fists and thrust them into his pockets. He gazed down at her bent head and waited numbly for the uncontrolled weeping to subside. At last her body quietened and she took her hands, wet with tears, down from her flushed face. She stared down unseeingly at the sun-dappled ground at her feet.

Davy broke the silence.

'Why won't he marry you?' His voice was harsh.

She looked up at him startled for a moment as though she had forgotten that he was there.

'Because he's married already,' she said flatly. 'He was married a fortnight ago. She's older than him and she's got a face like a horse. But she's rich and he needs the money. The mill's nearly bankrupt, you know,' she went on, as though she owed him an explanation. 'He couldn't afford to marry a poor Rector's daughter.'

'Did he know? About the baby, I mean,' Davy asked, painfully.

'Oh yes, he knew.'

'My God, what a swine!'

She shrugged and continued to gaze at the ground a small, silent, remote figure. The pain in Davy's chest made breathing difficult. He stood rigid and his fists opened and closed spasmodically in his pockets. He thought he should feel pity for her but his emotions were numb. At length she raised her head and squared her small shoulders. Her face had paled and her eyes glittered feverishly under fine dark brows like wings.

'I'm not going to have this baby,' she said deliberately. 'I'll kill myself first.'

He was shocked out of his numbness.

'Elinor!' he cried, reaching out and grasping her wrist. 'Don't! Don't say that!' His hand tightened as she tried to twist out of his grip. 'Promise me you won't do anything daft.'

She laughed wildly, and took a step closer to him. Her pale face with the brilliant blue eyes was lifted to his, her lips drawn back over small white teeth.

'Do you still want to marry me, Davy" she taunted, her eyes glinting maliciously.

The hot blood flooded Davy's face and his grip on her wrist tightened again. He pulled her against his body savagely and crushed the mocking smile with his lips. For a moment she struggled fiercely and they swayed together under the tree. Then her body suddenly went still and she held herself rigid under his kiss. It was a total withdrawal and he sensed it. He let her go and stepped back, his eyes on her face. She stared back at him, rubbing her wrist with long, slim fingers.

'You're a fool, Davy Rees.' Her voice was low and contemptuous.

'I know,' he answered and thrusting his hands back in his pockets he turned from her and began to walk away. After he had gone a few yards he halted and looked over her shoulder.

'Fool enough to marry you,' he said bitterly.

Her eyes on his retreating back were expressionless and with an indifferent shrug she sat down again with her back to the tree and stared out across the empty, sun-baked field.

That night Davy sought an interview with the Rector. It was embarrassing and painful and the old man wept openly. When it was over he rose with simple dignity and offered Davy his hand. He asked him to wait in the study while he went to Elinor and Davy sat and stared out of the window at the front lawn, where roses were filling the warm air with their heavy, sweet perfume and a flight of swifts circled and swooped between the two cedar trees which stood like sentinels at the far end. The air was still and the sky was almost lavender with tinges of pink showing in the west. He sat in the same armchair in which he had sat opposite Geraint on the night of his last encounter with Elinor. He felt empty, drained, and his hands lay quiet along the arms of the chair. Eventually the door opened and closed quietly and the Rector came back into the room. He looked distressed and when Davy rose to his feet, the old man's eyes roamed round the room before they rested on Davy's face. Davy felt a sharp pang as he realized that the expression in the Rector's eyes was pity. So she had refused. He straightened his shoulders and waited for the Rector to speak.

At length the old man cleared his throat and spoke in a tired voice.

'Elinor will marry you, Davy. But tell me, my boy, are you sure about this? I admit, I shall not be sorry. But have you really thought about it, lad?'

'I have thought about it,' said Davy, tonelessly. 'And yes, I am sure that I want to do it. Oh, make no mistake. I know that Elinor doesn't care tuppence about me. But at least I am going into it with my eyes open.' He gave a short laugh.

The Rector shifted uncomfortably.

'Yes, yes, I see. Well now, we must pray that Elinor will come to realize which side her bread is buttered. You are a good man. She must come to see that.'

He went over to the armchair and dropped into it heavily. He shook his white head and tugged at his moustache.

'When my wife died and I was left with Geraint and Elinor, it was hard. I left them too much to Mrs Buxton, I'm afraid. Oh, she has been a good woman, like a mother to them indeed. But she spoilt them. And I, oh dear me, I am to blame for a lot, Davy. But I want you to know that I am thankful for what you have offered tonight, I will do all I can to see you settled, I promise. Anyway. Go to Elinor now. She is waiting in the parlour. And Davy,' as Davy paused with his hand on the doorknob, 'God bless you, lad.'

Davy muttered his thanks and let himself out of the room. As he closed the door behind him he leant against it for a moment, and breathed deeply and painfully. He drew himself up and crossed the hall slowly to the closed door of the parlour. He knocked but there was no sound inside. He opened the door and went in and she was sitting upright on a high-backed chair against the wall, her feet together and hands folded in her lap. Her hair was down and tied with a wide blue ribbon and she looked young and defenceless. Except for her eyes.

They stared at each other silently for a moment. When she spoke she sounded like a child repeating a lesson.

'Thank you for asking me to marry you,' she said.

Davy remained mute, standing with his back to the door.

'I wish I could say that you won't regret it. But I know you will.' Her gaze was impersonal but when he showed no reaction she flushed and rose to her feet swiftly. She stood straight as a wand, hands clenched at her side, blue eyes blazing.

'Understand, Davy Rees. I have said yes because I have to. You mean nothing to me. Nothing! If we go through with this farce I will play my part. But expect nothing of me.'

When he still remained silent her eyebrows came down in a frown and she shook her head.

'Why are you doing this?' she said, curiously. 'I don't understand. I know you say you love me. But haven't you got any pride? Do you really want to marry someone who doesn't want you and take on somebody else's brat?'

'Why?' he echoed, bitterly, at last. 'You can't understand, can you Elinor?'

'No!' She flung the words at him furiously then, her mouth coming down at the corners, 'I doubt you'll have to father any brat, anyway. Not if I can help it.'

'Stop that!' he cried and stepped forward, but she flung her hands up as if to ward off a blow.

'Don't you touch me!' she hissed. 'Not ever!'

The door opened and closed quietly and he was gone. She stared for a moment at the closed door then dropped back on to the chair and the empty room was filled with her desolate weeping.

☆   ☆   ☆

The wedding was a quiet affair with only the two families present. The Rector officiated and Elinor's uncle from Bala came down to give the bride away. The only thing which prevented Davy from thinking that it was all a strange confused dream was his high white collar, so stiffly starched by Mama that it dug into his neck and chafed the skin to a sore red ring. Elinor was pale and outwardly composed but she hesitated so long over the responses that the Rector was thrown into a mild panic and the rhetorical questions took on a tone of desperation. At last it was over and the two families gathered at the Rectory, the Rees' stiff in their best clothes and still looking slightly bewildered.

After receiving good wishes with a set and slightly mocking smile on her pale face, Elinor had disappeared upstairs to change out of the cream shantung dress and wide leghorn hat which she had worn at the altar. There was to be no honeymoon and Plas Gwyn had been made ready for them, adequately furnished with overflow from the Rectory.

Plas Gwyn was a tall narrow house on the opposite side of the road from the Rectory, and within the Church living, which had been empty for more than a year. It had a garden on the left and a small walled courtyard on the right enclosed in big green double doors. Mrs Buxton was to move in with them as housekeeper, leaving Nan in charge at the Rectory.

Elinor had shown no interest at all in the furnishing of her future home and Mrs Buxton had taken over the task, leading Nan in a flurry of scrubbing and polishing, with windows flung open to the summer air. The small courtyard at the side rang with the noise of carpets being beaten and buckets being filled with coal for unnecessary fires to 'air the house'. When asked to choose colours and materials for curtains and cushions, bedspreads and chair covers, Elinor showed supreme indifference, merely remarking sharply, 'Do what you like.' Davy, wandering round the house when Mrs Buxton had finally pronounced it ready, looked around him with no sense of belonging, and it was just one more factor in the unreal and confused sequence of events which followed on from the painful evening of his proposal.

He stood now with a small glass of sherry in his hands in the Rectory parlour and looked round him. Mama, Llew and Meg sat uncomfortably on chairs against the wall, Meg nursing little Esther and Owen leaning against Llew's knee, regarding with some diffidence the large currant bun which Mrs Buxton had thrust into his hand. Dada in his best suit and his head high above his starched wing collar, was standing with the Rector and the Rector's brother by the window, nodding sagely and deferentially as they made polite and kindly conversation. He kept a wary eye on the delicate sherry glass in his hand and occasionally raised the amber liquid to his mouth with a stoical expression as though it were nasty medicine which he was drinking for his own good. Mama's forehead was puckered in a worried frown which was wiped off and replaced by a polite smile when the Rector looked across at her or Mrs Buxton hovered with a plateful of salmon or cucumber sandwiches. But when her dark eyes rested on Davy the frown reappeared and there was pained bewilderment on her face.

Davy met her eyes across the room and smiled reassuringly,

but there was an emptiness in him and he longed for an end to the unreality of the stiff little gathering. When Nan had brought his drink she had wished him happiness politely, but leaning closer so that the rest of the room were unable to hear, she whispered to him with a different tone.

'Good luck, Davy. You're going to need it. You're a damn fool.'

Before he could reply she had moved off with her tray of sherry glasses, nodding and smiling to the guests, trim and sturdy in her fresh green dress and starched white pinafore, her head tipped as though pulled back by the heavy knot of straight coarse hair, as yellow as stooks of ripened corn, which lay against the back of her short creamy neck.

At last Mama rose and signalled that it was time to go. Dada set his empty glass down gingerly on a small table and cleared his throat.

'Thank you for us, indeed, Mr Pryce,' he said. 'It was a very nice wedding indeed, and proud we are that our Davy and your Elinor have made this match.'

There was some shuffling and a murmur of embarrassed assent and then his family were gone and a terrible loneliness came over Davy as he squared his shoulders and prepared to face married life.

14

Turnkeys and Outings

The best of the crisp October day was over as Davy emerged from the Church School at half past four. Sharp night frosts and brilliant sunshine in the day had highlighted an Autumn where the countryside was aflame with gold and bronze and russet as the trees burst forth in a last defiant spectacular before they shed their leaves and settled to a bare and creaking winter. Under his feet as he crossed the playground acorns crunched and leaves rustled. Lately the playground had been the scene of conker battles and here and there mangled conkers on the end of grubby bits of string lay about in witness to sorry defeat at the hands of 'tenners', 'twelvers' or 'fifteeners'. The girls had made acorn necklaces with purloined darning needles and bits of wool, or had searched for spent matchsticks to stick in the sides of acorns to make pipes. Those with an over-stock of matches usually brought a potato from home and made a 'hedgehog' by sticking a forest of matches all round the potato and inking in two eyes at the front end. The countryside provided the children with a host of materials for their occupation at this time of year.

As he emerged through the gates he was meditating on the various 'seasons' of games which rotated by some sort of divine edict revealed only to the children and, of course, the shopkeepers who always seemed to have a plentiful supply of the right playthings at the right season. At the moment it was skipping and the better-off girls had their own individual skipping ropes with brightly painted wooden handles. Others, less privileged, would have acquired pieces of rope, knotted at the ends, the knots large enough to fit in the palms of their hands. Even more popular was the long piece of rope which

201

served the many and the playground rang with shrill voices chanting the rhymes which accompanied the swish of the rope and the steady thump of booted feet. Even the boys would be tempted to join in the communal skipping, albeit in a lordly and patronizing manner.

> All in together now,
> Never mind the weather now.
> Salt, mustard, vinegar, pepper!

A frenzied burst of speed would accompany the cry of 'Pepper' which would increase until finally the skippers got tangled up in the rope and were 'out'.

He wondered what would follow next? Would it be the top and whip season or the season for ball games, hoops – known locally as bowlders – or hopscotch? Occasionally the boys joined in these 'seasons' or indulged in their own 'season' of marbles, but football remained their staple recreation, mostly using a pigs bladder acquired from the slaughterhouse in Stone Street, blown up and tied at both ends.

As Davy came out on to Kerry Road, just opposite the school gates a man from the local board had a manhole up in the middle of the road and was vigorously turning a long iron turnkey which opened the stopcock at the bottom of the hole. It was market day and little knots of farmers and their wives stood about gossiping before setting off back to the hills on ponies or in their waiting traps. A few were 'market peart' since the pubs had been open all day and by night those under the weather would rely on the homing instinct of their patient ponies to get them home. Just at that moment a farmer, a small spare man in leggings, with his bowler hat tipped to the back of his head, staggered out of the side door of the Queen's Head. He tottered to the edge of the pavement and swayed giddily, peering round with bleary, owlish eyes. Spotting the man twisting the turnkey into the bowels of the earth he stared at him for a moment then advanced with a menacing air.

'So you're the bugger that's making everythin' go round an' round!' he shouted.

Swinging his arm he felled the astonished Local Board man. The impetus of the flailing arm further upset the farmer's balance and after staggering round wildly in a circle he disappeared into the manhole up to his armpits. He glared round in bewilderment making hoarse, inarticulate noises to the further delight of the hysterical onlookers. The Local Board man dragged himself to his feet cursing furiously and began to belabour the top half of the farmer with his turnkey. His victim roared in anguish and endeavoured to pull his bowler hat down over his ears to protect his head. The workman was eventually pulled away by a couple of laughing men who then hoisted the terrified farmer out of the hole. As he rose out of the earth a fierce jet of water from below helped him on his way.

'Now look what you've done, you owl fool!' shouted the Local Board man, beside himself with wrath, but the farmer was beyond caring as he was laid, soaked and gasping, on the pavement like a stranded, bewhiskered fish.

Davy was still chuckling to himself as he lifted the latch of the double wooden doors at the side of Plas Gwyn and entered the small courtyard. The smile died on his face when he was met by a pale and distraught Mrs Buxton.

'Oh, dear God, Mr Davy!' she sobbed, her eyes wild. 'It's Miss Elinor. She's half-killed herself. She's come off her horse!'

Davy stared at her for a moment then with a shaking hand led her back into the bright kitchen, with its polished dresser reflecting the glow of the fire. He sat her down in the wooden armchair and confronted her.

'Now tell me. Where is she? How bad is it?'

Mrs Buxton rocked back and fore in the chair, her hands clasped against her ample bosom.

'I've told her and told her, not to go riding that horse now. Dear God, she's six months gone. But she never listened. It was like as if she was bent on risking life and limb.'

'I know. I've begged her myself,' said Davy, distractedly. 'Where is she? Is she very badly hurt?'

Mrs Buxton shook her head.

'I don't know how bad. She was unconscious. They've took her to the infirmary. Go you and find out, Mr Davy,' she begged.

He turned on his heel swiftly and ran out. Mrs Buxton twisted her hands in her lap.

'I told her and told her,' she repeated to herself. 'But it was like she was doin' it a'purpose.'

On reaching the small infirmary Davy was shown into the

waiting room by the matron and told that the doctor was with Elinor and there would be some time to wait for news. When she left him he sat on a hard chair, his head bowed and his hands between his knees. His thoughts were chaotic but the one nagging question uppermost in his mind was born of the repeated assertions made by Elinor that she would never have this child.

She had consistently refused to take reasonable care during her pregnancy and with hard, glittering eyes had defied them all when they pleaded with her. She continued to gallop wildly across country on her pony and Mrs Buxton had tearfully predicted a miscarriage from the early days. In all she did she appeared to be driven by a crazy energy which left her exhausted by bed-time but brought no healthy sleep. Night after night Davy would wake to find the place beside him empty. Elinor would either be standing in the shadows immobile, gazing out of the window, or the room would be empty and he would hear her downstairs, moving restlessly about. She shrank away from physical contact and any attempt to reach her mind failed him. The only straw which he had to clutch at were the times when he was awakened in the night by her wild sobbing and then she would allow herself to be gathered into his arms while she cried herself to sleep again. At those times he lay awake in the darkness, savouring the nearness of her body and the scent from her hair, his tortured mind trying to penetrate the mists of their future together. But in the morning it was as though the contact had never been, and his attempts at conversation over breakfast were either met with total withdrawal or a hard and superficial gaiety which was almost harder to bear. Davy's own nerves suffered at this time and Mrs Buxton was driven to distraction.

He sat now, raising his head from time to time to stare unseeingly round the dreary brown-and-mustard painted walls of the waiting room, the rising panic making his mouth dry. He tried to calm his screaming nerves by reviewing the past months of their marriage, searching in his mind for signs of hope that anything at all was growing out of it. He had gone into the marriage with his eyes open but at no time had he foreseen the torture of her physical closeness coupled with the total rejection which left an aching void in his days. He rose, his heart beating wildly, at a sudden memory which forced itself

204

into his mind.

It was the memory of one particular night, in the early days of their marriage, when summer scents drifted through the window and filled the warm darkness of the room. He had lain beside her, staring into the gloom, the only sound her regular breathing. He turned his head on the pillow and in the faint light from the window, could make out the pale outline of her face, the mass of dark hair spilling around it on the pillow. She had pushed the covers back and the satiny skin of one smooth shoulder gleamed in the shadows. Overcome by love and longing he raised himself on one elbow and pressed his lips against the creamy skin. She stirred and reached out for him sleepily and suddenly she was in his arms, responding with a wild passion which seemed to take possession of his very soul. At the end he spoke her name, his voice trembling with love, but she slipped from his arms with a choking cry and ran from the room. She did not come back to bed that night and next morning she was more cold and withdrawn than ever, refusing to meet his eyes. His tentative advances the following night were met with a furious rejection and he never again attempted to break through the barrier, his hurt pride the only thing left to sustain him through the tortuous path of their relationship.

Dusk was falling outside when the door opened and Dr Bellamy came in. Davy turned swiftly from the window where he had lain his feverish forehead against the cold glass. He waited for the tall thin doctor to speak, his heart beating wildly.

'What drove your wife to such foolishness at this time is beyond me,' Dr Bellamy said, angrily. 'Oh yes, she's alive. She'll be all right. She's lost the child, of course. But worse than that she's injured herself in a way that it would be very dangerous for her to attempt to have another baby.'

Davy stared at him wordlessly and the doctor continued.

'Do you understand that, Mr Rees? There must be no attempt at more children.' Then, his voice more sympathetic, 'I know it's not an easy thing to advise, you're both young. But the risk would be very great. She's a healthy young woman and apart from that she'll soon be well again. Dear God!' he went on, the angry note returning, 'to be out riding at six months! I never heard of such a thing. Criminal it was!'

Davy nodded dully and the doctor opened the door and

waved him through.

'You can go and see her now. Don't stay too long.'

She lay in the narrow hospital bed, so white and still that Davy caught his breath. He hesitated, then leaned over and touched her cheek.

'Elinor?' he whispered.

Her eyes came open with an effort and found his face. A flicker of expression came and went in their blue depths for a moment and her lips moved.

He leaned closer eagerly.

'I'm glad,' she whispered and he caught a momentary gleam in her eyes before they closed and he was again shut out.

☆   ☆   ☆

Elinor made a good recovery and by Christmas a faint colour was returning to her cheeks. They spent a quiet Christmas at the Rectory, with Geraint home on leave and Mama and Dada invited for tea. Elinor was on her best behaviour, docile and almost childlike with her father, polite to Mama and Dada. She accepted Geraint's brotherly teasing with unusual tolerance and from time to time a puzzled frown would appear on his face as he watched her.

Davy had lived through the months of Elinor's convalescence a prey to conflicting emotions. Their relationship was coolly polite and the only time she showed irritation was when he displayed any solicitousness over her health. He was still unable to reach her and more and more he turned in on himself, giving all his energies to his teaching and working late into the night sometimes or immersing himself in reading. As soon as she had come from the infirmary she had insisted on separate rooms, stating coolly that she was sleeping badly and would only disturb him. He accepted with a hopeless shrug. In some ways it was almost a relief, since he felt he could no longer bear the torture of her physical nearness and her total rejection of him.

In the daytime when Davy was at school she wandered the house restlessly, impatient of Mrs Buxton's clucking concern. Sometimes she would take out her smart town clothes and lay them out across her bed. She would try on one outfit after another in front of the long mirror set beside the window, then abandon them for Mrs Buxton to smooth and hang back in the wardrobe. Occasionally she would pick up a book or a magazine and read for half an hour, only to throw it aside impatiently. In the late afternoons she usually sat in the parlour staring out at the gathering dusk and the dark, skeleton trees outlined against the cold wintery landscape. Finding her thus one afternoon after school, Davy had hesitated by the parlour door. She had turned to him and he had felt a stab of pity at the expression on her face.

'I hate the winters!' she said in a low, bitter voice. 'I feel trapped. Oh, why am I here?' There was desperation in her cry. 'Why doesn't the spring hurry and come?'

But he had no comfort for her and he turned away in silence and left her staring after him.

Spring came at last, the warmer air melting the winter snow and fresh green appearing in the hedges and on the trees. Primroses starred the banks and rooks returned to nest in the tall trees along the Rectory drive, circling around the topmost branches and cawing loudly.

Down in the town the people welcomed the warmer air. It was a struggle during the winter to keep warm. The woollen trade had been in decline since 1893, the handlooms which were operated in weaving rooms above small one-up-one-down cottages giving way to the larger factories and mills. These themselves were becoming fewer and were amalgamating to stave off closure and had reduced the weavers' wages. This had led to a strike of the weavers but the resultant hardship had eaten deeply into the people. The mill-owners paid fifteen shillings a week to the top weavers and considered this a fair wage. The Pryce Jones family which owned the large factory and warehouse and employed some five hundred people gave coal to help the most distressed cases in the small streets of the town, but the winter had been hard and killing and the spring was welcomed by the poor and soon the doors of the small cottages were opening and their inhabitants expanding to the soft spring air.

Although not a millworker LLew became deeply involved in their struggles, to Mama and Dada's chagrin. He was getting the name of an agitator in the town. From time to time he came to Plas Gwyn, pacing up and down in Davy's small study, his thin pale face intense and his eyes gleaming fanatically. Davy and he talked well into the night about the poverty and troubles of labour, but while Davy turned to reading the emerging social philosophers, Llew was impatient of theory and spent his evenings down among the workers in the back streets.

With the coming of the spring, Elinor's restlessness intensified. The Rector himself had ordered her pony to be sold and she now divided her time between wandering the Brimmon fields and woods or moving through the shopping streets of the town, her quick impatient steps tapping along the pavements and her stylish town clothes turning heads. She rarely entered the shops but stopped to look in the windows disinterestedly before restlessly moving on. As health returned to her so her tenseness increased, but with Davy she was a cool polite stranger and this he found harder to bear than the wildness and tantrums. He lived with an obsession that one day he would come home and find her gone. He watched her and waited but he made no advance to her.

He came home from school one Friday at the end of March to find her sitting by the French window which opened on to the tiny ornamental garden at the side of the house. The sun was warm on the threshold and the perfume of gilly flowers drifted into the room. Elinor was sitting turning the pages of a magazine in a desultory manner and when he entered the room she looked up at him briefly.

'Your father called.'

'Yes?' He waited with his hand on the doorknob.

'He's taking your mother and Owen to Manafon on Sunday. He called to ask if we wanted to go along.'

'I don't suppose that would be your idea of a Sunday outing,' he said with a short laugh.

She shrugged.

'I don't mind. It's a chance to go out.' She continued leafing through the magazine.

Davy looked across at her bent head.

'Oh, well. The weather's nice. A day in the country will do you good.'

She frowned and twisted her body irritably, then she rose and threw the magazine down on the chair.

'Tea will be ready,' she said curtly and preceded him out of the room.

At two o'clock on Sunday Dada was at the door with the trap. It was no longer Blod who drew it as the little brown mare had died. Dada had acquired a sturdy Welsh cob now which he called Mogg and the new pony's coat shone in the spring sunshine. The polished harness jingled as the cob stamped impatiently and Dada sat up front beaming and as proud as Ben Hur as Davy helped Elinor into the trap and took his seat beside her. Mama nodded and smiled opposite but her eyes remained wary as they always were in Elinor's presence. Owen sat beside Mama, cap askew on his dark curls and eyes sparkling with excitement.

'We're going to see Auntie Martha and Ifan and Luke,' he told Davy, grinning.

'Aye, Owen. You like to go to Manafon, yes?'

The boy nodded eagerly and wriggled in his seat as Dada cracked the whip and they bowled off down Kerry Road.

'I like Auntie Martha and 'specially Ifan. Ifan takes me down to the river to fish and shows me the birds' nests. But I mustn't touch, is it? Ifan don' let me touch.'

Davy nodded and remembered how he loved gentle Ifan and all the fascinating mysteries of the stream and the country-side which Ifan had introduced to him with dumb gentleness and understanding. He remembered Granny Evans, too, dead now these seven years and saw again vividly the tiny figure in the wooden armchair by the fire, with the sunken mouth, the birdlike eyes and sudden dozes.

'What about Luke?' he asked Owen, smiling but curious.

Owen ducked his head and twisted the fringes of Mama's shawl.

'He has a nice pony,' he said evasively. 'I would like to ride it.'

'Hush now,' Mama scolded. 'You are too little yet for galloping on ponies. Sit up now, like a good boy. You have not said good-day yet to your Auntie Elinor. Where are your manners, boy.'

Owen peeped up at Elinor warily from under the peak of his cap.

'Good day, Auntie Elinor,' he repeated obediently and Elinor nodded coolly, sitting upright beside Davy. She looked particularly lovely today, thought Davy, his throat constricted with longing. She wore a suit of soft heliotrope wool with a shantung blouse, its high collar elaborately tucked and edged with ecru lace. Her wide leghorn hat was held on with a mauve chiffon scarf tied in a bow and her glossy curls peeped out above dark-fringed, violet blue eyes. Her skin was translucent, with a soft pink flush in her cheeks from the sun and in that moment Davy found it hard to believe in her coldness.

Owen was staring at her more boldly now, his usual shyness in her presence forgotten momentarily.

'You are beautiful, aren't you, Auntie Elinor,' he said suddenly and then flushed and hid his face in Mama's shawl.

Elinor laughed almost gaily and Mama gave an indulgent smile. Suddenly Davy felt almost happy, as they rattled down Pool Road in the spring afternoon, Dada proud on his seat and clucking to Mogg as they passed under the trees in their new soft green foliage and between hedgerows thick with primroses and violets and fields dappled with drifts of wild daffodils.

As they bowled through Manafon village, sleeping as usual in its Sunday calm, Dada looked longingly at the whitewashed Beehive Inn, but Mama scowled and pinched his arm warningly. Reluctantly he flicked the reins and Mogg pulled them on past. Davy turned a laugh into a cough and Mama looked at him with suspicion. At last they pulled up with a flourish outside the Walkmill and there was Auntie Martha coming out of the door to greet them.

Davy had an especially warm affection for Auntie Martha and he proudly led Elinor forward, while Dada took Mogg on round to the field. Elinor answered Auntie Martha's welcome with a charming smile but Davy was aware of the shrewd appraising look in Auntie Martha's eyes. After a warm hug for Owen she led them in, down the cool passage and into the long kitchen which Davy loved so much. He was still conscious of Granny Evan's empty armchair and when Auntie Martha ushered Elinor into it the contrast struck him as between the fresh and beautiful girl and the ancient old woman who used to occupy it.

'Where is Ifan?' piped Owen, looking round eagerly and Auntie Martha and Davy smiled at each other, remembering that other small boy whose first question was 'Where is Ifan?'

'Ah, he will be down the meadow or at the stream, no doubt, Owen *bach*. Go you and find him, is it, while I wet the tea.'

She opened the back door and Owen ran out into the sunlit

yard and watching, Davy longed to run after him and find Ifan.

'Ifan is always out in the fields or fishing in the stream or just sitting,' Auntie Martha explained to Elinor as she settled Mama on the other side of the fire and spooned tea into the fat brown pot warming on the hob. 'Indeed I do not have the men underfoot much, I'll say that. When Luke is not working he is with those old ponies of his.' She turned to Davy. 'He has a new pony now. Gypsy was getting too slow, so he reckoned. How that boy has not broke his neck on those old horses I don't know. Indeed what good to spend money on another horse I did ask him. Gypsy is still strong to pull the cart and will take him and me where we want to go. No need for this tearing round the countryside like the devil is on his tail. Indeed, I do sometimes think he is,' she concluded with a sigh. 'Well come you now and have this cup of tea in your hand and we will have tea tidy later on.'

Elinor and Davy sipped their tea in silence while Auntie Martha and Mama caught up with each other's news and Dada looked on beaming and putting his oar in now and then. When he handed up his cup for a refill he wiped his moustache with his handkerchief and then blew his nose.

'There is no sign of Luke courting then, Martha?' he asked, his eyes twinkling.

'Courting, tush!' Auntie Martha grumbled. 'No sign of courting at all. I wish he was. Maybe he'd steady down a bit then.'

'He is a fine young fellow, indeed,' observed Mama. 'Very handsome now, and a good worker too.'

'Well now, Susan, not so young is it, any more. Luke is knocking on now, don't forget, and high time to settle down.'

'That's as may be,' said Dada, 'but you would miss him here, did he take a notion to go off to marry and settle on his own.'

'No need for him to go off anywhere,' Auntie Martha said, shortly, 'did he take a notion for a tidy girl there is room enough here for them. I am not getting any younger and I would not mind to take a bit of a back seat.'

'And what of Ifan?' asked Mama, very gentle.

Auntie Martha set her cup down on the saucer slowly and stared in front of her.

211

'Ah, God help me,' she whispered, her eyes bleak. 'that I do not know. I do lie awake nights very often wondering about Ifan if anything happens to me. Luke – well, Luke has no patience with Ifan. And then I do think, if Luke were to marry, would his woman mind to Ifan after me? Sometimes I do pray the Lord will take him before me,' she said softly. 'That would be the best, I am thinking.'

'Harrumph!' snorted Dada. 'There's morbid, girl!'

'Why yes, indeed,' cried Auntie Martha. 'Where is my manners? These young people do not want to listen to old talk like that. Now you, Davy, take your little wife out into the sunshine and show her round. She do not want to sit in here with an old lot like us.'

'Right, Auntie Martha,' said Davy, rising. 'We will go and see if Own has found that Ifan yet. Come on, Elinor, I will take you down to the stream. It is pretty there.'

He led her out through the back door and Auntie Martha poured another cup of tea for herself and Mama and Dada.

'She is a beautiful girl, indeed,' she said, cocking a speculative eye at Mama, who stared down into her teacup with a deep sigh.

'Aye. Good looking she is, no doubt. But she do not make my Davy happy. Better she would have a face like an old boot if she would make my boy to smile again. Really smile,' she added with vehemence.

'*Twt*, Susan,' grunted Dada. 'The girl is young yet and she have been spoiled. She will come to be a tidy wife to him, given time.'

Mama shook her head obstinately.

'No, I do not believe it. She have no warmth in her. She is not the right one for our Davy.'

'Well,' said Auntie Martha, soothingly, 'time will tell. Like Will says, she is young yet. And she have just lost a little babby. That will have hit her hard, surely so.'

Mama raised her eyebrows and pursed her mouth and said nothing.

Davy reached for Elinor's hand as they crossed the field where the cowslips were just showing in bud above their soft dark green leaves. She suffered her hand to remain in his and indeed looked almost happy as she let her wide hat slide to the back of her neck and picked her way through young thistles and over cowpats in her dainty shoes. As they approached the wicket gate that led onto the path down to the stream, Davy stopped. He took her other hand and pulled her round to face him. She stood very still, looking up at him and her eyes were watchful.

'Just to tell you about Ifan,' he said, aware of her body tensing.

'I know about Ifan. He is the idiot son, isn't he?'

Davy winced.

'Ifan is – well, simple, I suppose. I have never thought of him as an idiot. Ifan is special. He is gentle and good. I think he sees things we don't see and understands things we don't understand. Please don't think of him as an idiot,' he pleaded, bending his dark gaze gently on her upturned face.

She shrugged and pulled her hands away.

'I do not like simple-minded people. They make me feel uncomfortable. I'm never sure what they'll do.'

'But you will not feel like that about Ifan,' said Davy, eagerly. 'Everyone loves him.'

'Even his brother?' Her small smile held a hint of malice.

'Ah, Luke,' Davy looked thoughtful. 'You know, I have wondered if Luke might not just be jealous of Ifan.'

Her eyebrows went up.

'Jealous of an idiot?'

'Jealous because everyone loves Ifan. Jealous, I suppose, of something he does not understand. Oh, I don't know. Luke is a handsome chap, strong and healthy, and he works hard, I'll grant him that. And he'll get the farm after Auntie Martha, of course, although Ifan is the oldest. But there is something about Luke.' He shook his head. 'Well, never mind. Come on, let's find Ifan. No doubt Owen has run him to earth by now.'

He opened the gate to let her through and took her arm to steady her down the steep and narrow path that led to the river. She held her skirts away from the clinging sloe bushes and brambles which edged the path as they made their way under spreading trees down to the water's edge. There beside a willow, which drooped its fresh green on to the surface of the water sat Ifan, his massive head resting on his drawn-up knees and Owen beside him, the boy's head leaning against his arm trustingly. Davy smiled at the sight, remembering from his own childhood the instinct of all small creatures to draw near to

213

that gentle, almost primaeval, source of understanding and comfort which was beyond ordinary words. It was the same instinct which caused the wild creatures of the wood and fields to trust the simple man.

The man and the boy looked up at their approach, Owen's eyes dreamy and content. A wide smile spread across Ifan's face as his pale blue eyes lighted on Davy.

Davy drew Elinor forward.

'Here is my wife, Elinor,' he said smiling and putting a proud arm round Elinor's shoulders.

Ifan's happy smile widened as he gazed at the lovely picture the girl made against the mossy background of the steep bank, her slim straight body lit by the sunlight which filtered through the fresh spring green of the trees. He nodded his shaggy head approvingly.

'Pretty,' he said in his guttural voice. 'Pretty like bird.'

Elinor gazed for a long moment at the man, seeing the large unwieldy head with its straggling thin locks of fair hair with streaks of grey near the scalp. The wide smile showed large teeth, clean but misshapen, and a growth of greying stubble covering the long chin. His high domed forehead was smooth and uncreased and his large pointed ears stuck out from his head like wings. His rough flannel shirt was unbuttoned and showed a matt of fairish hair across a bony chest. As his pale eyes continued their gaze, filled with a child-like delight in her loveliness, Davy felt her shrink back under his arm as she drew in a sharp breath of revulsion. His grip on her shoulder tightened.

'Elinor! Please!' His urgent whisper was close to her ear but she tore herself out of his grasp and turned to scramble wildly up the steep slope. Davy watched her go, a hot anger flaring up in him. Then he shrugged and turned back to Ifan and Owen and slid down to sit on the mossy bank beside them. Ifan's eyes were puzzled as he stared up the slope where Elinor had disappeared, but his smile was still happy as he nodded his shaggy head at Davy, and Owen settled down between the two men with a merry little laugh.

Once through the wicket and on to the field Elinor slowed her steps and fought for breath. As she picked her way across the grass there was an ugly frown on her face and the corners of her mouth were down in a grimace of disgust. Suddenly the

sound of hooves careering across the springy turf startled her
and she paused, shading her eyes against the sun. She made out
the dark figure of a man galloping towards her on a black horse
and she stood very still, watching curiously as he approached.
He reined his horse in a few paces from her and sat immobile,
looking down without speaking.

She saw a stocky, broad-shouldered fellow with a coarsely
handsome face, dark skinned with thick black hair which
curled round his ears. Bold dark eyes searched her face and
then ran in a hard gaze over her body. She flushed and
straightened her shoulders, a strange shiver passing through
her.

'You are Luke, I suppose?' She gazed up at him coolly.

He did not reply at once but kept his eyes on her, absently
patting the neck of the restless animal beneath him. The horse
flung its head up and whinnied impatiently, moving sideways
threateningly towards the girl. She stood her ground, chin
lifted, and the man gave a grim smile as he pulled on the rein
and cursed the horse. He was dressed in heavy black serge
trousers and a shirt of cream flannel which was open to show
the strong brown column of his neck. His sleeves were rolled up
and his thick arms were closely covered in black hair.

'Davy's new wife, is it?' His voice was rough and there was
amusement in his eyes. She nodded and her gaze wandered
over the sleek black horse, its muscles tensed and impatient
under the gleaming coat.

Luke watched her, his full lips parted over strong white
teeth.

'I heard about it. Young Davy's done all right for himself.'

She looked up into the bold dark face, a hint of mischief in
her blue eyes.

'Think so?' she said and gave a short laugh.

'Well, so the old men say. The old women are not so sure, is
it?' He grinned back at her.

Her eyebrows went up like dark wings.

'You've got the cheek of the devil!'

'So they say.'

She moved in close to the horse as though drawn by an
invisible magnet and ran a hand over its smooth hide.

'Like horses?' he asked, his voice less rough.

'Yes. Better than people, I think.'

'Me too. You can trust horses, isn't it?'

'But not people?'

He shrugged and steadied the horse again as she moved round to the front of the animal and stroked its smooth black nose.

'Where's Davy?' he asked.

She gave a scornful jerk of her head in the direction of the wicket gate.

'Down by the river with Ifan and Owen.'

The corners of his mouth came down and his dark eyes narrowed between their long spiky black lashes.

'Good God! Sitting with that idiot. And him supposed to be a clever chap, schoolmaster and all. You'd think he'd find something better to do. Like stay with his pretty little wife.' His dark eyes glinted and he grinned. 'Why aren't you with them? Couldn't stomach our simple Ifan, eh?'

She gave an exaggerated shudder.

'I don't blame you,' he said, laughing.

'Look!' she said, eagerly, moving round to his side again, her face upturned to his. 'Can I ride your horse? I haven't been on a horse since – well, for ages. Please?'

He looked down at her, taking in the violet eyes and the flush on her creamy skin. She smiled up at him provocatively and he laughed aloud.

'Used to getting what you want, aren't you? All right, but go easy with him, he's touchy.'

He threw his leg over the horse's back and dismounted, landing very close to her. Before she could draw back he caught her roughly round the waist and with a flurry of skirts she was astride the horse. He laughed to see the colour deepen in her cheeks and handed her the reins.

'What's his name?' she asked, leaning forward to pat the horse's neck, determined that he should not have the satisfaction of seeing the confusion in her eyes caused by the roughness of his handling.

'Satan!' he cried with a wide grin and stepping back he watched her flick the reins and career wildly across the field, her hair falling loose and flying above the wide hat at the back of her head. His eyes followed as she circled the field, the horse's hooves pounding rhythmically, until a shout from behind made him turn, frowning, in the direction of the wicket.

Davy ran forward, his eyes on the flying figure on the black horse. He shook Luke's arm angrily.

'For God's sake, man! She shouldn't be riding! Elinor!' he shouted. 'Elinor! Stop!'

Luke grinned as he watched the girl gallop by unheeding.

'Leave her be, man. She's enjoying herself. She can handle him. They're two of a kind, I am thinking.'

'You put her up to this!'

'No. She asked to ride him. I couldn't refuse the lady now, could I?'

Davy watched helplessly as Elinor circled the field again, faster and faster, bent low over the horse's neck, something akin in the wildly careering horse and the girl clinging to its back, hair streaming out to match the flying black mane.

At last she reined in the sweating horse and cantered back to where they stood. She sat, breathing quickly, with chin lifted and cheeks flushed, patting the horse's neck as he tossed his head and pawed the ground, his breath jetting noisily through his nostrils.

'Well done,' grinned Luke. 'You looked if you enjoyed that.'

'I did. Thanks. He's grand. I wish he was mine.' She dismounted and tossed the reins to Luke, avoiding Davy's eyes.

'You know you shouldn't be riding yet,' said Davy in a low voice.

'Oh, for God's sake!' She turned an angry face to him, her eyes shooting sparks. 'Leave me alone!' She turned on her heel and flung off in the direction of the house, her hair still loose over her shoulders which were squared defiantly.

Luke laughed as he watched her go.

'Got your hands full there, Davy boy. Right little madam, she is. You'll have to ride her with a loose rein, I'm thinking.'

He jumped on Satan's back and as he pulled on the rein the horse circled round Davy, tossing its head with impatience.

'She's like Satan here,' he went on with a malicious grin. 'A bit wild, like. I doubt if you're the man to tame her, though.'

He circled Davy once more and then galloped off across the field.

Davy stood looking after him for a moment and then turned and walked slowly in the direction that Elinor had gone. His thoughts were bitter as he balled his fists deep in his pockets. The golden spell of spring in Manafon was shattered for the rest of the afternoon and he was almost glad when the time came to leave.

15

Hooters and Hoses

It was at breakfast the following Thursday morning in the Rees household and Dada had just pushed his porridge bowl from him and picking up his mug, sipped hot strong tea noisily through his moustache. Owen was struggling through the last few mouthfuls of his porridge, scraping manfully at the blue-ringed bowl which he had tipped towards him.

'That little *ferch'i* is coming on well, indeed.' Dada addressed Mama, who had Esther on her knee and was spooning mouthfuls of thinned down oatmeal into the rosy mouth, opened like a bird.

'Aye, well enough,' said Mama proudly as she caught the drips on Esther's small pink chin with the spoon and poked them back into her mouth. Two round cornflower-blue eyes focused on Dada and Esther kicked her plump bare feet and showed four small white teeth in delight.

'Da-da,' she crowed, spilling the porridge back out of her mouth.

'There now,' said Mama crossly. 'Leave her be or I will never get her fed.'

'*Diawl!*' said Dada, hurt. 'Only looking I was. But she do know her old Dada, don't you then, my little piglet?'

'She is no piglet, either,' said Mama, indignant. 'And you should make her to call you Grandad. Don't forget that Llew is her Dada.'

'I do not forget,' said Dada, on the defensive. 'It is her who does forget. And she cannot get her little tongue round "Grandad" yet. She is only just a year old now.'

'Aye, well,' nodded Mama, cleaning Esther's face with a damp flannel. 'The trouble is she do hardly see her Dada. No sooner he do get home from work and have a bite in his mouth than he is washed and out again, down that old Ladywell or up on Penygloddfa, into some old talk with the weavers, like as not. I do wish he would mind his business and leave the weavers and the millworkers to theirs. I do not see why he do have to get mixed up with them. Better he stay at home and give some time to his little ones.'

'Hush, now,' grunted Dada, an eye on Owen, who was sitting very still, staring into his empty porridge bowl. 'Little rabbits have big ears, isn't it?'

Mama sighed and rose to put Esther down in the old wooden high chair, fastening her in with a shawl tied in a knot at the back. The baby kicked her heels and beat on the tray of the chair with plump pink fists, showing her teeth in a happy grin.

'Like our Meg she is,' said Mama, tucking some straying locks of hair back under her hair pins. 'Good as gold and very contented. She is not much trouble, fair play, but I am that glad to see Meg get home anyway, to see to these two. Maybe I am getting too old for this old game.'

'Go on with you, girl,' Dada grinned. 'You do enjoy it. But indeed that Meggie is a born mother. She do love these two.'

'Ah. It is babies of her own she should be having,' said Mama, beginning to clear the breakfast things.

Owen watched her in silence for a moment, a pucker creasing his forehead. At last, plucking at the edge of the table, his face lowered, he said in a small voice.

'When Meggie do have her own babies she will not want me and Esther, is it?'

'*Diawl!*' cried Dada. 'What did I tell you about big ears, woman.' He put his hand on Owen's dark head. 'Look you, boy. Meggie will always want you and this small one here, I am telling you. Did she have a dozen babies you will still be her boy, mark you, and this one here will still be her girl. Now then.'

Owen cheered up and slid down off his chair.

'Run you and get a good wash and a comb through that hair, ready for school,' said Mama, turning him toward the back kitchen. 'And pull up them socks,' she called after him. 'They are round your boots like concertinas, boy.'

'Aye,' grunted Dada, rising. 'I shall have to get going. If I don't hasten I shall meet myself coming back. What is the time on that old clock?'

'It is nearly eight,' said Mama briskly. 'I must get this bread in or I will be all behind like an old cow's tail.'

'What was that?' asked Dada suddenly, cocking his head as a hooter sounded urgent blasts in the distance.

'What?' grunted Mama, poking the fire to make a good hot blaze to heat the oven.

'That hooter,' replied Dada, frowning.

'It will be the breakfast whistle at the Gwalia,' said Mama, impatient. 'I do hear it sometimes if the old wind is blowing this way.'

'No, no,' Dada was moving towards the door. 'It do sound more like the fire hooter.'

'Hm,' grunted Mama, not taking much notice. 'If I do not get more coal on quick there will be fire everywhere but in this old grate.' She rose stiffly and was moving toward the back kitchen to fetch the coal bucket when an exclamation from Dada, standing at the door, stopped her in her tracks. She joined him on the doorstep and peered over his shoulder.

The April morning was mild and cloudy and a freshening wind was blowing a pall of smoke across the river. The tops of the trees on the Rackfield were obscured by the thick dark grey cloud and and acrid smell filled their nostrils.

'Dear God!' whispered Mama, horrified. 'Where is it from, Will?'

At that moment Matt Owen came hurrying through the door of his cobbler's shop, dragging his club foot clumsily.

'It's the Gwalia!' he shouted across to them. 'I could see it from my back window. It looks bad,' and he hobbled off down the pavement, his leather apron flapping round his legs and his wispy grey hair blowing in the wind.

Mama's hand flew to her mouth.

'Oh, good God, Will, our Meggie!'

The Gwalia was the largest mill in the town, making tweeds, and the mill where Meg worked.

'Give me my cap, girl,' Dada shouted. 'I will go down to see.'

Mama reached his cap down with a shaking hand and jamming it on his white hair he set off at a trot down the road. As Mama watched people were coming running from all directions, heading towards the wooden footbridge known as the Ha'penny Bridge, after the toll that was levied there many years back. The Gwalia Mill stood in a field at the far end of the bridge and through the thick cloud of smoke which was blowing from that direction Mama could make out the shadowy forms of people streaming over the bridge in the direction of the mill.

With a strangled cry she rushed back into the house, calling to Owen. Snatching up the baby from the high chair, she hurriedly wrapped the shawl round her own body and encased the baby in it. Grabbing the astonished Owen by the hand she hurried out into the morning, her breath coming in quick gasps of fear. With white set face and heart pounding she joined the hurrying people and was jostled as they ran past her alongside the Bridge Wall, calling out to each other excitedly, their eyes turned towards the source of the thick smoke. Flames could now be seen licking up against a darkening sky and with a sob Mama quickened her steps, with Owen, white and scared, running and stumbling at her side as she dragged him along. The baby peered out of the shawl, her round head bobbing up and down as Mama ran. She emitted a series of small sneezes which creased her face, as wisps of smoke blew across them, then showed her four teeth in a happy grin, enjoying the bobbing motion.

As Mama headed for the Ha'penny Bridge, Owen was suddenly snatched from her grasp and she turned, startled, to see Davy at her side, lifting Owen to his shoulder.

'Go back home, Mama!' he shouted. 'Take the baby back home. I will see to Owen.'

She shook her head wildly.

'Meggie!' she cried. 'Our Meggie!'

He shouted at her again but they had reached the narrow bridge and his voice was lost in the cries of the people who bumped and pushed them on to the bridge in the stampede to get across. Over two hundred people were employed at the mill and nearly everyone in the town had a relative or neighbour working there.

Mama was borne along in the crowd as it struggled through the narrow confines of the wooden handrails of the bridge and was squeezed out at the other end like a cork out of a bottle. Men, women and children streamed up on to the Wire Walk, the footpath which bordered the field in which the Mill stood and which was now packed with people pressed against the wire fence which enclosed the field. Mama pushed her way through the press of bodies and fetched up against a fence post, where she clung with one arm, clutching Esther to her with the other under the safety of the old grey shawl. She gave a moan as her terrified eyes took in the scene below.

It was the tall warehouse attached to the side of the weaving sheds which was on fire. This warehouse had been built onto the side of the mill itself to hold the raw materials and bales of wool, and these materials were feeding the hungry flames which shot spectacularly thirty feet up into the sky and poured through broken windows, roaring and hissing as they consumed the oily and inflammable bales inside. The men of the town fire brigade were playing jets of water from leaky hoses in a desperate attempt to prevent the fire from spreading to the weaving sheds. The wind freshened still more, blowing strongly in a south-westerly direction fortunately, for though it fanned the roaring fire, it was blowing it away from the main building of the mill where the looms were. The firemen were cursing and struggling, frustrated by poor water pressure and hoses found to be full of holes. The agitated crowd shouted in fury and disgust as from time to time the falling pressure reduced the water jets.

'What the hell!' raged a man's voice behind Mama. 'They'd do better piddling on it than with those bloody hoses!'

Beyond the firemen and their inadequate equipment, mill-hands who had begun their work at six o'clock and had been at breakfast when the fire was discovered, were now hurrying in and out of the bottom half of the warehouse, dragging bales of wool out and bags of spooled thread. Women as well as men worked furiously to beat the flames which so far were confined to the two upper storeys. A number of men from the crowd leapt the fence and rushed down the field to help them, and Davy, having found Dada in the crowd, deposited Owen with him and leapt after them. He ran between the cursing firemen and jumped the hoses and when he reached the wide door of the warehouse he searched wildly among the hurrying, struggling figures who were dragging and pushing bales and bags through the door, their faces flushed and sweating with the intense heat, the men in shirt sleeves stumbling and cursing and the women, shawls tied round their heads and faces blackened with smoke and dust, working steadily and silently beside them.

Davy shouted hoarsely, calling Meg's name and running from one shawled woman to another. He stumbled against two men struggling with a huge bale of wool and was furiously cursed as he sprawled on the floor, knocking the breath out of his body. As he scrambled to his feet a huge roar sounded from above and an enormous beam crashed through the ceiling at the far end of the room, landing on a stack of bales in a sheet of flame and sparks like fireworks. There were screams from three women who had been tugging at one of the bales in the stack and Davy could see that the clothes of two of them were alight and a third had been knocked out by a glancing blow from the beam. The two men who had cursed him now dropped their bale and ran toward the women on Davy's heels.

One shawled figure was running toward Davy, screaming and beating with her hands at the shawl round her head which was alight with flames. Fire licked at the bottom of her skirts and she twisted and turned, reeling round. Davy shouted to her as he whipped off his jacket, but before he could throw it over her she had collapsed on to the floor in a senseless heap. He flung the coat across her head, smothering the burning shawl and then beat at her smouldering skirt. Afterwards he knelt beside her and gently turned her on to her back.

As he pushed the scorched shawl from her face, at first he failed to recognize her. Her face was blackened with smoke and dust, the skin on the one side seared horribly from her eye to her chin. Her fair hair was shrivelled into scorched tufts and her eyebrows were gone. Recognition came as he leaned closer to see if she was breathing.

'Meggie!' he whispered, his eyes wide with horror, and then he cried aloud, 'Oh my God! Meggie!'

He was sobbing raggedly as he picked up one hand with its pitifully burned palm and felt the wrist for a pulse. It beat faintly and he choked with relief.

At that moment there was a shout from behind him as firemen ran in through the door.

'Out! Out! Quick! The lot'll come down in a minute!'

He slipped his arm under Meg's inert body and struggled to his feet. With the help of one of the firemen he stumbled out through the door with his burden and the firemen urged him

224

well away from the blazing building. He sank down on the grass cradling Meg in his arms as the tall thin form of Dr Bellamy ran up to them. The doctor took one look at the unconscious girl and gave a groan of pity. He disappeared for a moment and returned with two men, who carried a stretcher. Davy and the men between them lowered the girl carefully on to it.

'We'll take her to the infirmary,' the doctor said to Davy, putting a kindly hand on his shoulder. 'Poor little girl, it is as well she has fainted.'

Davy watched as Meg was carried carefully up the field to the 'Oh's' and 'Ah's' of pity from the nearest onlookers.

'I must tell my mother and my father,' Davy muttered, his voice sticking in his throat. 'I will come to the infirmary after.'

'Right, lad. Now I must see to the other two,' and the doctor hurried away.

Davy's feet were leaden as he stumbled up the slope. Hands reached out to help him over the wire fence and the murmuring crowd parted as he made his way to where he had left Dada and Owen.

Dada's face worked pitifully as Davy put his arm round his shoulders.

'Meggie?' he asked, searching Davy's face with brimming blue eyes.

Davy nodded. 'She is burned, Dada, but she is alive, thank God. They have taken her to the infirmary. Come you, we will find Mama and you must take her home. I will go the infirmary.'

His arm still round Dada's shaking shoulders they pushed their way through the crowd and found Mama still clutching the fence post, Esther asleep in her arms. Her eyes closed and she swayed against the post as Davy whispered the news, then her shoulders straightened in a characteristic movement and she suffered herself to be led away in Dada's encircling arm, towards the bridge, Owen clinging, pale and silent, to Dada's other hand.

Davy watched them go and then turned and took one last bitter look at the blazing warehouse.

It was now one great red glare as the flames roared and crackled. The roof twisted and collapsed like toffee and the beams and rafters crashed through the floors down to the basement below. As Davy watched, the clamour of bells from another fire brigade sounded from the road above the Wire Walk and soon another detachment of men ran on to the field and were quickly at work with better hoses, sending jets of water onto the walls of the weaving sheds, which, thanks to the direction of the wind, were still untouched. The crowd cheered excitedly as the new army of men swung into action and their shouts rang in Davy's ears as he turned his back on the mad scene and made for the bridge and the infirmary.

☆ ☆ ☆

Meggie came home a week later. Davy hurried down from the school at four-thirty to find her sitting in Dada's wooden armchair, bandaged ankles resting on a cushion placed on the floor and bandaged hands lying in her lap. All that remained of her lovely hair was a few spikes at the front and snarled tresses at the back, where her scalp was too sore to allow of brushing. She turned a white face in his direction and he was stopped in his tracks by the shock of her appearance. When he had visited her at the infirmary the left side of her face had been covered with gauze, but now this had been removed to allow the air to heal and his heart contracted at the sight. The skin was drawn in an ugly liver-coloured pucker, with black scorched edges. Her left eye was half-closed and lashless, dragged down by the drawing-together of the skin on her cheek-bone and her mouth on that side was twisted grotesquely into the shrivelled flesh of her cheek. As he choked back a cry of pity she gave a lop-sided attempt at a smile and moved her head slowly from side to side on the blanket with which Mama had padded the back of the wooden armchair.

'It's all right, our Davy,' her voice was a whisper which came painfully through stiff lips. 'I am not as bad as I look. I am alive, isn't it, thanks to you.'

He shook his head and pulled out a chair from the table to sit opposite her.

'How are you feeling?' he asked, his voice shaking a little.

Before she could answer Mama came in from the back kitchen carrying a bowl of broth and a teaspoon.

'She is sore, but she is alive, and that's what matters,' she said with an edge to her voice. 'Don't sit there gawping, boy.

226

Shift and let me sit. Now, girl, we will try to get a bit of this old broth down you.'

She tied a clean tea towel gently round Meg's shoulders and drawing a chair close, began to spoon the warm broth into the girl's poor twisted mouth, while Esther looked on with interest, tied into her high chair with the old grey shawl.

Suddenly Davy became aware of the shadowy figure of Owen standing silent in the back kitchen doorway. The boy's face was pale and his dark eyes large and bewildered.

'Come here, Owen, my old beauty.' Davy strode over and swung the little boy up on to his shoulder. 'How would you like to come to have your tea with me and Auntie Elinor? Strawberry jam and currant cake, is it?'

Owen's eyes slid sideways to Meg who nodded to him between mouthfuls of broth.

'There's nice, our Owen,' she whispered, winking with her good eye.

'Aye, go you with your Uncle Davy, boy,' encouraged Mama. 'I will see to this old girl and then get tea for your Dada and Grandad. I have not got any currant cake and only old gooseberry jam.'

With a last anxious look at Meg Owen nodded and Davy set him down on the floor.

'I will go for my tea now and bring Owen back later, then,' said Davy, forcing a cheerful note into his voice. 'Just called in to see for you, our Meg. You will be all right girl. That will soon clear up and you will be right as rain again.'

Meg gave a faint nod and closed her eyes for a moment. When she opened them again a tear trickled slowly from under the puckered left eyelid and hung above the scorched flesh of her cheek.

Davy turned away quickly.

'Come on, Owen, lad. Let us go to see Auntie Elinor before she eats all that currant cake, is it?'

Owen was silent as he walked up Kerry Road, trying to match his steps to Davy's long legged stride. As they approached Plas Gwyn he slowed down and hesitated. Davy stopped and looked at him enquiringly.

'Uncle Davy?' the boy began in a low voice.

'What is it, lad?'

'Will Meggie's face get all right again, Uncle Davy?' Owen

peered up at Davy anxiously.

'Aye, I daresay.' Davy's voice was gruff. 'May be a bit of a scar, like. But she will still be our Meggie, won't she?'

'I don't care!' Owen said fiercely, his face flushing. 'Our Meggie is beautiful. I will still love her best in the world.'

'Good lad,' Davy squeezed his shoulder. 'You are right. Meggie is beautiful and always will be, no matter what. Now, how about this strawberry jam and currant cake. I don't know about you but I am starving.'

'Aye,' said Owen, grinning. 'I am starving, too. Is there right big strawberries in the jam, Uncle Davy?'

When Davy took Owen back down to No 46 that evening Esther had been put to bed and Mama was upstairs, settling Meggie for an early night.

'The girl is worn out,' said Llew, sitting on a chair opposite Dada. The tea things had been cleared and the fire stoked into a warm blaze and Llew was sitting forward, hands on his knees and a grim expression on his thin dark face.

'Go you and play in the back yard for a few minutes, Owen,' he told the boy. 'Mama will see to you going to bed when she has finished with Meg.'

When the boy had clattered out through the back kitchen, Dada nodded to Davy.

'Draw up a chair, boy. I am glad for you to come. This Llew here is working himself up into a temper about things that cannot be helped. Do you listen to him for a bit and let me be. I am tired of his old carry-on.'

Llew snorted and his face darkened.

'Carry-on, is it? Well, what happened at the Gwalia was the biggest carry'on.'

Davy shifted in his chair and cocked an enquiring eyebrow at Llew, while Dada frowned fiercely and blew through his moustache.

'Aye,' said Llew, a bitter eye on Dada. 'You can huff and puff, Dada, but they are asking questions in the town.'

'*Duw*!' snorted Dada. 'And giving their own answers, no doubt. Nothing is right and all is wrong for them. They will bury you before you are dead in this town.'

'Well, two are dead all right, through this lot,' Llew said angrily. 'And five are in the infirmary, besides the three women burned. Time for questions.'

'It was not the fire that killed that young fellow and the little girl,' Dada reminded, very patient. 'The fire was out when all those people did go poking round the ruins and have a wall fall down on them.'

'Oh, aye,' grunted Llew. 'It was a shambles, like everything else that day. Hoses leaking like bloody sieves, no pressure in the water. And then when the fire was out they were too damn busy seeing to the looms and so on in the weaving sheds and get the poor fool workers back on the job quick, to think of stopping the crowds that were poking around the ruins like ghouls.'

'Aye, it was pretty bad that,' agreed Davy. 'But there were still firemen and policemen there and they did try to turn the people back, fair play.'

Llew grunted.

'There should have been proper control there. That chap and the little girl with their heads crushed in and five girls with broken limbs. And all they cared about was their bloody machinery.'

'Now then, boy,' Dada banged his fist on the arm of his chair. 'There will be a bit less of that old swearing for a start. You mind, boy, who would put food in their bellies if those workers were laid off too long.'

'It was not the food for bellies but the money for their purses that the managers were worrying about,' answered Llew, unrepentant. 'But that is not the big question, is it? What started the fire, they are asking in town. Or who?' he added, darkly.

'That is dangerous talk, Llew, and you know it,' cautioned Davy.

'Aye, well. The owners will be all right. Plenty of insurance, isn't it? But nothing will bring back the dead. Nor put our Meg's face right,' Llew added bitterly. 'She will be scarred now for life.'

'Hush, you,' hissed Dada, very fierce. 'The girl will hear you. She has enough, without your old talk.'

Llew stared into the fire, an ugly expression on his face.

'If I thought –,' he began after a while, then stopped.

'For God's sake, Llew,' said Davy. 'Leave it. You will do no good to anybody.'

Llew looked at him and shook his head.

'Can you understand those murderous bastards sending workers into a blazing building to rescue a few bloody bales of wool?'

Dada banged on the arm of his chair again and his moustache bristled.

'Enough now, boy!' he growled. 'That will do from you. That tongue of yours will hang you one of these days. I do not want to hear any more from you.'

Llew got up violently and made for the door. He paused there and looked back at them, bitter fury on his face.

'That girl upstairs, scarred for life. Two dead and others maimed. And you do not want any old talk! You, our Davy. You should know better. Where has all your old reading got you? You are all theory, man. Theory doesn't help her.' He pointed a trembling finger at the ceiling. 'I am sick in my stomach!' he shouted and banged the door as he flung out.

Dada frowned into the fire.

'That boy does worry me no end. I do not know where all his old talk is going to land him. You mind,' he said, dropping his voice. 'If that old mill was fired for the insurance money, would they have worked so hard to save any of it?'

Davy made no answer for a while but stared in front of him thoughtfully.

'If they did,' he said at last. 'Our Llew is right. There are questions. But they will not be asked openly. Nor answered if they were asked. People are afraid. They want jobs, not trouble. There is trouble enough in this town. The wool trade is dying on its feet and what is to replace it? Already people are moving up to Huddersfield and Bradford. What will be left in a few years time? Unemployment and poverty or emigration to England. The usual tale,' he added, bitterly.

Dada grunted and drummed on the arm of his chair with his fingers.

Davy gave a short laugh.

'There is a bit more of old theory for you. But what is the good of Llew and the others encouraging the workers to band together for better pay and conditions. The bosses have the upper hand. When there are not enough jobs to go round the bosses always have the upper hand. Take it or leave it is their cry. And there is no choice unless you want to end up on the Parish or in the workhouse.' He sighed wearily. 'I see Llew's

230

point. Socialism is great in theory. But theory doesn't feed empty bellies.'

'Nor will our Llew,' said Dada flatly.

'No. That is the trouble. Trying to put it into practice as things are is no good either. You can tell the workers to withdraw their labour. And where does that get them? The mills are closing anyway and the owners will get out before they lose the lot. I suppose what we need is a revolution like in France. But it will not happen here. The class system is too deeply entrenched. I cannot see them chopping the heads of the aristocracy here!'

'What is this chopping off heads?' asked Mama, appearing from the direction of the stairs.

'God knows,' said Dada, bewildered. 'There is awful talk here with these boys. Llew is questions and our Davy is chopping heads. I do not understand old talk like this. I am getting old, isn't it?' he added with pathos.

Mama snorted.

'I am getting old, too, but I do not have time to do all this old talking. I do get on with it.'

Davy rose to his feet, laughing.

'Better that way, Mama. Talk is not getting us very far, indeed. How is Meg now?'

'She will do.' Mama's worried frown belied her words. 'But what shape she will be in I do not know.' She pulled a chair out from the table and sat down heavily. 'She is in pain, but that will pass. Her hands and legs are not too bad. But her face. Never will that come right I doubt. She was that pretty, too,' she said wistfully, clasping and unclasping her hands on the table.

'Come on, Mama,' said Davy, gently putting a hand on her shoulder. 'Owen said it all. Meggie will still be Meggie whatever, and beautiful to us, isn't it?'

Mama sighed.

'Aye, you are right. And talking of Owen, where is he to? Time for him to go to his bed.' She squared her shoulders and got up. She went out through the back kitchen, calling to the boy, and Dada reached for the poker to stir the fire.

'There is a good woman,' he said. 'Do not you lot forget it. Bring no shame on her, any of you, or you will have me to answer to.'

231

Davy nodded.

'I know, Dada. Salt of the earth she is. We all know it.'

'Aye, well,' Dada grunted, putting the poker down. 'Look to it. Or there will be heads chopped round here and I will be doing the chopping.'

16

Sherry and Monkshood

The summer should have been ended and yet the long golden days persisted as though reluctant to give way to autumn. After a poor May and even worse June, July had arrived bringing a heatwave that blazed unbroken through into August. That month was almost at an end and no sign of rain. There was a drought in the valley and water carts which had sprinkled the streets of the town every morning were now halted and instead brought round tanks of water from which the inhabitants filled their buckets in the parts of the town where the pressure was notoriously low and had now dried up.

The Severn meandered its shallow way languidly over its stony bed as it passed through the town and some of the women from the narrow streets bordering the river brought their washing down to the edges and laying it in the shallow water, beat at it with stones.

The Royal Welsh Warehouse, owned by the Pryce Jones family, organized an outing on a cleaned-up coal barge along the Shropshire Union Canal which had its terminal in the Canal Basin in Newtown. Ladies in large summer hats reclined on the seats of the barge and men in boaters adopted a nautical stance and shouted encouragement to the huge brown horse which plodded patiently along the towpath pulling them along. The ladies screamed with alarm in a most predictable manner as they rose and fell rocking through the locks and the men bravely called out soothing words to them while secretly eyeing the wet, dark slimy sides of the deep locks with trepidation.

Llew had insisted on taking Meg on the outing despite her reluctance. Her pretty hair had grown again and so had her

233

eyelashes and eyebrows and in right profile she was back to her normal self. But the livid scar which ran down the left side of her face still pulled at her eye a little although her mouth had healed into its own sweet lines.

At some stage during the summer Meg had come to terms with it and no longer tried to hide it with her hand or pull forward her growing hair. Her eyes once more looked out on the world with their usual gentle expression and those close to her became used to, and hardly noticed the ugly disfigurement. She had been back at work since the middle of June, but apart from that she went out little and devoted herself to Owen and Esther and to helping Mama in the house. Now, after the initial embarrassment of being with strangers, she was hugely enjoying the trip down the canal under Llew's protective gaze, as they slid between the banks, lush with summer growth and enjoyed the occasional patch of dappled shade cast by the overhanging branches of the leafy trees. Picnic baskets provided by the firm sat squarely in the bottom of the barge, for it was an all-day trip and they were to eat their lunch in a pretty spot near Welshpool before making a leisurely journey back.

Left at home, Mama had charge of Esther, now toddling around everywhere on plump legs and poking inquisitive fingers into everything to try Mama's patience. Dada had promised to take Owen to Manafon and had invited Davy and Elinor to go with them. Enervated by the dry heat and bored and restless, Elinor shrugged and agreed and they set off after dinner in the trap, Elinor cool and remote in gentian blue silk under a large hat and Davy in shirt sleeves and a straw boater teasing Owen, whose eyes shone with excitement.

As it was Saturday the Beehive was open as they drew into the village and Dada looked round at Davy with a grin.

'I do think that this Mogg here could do with a drink to stay her to climb up to the Walkmill,' he announced. He tugged at his starched collar. 'Indeed, I am near choked myself. It is this old dust that Mogg kicks up, see, or I would not bother. Can I bring you one out, boy?'

'We will all go in,' said Elinor coolly, before Davy could answer. 'I am not sitting out here in this heat.'

Dada's blue eyes were surprised but he nodded and twinkled at her appreciatively.

'Right you, girl. We will go in the snug. It will be more

private like and we can take Owen with us.'

The boy hurriedly scrambled down from the trap and trotted after them before anyone could change their minds. Dada endeavoured to usher them into the back room, but Elinor, with a swish of blue skirts, her chin high, sailed calmly into the public bar bringing conversation to a halt. As Davy and Dada exchanged helpless glances she looked around and chose a seat on the settle by the fireplace, which held a large potted fern in lieu of a fire. The only other inhabitant of the seat, a small man with a weasly face and cross eyes rose hurriedly with a startled look and, touching his cap, backed away towards the bar.

'I will take a glass of sherry,' Elinor announced in a clear voice which fell like a pebble in the pool of silence and brought heads craning forward.

'I will get these,' said Davy to Dada, who was standing uncertainly in the middle of the floor, a hand on Owen's shoulder. As Dada seated himself opposite Elinor with Owen at his side, feet dangling six inches above the ground, Davy ordered the drinks from a tall, thin lugubrious looking individual with drooping brown moustaches, who had at some time replaced the round cottage-loaf lady whom Davy remembered.

A long five minutes passed before conversation filtered back into the bar, while the intruders sipped their drinks and avoided the curious glances cast in their direction. Eventually Elinor set her empty glass down on the table and rose, drawing on her gloves and smoothing the fingers calmly. With complete unconcern she looked all round and with a smile and a nod to the staring men of the village, picked up her skirts daintily and glided towards the door.

Davy and Dada quickly swallowed the last of their ale and pushing Owen before them, followed her out with a hasty nod to the barman. An outbreak of excited voices followed them as they made their way back to the trap and as they climbed in, Mogg's reproachful eyes reminded Dada of the initial reason for the stop.

'Plenty of water you will have soon, my beauty,' soothed a breathless Dada as he flicked the reins and they proceeded through the village at a trot, one or two women at the doors of the cottages watching their progress with hawk-eyed interest.

Auntie Martha's welcome was as warm as the weather and

they were soon seated with 'a cup of tea in your hand.' Seated behind the big brown teapot, she nodded and smiled as they gave her the family news. The fire which had been stirred to boil the kettle settled to a glow, but the thick walls kept the long kitchen cool and the windows, open at both ends, let in the summer scents on a soft breeze which stirred the curtains. Soon Owen slipped down off his chair and slipped out of the back door. Davy and Auntie Martha smiled at each other, knowing he would be off in search of Ifan.

'Where are your menfolk?' asked Dada, putting down his empty cup and settling his stocky frame in Granny Evan's old wooden armchair with a contented grunt.

'Oh, the usual,' laughed Auntie Martha. 'No doubt Ifan will be down at the stream and Luke in the stable or galloping about like all possessed. The hay is all in and we are taking it a bit easy this afternoon, isn't it?'

'Good hay this year, sure to,' said Dada, hands clasped across his stomach, blue eyes drowsy.

'Indeed. We have had the weather for it. But dry it is round here now. We are carrying water up from the stream for the stock. There is not much in the old well, just enough for the house. Ifan do bring us all our water. He is good in the hay, too. Strong, you know. Oh, Ifan does do a fair bit around if you set him to it,' she said, quietly.

'Aye, well, there is no harm in Ifan,' replied Dada gruffly, 'he is quiet and do give no trouble, dare say.'

'No trouble at all,' said Auntie Martha in a firm voice. 'I just wish Luke – oh well,' she sighed. 'Luke has no patience with Ifan, poor boy. But there, Ifan is happy in his fashion. Happier than most folks, I do think. He goes his own way and bothers nobody.' She tucked some stray wisps of greying hair back into the bun on top of her head and squared her shoulders in a manner reminiscent of Mama. 'More tea, anybody?'

As she filled Dada's cup and Davy passed his up, the conversation passed on to Meg's progress, Auntie Martha tutting and soothing in turn, and no-one noticed Elinor rise silently and slip from the room.

She let herself out of the back door and closed it quietly behind her. She hesitated, standing in the dusty yard in the warm sun. Then she lifted her skirts from the dirt and made her way in the direction of the stables.

She peered over the half door into the dim interior. The two horses, Gypsy and Satan, were in their stalls and Luke was brushing Satan's gleaming black coat vigorously, whistling through his teeth. She watched him for a while, the sun warm on her back, taking in the movement of his short powerful arms and the rippling muscles of his back under his shirt. A lock of dark hair hung over his forehead which was beaded with sweat.

'Hello. Can I come in?'

Her clear voice startled him and he spun round to face her. He shrugged and turned back to his work.

'If you want.' His tone was indifferent and he resumed his brushing. The two horses turned their heads to stare at the intruder, Gypsy's brown eyes gentle and Satan's showing the whites in nervous wariness.

She leaned over and unlatched the door, stepping into the shadow of the interior and carefully fastening the door behind her. Her feet rustled in the straw as she moved across to the stalls, giving Gypsy a pat on her rump as passing. She halted beside the second stall and stood watching. Luke carried on working, a frown on his face, as Satan moved restlessly under the grooming. After a moment he threw down the brush with an impatient curse and turned round.

'He doesn't like strangers about. Makes him nervous.' His voice was surly.

'Thanks. That's a nice welcome.'

He thrust his hands in his pockets and stared at her.

'What do you want?'

Her eyebrows flew up.

'Well! Lovely manners you have. I came to see the horses.'

He stepped back as she entered the stall and ran her hand over Satan's shiny flanks. The horse shook his head and stamped the hoof nearest her.

'Watch out! I told you strangers make him nervous.'

She turned to face him. He was close enough for her to smell the sweat on his body. Her pulse quickened as a primitive awareness of the male animal in him shot through her body. She leaned defiantly against the restless flank of the horse, her blue eyes mocking.

'Better come away,' he warned. 'You're going to get kicked.'

She laughed daringly.

'I'm not afraid of horses. I told you once, I like them better than people.'

His dark eyes were bent intently on her tilted, laughing face and a sudden tremor shook his stocky frame. As though aware of something electric in the air, Satan rolled his eyes at them and tossed his head. He shifted his rear end suddenly with an impatient stamp and Elinor stumbled backwards.

Luke swore and his arm shot out and caught her wrist in a rough grasp, pulling her away.

'Stupid little bitch!' He ground out the words through his teeth. He caught her shoulders and spun her round, pushing her roughly against the side of the stall.

'Take your hands off me!' she blazed and he stepped back. Straightening up she rubbed at her wrist, her black eyebrows down in a frown.

His face darkened and he turned abruptly. Picking up the brush he spat on to the straw and resumed brushing with sharp angry strokes.

She watched him in silence for a while, still rubbing at her wrist absently, her eyes narrowed. The rhythmic movement of the brush, the smell of straw and horseflesh and the male smell of the nearby man seemed to produce a hypnotic effect on her. Despite the languorous warmth of the air in the dimly-lit stable a sudden shiver passed through her. Again sensing something, Satan turned his head and his ears went back. His flanks quivered and he stamped a hoof menacingly. Elinor gasped and stepped back as Luke swung round with a curse and hurled the brush into a corner of the stall. His fists were clenched and the corners of his mouth drawn down and she put up a warding hand as he took a step forward. Suddenly he stopped and took a deep breath, dropping his hands loosely at his sides.

'Why don't you get out of here?' he said softly and moved closer still so that as her back pressed against the side of the stall his dark face was over her, eyes glinting under black brows. Suddenly he grasped her shoulders roughly and pressed them back against the wooden partition. She tried to move but his weight pinned her back and she stared up into his mocking face mesmerized, her breath coming rapidly through parted lips. For a long moment his dark eyes gazed down into her face and then he allowed them to wander with deliberate insolence downwards over her long white neck to her bosom, heaving under the tight blue basque of her dress. A quick flush stained her cheeks and she twisted under his hands, reaching up to grasp his wrists. One of the buttons flew off her bodice and the blue silk gaped open over the soft white swell of her breast. Suddenly his mouth came down on hers, hard and bruising, stopping her breath and his fingers dug painfully into her shoulders. Then, as suddenly, he released her and stepped back, eyes narrowed, full red lips drawn back in a mocking grin.

'Was that what you were waiting for, then?' he asked.

She pulled herself upright, speechless with fury and insult.

'Now go you back to your schoolmaster husband.' He gave a short bark of laughter and walked over to the corner of the stall, where he bent and picked up the brush from where he had flung it among the straw. She put a shaking hand up to her bruised mouth which still burned from his lips, then with a strangled sob of outrage, ran through the straw to the door. Blinded by angry tears she fumbled with the latch and let herself out into the sunlit yard again. His tuneless whistle followed her tauntingly as he resumed his brushing.

She hesitated for a moment, looking around her wildly, her dark hair hanging loose around her face and one hand still pressed against her stinging lips. Unconscious of the gaping bodice of her dress she turned her back on the house and ran stumblingly across the field toward the wicket gate which opened on to the steep path down to the stream.

She reached the gate just as Owen was coming through and he stopped, staring wide-eyed at her dishevelled appearance.

'Auntie Elinor? Is it time for tea? I was just coming to see.'

Without a word she brushed past him, leaving him gazing after her in surprise.

Elinor ran blindly on, hardly noticing Owen, and stumbled on down the steep path, briars catching at the silk of her dress. She gave a cry as her loose hair tangled with a spiky blackthorn branch and tore it free with furious hands. She caught the heel of her shoe against an exposed root and fell to her knees. Half sobbing, she scrambled to her feet and then as she raised her eyes, stood transfixed with a gasp of shock.

Inches away from her stood Ifan, on his lumbering way up the path. His light blue eyes regarded her watchfully as she stood rooted to the ground. Then his wide mouth opened in a delighted grin and he nodded his large head up and down, the wisps of fair hair moving gently above his domed forehead. She took in the width of his bony shoulders under the flannel shirt, open above his pale chest, and the long ape-like arms which hung down at his sides. For a moment she stared at his grinning face, petrified, and then with a low moan of terror stepped back off the path, her shoulders coming up against the solid trunk of a tree.

'Go away!' she whispered, her eyes dilated with fear.

The wide smile died on his face and his pale eyes were puzzled. He put his large head on one side but he did not move. She drew in a ragged breath and pressed her back against the tree, while panic brought the bile to her throat. He looked up suddenly as a bird's wings whirred among the branches above and when his glance came down to rest on her again his eyes had cleared happily and the pleased smile was back on his face again. Suddenly he took a lumbering step towards her.

'Pretty,' he said wonderingly. 'Pretty like bird,' and he put out a large hairy hand and gently touched her cheek.

Elinor's piercing scream echoed through the trees. Ifan, startled, stepped back, his smile dying. He shook his head from side to side in bewilderment as she slowly sank to the ground and covered her face with her hands, cowering against the trunk of the tree. Running footsteps sounded above them and Davy burst through the bushes, slipping and stumbling down the path. His face pale with fright, he stopped short and gasped. His eyes moved from Ifan's bewildered face, to Elinor crouched at the foot of the tree, hysterical sobs shaking her body. His horrified glance took in the tangle of dark curls which hung loose about her face and the gaping bodice which showed a darkening bruise on one exposed shoulder.

'Oh, my God!' he whispered shakily. 'Oh no! God, no!'

He glanced back at Ifan and shook his head in disbelief. Quickly he knelt beside the hysterical girl and tried to draw her hands from her face.

'Elinor! Oh, my God, Elinor! Did he – did he – touch you?'

She shrank back, then nodding her head, broke out into wild weeping.

Davy straightened slowly and turned to Ifan, agony in his eyes. The puzzled look left Ifan's face and he smiled happily at Davy, nodding his heavy head.

240

'Pretty,' he said in his guttural voice, pointing to Elinor. 'Like bird.'

Davy closed his eyes, his mouth working.

'Oh no!' he muttered hoarsely. 'Not Ifan!'

Ifan stood, smiling and nodding, as Davy turned back to Elinor with a heavy heart. He raised her gently and half-led, half-carried her up the path, his heart like a stone in his breast.

A bird flew down and perched on a branch close to Ifan, who stood very still, watching it, joy lighting his pale blue eyes.

☆   ☆   ☆

Auntie Martha sat at the table, her hands clasped convulsively on the scrubbed top, her face white and stricken. Davy, sitting silently opposite, glanced from time to time at the girl sitting in Granny Evan's wooden armchair, face averted and one hand clutching the edges of her bodice together over her breast. Dada stood at the window, gazing out at the hens pecking unconcernedly in the dust of the yard. He shifted his shoulders from time to time as if to dislodge a heavy burden and his blue eyes were pained and bewildered. Owen sat unnoticed on a wooden chair in a corner of the kitchen, his eyes shifting watchfully from one face to another, deeply puzzled when they rested on Elinor.

But the main tension in the room seemed to emanate from Luke. He sat at the end of the table, his body rigid and his hands, which lay clenched on the table, showing white across the knuckles.

'You'll have to face it,' he was saying in a harsh voice. 'He's got to be put away. Locked up where he can't do any harm. Hell, it should have been done years ago. He's not safe.'

Auntie Martha winced painfully and shook her head.

'No,' she whispered through colourless lips. 'Not Ifan. Not locked up. I don't believe –. He's like a child.'

Luke's eyes glinted and he gave a short bark of laughter.

'Like a child, indeed! In his mind. But he is a man, isn't he? Roaming about. Not safe. I've told you before he should be put away. Asking for trouble it is. You can't watch him all the time. And now look.'

Auntie Martha shook her head again.

'He has always been harmless enough and quiet.' She bent

241

her head and twisted her fingers nervously. 'You cannot shut him up. It would finish him. Like caging one of the Lord's wild creatures.'

Luke gave an angry snort and got up, pushing his chair back roughly.

'For God's sake, woman! Where's your sense? You can't turn your back on this. I say he must be put away and I am going to see to it!'

Auntie Martha lifted bitter eyes to his face.

'That is what you want, isn't it boy? To have him put away. But you can't do that to him.'

'Can't I?' Luke's voice went dangerously quiet. 'We'll see about that. They'll certify him like a shot now he's shown he's dangerous.'

'Certify him?' she whispered slowly. 'Oh, God. Ifan?'

Dada gave a sudden cough and turned back from the window.

'I do think we had better go,' he said, addressing Davy, who sat with lowered eyes, silent and brooding. He roused himself wearily and went over to touch Elinor on the shoulder. Her face still averted, she clutched the bodice of her dress more tightly and moved over to the door, his arm supporting her. She carefully avoided looking at Luke whose dark eyes followed her, his mouth down at the corners and a strange expression on his face.

Dada put his hand on Auntie Martha's slumped shoulders.

'There now, girl,' he said, clearing his throat uncomfortably. 'Don't take on. There is no great harm done, is it? We will get the girl home now. A fright she has had. Perhaps the boy did mean no harm.' His voice trailed away as a tremor passed through her body. Then with an effort she drew her shoulders back and rose with painful dignity.

'Aye,' she said quietly. 'Best get her home, Will.' She watched as Elinor and Davy went out. 'I am sorry for what has happened, indeed. It is hard for me to believe – well, you know. Ifan is so gentle, so soft indeed. He does love all God's creatures. He has never hurt a fly before. I don't understand,' she ended with a hopeless gesture.

Owen slid from his seat in the corner and came to stand by Dada, who was tugging at his moustache, his blue eyes clouded. The boy looked up at each face in turn with an anxious frown.

'But I saw Auntie Elinor at the gate. She was – her dress was –.' He stopped short, startled by a violent sound from Luke, whose threatening look took the wind out of his sails.

'*Diawl*!' said Dada, putting a restraining hand on Owen's shoulder. 'I forgot about this little rabbit with the big ears. Hush now, boy. Not for you to talk now, is it? Come you, we must go. Say your thanks to Auntie Martha now, and let us get off home.'

Owen dropped his eyes, chastened by Luke's dark look and Dada's hard grip on his shoulder.

'But I didn't get my tea,' he ventured in a small voice.

Dada grunted, embarrassed.

'Next time, Owen *bach*.' And Auntie Martha smiled down at him, her eyes very sad.

When they had gone Martha lowered herself heavily into the old wooden armchair and sat in silence, staring into the fire. Luke watched her for a while, chewing his full bottom lip, a black frown on his face. When at last she got up wearily and went toward the back kitchen he barred her way, his body tense.

'I am going tomorrow morning. I will ride to Berriew and fetch Dr Thomas. He will see to it. Don't you see?' he burst out as she put up a silencing hand. 'It is better this way. You will never be sure now. Better for him, better for all.'

'Better for you, isn't it, boy?' Her voice was a painful whisper.

'For God's sake!' he cried harshly, putting out a hand, but she moved aside with a look which made him drop his hand and ball his fists. As she continued through the door his face hardened and his mouth was sullen.

'In the morning,' he said deliberately.

He saw her wince but she did not reply and he turned away with an impatient mutter and went to stand at the window to stare out with brooding eyes.

Martha lay in bed, staring into the darkness, her hands clasped above the white honeycomb quilt. Her mind went back over the years, images coming and going. From time to time she shifted her body restlessly and a deep sigh escaped her. The old clock on the chest of drawers ticked steadily and her eyes felt hot and dry. Thoughts chased each other wearily through her tired mind and eventually she raised herself on her elbow and fumbled for the matches on the small bedside table with its wicker top and bamboo legs. She struck a match and lit the candle which was stuck in an old blue enamelled candlestick. She peered at the clock and saw that the hands pointed to almost half past three. A sudden feeling of panic gripped her. She flung back the covers and swung her feet to the ground. She sat on the edge of the bed irresolutely for a moment in the flickering light of the candle. Then she rose, picked up the candlestick and crossed the room, her tall figure in a long white flannel nightdress throwing a gaunt shadow across the wall. She let herself silently out of the door and onto the landing, and crossed to the door of Ifan's room. Softly she lifted the latch and eased the door open. Raising the candle above her head, she stood in the doorway, resting her shoulder against the doorpost. The flickering yellow light fell on the narrow iron bed where Ifan lay on his back, his big head propped on a fat white pillow, his arms resting above the covers, palms upwards. His breathing was soft and regular and his wide, ugly face was peaceful, pale eyelashes resting above the prominent cheek-bones on which greying stubble glistened to silver in the candlelight. She stood for a long time, silent and immobile in the doorway, her sad dark eyes resting on the figure of her firstborn, unconscious of the cold linoleum under her flat bare feet or the drops of hot candlegrease which fell on to the hand which held the candlestick.

At long last the candle guttered and with a soft flutter the flame died. She stirred and her eyes went to the window where a faint grey light was creeping in. She gave a long, deep sigh and with a last look at the man who lay in untroubled sleep, she turned and closed the door gently behind her. Back in her own room she began to dress in the first faint light of the morning. She combed her greying hair and pinned it up carefully. She paused and stared at the shadowy reflection in the mirror curiously, then she straightened her shoulders with an effort and went quickly down the stairs.

She lit the fire, her movements deliberate, and when the flames were licking up the chimney, filled the big kettle from

244

the clean water bucket in the back kitchen and hung it on the hook above the crackling wood. Then she quietly let herself out of the back door and quickly crossed the yard and entered the field. The dawn sky was pearly and the air clear and sweet. The birds in the trees and hedges were singing their dawn chorus and overhead a pee-wit hovered, his two-note song faint and poignant against the morning sky. Her hurrying feet carried her swiftly through the dew-beaded grass towards the wicket gate, down the steep path and along the bank of the stream. She stopped where the ground was soft and marshy under her feet, beneath the spreading leafy branches of an old alder. She hesitated for a moment then knelt and began to gather long spikes of blue blossoms, their flowers shaped like a monk's hood. The stems were tough and strong and she tore them out of the soft ground by the roots. When she had a thick bunch of them she straightened, weariness flooding her body and swayed for a moment. Then steadying herself with a hand on the gnarled trunk of the alder, she turned and retraced her steps, mounting the steep path with an effort.

Back at the house she let herself in again silently and pouring water into an enamel bowl which stood on the sturdy wooden trestle in the back kitchen, carefully washed the earth from the roots of the monkshood, the deadly poisonous aconite, saving half a dozen plants, which she carefully put aside. Then she crushed the plants into a large saucepan and carrying it through to the fire, poured the now boiling water from the kettle over the tangled mass of roots, stems, leaves and purple-blue flowers. She set the saucepan on the trivet over the glowing wood of the fire and after watching it bubble for a while, she fetched a big white jug and set it down on the table in readiness for the brew. She watched again, her eyes going impatiently from the bubbling saucepan to the clock on the mantelpiece.

The hands pointed to quarter to six when she lifted the saucepan off the trivet and using an old colander, strained the dark liquid into the jug. It came half-way up the jug, a steaming, dirty-coloured brew. For a brief moment she stared down into the jug and a shiver passed through her. Then she took a deep breath and carried the jug through to the scullery where she set it at the back of the high shelf. She tipped the residue from the colander onto the back of the fire, where it

245

sizzled damply. Covering it with a piece of wood from a pile drying in the hearth, she then scrubbed the colander and the saucepan with the remains of the boiling water in the kettle and put them away. The remaining small bunch of the monkshood she thrust out of sight behind a flour bin in the corner of the back kitchen. She looked around her carefully, refilled the kettle and set it back on its hook and after laying the table for breakfast, went to call her two sons.

They ate their breakfast in silence, Martha's eyes bent on her plate and Luke glancing across at her from time to time, a frown drawing his heavy dark brows together. Ifan spooned porridge into his large mouth happily, pale blue eyes serene and unclouded. Eventually Luke rose and pushed back his chair. He looked down at Martha's bent, greying head.

'I am going to saddle up Satan and go to Berriew now.' His voice was flat and he waited for her answer.

She raised her eyes and looked at him steadily.

'You have made up your mind, then, boy?'

He gave an impatient nod and turned to go out.

'I should be back in a couple of hours,' he said over his shoulder. 'I will be bringing Dr Thomas and whoever else he says is needed.'

He caught Ifan's innocent gaze and looked away quickly.

Martha looked across at Ifan, who set his spoon down in his bowl and grinned across at her. Her throat worked for a moment and then she rose and squared her shoulders.

'Go you, then,' she said to Luke. 'I cannot stop you.' She paused and glanced again at Ifan, her eyes full of a tearless grief. 'Maybe it is all for the best, at that. I will not always be here to look to him.'

She began to clear the table as Luke, with a grim expression, went out through the door.

Martha carried the breakfast things out into the back kitchen and setting them in the enamel bowl, watched through the window until she saw Luke, mounted on Satan, ride off with a clatter of hooves on the hard dry earth of the yard. She took a deep breath, lifted the jug down from the shelf and filled a large mug with the cloudy liquid. Then she carried it carefully into the kitchen and set it before Ifan. He raised his large head and looked enquiringly at her.

'Drink, good boy,' she said hoarsely and nodded at the mug.

He picked it up obediently and gulped half of it down, his Adam's apple moving in his thick throat as he swallowed convulsively. Then his face twisted into a grimace and he set the mug down, shaking his head. Martha picked it up again and pressed it back into his hand.

'Come you, good boy, finish it off,' she urged. 'Drink, Ifan. Medicine it is. Drink it for me, is it?'

He frowned down at the mug in his hand, then as she urged his large hand towards his mouth, swallowed the rest down quickly, a shudder passing through his bony frame. Martha refilled the mug with the remainder from the jug and again urged him to drink. Again he swallowed obediently, making a face, his pale eyes questioning her over the rim of the mug. When the last drop was gone and he had wiped his wide mouth with the back of his hand, she fetched the bunch of blue flowers from their hiding place and took his arm.

'Come, my beauty,' she said, smiling gently. 'We will go for a walk down to the stream.'

She led him across the yard and through the field, matching her step to his loping stride. Halfway across the field he stopped and watched in wonder, screwing his pale eyes against the sun, as a wild goose flew against the morning sky. He gazed after it with a joyful smile, then he gave a grunt and the smile died as he clutched his stomach. His blue eyes clouded and he frowned. Martha drew in a painful breath but the spasm passed and his face cleared. With encouraging murmurs she urged him on through the wicket and pushing him gently before her, descended the path, clutching the blue flowered plants in a hand now damp with cold sweat. She drew him along to the spot where she had picked the monkshood and he leaned heavily against the rough bark of the alder as another, more violent spasm shook his body. He sank down on to the grass, a grey pallor spreading over his wide face, clutching his stomach with both hands, beads of clammy sweat on his high, domed forehead.

Martha watched, her body rigid, and anguish twisting her face as spasm after spasm shook him and he groaned, turning agonized, pleading eyes up to her.

'Oh, God forgive me,' she whispered, tears streaming down her cheeks. 'But this is better, my son. God help us.'

She knelt beside him and with the hem of her white apron

247

gently wiped the cold sweat off his forehead. He reached up and clutched her hand convulsively and as a great shudder passed through his big frame, she pressed his shoulders back against the soft mossy bank and cradled his head against her breast, her tears falling onto the sparse greying locks which barely covered his pale scalp.

At last his body relaxed and his pale lids closed over his bewildered blue eyes. She laid his head gently down on the moss and pressed his fingers round the stalks of the blue flowers. As she laid his hand across his breast his eyelids fluttered open and his hazy eyes looked at her then down to the blue flowers in his hand. A faint smile came and went on his colourless lips and a guttural whisper came painfully from his throat.

She bent closer to lay her lips against his forehead and caught the words as they died on a breath.

'Pretty. Like bird.'

Ifan sighed and his grasp on the blue flowers loosened. They spilled across his chest as the sweet notes of a blackbird poured out from the top of the alder tree and Martha gently and lovingly closed the pale lids over blue eyes which would see no more birds in this world.

She sat for a long time beside him, staring out across the stream which ran, shining in the morning sun, through the banks of willowherb and rushes. The tears had dried on cheeks which were suddenly old and tired. At last she leant down with a deep sigh and kissed her son once more on his forehead. Then she dragged herself painfully to her feet and made her way up the steep path and across the field to the house. Once inside she looked round vaguely for a moment then she squared her shoulders with an effort, washed her face and began on the breakfast dishes, paying careful attention to the big mug and the white jug, washing away their deadly dregs.

When Luke returned later in the morning with Dr Thomas and two strange men she was sitting at the kitchen table, staring through the open window. She stood up and faced them calmly. When they eventually enquired where Ifan was, she smiled.

'By the stream, no doubt,' she answered softly. 'Where he always is. He does like to sit by the stream.'

'Will you fetch him in, Luke,' said old Dr Thomas and came to lay a comforting arm across Martha's shoulders.

'Aye,' said Martha, looking across at Luke with a strange, almost pitying expression. 'Go you and fetch him, Luke my son. There's a good boy.'

17

Revelations and Moving Pictures

Davy sat at the table in Mama's kitchen and sipped hot strong tea. The long summer holidays were coming to an end and he would soon be back at hammering knowledge into the heads of his charges, with varying degrees of success. The long dry spell looked like breaking this morning and outside the window he could see clouds scudding across the sky in a freshening breeze.

Mama was rescuing Esther from the coal bucket where she had been investigating the interesting black lumps. With a smutty face wreathed in smiles and plump blackened hands held aloft, she was being led by a tutting Mama in search of the flannel. Mama's scolding voice reached Davy from the back kitchen.

'You limb of Satan, you! Can't turn my back for a minute. You will wear me out yet, girl. You are looking like a collier from South Wales. There now, look at your pinafore. Clean on this morning too. Well, it will have to do till dinner with you.'

She reappeared and sat Esther in her high chair, a buttered crust of bread in the newly washed pink hands. Esther attacked the crust with small white teeth and her blue eyes beamed at Davy over a round buttery nose.

'I will just sit for a minute before I do the potatoes,' said Mama with a sigh, sinking onto a chair opposite Davy and pouring herself a cup of tea. 'She does wear on me a bit. Into everything now, she is. I am glad when Meg does get home and take her off my hands. The girl does have more patience than me.'

'Meggie is a grand girl,' agreed Davy, grinning back at Esther.

'Luke called yesterday,' said Mama between sips. 'Into town

to pay the old funeral bill he was. Martha do like things straight. Always been the same.'

'How is Auntie Martha? Did he say?'

'Luke does not say much at the best of times,' sniffed Mama. 'A bit hang-dog he does look, just now. He did say Martha was all right, whatever that may mean. Martha will bear what she has got to bear. But she did look a lot older at the funeral. She did set great store by that Ifan, and indeed I did like him, better than Luke myself, for all his simple ways. I did never see any harm in him.'

Davy shifted uncomfortably but he said nothing.

'I suppose it was the way of it,' said Mama reflectively. 'For him to go like that. Eating them old poisonous things. And Luke gone off for the man to put him away. As if he knew, somehow. You do not think − ?' Mama looked a question mark.

'It was an accident,' said Davy sharply. 'They said at the inquest. Ifan was always eating things off the hedges, leaves and berries and such-like. Death by misadventure, they said.'

'Aye,' said Mama, very thoughtful. 'Some old long word. But it do seem very odd to me. Like he knew, you know? It would have been very bad on Ifan if they had locked him up. Finished him, it would. He was always out roaming. Let to go free.'

Davy frowned.

'Let us not talk about it any more, Mama.'

'Aye, you are right boy. No good to talk now. What's done is done and can't be undone. Maybe it is all for the best. What would have become of the poor soul when Martha went I do not know. That Luke − well, he had no time for Ifan.' She sighed and finished her tea then gathered up the cups to carry into the back kitchen. In the doorway she collided with Owen who had been standing silent in the shadow.

'Nemma God, boy! What are you doing standing there. Out of my way now. I must get on.'

Owen came forward and stood at the table, his dark eyes fixed on Davy's face.

'Uncle Davy?' he said tentatively.

Davy came out of a dark revery with an effort.

'Hello, Owen.' His voice was heavy.

'Uncle Davy,' Owen began again. 'Ifan was good, wasn't

251

he?'

'Aye, Owen, Ifan was good.' A flicker of pain crossed Davy's face.

'Then why were they saying things about him hurting Auntie Elinor?'

'Hush now, boy,' said Davy roughly. 'You do not understand.'

'Ifan was good,' said Owen, his face obstinate. 'Ifan didn't hurt people. He was kind. He didn't tear her dress and – and – what they said.' His face was flushed but he kept his eyes steady on Davy's forbidding face. 'I saw Auntie Elinor. By the wicket. Her dress was torn and her hair was hanging down. Before ever she went down the path. I saw her. She was running and she was out of breath.'

Davy stared at the boy, frowning.

'Look, Owen. You do not know what you are talking about. Leave it, it is not your business.'

Owen's eyes filled with tears and he grasped the edge of the table.

'I don't care!' he choked. 'Ifan didn't do it. I know. I saw her by the wicket. And now Ifan is dead. And I loved Ifan.' The tears rained down his cheeks and he hung onto the table, his small shoulders shaking.

Dark thoughts chased round in Davy's mind as he stared at the sobbing boy. Mama came in with a saucepan of potatoes which she set above the fire on a trivet. She wiped her hands on her apron and frowned.

'Now what!' she said, sharply. 'What have you been doing to make him cry like that, boy?'

'Nothing,' replied Davy absently, his eyes still on Owen.

'Funny nothing!' Mama's voice was tart. 'Stop your row now, boy, and go out to play. Good job when it's time for school with you. These old holidays is too long. Off you go now. I will shout you when your dinner is ready.'

Owen went out slowly, his head down and sniffing hard.

'I don't know what is with the boy,' said Mama, impatient. 'Moping like an old hen with wet tail feathers he has been.'

Davy rose and put his cap on.

'I must go back up home,' he said, a tired slump to his shoulders. 'Dinner will be ready soon. Did I tell you Elinor is going to London to stop with her Auntie Lou for a couple of

252

weeks? She needs a change, I suppose. She is going tomorrow morning on the train.'

'Hm,' Mama grunted. 'Trouble with that girl she has not got enough to do. With that woman to do all the housework and no small ones round her.'

Davy turned away, hurt in his face, and Mama was frowning as the door closed behind him.

That afternoon the first rain for weeks fell lightly on the parched earth. The air was cooler and Davy in his study, as Mrs Buxton primly called the small room where he worked, was staring at a book open before him, without taking in any of the words on the pages. From time to time he raised heavy eyes and watched as raindrops trickled down the window pane. He slumped over the table, a strange emotionless lassitude pervading his body and mind.

Elinor was upstairs, packing two large suitcases in readiness for her departure in the morning. When she had told Davy she wanted to go to London for a while he had agreed, almost with a feeling of relief. Since the day at Manafon she had been more withdrawn than ever, spending most of her time sitting at the window, staring out, her face pale and expressionless. Davy escaped from the house as often as he could, helping Dada in the garden, or calling down at Pool Road to take Owen and Esther by the hand, up into the Rectory field.

This afternoon his confused mind kept returning to what Owen had said. When his thoughts took a certain turn he shied away from them but all the time a question was building up in him which he knew would have to be answered. At length he got up and walked restlessly round the room, pausing from time to time to gaze unseeingly out at the soft rain which fell on the little garden, washing the dusty leaves of the laurel tree and gently shaking the flowers in the border. The window was open a few inches at the bottom and the cooling air was fresh with the scent of newly-washed earth and the orangey tang from the white blossoms of a nearby philadelphus which shed a few damp petals onto the rain-darkened soil. His head ached and he pinched the bridge of his thin straight nose and blinked wearily. Then he stopped at the table and placing both hands on the edge, hung above it, staring down at the dark oak top. Straightening at last, he turned on his heel and left the room.

He mounted the stairs and knocked at Elinor's door. Her

clear sharp voice called him in and he saw her standing there, clad in white chemise, shapely legs encased in grey rayon stockings held up above the knee by pale blue garters encircled with tiny pink rosebuds. She was struggling with the lacing of her boned corselette, her face flushed with the effort, her dark curls tumbled about her shoulders.

Davy closed the door behind him and remained standing with his hand on the knob, staring at her. His mind registered her desirability but his senses remained totally untouched. He saw the creamy swell of her bosom above the chemise as she bent to tug at the laces of her stays and the glimpse of rounded white thigh between the top of the grey stockings and the pale blue broderie anglaise edging to the legs of her cotton knickers and was mildly surprised to find his pulse steady and his feelings amounting to indifference. He watched her almost dispassionately for a moment and she raised her flushed face and stared back at him between a curtain of glossy dark hair.

'Well, don't stand there,' she said sharply. 'As long as you're here, help me with these laces.'

He crossed the room and as she straightened up, her arms falling loosely at her sides, he took the laces in steady hands and laced her up. His face was expressionless and even when his fingers came into contact with warm flesh, there was no answering stir within his body. The scent of her reached him and was lost and he stepped back when he was finished and stood watching as she slipped into a petticoat. When she had smoothed it over her hips and adjusted the shoulder straps she paused, frowning a little under his silent gaze.

'Well? What did you want?'

'Just to get something straight.' His dark eyes were intent on her face and, still frowning, she reached for a dove-grey dress which was laid out across the bed.

'Get what straight?' Her fingers were busy undoing the buttons on the bodice of the dress. Davy watched, an association of ideas darkening his mind.

'That day at Manafon,' he said steadily. 'It wasn't Ifan, was it?'

Her body went very still and as she bent her head over the dress he was unable to see her face for the hair which fell on each side of it.

'Did Ifan really touch you at all?'

A small shudder passed through her and her head remained bent but she made no reply.

'Elinor,' he said deliberately. 'I want an answer.'

She straightened up then but still kept her face averted.

'Yes, he did touch me. He frightened me. He was horrible. He was like an animal.' Her voice faltered then became high-pitched. 'He touched my face! He came right close to me and touched my face! I was frightened. I didn't know what he'd do. He was just grinning, it was horrible, I tell you.'

Davy stepped forward and grasped her shoulders, pulling her round to face him. The colour in her face deepened but she stared up at him defiantly. His grip tightened.

'And that was all he did, wasn't it,' he insisted grimly. 'Wasn't it? He touched you on the face. He wasn't rough with you? He didn't pull your dress open? It wasn't Ifan, was it?'

She twisted violently out of his hands and stumbled backwards, fetching up against the marble-topped washstand.

'Being touched by that – that creature, was enough, wasn't it?' She stared back at him sullenly. 'He frightened me, I tell you. I'm afraid of people like that. He was so – so big and so horrible.'

A sudden picture of the gentle, unworldly Ifan came into Davy's mind and a painful lump came to his throat.

'Who was it, then?' His voice was bitter. 'Luke?'

Her flush deepened betrayingly.

'I only went to see the horses. Into the stable. That lout! Ugh!'

She turned away and fiddled nervously with the lid of the soap dish on the washstand. Davy stood silent, waiting, his heart like a stone. She turned with an impatient sound and glared at him.

'What does it matter now? Whichever one of those ignorant beasts did it. I don't ever want to go to that horrible place again. To be pawed by those animals.'

She picked up the grey dress and slipped it over her head. Her fingers were shaking as she fastened the bodice up to the high mandarin collar and then did up the buttons on the wrists of the leg o'mutton sleeves. Davy stood in silence as she went over to the dressing table and sitting down on the stool, picked up a hair brush and began to brush and pin up her hair.

At last he passed a weary hand over his face, his eyes bleak.

'The unforgivable thing,' he said coldly, 'is that you let us think it was Ifan. And now he's dead.'

She swung round on the stool, fist clenched tight on the hairbrush, blue eyes blazing.

'You're not trying to blame me for that?' she cried. 'That had nothing to do with me!'

He stared at her as though seeing her for the first time and she had to turn away under the intensity of his gaze.

'I wonder,' he said in a low voice and turned to leave the room, by-passing the two suitcases which stood in his path. He paused at the door and looked back at her.

'I wonder?'

After he had gone Elinor raised her eyes and stared at herself in the mirror for a long time. Then she dropped her head into her hands and wept bitterly.

Next morning Davy stood on the platform at Newtown station and watched the train pull out in a cloud of steam which enveloped the footbridge above the track and left a sulphurous taste in his mouth. Around him the porters called to each other and trucks rumbled along on iron wheels. Elinor did not come to the carriage window to look out and he stood still, gazing absently as the rear end of the train swayed out of sight round the bend. He gave a deep releasing sigh as some of the tension drained from his body. He left the platform and passed through the entrance room, with its booking office window now closed, his feet echoing hollow on the wooden floor. He descended the flight of stone steps slowly and stood in the road for a moment looking across at the squat red-brick buildings of the County School. A picture of Geraint came into his mind as he had been when they had come and gone through the wrought-iron gates together throughout their action-packed schooldays. Memories flooded back as he stood there, until he was recalled to the present by a shout which made him step back smartly onto the pavement to make way for the station cab. Old Reuben Owen was atop the driving seat, flourishing his whip above the patient little horse in the shafts, his little monkey face split in a brown-toothed grin.

'Aye-up, Davy boy. Thee't miles away. Nearly run thee down. Thee'st look as if thee'st lost a bob an' found a 'a'penny. Schoolmastering makin' thee brain soft, is it?'

'Thee shut thy trap, Reuben,' laughed Davy, dropping into the comical local dialect. 'Who dost thee think thee art? Lord

256

Davies of Llandinam?'

Reuben made a rude noise through pursed lips.

'Me ass to that owl bugger,' he shouted with a ribald chuckle. 'I'm a better man than 'im, any day. Giddup, Fan, you blue-assed fly,' and he flicked the whip to make the horse trot with a clatter over the pot-holed road.

As the small swaying vehicle passed Davy he saw the offended expressions on the prim faces of the two long-nosed elderly ladies sitting upright in the dim interior, and let out a convulsive chuckle. Cheered by the exchange he set off down the station road as a watery sun came out of a misty morning sky.

Reluctant to return to Plas Gwyn, empty now except for a gloomy and bereft Mrs Buxton, he continued up Kerry Road and turned down past the horse repository in the direction of Pilots Fields. The air was sweet as he paused on the plank bridge across the stream. A frog which had been sitting on a stone in the weak sunlight leaped with a startled plop into the water, scattering a small shoal of sticklebacks. Davy squinted up into the clearing sky as a few black specks high up crossed a shaft of sunlight.

> One for sorrow, two for joy,
> Three for a letter, four for a boy,
> Five for silver, six for gold,
> Seven for a secret, never to be told.

He counted seven specks and watched them out of sight.

'Never to be told,' he muttered. 'No. No good to tell now.'

'Talking to yourself, Davy Rees?' A low laugh behind him brought him round, startled. A pair of grey eyes looked up at him with amusement. 'You know what they say? First signs!'

'Aye, like hair on the palms of your hands,' he answered with a short embarrassed laugh. 'Where did you spring from, Nan?'

She held up a bunch of dark green leaves.

'Finding a bit of watercress for the Rector's lunch. He's having some cold meat today and he does like a bit of watercress with it. Plenty down there.' She pointed to a shady patch further down the stream where the water rippled beneath an overhanging willow. 'What are you doing down here,

257

anyway?'

'Oh, I've just been seeing Elinor off on the train to London. Going to stay with her Auntie Lou for a bit. I just felt like a walk.'

Nan was silent, her eyes fixed on the bunch of watercress.

'Well, she needed a change,' Davy said with an attempt at lightness. 'This old hot summer got her down a bit.'

'Hm,' she said, without looking up. 'Dare say.'

Her mouth tightened and she turned to go.

On an impulse Davy reached out and gently took hold of her arm, rounded under the cool yellow cotton sleeves of her dress.

'Stop a minute, Nan,' he pleaded. 'I haven't seen you for a while. Don't rush off.'

'I've got things to do,' she said, but she stopped and stood with bent head.

He took his hand from her arm and thrust both fists into his jacket pockets.

'Aye well. Dare say. Seems everybody but me's got something to do.'

'Oh, come on, old misery-guts,' she smiled. 'Stop feeling sorry for yourself. You'll have plenty to do soon when school opens and you're back to teaching them little arabs.'

He gave a wry laugh.

'Yes, I suppose I'm of some use.'

'Oh, Lord, we are down in the mouth this morning, aren't we.' Then she came closer and put her hand on his arm. 'What is it, Davy? Want to talk about it?'

He shrugged then shook his head.

'It's Elinor, isn't it?' she said, a bitter edge to her voice. She sensed his withdrawal and gave a short laugh. 'Don't worry. I don't want to poke my nose. It was a sorry day – oh well, none of my business.'

She began to pluck at a leaf of the watercress with tense fingers, her head bent.

'Funny, isn't it,' she went on in a low voice. 'Them two. Geraint and Elinor. I wonder sometimes where the Rector got them. Leastways, they don't take after him. There's something about them. I don't know how to say it but they're trouble, both of them. They get their own way no matter who they walk all over to get it.'

She looked up to see the closed look on Davy's face and gave a bitter little laugh.

'All right, all right, Davy Rees. No need to look like that. You're not the only one that's been hurt by them, God knows.'

'Geraint – ,' he began and stopped at the acid twist to her mouth.

'Oh yes, Geraint,' she said, her grey eyes bleak. 'Your big friend. The fine-feathered handsome soldier. Geraint!'

As he watched her face the old uncomfortable feeling was back in his stomach, remembered from the days of the boyhood friendship. He frowned, not wanting to go on.

'Geraint is all right,' he said defensively.

'Geraint is bad.' Her voice was flat. 'Geraint is bad inside. Like somebody said – "A goodly apple, rotten at the core." Well, that's Geraint. Rotten at the core. God help me, I should know,' she added in a painful whisper.

Davy stared at her.

'You?' he said hoarsely. 'You and Geraint?' Then remembered the scuffle in the hall at the Rectory one night.

She nodded.

'Oh aye. Me and Geraint.' Unconsciously she began to shred the leaves of the watercress with quick jerky movements. 'Me and Geraint. Laughable, isn't it, Davy Rees? Ha! Fine, handsome Geraint, taking advantage of his father's skivvy. Only I wasn't took advantage of. I went willing. Mazed, seems to me now, looking back.' She shook her head, her grey eyes dark with some painful memory. 'Aye, even when he hurt me and marked me and frightened me half out of me wits, I still went back for more, whenever he came home. He was like a magnet. I couldn't help myself. Like a sickness it was. Like some old fever. I hated him and loved him at the same time. I don't suppose you can grasp that, can you, Davy?' She looked up at him and his heart contracted at the pitiful expression in her eyes. He gave a weary sigh which came from the depths of his own private agony.

'I think I can,' he said sadly.

She dropped her eyes again and nodded.

'Aye. I dare say you can. Well, I'm over it now, thank God. The old fever has gone. There's nothing left. I belong to myself again. I can say "no" now and it don't hurt. It's like waking up after a bad dream.' She laughed harshly. 'You feel a bit shaky and it sticks in your mind, but it's daylight again, see. And nothing's as bad as the dream.'

She stared vaguely at the bare stalks of the watercress in her hand and Davy felt pity and another uncertain emotion well up inside him.

'Poor Nan,' he said softly and reached out to her.

The next moment her lonely figure was in his arms and she was weeping silently against his shoulder, the watercress stalks on the ground at their feet. He held her close against the rough cloth of his jacket and patted her gently on the back, his dark eyes gazing sadly over her head with its crown of coarse, corn-coloured hair. They stood for a long time, each drawing comfort from the contact until at last her weeping ceased and she drew away, sniffing, and raised the bottom of her pinafore to dry her eyes.

'I'm a fool, Davy Rees.' Her voice was muffled by the pinafore.

He looked down on her bent head and smiled.

'We are both fools, Nan Mostyn,' he said with gentle mockery. 'But you're cured. And I think maybe I am on the right road as well.'

She dropped the hem of the pinafore and her grey eyes, misted after the tears, held a wry expression.

'Aye, but there is hurt in the cure too,' she said with a sigh. 'A gap in things and which way next.'

He shrugged.

'God knows, I can't look forward yet. But you are free anyway, Nan. Free to make your own life. To get away if you want. Start fresh.'

'Start fresh,' she repeated, musingly. 'Aye, there's nothing binding me now. Nobody to answer to.' She gave her shoulders an impatient shake and blinked rapidly. She sniffed and raising the hem of the pinafore, rubbed her nose with it vigorously. Then she drew back her shoulders and laughed aloud.

'Nemma God, Davy Rees! We're a pair of loonies. Here's me with no watercress for the old man, nothing but a bunch of old stalks! I'd better get and pick some more. It'll be dinner time soon and me maudlin here like a hen with the gapes. Out of my way, good boy.'

He joined in her laughter and stepped aside to let her pass. He watched as she skirted the stream on sturdy legs, her yellow cotton dress a gay splash of colour in the sun, then she crouched in the shadow to gather the watercress gleaming darkly at the edge of the stream. She didn't look up again as he called a goodbye and he turned and made his way back across the mossy planks of the bridge and with head bent walked slowly homewards.

In the afternoon he wandered down to the Rectory garden to give Dada a hand to lift the shallots. He found release in the physical effort of pulling at the dry tops with their tawny globes of small onions, held firm in the earth by white stringy roots. They laid them out to dry off in the sun alongside the empty bed, the damp topsoil pulled up to show dry earth beneath, where yesterday's light rain had failed to penetrate.

'That drop of rain yesterday did not do much good,' grunted Dada. 'A good soaking we do want. I will spread a bit of muck on here tomorrow,' he went on, looking at the empty bed reflectively. 'Do it good.'

Davy massaged his aching back while Dada cocked a wry blue eye in his direction.

'You are not used to hard work boy, is it?'

Davy laughed.

'Makes a change anyway. Do me good.'

'Aye, too much old book learning you do have. It is not good for a man, too much. I did not have any and took no harm from lack of it. This is what is good,' and he bent down and took up a handful of dark earth, letting it trickle through his stubby fingers. 'You can dig down into this stuff, boy, and bury your troubles in it.'

'Then I would need to dig deep,' said Davy, his dark eyes bitter.

Dada straightened up and rubbed his hands on the seat of his moleskin trousers.

'A man makes his own troubles, mostly. Some is put on him, no doubt, but most times he can see it coming.'

Davy drew in a deep breath.

'You are right, Dada, no doubt. And some of us sit up and beg for it,' he added with a short laugh. 'Specially when we are blinded by other things.'

Dada grunted and began to gather up his garden tools. He turned and looked up beyond the high garden wall, where the grey slate roof of Plas Gwyn showed from the other side of the road.

261

'That old place is empty for you now, boy. Come you and have tea with your Mama and us. Do you good. Meggie and Llew will be home in a bit. Some old talk will be better than you brooding by yourself. And your Mama will have one more chick to cluck over. She does like that.'

'Right you, Dada,' said Davy. 'I will just go to tell Mrs Buxton and I will come on home.'

'Good boy,' Dada nodded and stumped off in the direction of the toolshed, pom-poming a tune through his moustache.

When Davy arrived at No 46 Mama was laying for tea and the big black kettle was singing above a glowing fire. Esther greeted him with a joyous grin as she toddled across the kitchen to him on her fat little legs. He swung her up to his shoulder and tickled her in her plump ribs, making her wriggle and squeal with mirth. Owen was seated on the old horsehair sofa under the window, with its crocheted antimacassar and fat puce-coloured cushions. He had his head in a book, but looked up at Davy and smiled shyly. His dark eyes searched Davy's face anxiously but he relaxed when Davy grinned at him and setting Esther down, came to sit beside him on the sofa.

'What's that you're reading, Owen boy?' he asked, rumpling the boy's hair.

Owen ducked away and showed him the front cover of the book.

'Owen Glyndwr, eh?' Davy exclaimed, eyes wide. 'Oh, deep stuff you are into now, lad. Your namesake too, isn't it?'

'He was a Welsh prince!' explained Owen, eyes shining. 'He did fight the English. Sometimes he beat them, too!'

'Indeed, yes,' Davy nodded. 'A great old warrior he was. But he lost in the end.'

'I have not come to that.' Owen frowned and shut the book.

'Never mind, Owen.' Davy put his arm round the boy's shoulder. 'Those must have been grand times indeed.'

'I wish I was living then,' said Owen fervently. 'I would have been one of Glyndwr's men and fought for him.'

Mama snorted as she rattled cups into their saucers.

'That boy's head is full of old tales and nonsense. He is never out of an old book. He is as bad as you, Davy.' But her voice had an edge of pride in it as she ordered Owen out to the back kitchen to wash before tea. 'Another scholar, he will be.' She nodded as she set down the big jug of milk.

'Looks like it.' Davy smiled and settled himself comfortably against the puce cushions, stretching his legs out, feeling a healing warmth in the homely atmosphere of the kitchen. Plas Gwyn and his life with Elinor seemed remote as he watched contentedly while Mama bustled in and out, side-stepping Esther as the small plump figure staggered around in her path.

He craned his neck to look out of the window as Dada's hobnailed boots were heard, stumping over the cobbles of the back yard, his sturdy old body erect and a reedy whistle accompanying his entry through the back door. Mama came in to wet the tea in the big teapot and Dada followed shortly after, cheeks pink from his wash, his hand on Owen's head, which had damp spikes of hair standing erect above his ears. They had no sooner seated themselves than Llew arrived, followed shortly by Meg, her disfigured face serene and smiling. The children made room for her to sit between them on the bench and pressed against her as she popped morsels into Esther's mouth, open like a bird's, and encouraged Owen to eat up his crusts to make his hair curl.

Talk flowed between gulps of hot tea and mouthfuls of fresh sweet bread, spread with salty butter and gooseberry jam or folded over thick chunks of red cheese. Llew was relaxed and cheerful, teasing the children and chaffing with Dada.

'There are pictures tonight at the Victoria Hall,' he announced. 'I think I will go. Why not come, our Davy? Do you good. Join the rabble and watch *Secrets of the Old Manor*.'

Davy laughed.

'Aye, all right. I'll come with you, Llew. It will be a bit of a laugh, anyway.'

'I have never been to see this old magic lantern thing,' said Dada, blue eyes interested.

'Not magic lantern now, Dada,' grinned Llew. 'Moving pictures it is.'

'Moving pictures!' Dada's eyes were wide. 'What will they think of next, indeed.'

'How about coming with us now, Dada?' said Llew with a straight face. 'Experience for you it will be.'

'*Diawl*! I am too old for these new-fangled things.' Dada shook his head but his eyes slid speculatively in Mama's direction.

She sniffed and blew on her tea which she held in cupped

hands.

'Go you if you want to be an old fool.' She raised her eyes to the ceiling and shook her head. 'You are ripe for any old daftness. But good riddance, I say. Meg and me will have some peace to see to these small ones.'

Dada banged his fist on the table.

'Dammo, boys, I will come! Just this once, mark you. For to see, like.'

Mama smothered a laugh and her eyes twinkled across at Meg who gave an answering wink.

The three of them arrived at the Victoria Hall on time, where they were sold tickets by a plump middle-aged lady with yellow hair piled up in rolls and bangs on top of her head and two improbable rosy circles on her cheeks. She gave them their change with a girlish laugh which brought Dada's eyebrows up.

'Mutton dressed as lamb!' he muttered and Llew hastily took his arm and hurried him round the corner to the swing doors which led into the hall, where a small dapper man in a dark suit and such a high starched collar that he seemed unable to bend his head, held the tickets up to eye level to tear them in half. Dada watched this operation with interest.

'What good us buy these old tickets if this man here is going to tear them up?' he enquired of Davy in a stage whisper.

The small man peered at Dada suspiciously as he handed Llew three half tickets but he preceded them through the doors with a flourish. Dada hesitated inside the hall and stepped back on Davy's foot.

'*Diawl*! There is not much light in here!' he exclaimed. 'I do not see how we are going to see any pictures without a light.'

Davy, patient despite a sore toe, whispered reassuringly in his ear and pushed him after Llew and the little man. Images were beginning to flicker up on the screen as they were shown into their seats and Dada remained standing for a moment, fascinated, until irate cries from behind made Llew and Davy take an arm each and pull him down into his seat. There he sat, upright on the edge, his hands grasping the back of the seat in front of him and gazed hypnotized at the jerky movements of the characters of a short comedy film, who appeared to be running about frenetically, tumbling over each other and dodging falling masonry from a high building in an advanced

264

state of decay. Dada obviously saw nothing funny in this and wore a frown of consternation throughout, muttering scornful observations through his moustache. When the film finished the lights went up for a moment, bathing the auditorium in a sickly yellow glow.

Dada sat back and looked from one to the other of them in bewilderment.

'And that is the moving pictures, is it?' he asked Llew. 'I do not think much of it boy! Very clever, no doubt, but we have paid good money to watch some old fools running about like chickens with their heads off. Come you then, boys,' beginning to rise, 'let us get back home.'

On that the lights died again slowly, and they were in the dark once more.

'*Diawl!*' said Dada. 'What now?'

'Sit, Dada,' hissed Llew. 'There is more to come.'

Dada muttered under his breath but he sank back into his seat and remained silent as the title of the main picture flashed up on the screen. Suddenly a dramatic crash of chords from a piano situated down at the front below the stage made Dada jump. The piano player launched into a programme of music which changed to suit the action on the screen, sinister trills accompanying rather dim views of an old manor house surrounded by swaying trees. As the wind in the trees whipped up into a full scale storm the music rose to a frenzy and the shadowy figure of a woman at the keyboard raged up and down the keys, obviously thoroughly enjoying herself.

'Terrible weather they are having there,' observed Dada with a shake of his head.

The music softened to sentiment as the camera moved inside the house and followed after an ethereal looking young lady in a white dress, with haunted eyes and the back of her right hand apparently glued to her forehead.

'*Duw*,' said Dada in a loud whisper, very concerned, 'What is with that poor girl? She does not look well at all.'

He was sternly shushed from behind and subsided, blowing through his moustache, his eyes glued to the screen. Next the young lady was seen in the kitchen, preparing a tray, having with difficulty removed her hand from her forehead. She started back dramatically as a bell on the wall was seen to wag back and fore and the piano made tinkling noises. Then she

265

was seen carrying the tray into a vast and shadowy hall, where the figure of an evil-looking old man in evening dress sat at the top of a long table, flickering firelight showing white hair and goatee beard and a thin face almost as white, with black sunken eye sockets. Claw-like hands lifted coins from a huge black box on the table and counted them into piles while shoulders moved in a soundless evil chuckle. The young lady with the haunted eyes backed away and watched fearfully from the shadows, the back of her hand glued on to her forehead again.

Thereafter the piano playing rose and fell to accompany the flickering and confused narrative. A tall hero with luxuriant blond moustaches visited in secret from time to time and held hands with the haunted young lady, wearing an agonized expression in calf-like eyes. He was obviously forbidden the house. But not so a surly-looking, dark-visaged character who bowled up in a smart black carriage. From the dramatic sub-titles it became apparent that the ethereal girl was to be married off to the obviously-rich surly character by her miser father and was being urged by the blond lover to flee with him before this fate worse than death.

Dada watched the flickering tale unfold with dark mutterings at the machinations of the evil father and a great deal of gratuitous advice to the lovers, who hovered in dark corners, the young lady swaying about most alarmingly while her pale-faced swain entreated her to fly, with much arm-waving and exclamation marks at the end of the subtitles. This went on for so long that Dada lost patience with them.

'My good woman, will you make up your mind!' he cried in exasperation, leaning forward and drumming impatient fingers on the back of the seat in front of him.

The occupant of that seat, a thin woman, turned her head, her rather long nose inches from Dada's face as he peered tensely over her shoulder.

'Hush!' she hissed, sternly.

Dada drew back, startled.

'Hush, is it?' he said hotly, recovering himself and wagging an admonitory finger at the long nose. 'Somebody has got to tell her or she will go on all night, and that young chap will lose patience. He seems a tidy enough lad and I do think myself he could do better, indeed. Consumptive she looks to me.'

'Will you be quiet!' spluttered the long-nosed woman and Dada subsided back into his seat, wiping a fleck of her saliva from his cheek and muttering obstinately. Llew, shaking with silent laughter put a restraining hand on his arm.

While this exchange was going on the question on the flickering screen was resolved and the girl agreed to meet her lover outside the house that night. However, they were very obviously overheard by the old man, lurking behind a curtain, which brought a further excited comment from Dada.

'Where are their eyes!' he asked Llew, throwing up his hands in amazement, only to be shushed again. He sank back, breathing hard through his bristling moustache and watched in silence as the girl let herself out into the black and stormy night, still clad only in the white dress.

'She'll catch her death!' he muttered obstinately.

Suddenly he sat forward again, tense and quivering. The hero was creeping through the shrubbery towards her, while a sinister figure, revealed by a flash of lightning as his dark-visaged rival, stalked him from bush to bush with an upraised cudgel. The tension was too much for Dada. He leapt to his feet, waving his arms wildly and knocking the hat off the head of the long-nosed lady in front.

'Look out! Look out!' he cried. 'He's after you, man. Behind that bush!'

The long-suffering woman in the seat in front retrieved her hat from the floor and with hair awry stood up and set about Dada with hat and handbag. Astonished, he warded off the blows, while Davy and Llew dragged him back down on to his seat accompanied by catcalls and yells from around them. They kept him pinned down firmly in his seat through the final reels of the film, while good triumphed over evil, and it was a dazed and chastened Dada who finally tumbled out of the Victoria Hall into the fading light of a cool, sweet evening, his white hair on end and coat dishevelled.

He paused for a moment in the forecourt of the hall and looked around him then up at the clear sky with a puzzled frown. Then his blue eyes lightened and he gave a deep sigh.

'Cleared up nicely now,' he observed with relief and straightening his coat, set off cheerfully for home between his two slightly shaken sons.

18

Riddles and Tippit

October was almost at an end when Elinor returned from London. The weeks had passed quickly enough for Davy. Back to teaching in the daytime, he spent as little time as possible as Plas Gwyn, preferring the warm and welcoming atmosphere of 46 Pool Road, involved in political discussion with Llew, helping Owen with his lessons or playing with Esther. Mrs Buxton kept Plas Gwyn going but there was less for her to do these days. Davy's needs were few and he was rarely at home and without Elinor, the mainspring of her existence, she took to her rocking chair more and more. She was now ageing rapidly and her tired old eyes held a sadly reflective look. Two or three brief notes were all that Davy received from Elinor during her absence, each one telling him of her intention to stay a few more weeks, and these notes he had passed over to Mrs Buxton. She kept them behind the old marble clock on the mantelpiece in the kitchen and took them out every evening to read again and again during her lonely rocking. Davy was uncomfortably aware that the delay in Elinor's return brought him only a feeling of relief. When the final brief and cool note came announcing her return on the following Saturday, the last in October, Davy was forced to speculate on their future life together. He felt that he could look forward to nothing but the same strained atmosphere as before and it was with somewhat forced cheerfulness that he conveyed the news to the kitchen. The joy on the old woman's face made him feel guilty and he hurried off to school that morning with his mind full of confused thoughts.

When Saturday arrived he was on the station platform early, awaiting the London train. As this brought the second batch of mail in, the station was a bustle of rumbling trucks and porters at the ready. Mr John Ellis from the post office bowled up in his horse-drawn mail van and entered the station fussily, his postman's hat set square above his small, round face with its thick-lensed, steel-rimmed spectacles hiding watery little myopic eyes and its gingery mutton-chop whiskers bristling with self-importance. His dapper figure paraded up and down issuing orders in a high-pitched, squeaky voice to the porters, who took no notice of him at all, but cheerfully went about their business, chaffing with each other and with the handful of passengers waiting for the train to take them to destinations along the line to Aberystwyth.

Standing close to Davy was one of these passengers, an elderly and timid-looking figure of a countryman, his small bent form encased in his best Sunday black, his toecaps shining and a new-looking bowler hat resting on his whiskery ears. In his left hand he held a walking stick to which was attached a bundle tied about with black cloth. In his right he clutched his ticket from time to time, between dodging with startled sidesteps the trucks and porters which bore down on him. One of these porters suddenly stopped and looking more closely under the rim of the bowler, greeted the little man with friendly astonishment.

'Nemma God, Dick O'Rhosgoch! What art 'ee doin' 'ere? Never seen thee on a train before, mun!'

The little man peeped up at the porter and clutched his bundle and his ticket protectively to his hollow chest. Recognition dawned and with it relief.

'Twm the Pentre, is it?' he quavered. 'Well, indeed, I have not been on a train before. A bit moithered I am, see. I have got a ticket to go to Borth, isn't it. But where is the old train, then?'

'Be 'ere shortly, Dick,' grinned the porter, winking at Davy. 'What for are you off to Borth, then?'

'Well, I am going for to stay with my son, Ianto. You remember Ianto, yes? My eldest? He is farming close to Borth, isn't it. I am going for to see him, see.'

'Well, there is nice for you,' said the porter, nodding, an eye on the signal down the line. 'Here she comes! Keep back now, Dick. Dunna thee go falling over the edge now.'

The little man shrank back from the edge of the platform

269

and watched with round apprehensive eyes as the train came
chugging round the corner and, whistling shrilly, pulled into
the station, filling it with steam and noise. The little country
man forgotten, the porter began dragging mail bags from the
guards-van, while Davy's eyes searched the opening doors for a
glimpse of Elinor. At last he spotted her descending daintily to
the platform and looking round her with raised eyebrows. He
hurried forward to her side and she proffered a cool cheek for
his kiss. They exchanged a few stilted words and he began to
gather up her pieces of luggage. By the time he had tucked a
hatbox under one arm and a brown paper parcel under the
other and picked up the two heavy suitcases in his hands the
train had given a parting shriek and drawn noisily out of the
station.

As he made his burdened way in Elinor's wake he was
surprised to see the little figure of the country man standing
forlornly on the platform staring after the departing train with
a comic expression of dismay on his face. Just then, the porter,
Twm, came bustling by, pushing a truck loaded with mailbags.
He stopped and gaped at the little man, eyes wide.

'What the 'ell, Dick! I thought thee wast catching that train
to Borth?'

The little man turned tearfully to him, his face working.

'I did knock at two or three of them doors, but nobody did
ask me in!' he explained helplessly. 'An' then it was gone
without me!'

'Well, you silly owl bugger!' cried the porter, shaking his
head in wonder. 'You should never 'ave left Bwlchyfridd!
You'll 'ave to wait for the next train now, you owl oolert. Come
you on with me. You can wait in the parcel office. You'd never
believe, would you?' he appealed to Davy with weary exasperation and trundled on his way with hunched shoulders, the
little man tottering along after him, sniffing miserably. Keeping a straight face with an effort, Davy followed Elinor out of
the station.

Once at Plas Gywn, Davy had time to notice a radical
change in Elinor's appearance. She was very pale and her
violet eyes had dark smudges beneath them. She had obviously
lost weight and her smart town dress hung on her unbecom-
ingly. When they sat down to their midday meal she poked
indifferently at the food on her plate, while keeping up an

270

almost feverish flow of small talk about London, its shops and the theatres and places of interest she had visited. Unused to such talkativeness from her, Davy struggled to respond with a show of interest. Once, during an interruption in the flow while Mrs Buxton placed plates of apple tart and custard in front of them, Davy surprised a long speculative look from under Elinor's lashes, which puzzled him somewhat. After the meal she declared herself tired from her journey, and went up to her room to lie down, while Davy gave Mrs Buxton a hand to clear the table and carry the dishes through to the kitchen.

'That girl don't look well at all,' said the old woman, filling the enamel bowl in the sink with hot water for the washing up, her face puckered with worry. 'She is as thin as a lath. Her clothes are hanging on her.'

'She doesn't look too good,' agreed Davy, frowning as he piled dishes on the draining board. 'But maybe the tiredness after the journey makes her look worse.'

Mrs Buxton pushed her lower lip out and shook her head doubtfully without answering and he left the kitchen, a distracted frown on his face. He saw little of Elinor for the rest of the day. She reappeared in time for tea and afterwards went over to the Rectory to see her father, while Davy retired to the study with his books.

That night he was awakened in the early hours. The still, silvery light of the full moon outside silhouetted a slim silent figure standing at the window. Startled he raised himself up on his elbow and stared, blinking to clear his gaze.

'Elinor?'

The thin figure turned to face him. The moonlight showed her in her long white nightgown, dark hair in a cloud over her shoulders and hands clasped to her breast. For a moment she was silent and then a small sound, like a half-sob, escaped her.

'Elinor?' he queried again. 'What's wrong?'

She appeared to hesitate for a moment and then advanced towards his bed. She still stood without speaking and he frowned, puzzled.

'Bad dream?' he asked, his voice non-committal.

She nodded, standing suppliant in the shaft of moonlight.

'Can I come in with you, Davy?' Her whisper was childlike, but he was unable to make out the expression on her face.

He hesitated, his body very still. Then with an almost

271

imperceptible shrug he moved over in the bed to leave room for her. She slipped between the covers and gave a small shiver. Although he kept his distance from her he was aware of the tenseness of her body as she lay on her back, staring across at the window. He made no move to touch her and the minutes ticked by while they lay side by side silent in the eerie light filtering into the room. Suddenly she turned toward him and reaching over, put a tentative hand on his shoulder.

'Davy?'

'Yes?'

His answer was cool and unresponsive and she remained still for a moment, her breath uneven. Then she gave a soft, uncertain laugh and slid closer to his rigid body.

'I'm cold,' she murmured and touched his cheek with a small icy hand. 'Feel how cold.'

He turned his head on the pillow and stared at the pale outline of her face close to his shoulder. Her eyes were fathomless and the soft dark hair lay against his neck. He smelled the scent of it and something bitter and hurting stirred in him. His body fought to resist the dark emotion that flowed through it and his eyes were hard as he gazed at her. His hand went up to crush the cold fingers which still lay against his face and his mouth came down at the corners.

'Why, Elinor?' he whispered harshly and she drew in her breath with a quick gasp. She lay very still for a moment as though fighting some unknown conflict. At last she lifted her face to his with an effort, widened her eyes and made her voice soft.

'I thought you'd be glad!'

His eyes narrowed but his face became smooth and blank.

'You've left it a bit late,' he answered coolly.

Suddenly her body was convulsed with fury and she tugged her hand from his grasp with a wild cry. She tumbled from the bed and ran stumbling across the room, crying loudly and hysterically and he flung himself after her, catching her by the shoulders and swinging her round towards him. He clamped a hand across her mouth to stem the wild sobs.

'Hush!' he commanded harshly, 'Mrs Buxton –' then gave a gasp as she bit viciously at the palm of his hand. A dark and mad emotion swept through him and with an inarticulate cry he picked her up roughly and carried her, kicking and fighting like a wild cat, and flung her across the bed. She lay there for a moment, the breath knocked from her body, her eyes wide and dark, with a strange expression in their depths. Then, leaning over her he pinned her arms down with his hands and kissed her deliberately and bruisingly. For a moment she writhed convulsively under him then as he released her arms and gathered her up against him in a hard, merciless grasp, her mouth twisted in an ugly smile and her arms closed round his neck, drawing him down into a savage darkness.

When he woke in the morning she was gone. The pale light of the dawn was outlined by the window as he got slowly from the bed and went to stare out at the cold grey morning. The bells of St David's church pealed faintly through the morning mist and reminded him it was Sunday. A mixture of thoughts chased themselves through his mind as he stared at the outline of the trees along the Rectory drive, a few stubborn yellow leaves still clinging to them. A faint sparkle of frost rimed the grass on the little lawn as the moonlight faded into a greyer dawn. Davy sighed heavily and turned to get dressed. He poured water from the big toilet jug into the flowered basin on the marble-topped washstand and splashed his face vigorously holding the cold water against his cheeks and welcoming the icy stinging. His toilet complete he descended slowly to the small room where breakfast was set out.

Elinor was already seated behind the teapot and he watched her warily from the doorway before advancing into the room. Her face was pale and the smudges under her eyes were darker, but her hair was carefully dressed and she had on an immaculate beige shirtwaist blouse and dark brown skirt which only served to emphasize her thinness. She looked up from buttering a piece of toast and nodded coolly.

'Good morning.'

Davy mumbled a reply and seated himself opposite to her. She poured his tea and passed it to him in silence. He picked up the Sunday paper which had been laid beside his plate and hid behind it, trying to sort out his confused thoughts. The heavy silence persisted and at last he straightened his shoulders and folded the paper.

'Elinor? Look, about last night.'

Her eyebrows went up but she avoided his eyes.

'For God's sake,' she said impatiently. 'Do we have to have a

273

post mortem?'

He flinched and reached for a piece of toast to give his hands something to do.

'It's not quite that simple,' he replied curtly. 'You know what the doctor said.'

A dull flush crept up her face and her hand shook slightly as she stirred her tea.

'Well, it's done now, isn't it?' Her voice was sullen and she began to crumble the toast on her plate with nervous fingers. He looked at her face, paling again as the flush receded into blotches which seemed to highlight the shadows under her eyes, and the too prominent bones in her face. She certainly looked ill, he thought and suddenly he felt a wave of pity for her as he would feel pity for a stranger. He rose and went to her, putting a kindly hand on her shoulder.

'Don't you think you should go and see Dr Bellamy?' he asked gently. You don't look at all well.'

She flung his hand off and burying her face in her hands began to cry distractedly. He stood looking down at her bent head with a worried frown.

'Elinor. Something is wrong, isn't it? Won't you tell me?'

She rose clumsily and turned a contorted face to him.

'Why can't you leave me alone!' she cried in a hoarse voice. 'You get on my nerves! I never should have married you. I loathe you, can't you understand? You're always there, like a hurt dog, watching for something that doesn't exist. That never will. Oh, God,' she turned away, her shoulders slumped wearily, and went to stare out of the window. Davy stood in silence, his face white and his hands gripping the back of the chair she had vacated. Suddenly she turned back to him.

'I'm sorry,' she said, tonelessly. She closed her eyes for a moment and swayed, putting out a hand to steady herself by the window-sill. Then her eyes opened and she looked at him with a glimmer of pity in their violet depths.

'Forgive me, Davy. I should never have married you. It was for nothing in the end, was it?' she added with a bitter little smile. 'There was no bastard brat to give a name to, as it turned out. So your noble gesture was wasted.' She gave a short laugh. 'I've made a nice bit of hell for you, haven't I? Well, maybe not for much longer. Make your own life Davy. Forget me. I'm not worth your love.'

Davy removed his hands from the back of the chair and thrust them into his jacket pockets. He straightened and looked at her with steady dark eyes.

'No, Elinor,' he said, shaking his head. 'It was my fault. I went into it with my eyes open. You never wanted me and I knew it. But I was so mad about you that it didn't matter. I was a fool. I thought it would work out, I suppose. If I thought at all. I loved you very much,' he added in a low voice. 'But don't worry. That's over now. I've known that for a while. I don't think I feel anything at all now. Except that I'm very sorry for you, Elinor.'

For an instant the old spark was back in her eyes and her chin lifted.

'I don't want your pity!' she said in a hard voice. 'You don't have to be sorry for me. There's nothing to be sorry about. I do what I want to do. It's my life and I'll live it as I please. And end it as I please,' she added under her breath.

Davy bit his bottom lip and stared at her.

'Elinor, last night – .'

'Oh, last night!' she cried contemptuously. 'That was me. Not you. Do not think I'd have let you – ? You were a means to an end. Don't worry, it won't happen again. You can sleep in peace from now on!'

'I don't understand?' His voice was harsh. 'You did it deliberately? But why? Why? Tell me. You can't hurt me any more so don't worry.'

But she had turned back to the window again, her shoulders drooping and one thin pale hand stark against the dark red curtain.

'Please,' she said in a low voice. 'Please leave me alone. What's the good of all this? There's nothing more to say. I've said that I'm sorry, I can't do more. What's done is done. Please go.'

He watched her for a moment longer and then turned heavily and went to the door. As his hand reached for the knob she spoke again, something of the old crispness back in her voice.

'Oh, I shan't be coming to church this morning. If you see father just tell him I have a headache.'

Davy left the room and went slowly up the stairs to fetch his topcoat. Once in the bedroom he stared bitterly at the tumbled bed and the events of the night came hotly into his mind. He slumped on to the edge of the bed and sat with his face in his hands, dark, bewildering thoughts in a confused whirl. He remained there still and motionless for a long while, until the church bells began to peal again for the mid-morning service, breaking into the numb well of his mind. He rose and looked round the room unseeingly then he pulled himself together and taking coat and hat from the wardrobe, went down and let himself quietly out of the house.

The morning was cold and grey and he shivered slightly as he walked down Kerry Road. November was only a day or two away and already the dead hand of winter was on the trees and hedges and the last of the chrysanthemums in the gardens drooped brown and frost-spoiled. Churchgoers were wrapped in their winter coats, the old ladies with their fur tippets fastened close to their chins and the hands that clutched their prayer-books were woollen-mittened. Halfway to the church he was hailed by a bright voice and he turned, startled out of his brown revery.

'Hello, Davy!'

It was Nan, warmly wrapped in a long brown coat, her face fresh and pink with the cold, her grey eyes friendly above wide cheekbones. Her corn-coloured hair escaped exuberantly from under a close-fitting brown hat and her button boots tapped along the pavement sharply as she quickened her steps to catch up with him. She looked so vibrantly alive and her smile was so warm that he gave a quick answering smile in spite of himself.

'Alone this morning, is it, Davy? Where's Mrs Davy, then?'

'Elinor's not coming this morning. She's got a headache.'

She matched her steps to his and as he looked down at her sturdy, wide-hipped figure his heart lightened. There was something good and wholesome about Nan, from the decisive swing of her hips to the wide face, the firm chin and the clear steadfast grey eyes. His pulse gave a little skip as he followed her up the path to the tall grey church, their feet crunching on the gravel and the last few notes of the bells echoing from the square tower above them in the cold misty air. He let her precede him through the door and when she turned into a pew near the back he followed her on impulse and seated himself beside her. She gave him a quick, almost mischievous glance before bending her head and shoulders forward in an attitude

276

of prayer. He followed suit and when he raised his head and sat up found Mama's head craning round from the Rees' pew near the front, eyebrows raised in startled arcs and mouth pursed. He fought down a near hysterical desire to laugh at the expression on her face and instead set himself to finding the first hymn in the red hymn-book which he found on the narrow ledge in front of him. He stole a glance at Nan's face. Her eyes were bent demure on her own book but the corners of her wide mouth twitched and suddenly Davy felt happier than he had done for a long time.

When the morning service finished he left the pew abruptly. As he emerged into the churchyard she was close behind him. She gave him a quick glance and then turned and began to make her way along the path which led to the graveyard behind the church. He hesitated for a moment then followed her, welcoming the chance to avoid an encounter with Mama. He caught up with Nan as she stopped beside a narrow unmarked grave, the frosted grass neatly cut but unadorned. She stood in silence for some minutes looking down at the bare green rectangle, then raised calm grey eyes to his, not questioning his presence.

'Mam and our Alfie,' she said softly.

He nodded, remembering the wild October fair night so many years ago and seeing again the pale, thin child who lay dying in the cold kitchen by the light of a flickering candle.

'Poor little Alfie,' he said at last.

'Yes. And poor Mam. I didn't forgive her for a long time, you know. I had to grow up before I understood. God help her, I suppose she did her best for us. It was just too much for her. They're both better off,' she added with a trace of bitterness. 'Life can be awful hard, too, Davy.'

He nodded silently, his dark eyes with his own thoughts. They stood close together, their arms touching, without speaking, until suddenly she shivered and he took her cold hand in both of his. Their eyes met and for a brief moment the years fell away and they were two children sharing a remembered sorrow. Then he bent his head and gently touched her lips with his. It was like coming home after a long and tortuous journey.

She raised her free hand and brushed his mouth with a finger which trembled a little, then she drew away with a deep sigh and after a last glance at the green mound at their feet, walked slowly back to the main path.

Davy followed her as far as the church gates and there she gave him a suddenly shy smile and raised her hand in a small but decisive gesture of farewell. Her small, sturdy brown-clad figure disappeared in the direction of Kerry Road and Davy stood and watched her out of sight, feeling momentarily bereft. A voice from behind broke into his thoughts and he turned to greet the Rector, surplice over his arm and a kindly smile on his tired old face.

'You have not come in the trap today, then,' said Davy, suddenly aware of how the old man had aged recently. The eyes were still gentle and vague but his clean-shaven face showed its sad lines this morning, pinched by the cold air and although never a robust man, he looked very frail in his heavy black overcoat which hung loosely on his shoulders.

'No, indeed, Davy. It is not worth that your Dada should trouble himself to get the old trap out just for me. There is no-one else to come with me now, you see. And why the old ceremony when it is not far to walk. I think your father was a bit shocked when I told him so, yesterday,' he went on with a wry little smile. 'Come, my boy, we will walk up together. Where is Elinor this morning?'

'She had a headache.'

'Hm,' said the old man. 'She did not look at all well when she called yesterday. I don't see why she had to go down to London in the first place. She is a restless creature.' His voice took on a sad and bewildered note. 'Why does she not make herself content here. She has a good man for a husband and a nice home and Mrs Buxton, who thinks the world of her. But she is restless. They both are, Geraint too.'

'Have you heard from Geraint recently?' asked Davy, to turn the subject.

'About a fortnight ago. He does not write often. But the life seems to suit him. He is out in India now, of course you know. Wrote at some length about being sent up into the hills to quell some riot or uprising among the natives there.' The Rector sighed and shook his head. 'I don't understand at all. He sounded as though he enjoyed the danger and the fighting. I had hoped when he was small that he would grow into the Church and be called to the ministry. But I soon saw that was not to be. There is a side to him – well, there, we are not all the same, of course.' He laid a frail hand on Davy's arm and his eyes were gentle. 'I would have wished no more than that he had turned out like you, my boy. You are a good man.'

Davy flushed and stammered some reply and soon they reached the Rectory gates and Plas Gwyn opposite. The Rector nodded a vague farewell, lost in his thoughts again and Davy let himself into the house reluctantly.

Dinner and tea were eaten in comparative silence, which Davy found oppressive. Between the two meals Elinor rested upstairs and Davy wandered the house restlessly, depressed by the atmosphere. Down in the kitchen Mrs Buxton dozed by the fire, sighing and murmuring to herself, and the clocks in the various rooms ticked the afternoon away drearily. After tea Davy felt the need for escape and, letting himself out into the gathering dusk, made his way to No 46 Pool Road.

When he entered, the family were all seated round the fire, with the exception of Owen who was curled up on the old sofa with his head in a book, and Esther, who sat at the table, raised up in her chair with a pile of cushions, building a tower of wooden bricks. Dada bade him pull up a chair to the fire and Mama raised her eyes from a sock she was darning to give him a searching look. Meg smiled gently, the good side of her face toward him, pretty and pink from the heat of the fire. Llew, sitting next to her, grinned a welcome and Davy drew his chair up into the space they made for him. He settled himself among them with a sigh of relief and contentment, as the fire settled to a rich glow and the old brass oil lamp on the table shed a pool of soft light through its pristine clean, fat-bellied glass globe.

Mama opened the conversation, eyes intent on the darning needle which was swiftly closing the hole in the toe of the sock.

'Elinor was not at church this morning?'

Davy sighed inwardly.

'She had a headache, Mama.'

'Hm. Why did you not come up to sit by us? Instead of going to sit with Nan Mostyn. People were looking.'

'No harm,' said Davy patiently. 'I walked down with her and just slipped in next her, not thinking.'

'Hm,' grunted Mama again, reaching for the scissors to snip away the spare wool. 'Looked to folks like you came to church with her instead of your wife.'

'Oh, for God's sake, Mama,' muttered Llew, impatiently.

279

'You, boy. Watch your tongue,' Mama answered in a sharp voice. 'Too fond you are of calling on the Lord. You could do your calling in his own house a bit more often, too, mind.'

Llew shifted in his chair.

'Aye. Dare say. But there are a few calls He is not answering. Like from the people with no work and small ones with nothing in their bellies.'

Mama's lips tightened and Dada turned apprehensive eyes to her.

'Now then, now then, my boy. That will do.' He held up a warning hand. 'A bit more respect here, isn't it.'

'Respect for what, now?' asked Llew, eyes glinting in his thin, intense face. 'For the fat ones in their bowler hats and the women in their fur collars, dropping half-crowns in the plate? A half-crown is as much as some families get off the parish to keep them a week. If they are lucky. No doubt the mill-owners have made their profits. They can pull out now and sink their brass in the mills up in Lancashire and Yorkshire.'

Meg coughed warningly and turned to Davy to change the subject.

'Did Elinor enjoy her stay in London, then?'

'She does not say much about it,' Davy answered, eyes on the flickering flames of the fire. 'But she does not look well. Gone very thin. She has been rushing around, I dare day. All those grand shops to see and going to theatres and such like. I expect it is a more hectic life down there.'

Mama snorted softly as she smoothed the neat darn with her fingers, then putting the sock aside, she reached for another from the pile on the table.

'I do not understand this old London life at all,' she announced disapprovingly. 'Why to look at shops all day? Shops is for buying things which are wanted, not to look at, I do say. And what for go to these theatres every night. Have the people in London got no homes to go to?'

'It is a different way of life from ours, Mama,' laughed Davy. 'Not so slow.'

'Slow, is it?' Mama's eyebrows went up. 'I do not go slow in this house all day, mind, or I would get nothing done.'

Dada grunted and pursed his lips under his moustache.

'If them theatres are like the old moving pictures I went to in the Victoria Hall, they can keep them in London. The people

280

in them pictures were *twp*, mark you. They were like old sheep with the staggers. They wouldn't take telling, neither. I did try. But they were running around spare. Like Mary Ann y Golfa – here's me head, me arse is coming.'

'Will!' Mama's shocked cry pierced her sons' hysterical laughter.

Dada sank back, abashed, and tugged at his white whiskers.

'I am sorry girl. I did forget myself a minute. No harm meant, indeed. It did just slip out.'

'There are small ones here,' said Mama, bristling. 'And you say you cannot always get your tongue round the old English, but some words you do pick up, no trouble!'

Dada hid a sly grin with his hand and his eyes twinkled mischievously at Davy and Llew. Owen's voice piped up eagerly from the sofa.

'I have been counting. There are six of us now Uncle Davy's come. Enough for a game of Tippit.'

'Aye,' said Llew, grinning. 'Let us play Tippit. It is safer.'

'I have got this old darning to finish,' grumbled Mama, still bridling. 'Holes as big as your head in some of these socks.'

'Never mind, Mama,' said Meg. 'Play Tippit for a bit now, isn't it, and I will help you with the old socks later.'

Mama sighed and stabbed the needle into the sock before laying it back on the pile, grumbling under her breath. They all rose to put chairs back under the table and while Mama removed the pile of socks, Owen rooted in her sewing box for a suitable button for the game. Esther knocked her tower down with an air of finality.

'An' me play Tippit!' she clapped her plump pink hands and beamed round expectantly.

'You are for bed, my girl,' said Mama firmly, lifting her down from the chair and leading her out to the back to find the flannel to wipe her face and hands. Esther gazed reluctantly over her shoulder as she was led away, round blue eyes swimming with disappointment.

When Mama returned after settling Esther she took her place next to Meg and Owen on one side of the table, while Dada, Llew and Davy were seated on the bench on the other side.

'We will toss for first go,' said Llew, taking a halfpenny from his pocket and throwing it up. He caught it in one hand and slapped it quickly onto the back of the other, covering it closely.

'Right, Owen boy, heads or tails?'

'Tails!' cried Owen eagerly, but when Llew uncovered the coin it showed the fat-cheeked head of the old Victoria.

'Hard luck,' grinned Llew. 'First turn to us men.'

'Two heads to that old penny, shouldn't wonder,' murmured Mama, winking at Owen.

The three men sat up straight, shoulder to shoulder, hands behind their backs. With carefully blank faces they passed the button between them until it settled in one of their hands.

'Up!' called Llew, and six closed fists were raised onto the table and six eyes stared challengingly at the opposing team.

'You go first, Owen,' said Meg, smiling.

Owen stared hard at the six clenched fists as though he would penetrate the flesh and bones with his eyes. Was any one fist fatter than the other because it was closed round a button? He screwed up his face and took a deep breath.

'Off!' he cried, pointing to Davy's left hand. He held his breath while Davy opened his fist slowly. It was empty and he removed it from the table.

Owen studied the fists again, judiciously.

'Off!' He pointed to Dada's left hand. Again the fist was opened to reveal emptiness and then removed.

Owen's eyes glinted at the remaining four fists. He chewed his bottom lip, then ordered Davy's right hand off. Again it was empty and Owen let out his breath in relief. Three fists left on the table. He was doing well. Boldly he pointed to Dada's right hand.

'Off!' he called, a note of anxiety creeping into his voice. Slowly Dada opened the fist. It was empty and Meg clapped her hands in delight.

'Good old Owen! Tippit now!'

Owen stared at Llew's two fists and Llew stared back at him sphinx-like. Two fists left. Which held the button? Owen drew in a deep breath and plunged.

'Tippit!' he cried, tapping the back of Llew's right fist.

Llew grinned and slowly opened his hand. It was empty. He opened the other to reveal the brown button sitting triumphantly on his palm.

'Aw, heck!' cried Owen, disappointed.

'Never mind,' smiled Meg. 'You nearly did it. My turn to try now.'

But Meg had no more luck, ordering the fist that held the button off the table at her second try.

'There, see,' she said to Owen. 'I have done worse than you.'

Mama won the next game for them however, by correctly divining the excess of innocence in Dada's widened blue eyes and tipping his left fist, which held the button, at her fourth go. Owen clapped with glee and it was their turn to pass the button along behind their backs and respond to Meg's command.

'Up!' and the six fists were placed on the table, Owen rounding his small empty ones to make them look fat, as all three stared at the opposition with studied nonchalance.

The game proceeded, its fortunes fluctuating excitingly between the two teams. By half-past eight by the clock on the mantelpiece Owen's team had won by a narrow margin and he was bursting with pride and satisfaction as he made his way with some reluctance out to the back kitchen to wash ready for bed.

Mama brought cups to the table and wet the tea in the big teapot and they all sat at the table sipping and talking cosily. Owen reappeared with his hair in damp spikes round his face and after Mama had given him a mug of milk, which he was inclined to linger over, he was shooed off to bed. Davy rose soon afterwards and took his leave, with a wistful backward glance at the familiar faces around the old lamp. His steps were slow as he made his way back up Kerry Road. As he approached Plas Gwyn the only light showing was in Elinor's bedroom and he hesitated outside, depression descending on him again. Then his eyes turned to the outline of the Rectory showing faintly in the dark, behind the trees. An image of Nan came to him, grey eyes calm and smiling and thick corn-coloured hair escaping from its knot. The thought warmed him and he gave a little smile.

'Tippit!' he murmured, for no reason at all, and bowed in the direction of the Rectory. Then with a rueful laugh at his own daftness, he let himself in to Plas Gwyn.

19

Beginnings and Ends

November came and went with cold bitter winds and grey days. The last few tattered leaves were shaken from the trees, leaving them gaunt and bare against dark skies. Snow threatened but never materialized, except for a few flurries, and by the end of the month the wind had dropped and the days were shrouded in thick fog which hung along the valley like a blanket and crept upwards until the comfortable, confining hills were blotted out. When the people of the town raised their eyes for the reassurance of the familiar outlines, they had disappeared, and they were left with a disorientated feeling which affected the mood in their daily lives.

Poverty was on the increase as mills closed one after the other. The fire at the Gwalia was not the last of the controversial mill fires to happen and more and more people were thrown on to the far from tender mercies of the Parish relief. Pompous dignitaries in the town condemned the 'working classes' for their shiftlessness, overlooking the fact that a large percentage of the town could hardly be described as 'working' class any longer. Those who could left to join relatives and friends in the woollen mills of Huddersfield, Rochdale and Bradford, but a greater number were reluctant to leave their native valley or were unable to finance themselves for the move and stayed at home to eke out a living as best they could. Fortunately the Pryce Jones factory and warehouse were becoming well established and their labour force was expanding and they now became the largest employers of labour in the town. The decline of the little market town, once known as the Leeds of Wales was accelerating.

Davy saw evidence of social conditions in the Church

School. The more privileged still brought hunks of bread spread with good meat dripping to eat at playtime, and those less fortunate hung around them, eyes on the crusts, which they begged and generally got. Here and there evidence of the endemic prevalence of consumption showed in the feverish flush on otherwise pale and pinched faces.

Despite all these conditions, however, the natives of the town kept their wry buoyancy and the dry humour which was characteristic of the community of the narrow little valley in which the town nestled. The dialect mixture of Welsh and scraps of Yorkshire picked up from the immigrants of the previous century, lent itself to this particular brand of wry comedy. Comic tales abounded and 'characters' were regarded with humorous affection. Ale was cheap and helped to fudge the harsh outlines of daily life. As one wag in the Cross Guns put it –

'Life looks a hell of a sight easier when you see it through the bottom of a pint pot!'

Although the convivial season of Christmas was drawing near, Davy felt unable to look forward. The atmosphere in Plas Gwyn was uncomfortable. Elinor was more withdrawn than ever and seemed bent on keeping out of his way. Her health seemed to be deteriorating but if Davy ventured the suggestion that she should visit Dr Bellamy she turned on him with a spark of her old fury and cried out to be let alone. Mrs Buxton's face took on lines of worry and apprehension and her eyes followed Elinor's every movement until the girl turned on her too and brought on a look of hurt bewilderment with her cutting words.

Christmas was two days away when Davy arrived home on a Friday afternoon, a pile of books for marking weighing heavy in his battered old brown case. Only one place was laid at the tea table and he looked enquiringly at Mrs Buxton when she brought in the teapot in its knitted red cosy.

'Has Elinor had her tea, then?' he asked, filling the solitary cup with the strong, steaming brew.

Mrs Buxton's lips were pressed tightly together and she stood looking down at him with a strange expression on her face.

'She is in bed,' she answered shortly. 'She has been very sick.'

Davy frowned and stirred his tea.

'Look, Buxy, can't you get her to go to the doctor? She won't listen to me. She hasn't been right since she got back from London. Whatever is wrong with her, it needs seeing to. But she just gets in a temper if I mention doctor.'

Mrs Buxton folded her plump red hands across her stomach and stood looking at him curiously, without answering. His hand wavered above the plate of bread and butter as he stared back at her, puzzled. He withdrew his hand and drummed on the table with his fingers, meeting her stare defensively.

'I'm as worried as you are,' he insisted. 'I have thought of asking the doctor to call. Not warn her, like. But then, you know Elinor. She would get mad if I did that. She would take more notice of you. I've tried, God knows.'

'Bit late for a doctor, isn't it?' Mrs Buxton's cheeks flushed angrily, and her old eyes misted with tears.

Davy stared back, speechless. Mrs Buxton lifted the edge of her apron to her eyes and turned, lumbering out of the room with a heavy tread. Davy gazed after her for a moment, an awful suspicion dawning on him. Then he rose hastily and followed her into the kitchen.

She was sitting in her chair, rocking back and fore distractedly, a large handkerchief to her face, her white cap askew. Muffled sounds of distress came from behind the handkerchief and Davy leaned against the kitchen table, his face pale, staring at her with comprehension dawning on him.

'Mrs Buxton!' he said hoarsely. 'What is wrong with Elinor? Tell me!'

She stopped rocking and blew her nose with the handkerchief, wiping her moist eyes before she answered.

'Don't you know?' she said, dully. 'You should. It's your fault!' She gulped and stared down at her hands, twisting the handkerchief in her lap.

Davy closed his eyes and despair draining through his body. He slumped against the table.

'Oh God,' he whispered painfully. 'She's going to have a baby, isn't she?'

Mrs Buxton's only reply was a harsh sob and she began to rock back and fore again, her sagging body bent over.

Davy straightened wearily and pushed himself away from the table. He moved towards the door, his feet leaden.

286

'It'll kill her,' Mrs Buxton said without turning, her voice flat and he flinched and quickened his step to escape the bitter reproach in all the lines of the suffering old body.

He hesitated at the bottom of the stairs, his hand trembling on the bannister post, then slowly mounted, every step an effort. He stopped again outside the door of Elinor's room, then taking a deep breath he turned the knob and went in, closing the door quietly behind him.

She lay on her side in the big feather bed, knees drawn up, one hand under her cheek on the fat white pillow, the other resting still on the eiderdown. Her violet eyes, darkly ringed with exhaustion, stared out at nothingness. His heart contracted at the pallor of her face and the sharply outlined cheekbones. Her hair lay loose on the pillow, the glossy dark curls dulled now and drawn back harshly from her high, pale forehead. He went close to the bed and touched her hand gently. Her eyes closed and the fine black brows came together in a frown.

'Elinor?' There was pain in his voice. 'Why didn't you tell me?'

For a moment there was no response, then she withdrew her hand from beneath his and turned wearily onto her back. Propped up against the pillow she remained silent and then opened her eyes and looked at him expressionlessly. He sat himself down on the side of the bed, pity and despair darkening his eyes.

'Why didn't you tell me?' he repeated and she shifted restlessly under the covers. 'It's my fault. What can I do?' His voice was low and broken.

She made a gesture of weary rejection.

'Nothing. Just leave me alone.'

'There must be something. We must get the doctor at once. Oh God, Elinor, can you ever forgive me?'

She stared at him curiously and shook her head. There was a strange expression in her eyes which he was unable to read. Then she turned her head away from him.

'I've told you, there's nothing to be done. What can be done. It's too late now.' She turned her head back to him and she was frowning irritably. 'If you sit there looking at me like a whipped dog, you only make me feel worse. I can't stand it. Please go away!'

287

'At least let me get the doctor,' he pleaded.

She struggled to raise herself on an elbow.

'Can't you get it into your head?' she said, between clenched teeth. 'No doctor. Just keep out of my sight and leave me alone. You can't ride up on a white charger and rescue me this time,' she added with a caustic twist to her lips.

He stared at her helplessly, overwhelmed by pity and guilt. She sank back on to the pillow again and closed her eyes in a gesture of dismissal. He hesitated, then rose heavily and went out and down the stairs. He reached for his coat from a peg in the hall and shrugging into it, left the house.

The night was clear, with a moon casting a pale, silvery light over the frosted road outside. He drew in deep stinging breaths of the cold air and thrusting his hands in his pockets, stared up at the sky. The Milky Way showed as a misty path across the night blue and all the other stars twinkled like diamonds. He was bare-headed and he turned up his coat collar. He walked on up Kerry Road, face to the hills, the icy air stinging his cheeks and ears. Trees stretched up their spectre-fingered arms to the moon and cast ghostly shadows across the road. An owl hooted sadly from one of the still, motionless trees, as though echoing his thoughts and he shivered and quickened his pace. His solitary footsteps sounded crisply from the frosty surface of the road and were the only sound in a landscape which looked as though it were frozen for all time into a silvery, phantom world. He strode on, no clear thoughts in his head, and soon began to climb the steep slope known as the Vastre. By the time he reached the brow of the hill his breath was coming in sharp gasps as the icy air hit his lungs and he stopped and leaned against a gate in the hedge and stared down at the town below.

It lay in its narrow valley, bathed in moonlight. The steeples of the churches and the tall mill chimneys pointed fingers to the myriad stars in the sky and the rest of the buildings were outlined by exaggerated shadows and gleaming highlights. The river curled and divided the town like a flung-down white ribbon. Faint pinpoints of yellow street-lamps seemed to struggle against the sharper light of the moon and round the silver ribbon of river the little houses, their grey-slated roofs shining with frost, seemed to huddle together for warmth.

On his climb up he had forced himself not to think, emptying his mind of all the dark tumult that troubled it. Now

288

the first thought that rushed into his mind was a poignant feeling of love for the little town, lying compactly along the confines of the valley and only spreading very sparsely up the steep slopes surrounding it. The hills gathered around protectively, bathed in this ethereal light and he mused on how the isolation of the valley dictated the character of the people in the little town, making for its close community. He knew in that instant that he could never leave it, whatever happened, whatever its shortcomings and however deep his own personal despair. He thought of all the people in their houses down there and the conflicting nature of them. The narrowness of thought against the warm neighbourliness. The gossip, the dry humour, the comic and the tragic, the initial suspicion of strangers and then their slow, almost casual absorption into the community. They were his people, mixed good and bad, puritanical and bawdy, earthy and yet with an inherent Celtic understanding of things of the intellect. They were struggling subconsciously against the slow Anglicization which was taking place, hardly aware that it was happening but feeling, without understanding, the eroding of the old culture and way of life which was still untouched in the higher unreached communities of the hills.

At last, reluctantly, he turned his thoughts to the problems of his own life. He went back doggedly to that savage night in October, to Elinor's blatant invitation and his own hungry response. His bewildered mind searched for motives in an effort to resolve the conflict in his heart, but again and again he shied away from any answers. As though in escape he thought of Nan and a cold hand closed round his heart. He knew now that he loved her, his feelings like the contrast between the light and shadow in the valley below. His love for Nan was all light and clear, in contrast to the dark hunger for Elinor which had burned itself out against the coldness and hurting indifference of the years.

He stood for a long time, leaning against the frosty bars of the gate, unaware of the icy cold air penetrating to his body, his thoughts on a treadmill of bewilderment and guilt and a dread of the days to come. He raised his face to a pitiless moon and found no solution or help in its cold indifference. He stared down again at the little town and knew he must ride out his own private agony down there, with all its implication, and at last, with a feeling of numb resignation, he turned back to the road and began the descent to the valley, stamping his feet sharply as he went to bring back the feeling of them and huddling further into his turned up collar against the biting cold.

☆   ☆   ☆

The end came in April, as though part of the ending of the long winter, which had lingered on with cold winds and showers of snow denying the coming of spring. Suddenly in the third week of April the winter backed down and the air softened and warmed. Showers of gentle rain fell on a grateful earth, which hurried to make up for lost time and pushed vigour into the green shoots and opened the flowers in the gardens and hedgerows. A sigh of relief seemed to go through the town and the people came out of their winter huddle to welcome the sun which shone between the showers. The men hurried to the gardens and allotments in the lengthening evenings and the women opened doors and washed curtains and shook mats in a flurry of spring-cleaning.

An urgent message came for Davy in the middle of a Thursday morning, while he struggled with the reviving spirits of his class, who turned longing eyes to the unaccustomed sunlight which filtered through the dusty classroom windows. Leaving his charges to the far from tender mercies of Miss Bumford, a thin and sharp-tongued disciplinarian, with grey hair skewered to the top of her head and mauve chalk-ingrained hands ready to wield a stinging cane at the first sign of recalcitrance, he hurried up Kerry Road, panic bringing the bile to his throat.

When he got to Plas Gwyn the Rector was seated in the little parlour, his manner more vague and bewildered than ever. As Davy entered the room he looked up with a pitiful expression in his child-like eyes and when he saw Davy's face his mouth started working helplessly.

'What's happened?' Davy stammered, fright sharpened at the sight of his father-in-law.

The old man swallowed and made an effort to speak. He shook his head and pressed his hands together.

'The baby,' he brought out at last with difficulty. 'The

290

baby's coming. Too soon. Dr Bellamy is with her. Things are bad, Davy.' He tried to collect himself and sat up a little straighter. 'Sit down, my boy. There is nothing we can do. Only wait.'

Davy lowered his trembling body into the chair opposite the old man. He looked round the room helplessly and then back at the Rector.

'When did it start?' His voice was hoarse.

'Early this morning, I think,' said the old man wearily. 'She didn't call anyone. Mrs Buxton found her like that when she went up to take her a cup of tea after you went out. She fetched the doctor straight away. It is not good, I think.' His eyes misted with tears and he took out a large white handkerchief and blew his nose. 'Mrs Buxton is up with the doctor now. Elinor will have nobody else. I have fetched Nan across. She is in the kitchen now.'

On that Nan entered, bearing a tray with two cups of tea steaming on it. She set it down on the table and nodded to Davy, her face full of pity.

'There now, Davy,' she said quietly. 'Have this tea now, and you, Mr Pryce. It will do you good.'

She handed the tea out and Davy's cup rattled in its saucer as his shaking hand tried to hold it. He put it down on the small table at his side and pressed his hands together to still their trembling.

'How is she?' he asked in a low voice, his eyes raised to her face.

She shook her head, her grey eyes full of compassion as they rested on him. Then she put her hand on his shoulder briefly and left the room without answering. Davy got up and began to walk about restlessly. The pain of his guilt threatened to overwhelm him. From time to time he glanced across at the old man, slumped back in his chair and sipping tea abstractedly. Almost he wished the Rector would accuse him, would get angry and fling bitter words at him. But when the old man sighed and looked up there was nothing in his eyes but sorrow.

'Sit down, my boy,' he murmured gently. 'Drink your tea, now. It will help you.'

Davy lowered himself into the chair again and picking up his cup began to sip the cooling tea. The room was silent now, no sound but the old man's breathing and the clock ticking inexorably on the mantelpiece. Time seemed suspended in a tortured vacuum and when Dr Bellamy finally descended the stairs and entered the room with slow steps, Davy could only stare at him dully, his heart thudding in his breast.

The doctor looked at the old man first. The Rector sat forward, but as his eyes held the doctor's expression he sank back with a soft moan and moved his white head from side to side in rejection. As the doctor turned to him, Davy rose, his breathing suspended.

'You can go up,' Dr Bellamy said, his eyes cold as stones. 'The baby is dead. Your wife – ' he shook his head, his lips tight. 'I did what I could. But you were warned.' A spark of anger flared briefly in his eyes and then died away, leaving his face blank.

Davy winced painfully. He left the room and mounted the stairs with leaden feet. As he entered the bedroom Mrs Buxton rose from a chair by the window and lumbered past him towards the door. Her red-rimmed eyes avoided his as she closed the door behind her and he was left alone in the room with the still figure on the bed.

As he approached Elinor's eyelids fluttered open and a flicker of something crossed her white, exhausted face. He moved closer and took one of the pale hands which rested on the coverlet. His legs were trembling and he reached with his other hand for a chair. He sank into it, his knees touching the bed and his eyes bent on the sunken face against the pillow.

'Elinor?' he whispered brokenly.

The hand in his moved faintly and she seemed to be making an effort to speak.

He shook his head and laid a trembling finger against the pale lips.

'Rest,' he murmured. 'Don't try to talk. All I want to know. Can you forgive me?'

Her fine eyebrows came together and she moved her head weakly. Her blue eyes pleaded with him and her throat worked feebly as she tried to say something. He leaned closer, sensing that there was something she had to say. She took a ragged breath and gathered her last remaining strength.

'Nothing to forgive you.' The words came faintly through dry lips. 'You to forgive me. Not you. Not your baby.' She paused and closed her eyes for a second and Davy stared at her, feeling an icy shiver down his spine. Her eyes opened again and she took another rasping breath.

'My fault – that night. Ronald Purvis' baby. In London. Wanted you to think – yours.' Her pale lips twisted in the ghost of a bitter smile. 'What good now? Too late. I'm sorry. Made you suffer for nothing.' Her eyes darkened as they rested on his face and her hand moved in his again. 'Don't tell?' The whisper was urgent.

He shook his head slowly. For a moment the words refused to come through the confusion of emotion. Then with the first faint stirring of relief in his heart and pity now uppermost he gently pressed the thin hand which lay in his.

'I won't tell,' he murmured, then, 'Poor little Elinor.'

For a brief second a faint flicker of the old Elinor brought her eyebrows together and flared defiantly in her eyes. Then it was gone and the white lids fluttered down over the blue depths and she lay still.

Davy sat on, holding her hand in his, conscious only of a deep sadness replacing the tortured guilt which had haunted him like a nightmare. The room was silent and he sat as in a dream as her hand grew colder in his. He relived the years of boyish longing, the innocent worship and the ending of the dream, and all bitterness fell away from him. A shaft of sunlight suddenly pierced the drifting April clouds and shone softly onto the face on the pillow. For a moment Elinor looked like the little girl he remembered, but more peaceful, with all the restlessness and searching gone as if smoothed away.

He leant forward and touched her pale forehead with his lips, just as the door opened and the doctor and her father came silently in. He rose stiffly and made way for them his face calm now and his eyes bent pityingly on the old man. The doctor picked up the hand which Davy had laid down and felt for a pulse. Then he turned to the Rector and shook his head.

'She's gone, Mr Pryce,' he said gently and the old man silently sank to his knees beside the bed and clasped his hands, soft tears welling over his old cheeks.

The doctor turned to Davy then and Davy returned his glance unflinchingly.

'I am sorry, Mr Rees,' he said in more kindly tones. 'I did my best. The baby was already dead and there was no hope for your wife. I am sorry,' he repeated and held out a tentative hand. Davy shook it and nodded to the doctor without replying.

With one last backward glance at the still figure on the bed he left the room and went down to his little study. He shut himself in and taking a chair by the window sat staring out on the small garden. Gilly flowers were growing against the wall and tall red and yellow tulips filled the border around the little lawn, with forget-me-nots like a cushion around their feet. The blossom was beginning to open on the apple tree in the corner and the leaves on the trees and hedges were a fresh tender green against the April sky. He felt weighed down with sadness, a grief which was beyond tears, for everything that was fresh and new and beautiful and very, very fleeting. A line from his favourite poem came into his mind.

'Where Beauty cannot keep her lustrous eyes,
'Or new love pine at them beyond tomorrow.'

God knows, the thought painfully, he had pined at Elinor's eyes for the most of his life, and yet that was gone, buried under a response of indifference and hurt. He mused on her loveliness and her prideful ways and on the dark side of her nature which destroyed all that she was and all that she could have been. He leaned his hot forehead against the cool glass of the window. Her death was like a wound in his life and yet he knew in his heart that the wound would heal in time, salved by the gentler feelings of sorrow and pity, and not kept open and weeping by the tortures of guilt.

The door opened quietly and Nan came in. She came to him and put a gentle hand on his arm.

'Davy?' Her voice was soft and concerned. 'There is food in the kitchen if you can eat?'

He shook his head.

'No, thank you, Nan.'

She dropped her hand and smoothed her apron down.

'I am sorry, Davy,' she said in a low voice. 'Real sorry.'

He nodded without speaking and after searching his face for a moment with anxious grey eyes, she turned and quietly left the room.

After that he sat on for a long time, immobile. He was left alone and was oblivious to the muted sounds in the house as people came and went about the business of dignifying death. At one stage someone opened the door and looked in, then closed it gently and went away. The clock ticked and the time lengthened and at last he rose wearily and stiffly and hugging his chest with his arms, gave a compulsive shiver. Then he took a deep breath and squared his shoulders. He knew now that he could face the days to come, the immediate pressures he would have to face. He looked no further than that, just thankful that the conflict in his heart had been resolved through the healing silence of the April afternoon.

☆   ☆   ☆

The sun shone gently on the small dark-clad group gathered in the churchyard to lay Elinor to rest. Wreaths of fresh spring flowers lay on the grass round about, their tender and delicate colours contrasting with the sombre hues of the mourners and with the brilliant green of the new grass. Geraint, fortuitously back in Aldershot for a few months, had come home and stood now in his uniform beside his father, his face pale, withdrawn and expressionless. Davy stood with Mama and Dada and the rest of the Rees family, Dada sturdy and solemn, his white hair lifted by the gentle April breeze, Llew, thin intense face serious, stood shoulder to shoulder with Davy. Mama was dignified and respectable in her best black next to Meg, whose gentle blue eyes looked out of her disfigured face and rested compassionately on the stooped figure of the Rector, his bare white head bowed as his lips moved in silent prayer.

Davy sent a veiled glance in the direction of the tall, spare black-clad figure standing on the other side of Meg. It was Auntie Martha who had driven up alone in her trap this morning, drawn by old Gypsy, a spray of white Easter lilies on the seat beside her, sending up a poignant scent from their tiny orange centres. A spasm of pain clutched at Davy as he saw her now, standing straight and calm in her long black coat and a flat black hat of shiny straw, skewered to her grey hair. As though aware of his thoughts she turned her head and looked at him and her brown eyes were kind and understanding. Davy was glad she had come alone. He could not have borne to see Luke beside her, he thought.

The words of finality penetrated his consciousness and he

looked down as a handful of earth rattled onto the coffin. Tears welled up in his eyes as a brief picture of Elinor in all her loveliness came into his mind but they were tears of mourning for the passing of an elusive dream. Llew gripped his arm and led him away and he said goodbye to the reality of Elinor in his heart as he said goodbye to the image of the dream a long while ago.

Back at Plas Gwyn the funeral meats were set out, prepared by Nan and Mrs Buxton and after these had been partaken of, accompanied by the usual halting, low-toned conversation, the mourners began to stir and take their leave. The Rector and Geraint were the first to go and as Davy saw them to the door he had a sudden awareness that Geraint had avoided speaking to him throughout. The old man turned at the door and with a kindly hand on Davy's shoulder, murmured a few words which were lost as Davy looked at Geraint's cold, averted face with a quick, pained comprehension.

'Geraint?' he said hoarsely, as though grasping desperately at something slipping away.

As the Rector made his way shakily down the steps, Geraint turned and faced Davy. His lips came down at the corners and Davy winced at the expression in his eyes.

'You killed our Elinor.' His voice was hard and pitiless. 'I'll never forgive you.'

He turned abruptly and followed his father across the road to the Rectory gates.

Davy stared after him, bitterness sour in his mouth. He leaned wearily against the doorpost and heard again Elinor's last whispered plea.

'Don't tell?'

As soft murmurs and movement sounded in the hall behind him he straightened up and turned to his own family with relief. Auntie Martha was the last through the door. She put out her hand and took his.

'There now, Davy,' she said with a sad smile. 'I am real sorry. But you are young, boy. You must look forward now, isn't it?'

'Auntie Martha,' he said impulsively, putting out a hand to stay her. 'I've got something to tell you. Something I think you ought to know. It can't hurt Elinor now, if I just tell you. It's about Ifan – about that day – you know?'

She shook her head and drew the collar of her coat close round her throat as though the April sun no longer shone.

'No Davy,' she said, holding up a hand against his words. 'No. I do not want to hear what you have to tell me, boy. Mind you, maybe I know. Maybe I have always known. And what good to tell me what I already know? The time for telling was then, not now. What's done is done and nothing can alter, Davy boy. What good would come of the telling now? That I would think better of Ifan?' She smiled sadly. 'I have never thought bad of Ifan, see? For Elinor? Well, not for us to judge, the Lord did say. And you forget, lad. Luke is my son as well. Better for me while I live with him as his mother that there is no old telling. Better for me and better for Luke.'

She put up her hand again encased in its black cotton glove and touched his cheek. He stared back at her sombrely, taking in the new lines in her face and the aching sadness which lurked in the depths of her brown eyes. Suddenly he felt ashamed and as though she read his thoughts she shook her head.

'Yours is a sorrow you will get over, Davy. You are a good boy and your good times will come. I have got a good bit to explain to my Maker when I go, God knows. But it's funny too,' she mused, her eyes fixed far off. 'None of it seemed bad to me in the doing of it. Maybe that will count for something with Him.' She glanced at Davy's face and gave a wry little smile. 'Dammo, I am getting morbid in my old age. I never did like funerals, mind. Laying out is one thing. You can take a pride in that. But funerals is another thing altogether. I must go now or I will not be back to help Luke with the milking. Good day to you now and thank you for my tea. Come and see your old Auntie Martha again soon. Soon as you have got yourself sorted out, isn't it?'

'I will,' he answered, watching her go. 'And thank you, Auntie Martha.'

He watched her down the road. She was much thinner than when he had last seen her but the uncompromising set of her shoulders was unchanged, the narrowing back as straight as ever and the tilt of the head under the flat straw hat still as gallant as it had always been. As he turned to go in again he met Nan on her way out.

'I am going now, Davy,' she said. 'I must see to things at the Rectory. Mrs Buxton says she can manage now.'

For a moment he looked over his shoulder at the empty hall which led to all the sad and empty rooms and briefly panic flared in him. Watching his eyes understandingly Nan patted his arm.

'It will be all right, Davy,' she murmured, 'just don't stay in brooding. Get out plenty. Call to your Mama's. There is company there.'

He nodded.

'I will, don't fret. Thanks, Nan, for helping out.'

As she crossed Kerry Road and disappeared down the back drive of the Rectory, Davy gazed after her. There was that about her which reminded him of Auntie Martha as he watched her, and he had a sudden wild desire to run after her, to hold her and to cry out to her in his awful loneliness.

Slowly and reluctantly he turned back into the cold and empty house and closed the door.

20

Drums and Sunsets

Davy stood among the thronging crowds under a cloudless
blue sky in late June. Flags and bunting hung across the streets
of the town, scarcely moving in the still air. It was only ten
o'clock, but already the heat was showing in the flushed,
excited faces around him as the people crowded the pavements
and waited in buzzing anticipation for the next big band to
march down from the station.

It was the Warehouse sports day, the annual gala organized
by Pryce Jones Royal Welsh Warehouse. A carnival day of
great band contests and sports, cycle racing and tug-of-war, on
which the sun always seemed to shine by courtesy of Sir
Edward Pryce Jones, not the Almighty. The pubs were open all
day and already hummed with the voices of those who needed
refreshment or a chance to air their views on the rival merits of
various teams and competitors, or the comparative glories of
the various visiting bands from South and North Wales and
even from the English Midlands. As the bands arrived off the
train during the morning, they marched down from the
station, treating the eager crowds to a preview of their prowess,
blowing and banging out rousing marches, while the throng
judiciously commented on their rival merits in between waving
and cheering a welcome.

Davy stood in the forefront of the crowd, on Bridge Street,
with a restraining hand on Owen's shoulder, who teetered
precariously on the edge of the pavement, his small body tense
with excitement. With his free hand Davy tipped back the
straw boater from his hot forehead and shading his eyes gazed
up towards Kerry Road, where the feverish activity of the
crowd heralded the arrival of another band.

299

'Merthyr Colliery Band!'

The information was conveyed in a frenetic verbal telegraph along the lines of the crowds and gradually the muffled thump of the big drum could be heard in the distance, accompanied by the shrill and prolonged whistle of the departing train which had disgorged them. Soon they appeared, away at the top of Kerry Road, the martial music growing louder and the big brass instruments gleaming in the sun. A wave of cheering greeted them as they trumpeted and tromboned and banged their way down Kerry Road and across into Bridge Street. As they drew nearer the loud and stirring march sent a shiver through the watchers and as though responding to the electric current which passed through the crowd they increased their efforts, blowing into their instruments with such fervour that the sweat ran down from under their smart peaked caps and put a sheen on the small, dark, pit-scarred faces above the tight embracing collars of their plum-coloured uniforms. The drummer banged and twirled with an expression of grim determination and as he passed the skin of his huge drum sent out shockwaves which caught at the throats of the people watching. Heads appeared at the doors and windows of the pubs along the route, calling out beery encouragement, those on the pub doorsteps waving pint pots which sloshed perilously and were quickly quaffed by their owners to reduce the risk of loss.

Sections of the crowd along the route detached themselves from the main body as though drawn by a magnet and joined the children, who danced and skipped alongside the band. Owen made as though to dive into the surging escort but was held back by a laughing Davy, who stood firm with the others who waited for the next grand spectacle to pass. Shortly the excited cry spread down the ranks.

'Newtown Silver Band!'

Loyalty to the local bandsmen whipped the cheering to fever pitch as the Silver Band rounded the corner from New Road, sure of themselves on their home ground and giving of their scarlet-faced best. Individual bandsmen were encouraged by name and greeted with affectionate ribaldry.

'Come on, Dai lad. Put thee back into it. Thee't not blowing thee tea now!'

'Good owl 'Arry! They'm all out o' step beside thee, mun!'

'That's the 'ammer lads! A pint all round if Newtown wins!'

The last caused a faltering note in one or two instruments as the prospect brought destructive moisture to dry mouths but the rhythm was quickly recovered and they marched on with proud determination, brought up behind by the drummer, a very small wiry man, partially blinded by the peak of an over-large cap, and the rest of his view totally restricted by the enormous drum which he had to lean back perilously to accommodate above his small knees, which were moving like pistons in an effort to keep up. As he sweated along, arms flailing and deafened by the reverberations of his enveloping instrument, the band reached a fork, the main column bearing left past the Eagles pub and making for Broad Street. The drummer, insulated in his blind and deafened world, carried straight on alone up the incline towards the gas works, puffing and banging his lonely way, oblivious of his companions, disappearing in the other direction.

Suddenly his isolation seemed to penetrate to him and at the top of the bank he was seen to slow down and his flailing arms to falter and stop. In the ensuing silence he turned slowly and awkwardly, and pushing his cap to the back of his head he peered round the side of the drum with difficulty. The sudden delighted roar from the spell-bound crowd made him jump and the cap fell off its precarious perch at the back of his head. Confused, he tried to lean sideways to pick it up but the weight of the drum toppled him and he ended up on his back like a huge snail, his legs thrashing and squeals of anguish issuing from behind the instrument. A couple of bystanders, choking with mirth, detached themselves from the crowd and rushed up the bank to rescue him. They lugged him to his feet and while one steadied him the other picked up his cap and jammed it down on his head, where it slipped over his inadequate ears and covered his eyes. Then, taking an arm each, they lifted him and carried him, feet working helplessly in mid air, round the corner and off up the route which the band had taken.

The crowd had barely recovered from this incident when round the corner, pedalling furiously, came the Newtown cycling club, showing off their prowess to the cheering watchers, on their way to the Sports Grounds down Pool Road, where they were later to compete in the cycle race. Owen spotted Llew and jumping up and down excitedly, pointed him out to Davy.

'Look! My Dad! Bet he'll win. Da-ad!'

Llew grinned and raised a hand in salute as he flew past with his team, white duck trousers held firm with cycle clips above white boots, their torsos encased in long-sleeved white woollen vests.

When he had proudly watched his father out of sight Owen turned in time to see another spectacle appear round the corner which brought a startled squeak from him. The newcomer was ten foot tall, swaying from side to side and exchanging banter with the crowd. It was Long Tom, a six-foot tall, thin, lugubrious looking individual with long drooping moustache, atop a pair of stilts, which added another four feet to his height. It was Long Tom's practice on such occasions to mount his stilts and take round the collecting box in aid of the infirmary, in which an operation some years ago had saved his only daughter's life. The girl, now fifteen, was always seen skipping along beside the striding stilts, her merry little face in contrast to the drooping lines on the countenance of her father up aloft. Since Long Tom had refreshment pressed on him as he leaned down to the doorway of every pub on his route, the day usually ended with him sitting propped against a wall, legs and stilts stretching out into the road, a danger to passing pedestrians, some of whom were themselves not too steady on their feet by this time. At this stage the indefatigable daughter, Mary Ann, would cheerfully unstrap the stilts and rescue the collecting box and with stilts under one arm and the other steadying her dazed parent, would stagger home at his side, the collecting box heavy with pennies and silver to swell the infirmary's struggling coffers.

As he swayed by now, Mary Ann, dancing gaily at his side, was dressed in a white frock and a large matching bow on top of her pretty fair curls. She wore white stockings and her feet were encased in white kid button boots. Her round rosy face wore a happy smile and the bright blue eyes gazed up fondly on her father as he rocked above her, answering the affectionate chaffing of the crowd with his own droll unsmiling wit. Owen, standing still under Davy's hand, was struck by this vision of female beauty and promptly lost his heart for the first time. He followed her progress along the street with wide admiring eyes and a flutter in his young breast and when she and her giant companion passed from sight, gave such a deep

302

and wondering sigh that Davy, who had been watching with amusement the effect of Cupid's dart, squeezed his shoulder sympathetically.

'Come on, Owen lad, let's get off down to the sports field. The first heats of the races will be starting soon.'

Owen brightened and they joined the throng of people who, laughing and chattering gaily, were making their way down Pool Road towards the sports field, the women in their gay summer dresses and white straw hats, and the men in shirt sleeves, jackets slung over their shoulders, many with straw boaters worn rakishly above hot and smiling faces.

As they passed No 46 Davy and Owen waved a greeting to Mama and Meg, who stood on the steps of the house, Meg holding a rosy, waving Esther in her arms. Dada was still up at the Rectory, hurrying to finish his chores, for he was to take part in a quoiting competition during the afternoon and besides, he was the escort for Mama, Meg and Esther for the day.

On reaching the big field where the sports were held, Davy brought a tuppenny programme at the gate and soon he and Owen were making their way to the steep bank at the far end of the field where they seated themselves on the grass to enjoy a good view of all the proceedings in comfort.

Down in the centre of the field the crowd were roaring encouragement to two teams who were striving and struggling in the first heat of the tug-of-war, the Eagles Brewery versus the Station draymen. Leaning horizontally backwards on each end of the stout rope, heels dug in and faces purple and sweating with effort, they pulled for their lives, each team gaining ground alternately. In the end it was the Brewery men who collapsed first, some of their prowess being impaired by the fact that they had firstly had to deliver the beer for the beer tent, and naturally when they had the barrels set up, it was necessary to sample the contents to see that it had taken no harm on its journey down to the field. It was a hot day and the samples tended to be large – pint pot size in fact. Then second samples had to be taken to see that it was settling properly and finally a free pint each from the organizers of the beer tent as a reward for their efforts. The victorious draymen, with wistful looks in the direction of the beer tent, turned reluctant backs towards it, spat on burning palms and waited stoically for the next heat against a team of farm boys from Trefeglwys.

From their seat on the grassy bank Davy and Owen watched events through the late morning and soon the noonday sun was burning high and relentless from a cloudless blue sky. The beer tent was full and heaving with bodies as dry throats were slaked, victories celebrated or defeats drowned. A smaller crowd partook of tea in another tent, where scarlet-faced and perspiring ladies served cup after cup of the weak milky liquid to the more abstemious. Down in a corner of the field the strident music of the bands competed with the roars of the crowd and an impromptu choir from the beer tent.

They were watching the first heats of the cycle race when they were joined by Mama, Dada, Meg and Esther, who sank gratefully to the ground beside them, Mama with a large fawn parasol with which she shaded herself and Meg, while Esther toddled delightedly round the group, a sunbonnet tied under her plump chin.

'Dammo, it is hot!' grunted Dada, mopping his brow and puffing out his whiskers. 'A terrible thirst this old sun does give you, mind.' His blue eyes gazed innocently round, hardly resting at all on the beer tent.

'You are playing quoits at two o'clock,' stated Mama firmly. 'Maybe a cup of tea we will have before then.'

'A cup of tea,' echoed Dada mildly. 'A bit hot for tea, I am thinking. I am afraid it will make me sweat too much, see. My hands would be a bit slippy to hold the quoits, isn't it?'

'If you are thinking of disappearing into that old beer tent, then it will be your feet that are slippy by two o'clock,' returned Mama, sniffing.

Dada's eyes widened, very hurt.

'*Diawl*, no! Just one I was thinking of, to cool me, is all. I am not wanting to get rolling before the quoits match.'

'Nor after,' warned Mama, the parasol jerking.

'No indeed,' said Dada, hastily. 'I have no time for them that come to watch the sports and spend the day in the beer tent seeing nothing.'

'There's a few in there will see nothing,' grinned Davy. 'They have started early.'

'And they are in good voice, too,' remarked Dada, cocking an ear to take in the harmonizing of a hymn. 'Tenors they need, though, by the sound of it,' he added judiciously.

'Well, there is one tenor they are not going to have,' said Mama, giving him a hard look.

'Me?' said Dada, surprised. 'No, no, I was not meaning. Just saying. It is a pity when there is a weakness with the tenors, is all.'

'Those tenors in there will be very weak before much more of the day is through. Weak in the legs,' replied Mama.

Dada did not answer but began to pom-pom the hymn which was being sung with a devout fervour which is rarely commanded in church. A small crowd began to gather round the tent to listen and some to join in. As more drifted up, Dada rose to his feet.

'I will just go a bit nearer. I do like that old hymn and they are singing right tidy indeed.'

Mama gave a resigned sigh and raised her eyebrows in Meg's direction, who gave a little sympathetic laugh.

'You coming, boy?' invited Dada, turning back to Davy. Davy hesitated but Mama nodded to him.

'Aye, go you. Somebody should look to him.'

He followed Dada into the crowd where by dint of judicious elbowing and patient pushing, they finally managed to get in through the flap of the tent. There the heat was intense in the swimming, diffuse light, aggravated by the press of bodies. Pint pots were raised high for safety and guarded with rounded arms. Heads were flung back to give force to the harmonising, which was being conducted by a large sweating man perched atop an up-ended beer barrel which was already empty and otherwise redundant. Dada made the tortuous journey to the long trestle at the back of the tent, Davy carried along in his wake, bringing one or two singers to a scowling falter as he disturbed their stance. He ordered two pints from one of the perspiring dispensers of the foaming liquid and they both remained pressed against the trestle carefully shielding their pots from the crush. The beer was already tepid but they sipped it gratefully and, his dryness eased, Dada was soon adding his still passable tenor to his favourite hymn, *Jesu Lover of my Soul* to the tune *Aberystwyth*.

After an hour had passed and a second pint quaffed to the dregs, Davy reminded Dada of the quoiting match and drew the reluctant tenor back through the crush to emerge, still singing, into the hot sunshine outside. He delivered him firmly to the corner of the field where the competitors, mostly from the country districts around, were gathered, fingering the quoits and measuring the distance to the iron spike in the centre of the pitch with practised eyes. Leaving him safely with his cronies, Davy made his way back to the rest of the family and felt a warm glow expand in his chest when he saw that they had been joined by a figure in a fresh green cotton dress, whose thick, piled-up corn-coloured hair shone uncovered in the sunshine.

'Hello, Davy,' Nan greeted him with a suddenly shy smile, grey eyes uplifted above wide cheekbones, flushed with the heat.

'I am just telling this girl she should have a hat on,' said Mama, looking very friendly at Nan. 'She will get the sun-stroke with nothing on that head of hers.'

Nan shook her head and laughed.

'I love the sun. It will do me no harm.'

Davy settled himself contentedly at her side and suddenly the sunlit field and the crowds in their summer attire took on a new dimension, conscious as he was in all his senses of the girl at his side, who seemed to fit in so well with the family group.

Esther's tireless toddling was now slowing down with the heat and unaccustomed excitement and Nan, with a warm laugh, reached out sympathetic arms. Soon the head in the sunbonnet was resting against Nan's breast and the lids closed slowly over the bright blue eyes and Esther slept. Davy leaned back on his elbows, chewing a piece of grass, his straw boater tipped over his eyes, and from under the shelter of the brim, watched Nan as she sat at ease, cradling Esther's plump little body and murmuring placidly to Mama and Meg.

His heart swelled within him with a warm happiness and his feelings became part of the golden afternoon, where the gaily-coloured crowds on the sun-drenched field seemed to be held timeless in a protective bowl formed by the heat-hazed hills and perfumed by the earthy smell of the warm grass.

Llew came third in the cycle race and the Rees' agreed indignantly that he would have surely been first only for the incident of the dirty little mongrel dog which ran out onto the track causing him to swerve slightly. But when he joined them and displayed his medal, Owen's pride knew no bounds. Shortly afterwards Dada returned, triumphantly bearing a small cup which he had won at the quoits and so beaming with pride was he that Mama had not the heart to deny him the pint which he told them he needed as his tongue was cleaving to his mouth. So she took possession firmly of the cup and watched with a wry smile as he made his way to the beer tent, where *Sospan Fach* was getting a hammering now, although the tenors were taking on a coarser tone. Davy and Llew fetched cups of tea for all and ice cream cornets for Owen and Esther, to their delight.

The afternoon wore on. Races were run, bands blew and drummed their way through the competitions, the last heat of the tug-of-war was won by the final, desperate, sweating effort of the Station draymen, the beer and tea tents were packed to overflowing and the crowds grew slower and hoarser in their acclaim for the winners, all under a sun which hung hot and haze-ringed in a sky which was developing wispy streaks of goatsbeard cloud.

Suddenly the family group was startled by an almighty commotion of shouting and screams and turned in time to see the beer tent collapse and fold down over a heaving mass of thrashing bodies and muffled cries. Some wag in his cups had crept round to the back and unguarded side of the huge tent and had heaved out all the ground pegs. Llew and Davy flung themselves after the crowd who were rushing up to the rescue, while Mama rose to her feet, dropping the parasol.

'Will!' she cried and then, tearfully, 'where are you?'

Hands grasped at the remaining ground pegs and heaved them out of the dry earth. Slowly and with some difficulty the huge canvas was folded back to reveal a heaving pile of bodies, arms and legs flailing, open mouths gasping roars of fright and strangled curses, the whole mass exuding an overpowering smell of spilled beer. Gradually the top layer of tangled bodies were dragged clear accompanied by the dazed and muffled cries of those at the bottom of the pile. Davy and Llew finally discovered Dada on his back near the upended trestle, the breath knocked out of him, and pinned down by a large man in a white apron, who lay across him still clutching intact the big white jug with which he had been dispensing the ale. As they dragged the large man off his chest, Dada stirred painfully and focused bewildered and terrified eyes on his two sons, who stood over him, hardly able to restrain their laughter now that they saw he was whole and comparatively unscathed. They gave him a hand each and he sat up shakily and stared around him at the chaos and the bodies being lifted and borne away on all sides. He drew in a breath with difficulty and then jumped guiltily as Mama's white face appeared above him, between those of Llew and Davy.

'*Diawl!*' he quavered, passing a trembling hand over his face. 'What did happen? Everything went dark and I went down with a weight on me like a ton of bricks. I could have been killed!' Indignation lent a little strength to his returning voice.

The colour began to come back into Mama's face as it hung menacingly over him.

'Lucky for you you weren't!' she returned fiercely. 'You old fool!'

'I didn't do it!' Dada's face was a study in indignation as he sat there clutching his head in both hands. 'Minding my own business I was. Singing some bit but no harm, mind.' He looked round then squinted up at the sky accusingly. 'No need for all this, at all.'

'You may well look up there,' said Mama through tight lips. 'A judgement, no doubt. Get him up!' she commanded Llew and Davy, then wrinkling her nose, '*Ach y fi!* He do smell like an old brewery!'

The brothers, shaking with mirth, heaved Dada to his feet with difficulty. He stood swaying for a moment, taking in the scene around him with bewildered eyes. Bodies were laid out on the grass, mostly none the worse for the experience apart from cuts and bruises. Others staggered away in a dazed state helped by ministering arms, and stepping blindly over scattered pint pots or slithering on grass wet with spilled beer.

Dada shook his head and pulled himself together.

'Judgement, is it?' he said sternly to Mama. 'Why for a judgement? Weren't we singing hymns? Praising the Lord, with a drop of ale to help the voices, is all. And then struck down like that. He do not encourage poor creatures much, do He?' he muttered darkly.

Mama took his arm none too gently.

'Do not add blasphemy, boy. Come you, we will make for home. A tidy cup of tea I can do with. Old dishwater they are serving in that tent.'

However, her eyes were twinkling as she beckoned to Meg and the children and her hand was firmly through Dada's arm as she made her way towards the entrance, gathering her dignity about her, Meg in tow, carrying the parasol and leading Esther by the hand, with Owen bringing up the rear, carrying Dada's cup like it was eggshells.

Davy and Llew watched them out of sight grinning at each other in happy appreciation.

'Aye, well,' said Llew, looking down on the field below, where the last prizes were being presented and the last speeches were being made. 'I think I will make for home too. It's about all over I am thinking. Well,' he added, satisfaction in his voice, 'I have got a medal out of it anyway and Dada has got a cup. He has forgotten that for now, I think, but polishing it up he will be when he gets over his shock. Are you coming now, our Davy?'

Davy's eyes slid sideways to where Nan sat alone on the grass, her face serene as she watched the winding-up activities down below.

'I will be up shortly,' Davy's voice was casual.

Llew followed his glance and grinned.

'The sport is not over for you, then? Oh well, good luck, boy. You could do worse. A tidy girl, that. I have had leanings that way myself, but not much encouragement. She do not see me at all. I am thinking you will have more success, by the looks. I'll see you later on then.'

He lifted a hand and set off down the field. Davy stood for a moment looking after him then turned and went over to where Nan sat.

He lowered himself to sit beside her and she smiled a welcome but remained silent, watching the departing crowd make slowly for the gate and stream up the road. Davy watched her covertly, trying to see her as though for the first time, without the memories of the pale, tow-haired girl of his boyhood or the maidservant at the Rectory. Suddenly his mind cleared as though mists and confusion were swept away and he saw her as she was, a woman, with all that that meant. Warm, deep-breasted, with wide curving hips and rounded sturdy arms. The skin of her throat was creamy above the fresh green of her dress and her thick yellow hair like ripened corn seemed to complete the picture of fruitfulness. Her wide mouth was full, the soft lips parted slightly to show even white teeth and her grey eyes had serene depths to them. As he watched her a deep happiness grew in him and he had a sudden desire to take her there and then, to lose himself in the warm sweetness of her, to wipe out all the tortured desires and repressions of the past, all the painful memories and bitterness and to know only the release of a healing, satisfying, enveloping love.

She seemed to become aware of his eyes fixed on her and she turned her head, meeting the dark intensity of his gaze steadily. Suddenly it was as though she read his mind and a slow flush crept up her cheeks. Her eyes dropped to her hands which were clasped in her lap, but not before he had seen a half-confused question in them.

'Nan?' he said softly and something in his voice made her raise her head and meet his eyes again. She smiled and put out a hand and he took it in his, where it curled, warm and trusting as though it belonged there.

'Davy Rees!' she said with mock severity. 'I would thank you not to look at me like that. It is not nice.'

'How was I looking, then?' he asked, eyes wide and innocent.

'Eyes everywhere,' she murmured, dropping her gaze to the lone hand on her lap, which she opened to study the palm intently.

'Only looking!' Davy's voice was teasing. 'No harm meant.'

She withdrew her other hand from his and ran her fingers along the line of the palm she was studying.

'I have a long life-line,' she offered, gaze fixed. 'The heart line is broken a bit at the start but it goes on nice and steady after, like. What about yours?' She peeped up at him from under her lashes.

With a soft laugh he laid his hand palm up on her knee and she took it in a warm grasp and ran an exploratory finger along the lines. A faint tremor passed through him but he sat still and watchful as she gazed down at his hand, a lock of yellow hair escaping and lying across his wrist.

'You have a long life line, too,' she said with satisfaction. 'And your heart line is just like mine.'

'A bit broken at first and then nice and steady after?' he said.

She nodded and released his hand and tucked the stray lock of hair under a hairpin. They were silent for a while but there was an awareness between them. Davy became very absorbed in plucking bits of grass out of his turnups.

'Do you know something?' he ventured at last. 'I have never courted a girl yet. Not really courted as you might say.'

Without raising his eyes he was aware of her soft gaze bent on him.

'Funny you should say that,' she replied reflectively. 'I have never been courted by a fellow yet. Not really courted, you know?'

He took a deep breath and tilting his hat to the back of his head gazed dreamily up at the sky. The sun was sliding slowly towards the west and the shadows were mauve on the sides of the hills. A faint warm breeze was stirring the grass and the debris left by the crowd. Overhead a few puffs and wisps of cloud drifted across the hazy sky and the voices of the few people left sounded faintly from the field below, emphasizing a creeping quietness.

'It will be a lovely evening when it cools down a bit,' he remarked. 'I fancy a walk down Pilots Fields after tea. Will you come with me, Nan Mostyn?'

Her gaze wandered across the sky and took in the hills in the distance.

'It has the makings of a lovely evening, right enough,' she agreed, softly. 'Yes, I will walk with you, Davy Rees.'

CONTRACT LAW IN PERSPECTIVE

Cavendish
Publishing
Limited